Greig Beck grew up across the r
Sydney, Australia. His early d
sunbaking and reading science fict
went on to study computer scienc
financial software industry and later received an MBA. Today,
Greig spends his days writing, but still finds time to surf at his
beloved Bondi Beach. He lives in Sydney, with his wife, son
and an enormous black German shepherd.

Also by Greig Beck

BOOK OF THE DEAD

GREIG BECK

momentum

First published by Momentum in 2014
This edition published in 2015 by Momentum
Pan Macmillan Australia Pty Ltd
1 Market Street, Sydney 2000

A CIP record for this book is available at the National Library of Australia

Book of the Dead

EPUB format: 9781760082437
Mobi format: 9781760082444
Print on Demand format: 9781760082499

Cover design by Conzpiracy Digital Arts
Edited by Kate O'Donnell
Proofread by Laurie Ormond

Macmillan Digital Australia: www.macmillandigital.com.au

To report a typographical error, please visit momentumbooks.com.au/contact/

Visit www.momentumbooks.com.au to read more about all our books and to buy books online. You will also find features, author interviews and news of any author events.

To H.P. Lovecraft (1890 – 1937);
the first father of macabre horror.
Your legacy lives on, sir.

That is not dead which can eternal lie,
And with strange eons, even death may die
       H.P. Lovecraft, *The Call of Cthulhu*

Hell is empty, and all the devils are here
       William Shakespeare, *The Tempest*

The Book of the Dead, otherwise known as the Book, *The Necronomicon*, or the *Al Azif*, is an ancient grimoire of magnificent beauty and unspeakable horror. Many early-translated copies exist, but they contain little of the secrets of the Old Ones, and the incantations that deliver power over life and death. Rumor has it these details were intentionally omitted in the copies. The original remains lost to this day.

The Gated Deep

They slumber, a race far older than man's first word,
In a city more ancient than Lemuria's first brick.
The sleepers in the dirt, the burrowers below us all.
We who climb down into the depths find not just
caverns of wet and slime,
But carved faces beautiful in their hideousness,
carrying not one visage of mortal man.
Pathways spiral ever downward to hopelessness and
eternal blackness.
There, find mighty columns, towering edifices, and
streets too wide for a sapiens's feet.
A primal city long past anything the tiny human
mind could comprehend.
Gates of red granite so huge they could hold back
an army. Now swung wide.
Past them the Old Ones eternally slumber –
dreaming, and still reaching out to us.
And the Earth shall fall before they rise.

Abdul Alhazred, from the *Al Azif*
(*The Book of the Dead*)

Prologue

City of Damascus, Syria, 738 AD

Abdul Alhazred dodged his way down the street, weaving between stallholders and layabouts and mothers with too many small children. He passed the newly built Umayyad Mosque, and briefly contemplated entering, before swerving hard, knowing that there would be no sanctuary anywhere for him now.

He babbled and cursed in between ragged breaths, and even giggled as people stepped from his path, thinking he was mad. Alhazred threw back his head and roared with laughter. He *was* mad – the Mad Arab – insane, sent insane by the things he had seen, things he had uncovered through his travels and then his further studies.

He looked up, and saw birds circling above him, faster and faster – sparrows, wrens, shrikes, geese, and dozens more species all twisting together in a tornado of feathers and flesh.

He screamed at them, and cursed again at mankind's stupidity, *his* stupidity, and...curiosity. A scrap of information here, a whisper there, and he'd been off like a hound on a scent. He had travelled to the ruins of Babylon, and then meandered into the great red deserts of Arabia, that vast and empty sea of nothing but heat and sand and scorpions. And then he had found them – the caves; he wished now he hadn't. The legends said they were protected by djinn, evil spirits and monsters of death. He had found out too late that in their depths lay things far worse than that.

Alhazred felt the book under his robe. His fingers touched the soft cover of forbidden leather, and pictured the words he had transcribed within in a mixture of blood and charcoal as he had been instructed. Some of the words were incomprehensible even to him – the Old Ones spoke a harsh tongue the primitive mind of man could not possibly understand.

The book, the *Al Azif,* had taken him half a lifetime to write, and now he needed to hide it, get rid of it or pass it on, the ideas too important for mankind's future to be reclaimed now by the Old Ones or their vile servants. The information was not just for the living, but instead, was a book of the dead.

Alhazred had been given their secrets, told to him in fever dreams, in return for the betrayal of his race. But the more he wrote down, the more frightened he became, and the more his sanity left him. They had promised him a kingdom, but all he saw was slavery to masters who would look upon him in the same light as he viewed an ant.

He turned briefly, glimpsing from the corner of an eye the shape appear and then dissipate like oily smoke. *Too late: they'd found him.*

He had fled, stolen their plans, and disobeyed them. With his help, the Great Old One had expected to return to the world of man, to own it once again, but he had outsmarted them all, stopped them, or at least slowed them down.

He sucked in hot breaths, feeling the sweat pour down his body. He was nearly spent as he saw his target, a holy man leaving the mosque. Abdul put his head down and raced toward him. At the last second, he ripped the book from his robe, and jammed it into his hands. "Keep it safe, holy one. Mankind's fate depends on it."

He tore away and sprinted down a dark alley, but less than halfway to the end, the shape boiled up again, squeezing from the very cracks in the path and forming now into a shapeless mass of some viscous black substance, studded with disturbingly human eyes. Alhazred screamed: "*Shoggoth!*"

He looked high and higher as the thrashing tentacled mass grew. Lidless eyes swiveled toward him and a round sucking maw opened like a dark bottomless pit. He dropped his arms, surrendering. He was grabbed then, around the neck, the arms and waist, the black tendrils holding him tight, and sizzling and stinging like poisonous fire.

Abdul Alhazred, the Mad Arab, was lifted to the massive maw and jammed into that foul orifice. Mercifully, his mind left him completely as the jaws closed.

PART 1
And The Earth Shall Fall

Chapter 1

Red Oak, Iowa

Big Bill Anderson sat in his favorite chair – red faux leather, soft, deep, and comfortably shaped by decades of sitting into a perfect reverse image of his ample butt. His chinos were pulled up a little high, and his blue checked lumber shirt was a tad tight across the gut, but at his age, he'd earned the right to get a little out of shape.

He turned the page of his paper, looking down the ads for pet adoption, scanning the older dogs: Labradors, terriers, schnauzers. Most had pictures beside them, and insanely happy, beseeching, or frightened faces stared back at him, all wanting new homes, just one more game of fetch with an attentive new owner, or to be far away from the guy who used beat the shit out of them.

He stopped at one, a shepherd, five years old, big guy with the tip of one ear missing, eyes that were clear and sharp with whip-smart intelligence – *Rusty*.

"I wish, boy."

Bill had desperately wanted another dog ever since Bella had died ten years earlier. He felt that now he was retired, and had his days on his hands, he might be able to swing the old girl toward it one more time. He tore the page out and let it rest on the small side table beside a new cup of steaming tea.

The vacuum cleaner started in the other room, and he knew that Margaret would be pushing the infernal machine in under his feet any moment. He grimaced, imagining the rush of warm, stinking exhaust air, the roar of a jet engine, and her light smile revealing her perverse delight in either loud cleaning devices or another opportunity to simply bug him.

He leaned forward to look at the picture once again. "Maybe later, Rusty." Bill let his eyes slide to the small table. A huge roach was edging across its smooth top. He rolled up the paper, and whacked it. "Ha."

A vibration beneath his feet tickled his soles. He forgot the roach and frowned in the direction of the vacuum-cleaner noise. "What the hell setting has that woman got it on?"

Another vibration and he noticed the surface of his tea shimmy. He reached for the cup just as there came a thump from below. The vacuum went off, followed by silence for several seconds.

"Bill?" Margaret called from the other room, apprehension in the word.

"Wasn't me, honey." Bill sat still, silent, waiting. There was another thump, then another, the latest from overhead. "What the hell?"

A deeper thump, again from below, sounding like someone was shifting heavy furniture in their basement. An antique plate on the mantelpiece tilted forward and fell to the rug.

"Margie?" Bill slowly rose to his feet as his wife entered the room, her forehead creased, her hands wringing a cleaning cloth.

"Bill, are you...?"

Bill shook his head, turning it slowly, concentrating on listening, his arms out from his sides slightly, as though to help with his balance.

Several more thumps came from above, and Margaret squeaked and hunched her shoulders. Bill looked to the window. Outside, there seemed nothing unusual – the garden and, beyond that, the Wilsons' house, with the lemon tree just covered in green bulbs not yet ripe enough to pick overhanging the fence in between.

More thumps, and, as Bill watched, something black struck the lawn, and then another. Bill squinted – *birds*.

"Hey, birds are –"

Bill never finished that thought: another thump cracked the plaster in the walls, and the house actually seemed to drop a few inches.

"Whoa." Bill noticed Margaret's face was white, and her wringing hands continued to move up to her breasts, as though she was praying. She was shaking her head; her eyes were watering.

He smiled at her. "Stay there. We'll be fine."

There came a blast of thick heat, and then the house simply…fell. Bill felt himself become weightless, as if gravity had been suspended. Outside the windows went black at the same time as the power shut down. The only light was thrown down from above, and outside he could still see movement, but rapid, as though walls were shooting upwards past the windows.

There was a crash. Margaret screamed, and Bill was smashed to the floor. His wife of thirty-five years began to sob, and that hurt him more than anything else. He got to his knees, staying there for several seconds as he checked his numerous aches and bruises. He was relieved to find that nothing was broken – at sixty-five, bones were like kindling.

"Oh god." He gagged, and put a hand over his mouth and nose, as a God-awful stench filled the house. His brow ran with perspiration from the heat.

"Margie, you okay, girl?" He stayed on his knees and crawled toward her.

His wife lay on her side, moaning. He bet it was her hip; she'd had a replacement half a dozen years back, and still complained of it.

Bill went to an upturned table among the debris of furniture, broken pottery, papers, sheets of plaster, and something else – dozens more of the scurrying roaches.

"What the hell?" He bet it was an earthquake, and a big one by the feel of it. He scrambled around in the murky light, just the ghost of a glow coming in through the windows. He pulled a drawer and emptied it, rummaging until he found a small flashlight, and flicked it on.

Margaret was sitting up, holding her stomach. There was blood on her face.

"You okay?" he whispered, not knowing why quietness was important.

She nodded. "What happened?"

"I don't know yet." Bill used the table to push himself to his feet and walked to the window. He was right – there looked to be walls built all around them. He frowned as he followed them upward, and placing his face close to the glass he saw that the walls loomed hundreds of feet over the house. At the very top, there was sky...and maybe a lemon tree.

"Holy..." These weren't walls that had *sprung up*; instead the house had *fallen down* into some sort of pit.

He still had his cheek pressed to the glass when something rushed past. "*Christ on a cross!*" He pulled back as though electric shocked. The shadow had been huge: twice as big as a man.

"Bill, is there a fire?" Margaret had managed to get to one knee.

"You just stay there a moment, old girl. I got to check on something." Bill licked his lips and ran a forearm up over his head. It was blistering hot, and though he couldn't smell smoke, he could smell something that refused to be identified

– sulfur, methane, and fishy like. He remembered being at a beach when he was a kid, and there was a shark carcass high and dry on the sand, all bloated up in the hot sun – it was that sort of smell.

He turned his small light beam to the floor, checking the rubble, and then picked his way through it to the front door. The frame was warped, and deep cracks run up past the lintel, and across the ceiling. The house was warped. Forget about repairs; this is a knock-down job, he thought. Hannity's Insurance would have a fit.

He grasped the handle, and immediately jerked his hand away – it was damned hot. He gritted his teeth. "Man up," he whispered, and grabbed it again. The brass knob was hot, but not searingly so. He turned and tugged, and the door moved a quarter inch and them jammed tight. Plaster dust rained down onto his head and neck. Bill grunted and tugged again, and this time the door flew inwards.

A shock of horror ran through his entire body. He dropped the flashlight, and the breath caught in his throat. He didn't smell the vile air, or feel the inferno heat on his face; instead every atom of his being was focused on the thing that filled the doorway.

Octopus man, was the thought that jumped into his mind. The creature towered over him, all thrashing arms sticking from a bulbous head. He stared, his mind trying to assemble it into some sort of category of man or beast he recognized, and failing miserably. The thing was a massive amoeba-like creature made out of iridescent black slime. Multiple eyes floated over its surface, popping open to stare, before sinking back into the mass, and rising in another position.

Something wrapped around Bill's neck, wrists and waist all at once and began to drag him outside. It was hot and greasy against his flesh, and hurt like a jellyfish sting. He tried to pull against it, began to struggle, but made zero impact on the monster. As he was dragged along the remains of his lawn toward one of the walls of the pit, he managed to look back in time to see more of the lumpen things wedge themselves in through his doorframe.

He heard Margaret scream, and he began to weep. Big Bill Anderson, her protector, her rock, was now useless. He wished he had a dog, and a big one, as he was pulled toward the wall of dirt.

*

"Yo, Frank, racked and ready." Andy took one last look around as he teetered on the edge of the cavernous sinkhole. The grass behind him was littered with dead birds, which was why he specifically had been called in from his home base at Cedar Rapids.

Andrew Lincoln Bennet was an environmental geologist, and one of the best authorities on sinkholes in the state, if not the country. His job was to try and ascertain any connection between the land sink and the avian deaths. So far, he had no idea. The birds' lungs (he had hastily dissected a few on a trestle set up beside their van) showed no sign of gas inhalation, and their eyes were clear, so no toxin deployment either. Still, he had breathing equipment slung on his back as he knew methane, sulfur dioxide, and even chlorine gas could belch up from the earth with little warning, as if the planet had ingested something disagreeable.

Andy nodded to his second-in-command, Frank Kelso. Frank was twenty years older and knew rocks like they were his family, but Andy had the modern expertise and had seen a lot in his thirty-five years. Frank was more than happy to defer to his *young protégé,* as he liked to call him.

"One away," Frank, yelled, manning the winch, and gave him a thumbs-up.

Andy stepped back to quickly rappel down into the darkness. The sinkhole crater was more than two hundred feet across, and about twice that in depth – a biggie in anyone's books. Andy knew of larger ones – Louisiana had one at Lake Peigneur that went down fifteen hundred feet – it was huge. But the current record was held by a monster in China in the Chongqing Municipality, that was a thousand feet across and two thousand deep – it could have swallowed a small village. As he rappeled down, kicking off the wall, he thanked his lucky stars this one wasn't like that. The big ones could collapse, and a few hundred thousand tons of cascading rock and soil meant you just earned a free burial.

"How we lookin, hotshot?" Frank's voice squawked from his belt mic. Andy could imagine his buddy up top, standing a good fifty feet back from the edge in case the walls started to slide. He'd be fifty again in front of everyone else, keeping the police rescue, residents and general public well back until he, and others, had fully examined the site. The entire block would remain evacuated and sealed off until their work was done.

He touched down. "I'm okay; just hit bottom, pop."

He heard Frank whistle. Andy unsnapped the harness hook and grabbed a secondary flashlight dangling from his belt; he flicked it on, adding the beam to his helmet lamp's halogen, and looked around.

Andy's number-one priority was to locate Bill and Margaret Anderson, and his hopes rose. The house was virtually intact, sitting in the center of several feet of green lawn, now littered with carcasses of dead birds.

"*Bill Anderson*! Bill and Margaret Anderson, can you hear me?" He waited as his words bounced around the huge pit. After a few minutes, there was still silence. Light from above gave the scene a nighttime atmosphere. He looked closer at the house: aside from some cracking in the external structure

13

and the front door hanging off its frame, he might have expected to see Bill and Margaret sitting on the porch as if nothing was wrong.

"Structure's pretty good; I'm going in." As he approached he winced at the smell. Weird, he thought. Wonder if they've got a septic tank. He quickly checked the anemometer on his belt – the air quality was still good. Just leaking shit, he hoped.

Andy adjusted his helmet, sweat now streaming from his pores. As well as the smell, the heat was near unbearable, which was also weird, as he should be feeling lower temperatures at a few hundred feet. He knew there was no volcanic or geothermal activity in the area, and there hadn't been for close to a million years.

"*Bill Anderson?*"

Andy leaned forward to wave his light across the doorway and windows. He guessed if they were in there, they'd be damned confused and frightened. And if Bill had a gun, Andy was liable to catch a gutful of double ought if he went barging in.

He approached carefully, his feet crunching on something. He looked down to see hundreds of roaches moving about. "Nice." At the doorframe he rested his hand on the broken wood, and then snapped it back, revolted. Even though he wore gloves for the descent, he recoiled from the thick, viscous material that coated the rough leather. He shone his light on it – glistening, milky with darker streaks. He brought it close to his face.

"Aw, fuck." He ripped it away. It had to be the source of the smell enveloping the area. It was like fish, sulfur and crushed snails all in a jellied paste. He shone his light around at the walls, wondering where it had come from. In his decade and a half in geology, he had never come across anything like it occurring naturally above or below the ground. He brought his light back to the frame.

"Bill, I'm coming in, if that's okay." He shone his light inside. "If you can hear me, just make a sign...*anything*."

Andy counted off the few seconds – nothing but silence. He swallowed noisily, and then moved inside, avoiding the fallen furniture and going quickly from room to room. The smell was worse in the small building, and he held his breath as he searched. In a few minutes he had examined the house in detail, and stood again on the porch.

"Nothing, Frank; are we sure they were home?" He looked up to the sky, hundreds of feet overhead; suddenly wishing he was up there.

"Yep," Frank said. "Neighbor said he saw them only an hour before, and he's sure they didn't leave. Have you looked everywhere – the perimeter?"

"I'll do a final sweep now." Andy stepped off the porch. The lawn was littered with dead birds down here too, but incongruously, it otherwise seemed almost untouched by the drop into the pit – as if it had been lowered gently. Flowers in their beds still stood upright, their blooms straining towards sunlight they would never feel again. There was a wheelbarrow, with gloves laid over one handle, and a flagstone pathway ran for two dozen feet to abruptly stop at a wall of dirt and rock.

Andy circled the house. He had about twenty feet of space between himself and the walls of the sinkhole. They looked solid and not saturated, as he would have expected.

"What's wrong with this picture?" he whispered.

He knew sinkholes occur because groundwater erodes away porous limestone creating a *karst* feature below the surface shell. Eventually the ground just collapses into the void that's been created, and might have been there hiding for days, months or even years. But *water* is the key ingredient, and down here it was dry...and hot.

"Talk to me, Andy." Frank's voice sounded tight.

"It doesn't make sense – it's bone dry down here." Andy continued to pan his light.

"Maybe drained away. That pocket could be years old, and by now we have a total percolation effect. Water's long gone – it happens," Frank said.

"Yeah, but in limestone, and not in bedrock like this. This just feels...different." Andy walked to one of the walls and frowned – there was something on it, or pressed into it – a symbol or shape. He reached into his pocket and pulled out a small camera, taking a few images, and then turning to snap off some more pictures of the structure and size of the cavity.

He tucked the camera away and then reached out to touch the dark soil where the shape was indented. It was soft and spongy, like Styrofoam packing. He knew the earth was capable of some amazing feats – it could sink, rise up in columns or waves, it could spin like a whirlpool, and become as hard as rock or soft like quicksand. But this was something outside of his experience. Besides, as he'd said to Frank, down this far, it would have to be mostly bedrock, not soil.

Andy pulled a small plastic bottle out of a pocket and scraped some of the spongy soil into it. He capped it and had begun to turn away when he stopped, and then spun back, frowning. He lifted his flashlight, holding it up and centered while reaching into yet another of his numerous pockets. He carefully drew forth a flat folding knife that he expertly opened out one handed while keeping his eyes on the wall.

Andy used the blade to dig in gently, carefully, edging out the spongy soil, and letting it plop wetly at his feet. He used the tip of his blade to snag the object and drew it out: it was a sleeve – blue checked wool, thick, like you get in those hunting or lumber shirts. He tugged it free and held it up on the blade tip. Despite the dirt covering the material, it was clearly fairly new.

"How the hell did you get in there?" he whispered, and then looked briefly to the surface – not a chance that this thing had been buried by sedimentary processes. Anything down here would be tens of thousands of years old, at least. He flapped the dirt free and looked at it again; even from a foot from his face, he could smell the stink – the same fishy, sulfurous odor that was in the slime.

It was a sleeve with a shiny button still on the cuff end, shredded at the other. He moved his light a little closer – the ragged end was damp. It was hard to tell what it was in the whitening glare of the flashlight, but the fluid glistened, and he knew what he hoped it wasn't – *blood*.

"Jesus, Bill, what happened down here?"

He quickly checked his pockets. *Damn, no sample bags*. He cursed his poor preparation and ended up wadding the material up and tucking it in a spare pocket. He dug a little more into the soil without finding anything, and then turned away looking again towards the sunken house. It was tomb quiet, and a prickle lifted the hair on his neck.

"Ah, Frank..." Andy cleared his throat. "Frank, there's nothing here." He lifted his light again. The slime glistened back at him from the door. "If the Andersons were ever here, they're gone now."

"Probably never down there. They'll sure get a shock when they get home this evening." Frank didn't sound convincing.

Andy felt the sleeve wadded up in his pocket. "Sure...sure they will." He took one last look around, moving his light slowly over the property. Smears of the glistening slime reflected the beam back at him. The dark or confined spaces never worried him. Being a geologist meant caving, tight tunnels, basically a lot of underground work, but this down here...He felt the hairs on his neck rise, and stay risen like the hackles of a dog. This is a hundred percent pure weird, he thought.

Andy snorted softly. "Only in America."

"What was that?" Frank asked.

"Nothing." Andy reconnected himself to the drop line. "Grabbing some samples and coming up."

Chapter 2

Kirov, Russia

Viktor smoked the pungent cigarette slowly. He managed to tune out the sound of his five young children and screaming wife, Alina, as he read the morning paper. It'd be another long day driving the bus from the airport to the city and back. It was a twelve-hour shift now; it had been eleven hours only two years back, but the manager had cut staff with the remaining drivers working longer, or risking being cut themselves. The biggest joke on the drivers was that though the hours increased, the pay stayed the same. Big, big joke, he thought and blew more thick smoke into the tiny apartment.

His wife's voice went up a few decibels and he raised his eyes over the paper to look at her – he smiled and winked – still beautiful after five children. Alina had managed to turn her face beet-red from screaming at the young ones. Only Maria, their oldest at seven, ever listened to her. Alina straightened, blew hair from her forehead and grinned and shrugged.

He nodded in return. He'd work a hundred hours a week if it meant keeping food on this woman's table. She made it all worthwhile. He looked up at the stained walls and the roaches moving along the peeling picture rails. She deserves better, he thought glumly.

He sipped at a metallic-tasting coffee and winced – extra flavor thanks to the old copper pipes, he knew. He lowered the cup just as the table jumped.

"What is – ?" The table jumped again. Alina stopped moving, and the house quieted as the children ceased their mad dashing about. They all stood in silence. Alina and the five little ones turned big eyes towards him.

Something struck the window, making Viktor jump and little Rakael squeal. Viktor looked to the pane as another wet thump sounded against the glass – it was a bird, momentarily stuck on the sill, its beak shattered and bloody, its eyes round and mad. It fell away, leaving a streak of blood as it plummeted towards the earth.

Viktor started to rise to his feet. Earthquake? he wondered. Kirov had minor tremors all the time, but these buildings, most twice as old as his babushka, were little more than cheap, crumbling brick and powdery mortar – a good breeze, and they'd collapse like a deck of cards.

He felt a juddering vibration beneath his feet, and then a waft of hot, stinking air. Birds started to crash into the building as though being fired from a cannon. That's it, no more waiting, he thought. Better to be safe in the street, than crushed to muck in an old building.

"We go quick. Out, out." Alina took control, snatching up the two youngest and yelling instructions. Maria grabbed Rakael, and he took his eldest son by the hand. They went down the old steps two at a time, their feet squashing roaches on every riser, as the building started to grind. On the way down, doors opened and old gray heads poked out, but then were pulled back in as though on a leash.

"Get out!" Viktor yelled to them, but no one followed or even acknowledged him. In this building, like many others, neighbors rarely talked, and all were strangers to each other.

Viktor kicked open the downstairs doors and rushed into the freezing street, not stopping until they were on the opposite sidewalk. He checked his brood were all with him, and put an arm around Alina. Only then did he look back.

The building shimmied, rose a couple of feet, and then, staggeringly, dropped into the ground as though on a fast elevator. It didn't fall and then stop, crumble, or even collapse. It simply *went down*, and kept *going down*.

Viktor could hear the crushing grind of earth and brick as the three-story edifice disappeared into a massive black void. There was silence for a minute or two. Then the screams came.

Chapter 3

Matt Kearns pushed long hair back off his face, and then ran across Massachusetts Avenue towards the Qdoba Mexican Grill. He kept a hand over his leather satchel on one shoulder and pushed open the small door, inhaling the scent of chilli, spices, and roasting meat.

"O-ooh, yeah."

His interview with the board in at the Harvard Lamont Library had gone well – *very* well – and he expected an offer to come through within the week. After all, he was still one of the top paleolinguists in the world, had an understanding of more ancient languages than anyone else in the USA, *and* was witty and charming – Why shouldn't they love me? he thought, and grinned, as he was shown to a table.

He snatched a copy of that day's newspaper from the rack and slid into the booth. If he got the job, he'd start teaching a basic languages class at the Resource Center. Low down the ladder, but he'd be home, and that was all that mattered. Besides, he was sure he could climb back to full tenure quickly.

He waved to a pretty waitress and she nodded in return, and then made a beeline toward him. He looked around – the diner was near empty, save for a few foreign students, a large family eating without talking or even making eye contact with each other, and a solitary coffee drinker.

Matt lifted the satchel over his head, leaning it on the seat beside him as the waitress stopped.

"Welcome to Qdoba Mexican Grill. My name is Andrea. We have specials today that–"

"I know." Matt smiled. "It's *all* good, Andrea." He smiled, sweeping his hair back again. She nodded, and her eyes lingered just a few seconds longer than was necessary, before flicking away.

He smiled. Still got it, he thought, as he looked down the menu quickly, already knowing what he wanted: chicken quesadilla – one enormous corn tortilla filled with spicy chicken, bell peppers and melted cheese, then folded in half and lightly toasted – heaven on a plate. He used to have them once a week when he worked here three years earlier...and he planned on resuming the same delightful habit now he had returned.

"Andrea, I'll have the prince of tortillas – *quesadilla de pollo, por favor.*" He grinned and winked. Andrea giggled as she wrote and then headed to the kitchen.

Matt dropped the small laminated sheet, picked up the newspaper, and flicked through the headlines while he waited – financial crisis in France worsening; the Middle East still beating itself back to the Stone Age; and another picture of the President grinning and swinging a golf club. He sighed and continued flicking through, only glancing at the stories, until – *Unexplained bird deaths accompany sinkholes.* "Huh?" Matt frowned and read quickly.

Huge sinkholes have opened up across the country, over forty to date. Some are over two hundred feet across. Geologists have been left baffled.

"Now *that* is interesting", he whispered.

Matt didn't know that much about geology, but he did know that sinkholes had been around forever and occurred when too much groundwater dissolved away the subsurface layers. The ground just fell into a void. They were common in places like Florida with a lot of rain and lots of limestone rock below the soil surface. But they were near unheard of in places like Idaho, Montana, Wyoming and Colorado, which were way up in the mountains.

And what's with the birds? he wondered. Intrigued now, he swiveled and reached for his satchel, taking out a slim computer and opening it on the table. In a few moments he had powered it up and found the restaurant's wifi and was entering the headline. He selected one of the most detailed results and quickly read down the page.

In Red Oak, Iowa, expert environmental geologist, Andrew Bennet, who was first into the hole, stated that the cause for the Iowa sinkhole and others was unknown, as the ground was geologically solid, and no severe rain or underground stream activity were present to cause the subsurface erosion. In addition, investigators could find no link between the bird deaths and the sinkhole. Other than a noxious odor, no gases were detected, and no identifiable toxins had been found on the site. Other samples collected were still being analyzed.

Hmm, 'and the Earth shall fall', Matt thought, remembering a scrap from some unknown ancient Arabic prophecy. The pretty waitress appeared beside him, balancing a huge plate on the tips of the fingers of one hand.

"The prince of tortillas...for a prince." Color rose in her cheeks at the blatant flirting, and she slid the plate in front of him.

The quesadilla looked magnificent. Matt looked up at her and flashed his most charming smile. "Beautiful...and the quesadilla looks pretty good too."

The waitresses face went a shade redder and she scampered away, looking back over her shoulder when she got to the kitchen door. Matt looked back down at the food, his mouth watering.

As he ate, he used one hand to find more results for recent sinkholes and was near overwhelmed with the hits – too many to count, and all over the world. Some had pictures – massive dark craters, in some cases hundreds of feet deep. There were a few from the Iowa hole – shots of a lonely house down deep in the darkness, and then a picture of the wall and the symbol. He leaned forward.

"Hello there, what are you?"

Matt knew hundreds of languages, and spoke most. He had studied dialects living and dead all his life, and he knew a communication symbol when he saw one. This picked at his deep memory, but still wouldn't surface. He shook his head, and then read on. The final details almost obscured the geological impact – people were missing – dropped down into the holes and not recovered.

"Wow," Matt said, whistling softly and then inserting another mouthful of quesadilla. What's with that? he wondered. *Can't* be recovered, as the sinkholes are still active, or something else? Hmm, those damned holes must be deep, he concluded.

And the earth really shall fall, he thought, frowning as he read on. The final pages of the paper surprised him – in the missing-pets section, there used to be maybe a single column of furry faces staring out. Instead there were endless appeals for Bitsy the black and white cat, Big Jim the Rottweiler or Sam the retriever – dozens and dozens, all gone missing.

Times sure have changed, he thought and tore out the sinkhole article and the images from the paper. Matt jumped as his phone buzzed in his pocket, and seeing the unknown number he contemplated letting it go to message.

He shrugged – he wasn't exactly pressed for time, so he stuck it to his ear.

"Hello?"

He listened for a few seconds and nodded. "I've been known to do consulting, but my rates are – " His eyebrows shot up. "Wow, I mean, sure, I think I can make that. A day's work sounds interesting and coincidently I was just reading about – Yes, I understand." He hung up and snorted. Government loves spending other people's money. Still, a day's consultancy at *those* rates with all expenses paid would take care of his rent for the next week. Why not? he wondered and looked again at the strange symbol, straining to remember its implication – nothing came.

After a few seconds he had to look away. He took a bite of his quesadilla even though for some reason he felt a bit queasy.

*

Sun Valley, Idaho

Deputy Will Kramer walked the girl up her front steps, and then checked her house from top to bottom before she would let him leave. Her face was pale, which made the dark rings under her eyes all the more prominent.

After twenty minutes, he left her standing in the hallway, every light blazing in the house. He placed one of his police cards on the hall table, tapping it and asking her to call him if she remembered anything, or had any concerns. She never moved a muscle.

Kramer whistled air through compressed lips. She'd gone out for a date with her boyfriend, and something had scared them – *a monster*, she had called it. Now her boyfriend was missing, and she looked about a hair's breadth away from running screaming down the street and all the way out of town.

He stood at the open door, and touched his hat. She still didn't move, just stood with her shoulders slumped and hair forward over her face.

"Alison, I'll call if we find out anything, okay?" There was the slightest hint of a nod. Kramer exhaled and shut the door.

Doesn't look like any breakup I ever seen, he thought as he jumped back in his cruiser and eased away from the curb. He headed straight over to the missing man's house. Mr Marc Rice lived right on Knob Hill Park at the end of Alpine Lane – ten minutes away.

Kramer slowed as he turned into the street. It was coming up to three in the morning, and it was tomb silent. He wound down the window as he pulled over exactly where Alison had told them she had seen her boyfriend for the last time, earlier in the evening. He switched off his car, and listened to the engine tick as it cooled – there was nothing else – no sound, no motion.

His eye caught movement and his neck wrenched as he swung around quickly. Several large fat cockroaches were heading single file along the gutter toward the park. They moved quick and with purpose. In a moment, they had entered the grassed area and vanished into the dark void.

"Good riddance," he whispered.

Looking to the sidewalk, he saw that it still glistened from the spillage mentioned in the report. He grimaced as several cockroaches stopped at its edge, seemed to taste it, and then headed at top speed into the park. He pushed open the door, stepped out and stretched his back.

Kramer wrinkled his nose; the air stank of a strange fishy odor. "Phew, garbage day."

He pulled his long black flashlight free and held it up in his fist. He then touched the button on the mic attached to his shoulder. "Sal, going to check out the park at Knob Hill. Over."

"Okay, Will: stay in contact and take care," the voice said in among the crush of electronic noise.

"You got it. Kramer out." He swung the flashlight around. There was nothing but the foul odor. Stepping up onto the pavement, he saw that the black spillage marks had mostly dried, but still left a silvery snail trail that shone stickily in his beam.

"Nice." He walked slowly toward the park, unconsciously placing his steps to avoid crushing leaves, roaches, or making any noise. He didn't know why, but he had the urge to be as silent as humanly possible. He came to the park edge and its fringe of trees. For the most part the park was empty save for scrubby bushes and a huge rocky outcrop that gave the area its name. Normally this time of year it was dry and smelled of dust, and not much else.

Knob Hill Park wasn't exactly a showpiece, like some of the national park areas closer to Bald Mountain that had willows, alders, cottonwoods, and sedges with Idaho fescue and bluebunch wheatgrass growing underneath. This was more an open space favored by dirt bike riders on weekends, much to the chagrin of the peace-loving residents nearby.

Kramer exhaled through pressed lips and shook his head. He doubted it would even be used for that any more, now that a *huge sinkhole* had opened up in its center. He walked out a few dozen feet, breathing through his mouth to avoid the sulfurous odors wafting over the dry ground. He panned his light slowly over the landscape.

"Jesus *Christ*." He started, and felt his neck and scalp tingle from the shock. *Someone was there*. Still as a post, but around fifty feet further in, standing there in the dark. Kramer couldn't tell if the guy was facing him or not. However, he looked big, bigger then him, and damned bulky. Marc Rice had been a little dude, according to his girl.

"That you, Clem?" Kramer squinted. "Trying to give me a heart attack here?" Big Clem Johnson was an ex-wrestler, six-eight easy, but this guy seemed even bigger.

Kramer reached down to unclip his gun while keeping the beam of his light on the figure. He advanced a half dozen feet. "Sir, you need a hand?" He waited, but the figure didn't flinch.

He swore softly, and angled his head to touch the mic button on his shoulder. "Got someone in Knob Hill Park. Not responding to instructions." He went to take another step, but felt his primitive core rebel. "Ah, Sal, are there any cars in the area you could send?"

"Will, is there a problem?" Her voice contained a hint of concern.

Kramer smiled. "No, no, just like to have some backup. This guy is no lightweight and isn't talking." He let go of the microphone, and stood a little straighter. Kramer, at six-two, was a fair-sized man, and broad across the shoulders. But he guessed he fell about a foot shy of this guy and was outweighed by a hundred pounds.

"Sir." He drew his gun. In the entire time he had been in the force, he had only drawn it once, when a car chase dropped a load of out-of-town gang-bangers on their doorstep a few years back. Even then, he hadn't needed to fire it.

He stopped his approach, and started to crab to the side, trying to see under what he assumed was a hood or shawl up over the guy's head. He tried again with the light, but couldn't see to pick out any definition – inside the hood, it just looked empty – and wet.

"Sir, you need to answer me. Sir." Kramer swallowed, feeling the pulse of his heart in his chest and neck. He had advanced to within ten feet of the figure, and up closer he seemed even bigger than ever...Or is this guy *actually getting bigger?* he wondered. One thing was for sure, this was no resident.

Kramer resorted to breathing through his mouth as the smell up close was revolting, and he wondered whether the guy had shit himself. He took another step, but felt his stomach roil, from nerves. His feet were begging to challenge his commands, as if his body recognized danger that his brain was too dumb to notice.

Where the fuck is that backup? He ground his teeth.

Maybe a warning shot, he thought. He looked back briefly at the houses through the line of trees. Better not: he'd panic them. He turned back and saw that the thing had shifted, only slightly, but the bulkiness had...rearranged. Then an eye opened inside the hood – he was close enough to see in the beam of a park safety light that it was an amazing grey-blue. It blinked once, and then another opened beside it. Then, to Kramer's horror, another eye opened – an inch above the first two.

"What the fuck?" Kramer lifted his gun in one hand like he'd been trained – gun up, and resting on the lower wrist of the flashlight hand with the light turned toward the target. He strained, working hard to stop the shaking in his limbs as more and more orbs popped open on the thing, and just as quickly bubbled back into the body. The slimy black was no cape or hood or suit: it *was* the thing. What freaked him the most was that he knew all the eyes saw him, looked at him, sized him up, and stared with interest. Soon other pustules and protuberances bulged and formed, and Kramer's nerves gave out. He dragged one foot back a half step.

It was if that stumble was the trigger for the thing to explode into movement. It went from a roughly man-shaped column of blackness to a ragged tentacled monstrosity in a second – and in even less time it was a wave of goo enveloping him.

Kramer felt the thing cover his entire body, and every dot of his exposed skin felt compressed, hot and greasy, and then the pain came – it was like being bathed in battery acid. He still held his gun and fired and fired, over and over, the bullets punching holes in the dark flesh, but the holes quickly closed over. It made no difference to its hold on him.

In the last seconds of his consciousness, he felt himself lifted and something warm and wet worm its way into his mouth and force itself down his throat and into his stomach. He would have vomited if he could.

Alison's monster, he thought as he felt himself being carried, and he knew exactly where – the sinkhole.

Chapter 4

Darayya, outskirts of Damascus, Syria

Alfarouq skipped down the early-morning street. Dust puffed up as his battered shoes touched what remained of the sidewalk – broken roof tiles, decrepit cardboard boxes, smashed windows and miles of rubble littered the bloodstained concrete. The only real traffic was the occasional beat-up truck, and perhaps a cruising military vehicle on the lookout for snipers, insurgents or other slow-moving targets. Violence was now so common and enduring that ten-year-old 'Fookie' remembered little else.

Darayya City was one of the oldest in Syria, and home to over seventy-five thousand people. It was said it was where Paul the Apostle had his conversion to Christianity – *on the road to Damascus*, as the saying went. Christians, Jews, Yazidis, Druzes, all gone now: chased out. Fookie shrugged. Everyone would be gone soon, and then who would be left to fight? He thought about it, and then made up his mind – maybe a good thing.

Fookie picked up a metal rod and banged it on the ground, making a hollow clang that reverberated down the street, fading away to silence...almost. A single fat roach marched out from under a broken box, and he banged the steel rod down again, crushing it in half. "I'm boss here," he said to its remains.

Lifting his head, he could just hear the faint sound of a radio playing somewhere, and he headed toward it, hoping some of his friends had woken and were gathering for another idle day on the streets.

He kicked at a soda bottle, sending it spinning down the road, and watched as it whirled to a stop. Something crashed into the ground beside it in a dark and wet explosion. Fookie frowned and took a few steps closer. Another thing struck the littered street further away, breaking glass, and sending a small billow of dust into the air. Then came another and another. One of the things flapped once, weakly, and then lay still. A blackbird, then, he guessed.

He approached one of the smashed birds and lifted his rod, ready to poke at it, but paused mid-reach as the street rumbled beneath him. Fookie looked up and saw a few windows open and heads stick out; scowling faces stared down at him, as though somehow he was the cause of the deep vibrations.

Fookie looked above their heads, then higher – the brightening sky was filled with circling birds – not all the same – some huge crows, some starlings, pigeons and tiny fast-moving sparrows that darted in among the tornado of feathers and fury. They took turns peeling off, and then dive-bombing the ground, committing suicide in some sort of strange attack on the Earth.

Another vibration, shallow this time, as though something was getting nearer. Fookie looked around, confused, and not a little frightened now. The ground jumped up and down, and mortar and tiles fell from roofs to explode on the already debris-littered street. As if a signal had been given, the remaining birds all started to dive at the ground, striking hard, dying instantly. They were silent missiles of flesh and feather; their fury was unbounded.

Fookie placed his hands up over his head and ran for a tattered awning as the birds continued to explode in red wetness around him.

"Crazy," he screamed once under cover. He pointed his rod at the small bodies beginning to pile up in the street. "Crazy."

He could hear alarms going off, and shouts of confusion and also of terror. Fookie thought it might be a good idea to retreat home for a while and looked up to check for more birds. The sky seemed empty so he ran hard – just as the ground gave a mighty heave. Right then, from out of every doorway, window, drain, and crack in the pavement, roaches streamed in long lines, falling over each other, excited, skittering and scattering, moving faster than anything Fookie had ever seen.

He screamed, but his voice was drowned out as a huge crack ran down the center of the road, unzipping to reveal blackness that was like a river of night opening at his feet. The roaches piled into it like lemmings on their suicide dive. A vile gas belched upward and then a jet of hot air that made the young boy gag as he ran. He held his nose, crying now. Fookie ran harder, in a wide-legged style, looking like a ragged sailor trying to keep his balance on the heaving deck of a ship at sea. He leaped over the crack that was widening from an inch to many feet in a blink. The ground on the other side fell a foot, then immediately rose about a dozen feet. Fookie tripped and fell forward onto his face. He lifted his head and looked back over his shoulder. The buildings, the street, the piles of dead birds, hung there momentarily, before dropping...and dropping and dropping. A deafening roar filled the air as though some giant beast was in its death throes.

Dust rose in sheets as the buildings slid downward. As Fookie stared, he had the impression of terrified faces pressed against windows that had been three stories in the air, but were sinking now into a void that continued to grow. There was a howling, perhaps of stone and steel being crushed, or was it the sound of a thousand voices collectively shrieking their horror?

Fookie's nerve broke and he also screamed again, backing away crablike, as the ground continued to grind beneath him. He squeezed his eyes tight and covered his ears for many minutes until the ground stopped shaking. When he finally peeped from just one eye, there were settling clouds of dust, and a monstrous pit, bigger even than the Aarjess Soccer Stadium.

The entire block, Fookie's block, had been swallowed.

*

Hussein ben Albadi, former Doctor of Anthropology at the University of Damascus, felt the pull of vertigo as he stood at the edge of the enormous crater or pit or whatever it was that had opened up in the earth. Even standing right at its edge, and seeing the massive emptiness before him, he found it hard to believe.

Thousands of people had been evacuated from the surrounding suburbs, but still there were hundreds of figures lining the rim: people who, like him, had come to gaze into the crater's depths. Government forces, rebels, fanatics had all suspended hostilities to stand shoulder to shoulder with disbelieving neighbors.

Albadi crouched, as he didn't trust his shaking legs so close to something that overwhelmed his senses. Looking down, where the light still allowed details to be seen, there was a cross section of the surface world, as if someone had sliced a child's birthday cake, and the layers of icing, sponge and cream were all laid bare. Except here, it wasn't sugar and sweets on display, but half basements with furniture stacked against walls, an underground car park with a single car left hanging precariously at the edge of nothingness, the other vehicles having been swallowed by the monstrous pit, and broken pipes, the water pouring from their severed ends turning to mist long before it disappeared into the darkness. Further down, and just before everything disappeared in darkness, he saw what was below human intrusion into the thin outer skin of our world. The soil here became bedrock. Whatever had occurred had pulled down buildings, streets, soil, and even hundreds of feet of solid stone.

Albadi couldn't even guess at how far it went down but, like a few others at the edge, he had a small pair of field glasses that he used to peer into the depths. Once or twice he thought he saw movement but quickly discounted it as a trick of the near non-existent light against the dark and darker shadows.

A few hundred feet along, someone lit and dropped a red smoking flare into the depths. Some pulled back momentarily, fearful the dot of heat and light would ignite flammable gasses, but eventually curiosity won out, and they crept back to watch it drop lower and lower, until it became a flaring spark that finally landed, creating a small pool of hellish red light on the sunken architecture about a thousand feet below them.

Albadi exhaled and felt slightly dizzy. He perspired profusely, and didn't feel well at all. Apart from the feeling of empathetic shock at the knowledge that hundreds of people were either dead or trapped down in the depths of the crater, there was something else – a feeling of unease and foreboding that made his gut roil. When he had read about the people going missing, and the holes opening up, he had been dreading this. Could it be true? he wondered.

He and a few other academics had taken it upon themselves to preserve the great literary history, the precious works in the ancient Damascan library, from terrorists and looters. Albadi and the other men and women had worked with a mix of speed and care as they packed up the ancient books, manuscripts and scrolls. However, there had been one discovery that had frozen him. Wrapped in an oilcloth, hidden from sight between two religious texts, it was just a copy of an earlier work, but still, from the first page, it had taken his breath away. Fanciful blasphemy, he had thought from the scraps he had been able to read.

But now? Albadi, still crouching, turned and threw up onto the ground. After a moment, he wiped his mouth with a sleeve and got to his feet, pushing quickly back through the crowd. The more distance he put between himself and the pit, the better he felt. It was strange: he didn't see the crater as a geological oddity, but instead some evidence of infection, a canker on the face of the Earth from which an evil and pustulant scourge would soon burst forth.

The Book said this would happen. He needed to be home. The Book also said there was worse to come.

Chapter 5

United States Army Forces Command, Fort Bragg, North Carolina

General Henry Decker looked at the image on the wall screen, hands on his hips. Beside him, Major Joshua Abrams walked forward, holding up an arm and sweeping it across the picture.

"Two thousand feet wide, give or take. And goes straight down about a thousand. No survivors." He turned to Decker. "This is in Syria. It's bone dry, and only suffers sinkholes rarely in its lowland marsh areas." He shook his head. "No reason for it, sir."

"Just like in Iowa, and in Kansas, Montana, Utah, and…" Decker's forehead creased. "Just how many other places now?"

"Five hundred confirmed significant sites…just in the USA. Over four thousand worldwide, and they're getting bigger and deeper, as we can see from this monster."

"Jesus Christ, this is not normal," Decker said.

"Far from it, sir. Right across the States we suffer from sinkholes, but the things that make this series of events very abnormal are the size and depths, and the absence of ground water. In fact most of these are opening up in geologically very old and dry areas."

Decker frowned. "Theories?"

Abrams shook his head. "Plenty, but none that make sense." He brought up another image, this one of the Iowa hole, and also a shot of Andy Bennet. "This guy, a geologist, was first into the Iowa hole. He took several samples from the base. Seems to know what he's doing. Results are yet to be confirmed, but the material recovered at the bottom of the pit was biological...*primordial* biological."

"What the hell does that mean? Primordial as in some ancient animal? This isn't getting any clearer, Josh." Decker's jaws worked.

Abrams exhaled and shrugged. "Yes and no. More like basic tissue matter, with a simple cell structure – protoplasmic almost."

Abrams picked up a small remote and changed the screen image again. Next was a report, heavily redacted. "There's more. Mr Bennet also wrote a report that is now in our hands." The next image cleared away the blackout stripes over the words. "In it, he says the earth walls at the bottom of the sinkhole were spongy, but not as in damp. More like the soil was resolidifying, as though it had been made soft, not by water, but by some other means, and it was that which caused the house to drop."

"I'm not liking the sound of this." Decker stared evenly at the image. "We're testing vibration weapons that can soften entire surface structures. Maybe someone else is trying out something similar on us."

"Maybe, but I don't think so." Abrams turned the page. "And this is where it gets weird. Bennet also recovered something from down in the pit – from within the wall actually – this sleeve." He shrugged. "Unremarkable by itself, but it was *in the wall*, looked *dragged in*, as Bennet put it.

We sequestered the sample and had our own labs analyze it – weird on top of weird. We did a DNA test with some epithelials on the material against one of Bill Anderson's surviving relatives – we got an immediate hit and confirmed the shirt definitely belonged to our missing man."

Abrams sat on the table's edge, pulling at his lip for a moment. "We found something else on that sleeve, some fluid: not blood as Mr Bennet first wrote in his report, but something else – once again biological."

Abrams reached over to enlarge the image of the ragged end of the sleeve. He sat staring for a few seconds.

The general leaned forward. "Well, go on."

"Saliva...or something like saliva." Abrams said slowly.

"Something *like* saliva, huh?" Decker groaned. "Major, can you please get to it? Was it saliva or not, and what the hell dribbled it onto the arm of our missing Mr Anderson – did they have a dog?"

"No." Abrams exhaled, knowing his superior officer was already getting fed up with the unexplained phenomena – so was he, for that matter. "Okay, let me lay out what we got back from the labs – the substance is *like* saliva in that contains sodium, potassium, calcium, magnesium chloride, bicarbonate, phosphate, and trace amounts of iodine, plus a truckload of amino acid chains all in a solution of mucopolysaccharides and glyco-pseudo proteins – mucus – exactly as in saliva."

Decker folded his arms, his face hardening. Abrams continued, picking up the pace. "But the lab boys are stumped as the proteins don't make sense. They're biological, but biological straight out of a nightmare – could be mammal, could be reptile, could even be jellyfish with all the mismatch of DNA strands they've identified so far...And some don't match *anything* in the global genetic libraries."

"So we have no idea what left these weird traces behind?" Decker asked.

"Maybe we do. VELA picked up movement in a few of its last scans." Abrams changed the image on the screen again. The new picture showed the massive Syrian sinkhole viewed from about ten thousand feet. He clicked through the images as the satellite drilled down further, and further, until the screen darkened as the VELA magnification dived into the heart of the pit.

"It's what made us have another look."

"Survivors?" Decker eyebrows were raised.

"That's what we thought until we got the IT guys to clean up the images." Abrams moved through a number of pictures, and the grainy darkness became sharper, more focused.

"Holy shit, what is that? A deformed bear?" Decker craned forward.

There were now three images, side by side, taken over a few seconds. In the first, something large and dark moved towards a human body. In the next, the thing was seen to be dragging the corpse by one leg toward the pit wall. In the final frame, it had vanished – seemingly into the dirt.

Abrams shook his head, eyes fixed on the screen. "We have no idea what that was. But according to the Syrians, who have now ventured into the sinkhole, there were no survivors. However, we have heard via informal channels that this isn't the entire story: they *assumed* there were no survivors, because they didn't find anyone down there – living or dead."

"Jesus." Decker exhaled. "So whatever that was, it wasn't the only one."

"No, we don't think so," Abrams said. "Not if we estimate how quickly the hundreds of bodies were removed."

"Removed? To where?"

Abrams shrugged.

Decker turned back to the screen. "Well, whatever it was, it was below ground – thank god for that. We can at least contain it."

Abrams shook his head. "Maybe, maybe not. We are starting to find traces of this substance above ground – in Arizona, Utah, Iowa, Idaho, Texas: the list goes on." He looked up. "Something else..."

"Jesus Christ, *there's something else?*"

"Pets, dogs, cats, local wildlife – they started to go missing just after these phenomena started. We thought that the animals, being sensitive, might have just hightailed it." He exhaled. "But now people are also vanishing." He called up more images. "And there are these...clues, hopefully."

Decker leaned in to examine the images on the screen. "Is that...a language? Have we translated it?"

"We don't know what it is. Our own experts say it *could be* a language, but none they know of – or at least none they know of existing today, or even in the recent past. But we haven't yet consulted a few of the experts on ancient languages and symbolism."

"Then do it. Someone is trying to tell us something – we need to know what it is." Decker rubbed two gnarled hands through his hair. "Jesus Christ, Josh, I feel I know less now than when you started talking. We need to be on the front foot here – skip to what we're doing about it."

Abrams nodded. "The events, so far, seem random, unpredictable; so for the time, we should stick with what clues we have, and pursue them. The geologist, Bennet, reported the sleeve was in the wall, and that the walls were solidifying, like they had *been* soft. Maybe that's how this thing occurred. The major activity is below ground; Bennet wanted to excavate." He shrugged. "Maybe we should let him."

"Yes." Decker stared for a moment. "I need answers, and so far I feel we're in the eye of a shit storm without an umbrella." He half turned. "Have you got the media nailed down? Don't need Joe Public banging on our door until we know what we're dealing with."

"We've got a lid on it for now, sir." Abrams from his notes. "The majors from the television networks, radio and newspapers are all onboard. Also, the internet carriers – we needed to wave the National Security Act at them, but they'll play ball. A few local news jockeys may try and run a story, but we've got counter-information ready to go." Abrams half smiled. "For now, we own the data flow."

Decker grunted. "Good man. Make it happen, Joshua."

Abrams gathered his folders. "Already in motion, sir. I've dispatched one of my best people with a team of engineers down to Iowa. They're going to pick up a languages expert on the way, rendezvous with Bennet and commence a subsurface excavation." He turned to the screen, and the shredded blue-checked sleeve. "If there's anything down there, we'll find it."

*

"Holy shit." Matt eased the rental to the curb.

He pulled the scrap of paper from the dash and read the address again – this was it all right, but where he was expecting to see the hole in the ground where Bill and Margie Anderson's house used to be, there was a huge inflated dome covering the entire site. Barriers were set up and two military men stood casually at the entrance.

He was due to meet up with some army guy, but had decided to swing by to look at the site first. He pushed open his door and stepped out. Down the road an SUV pulled in, and behind the wheel a big, older guy in a cap glared at him.

Matt nodded – the guy just kept glaring.

"Sheesh, welcome to Pleasantville." Matt smiled and walked toward the barriers. He noticed the front flap of the dome billowing slightly and knew that meant negative air –

a decontamination entrance. This was a big deal; something must have turned up in the sinkhole. He felt a prickle of apprehension on his neck.

Matt pushed aside one of the wooden barriers and flashed his friendliest smile at the closest guard. "Hi there."

The man did little more than square his stance, but remained at ease. "Good morning, sir."

Matt nodded. "I'm Matt Kearns, Professor Matt Kearns. I'm expected, well, not really, but I was sort of invited..."

"Sir, do you have an appointment?" The guy looked bored, but his eyes were stone chips in a granite-hard face.

"Yes and no; sort of. I was invited down, but not yet. Do you think I can speak to...?"

Suddenly, the entrance flap was thrown back and another soldier appeared – a woman. She looked briefly down at a clipboard, smiled and then stuck out a hand. "Professor Matthew Kearns; I'm glad you could make it."

The two huge guards stepped aside like double doors being thrown open. Matt's hand automatically came up to meet hers. "No problem. But I didn't know I needed an appointment or that you were even here. What's going on, and why are you guys, I mean the military, involved?"

"I'm so sorry, we've been trying to get hold of you, through your office, your home, text messages." She shrugged.

Matt reached into his pocket and pulled out his phone – three new messages waiting for him. He read quickly, and then sighed. "Captain Kovitz? *You're* the military guy?"

She nodded. "That's me. But you can call me Tania. We've kinda been waiting for you. I work for the military's Federal Archeology Division."

Matt had never heard of a Federal Archeology Division, but he *had* always wondered how it was the army managed to turn up so quickly to Civil War sites to begin excavation. These guys obviously worked fast.

She smiled as he looked at her properly. The more he stared the more he liked what he saw – clear blue eyes and blond hair pulled back tight, with a spray of freckles across her nose. Even though she only seemed to be in her early thirties, about his age, she had lines around her mouth and eyes, signifying years of outdoor work.

"So, is there something of archeological value here?" He pointed to the dome. "And that looks like a contamination shroud."

She continued smiling, not bothering to look over her shoulder. "It's just to give us some space and privacy as we work. Remember, we haven't yet found Mr and Mrs Anderson. If we do discover them, best not to have a news chopper broadcast it before we've had a chance to inform relatives."

Sounds reasonable, he thought. "Or worry the neighbors, I guess. Makes sense."

"Come on in." She turned and nodded briefly to the two guards who came to attention as she passed.

She pushed the flap aside and held it open for him. Matt felt the rush of warm air bathe his face. There was the smell of something unfamiliar that nevertheless picked at his memory.

Inside, the plastic dome cast a white glow over everything. Matt saw that the sides of the enormous hole had been reinforced with ribs of some type of synthetic material, and a cage elevator stood open and waiting at its edge. On the far side, a small crane was anchored to the ground, and it was silently lowering more equipment to the sinkhole's floor.

A young man, also roughly about his own age, leaned against a railing with arms folded. His eyes flicked to Matt, but then went directly to Tania. The guy didn't look military.

"Matt, I'd like you to meet – "

"Howdy." He came forward and stuck out his hand. "Andy Bennet, geology, nice to meet you. You're another archeologist, huh?"

Matt shook the hand. It was rough and callused, and he was sure his felt the exact opposite. "Nice to meet you too, Andy. I'm Matt Kearns, and I just work with old languages. Nothing as glamorous as archeology, I'm afraid." Matt went to lean out over the railing, and saw that floodlights illumin-ated the depths. Several people wandered about around the sunken house in bulky suits.

"Don't sell yourself short, Professor. You're probably the best in your field – both of you are. It's why you're here," Tania said joining him at the railing.

Matt whistled softly. "Wow, how long have all you guys been here?"

"About twelve hours; we got here last night." She looked out over the space, pride on her features.

"And you archeologists always wear HAZMATs?" He turned and raised an eyebrow.

Tania shrugged. "Sure, if some brilliant young geologist by the name of Andrew Bennet has said there was a strange substance in the hole that might turn out to be toxic." She briefly nodded to Andy, and then tilted her head. "I've already been down there, and look..." she patted her chest "...still hale and hearty. But military rule number one: better to be safe than sorry, right?"

There was a commotion behind them, and Tania turned momentarily to see one of the guards stick his head past the front flap. "Captain, his partner?"

"It's okay, lieutenant, let him pass." She turned to Andy. "Oops."

Frank bustled in, looking red-faced and pissed off. "Goddamn army assho–" He saw Tania and his lips clamped shut. He smiled and half bowed. "Ma'am." He turned to glare at Andy, then Matt, and then looked out over the work going on. "Holy shit...sorry."

Tania introduced herself, but Frank couldn't take his eyes off the work in the sinkhole. He took off his cap and wiped his brow. "Looks like someone's been busy."

"Federal Archeology Division," Andy said, and jerked a thumb at Matt. "And a languages guy."

Matt went to stick his hand out.

"Bullshit." Frank waved the hand away. "Pardon my French, Captain. But I've been on sites where you guys have turned up, and at most you get some pencil-neck with a mobile ground-penetrating radar and a clipboard, and that's about it."

Tania held up her board and shrugged. "That makes me the pencil-neck, I guess." She motioned to the work going on. "Gentlemen, we can cross a river, a deep gorge or burrow through a mountain if circumstances demand it...and we think they demand it here." She turned back to Andy. "Mr Bennet, your report brought us here, that, and the hundreds of these holes opening up right across the country." She stared down into the pit. "We're looking for answers, and I think you are too. You said in your report you wanted to excavate." She pointed to a rack of suits. "Put those on, gentlemen, and then let's go excavate."

*

Matt leant against the cage wall in the elevator and let his eyes wander over to the other occupants, which wasn't easy to do with the HAZMAT suit's hood over his head. Andy Bennet was pretty intense, but seemed professional. He noticed that the geologist rarely took his eyes from Tania, and guessed he was smitten.

He admired the guy's fortitude. Matt had a problem with caves, though perhaps once, a long time ago, he could have descended by himself. But not any more. Andy's partner, Frank, looked ready to explode, and that wasn't just the from the ill-fitting suit. Matt grinned, and looked across to see Tania, ice cool and smiling back at him. He nodded in return.

Matt doubted that the glyphic writing Andy had discovered in the sinkhole had anything to do with the land drop, but as he had been only a few hours away, it was worth having him come and look them over. If they were anything like the image he had seen in the newspaper, he doubted he'd be able to help. But he was interested, and he still he got paid whether he *could* help or not – money for old rope, as his father used to say.

He noticed that Andy held tight to the railing in the five-man cage and listened to Tania deliver a continuous stream of information as they slowly descended. She explained the different machines, people involved, and what their overall expectations were based on his report. At one point she had Andy point out to them where exactly he had found his samples, her voice piped to all their suits via a two-way radio.

Matt pulled at his visor. Tania had explained that for now they would need to use what was termed a *Level-A suit* – the highest grade of protection against vapors, gases, mists, and particles. Even though it was warm outside, and he was encased in a single piece whole-body garment of thick, impermeable material, the suit contained a personal canister of breathable air that was ice-cool against his skin. Fresh air and air conditioning: bearable, he thought as he adjusted the hood again. Apart from this stupid visor. He held it in place for a second or two.

Matt had to swivel most of his upper body to look at the military woman. The full-face piece – a large curved sheet of clear material – was difficult to get used to, and allowed zero peripheral vision.

On the other side of Tania, Frank gripped the bar, hard. The older man's large and overweight frame pushed at his suit front, and even behind the faceplate he was visibly flushed.

Matt nudged Andy, and motioned towards his colleague.

Andy turned and peered at Frank. "Okay there, big guy?"

Frank flashed him a look, and then nodded jerkily. He added a small salute.

The cage eased to a stop and Tania pushed open the gate. "Gentlemen." They stepped out, and Tania shut the gate. "Follow me."

She took the lead and they walked single file. The amount of light and activity created a show-room environment that made everything seem garish and movie-set-like. Still, Matt was thankful for the extra light as it mostly dispelled the sensation of foreboding he had experienced travelling down.

The four of them skirted other people in similar suits who were working in teams, either collecting the dead birds, scraping samples from door frames and window sills, or waving what looked like Geiger counters at different sections of the newly fortified walls.

"What killed the birds?" Andy asked.

Tania looked from the geologist to the men dragging the bags of feathered corpses. "The birds killed the birds – did it themselves. Just flew into the ground." She stopped beside a stack of shovels and picks ranging from full ditch-digging size right down to gem-collector picks.

Andy picked up one of the tiny hammers and turned. "Where do we start?"

Mat snorted, liking the guy.

"Very funny." Tania took it from him. "I didn't know geologists had such sophisticated senses of humor." She smiled and dropped the tiny tool back onto the pile. "And we can start wherever you say – you get to show us where you found the sleeve, and we'll commence there. Further to your report, we'd also like your advice and commentary on what the consistency of the soil looks like as we excavate – any changes or anomalies."

She swiveled to Matt. "And Professor Kearns here can give us his insights into the symbols."

"So it was a language?" Andy asked, eyebrows raised behind the Perspex.

Matt shrugged. "Might be nothing more than a formation anomaly. Once I've seen the site, and also any evidence of other communication, I'll be able to judge whether it was human in origin or not."

"Excellent," Tania said. "Are we good?"

Frank and Matt nodded, and Andy bowed, and held out an arm. "This way."

Tania waved over a couple of men and motioned for them to bring the digging equipment. Andy approached a section of wall and leaned in close. "Here."

Matt stepped up beside him.

"This is where the shirt sleeve was...and the carving or whatever it was." He waved his arm over a wall now pocked with digging marks.

Matt reached out and touched it. It was quite solid. "You said it was soft?"

Andy reached out and stuck a finger in. "It was softer than this." He turned and looked over their shoulders. "Can we...?"

Tania spun. "Turn that light over here."

One of the halogen stands was swung around and they were lit up like stage actors. Andy backed up a step.

"Notice something strange, Frank?"

The older man folded his arms. "Yup; most of the surrounding strata down this far is Cambrian-age bedrock, some shale, and a little limestone for good measure. Most that is, except that section right there." Frank pointed with a thumb to the ten-foot-wide area Andy had just been examining up close.

"Bingo. It's hardening up now, but still not rock." He held a hand out to Matt. "Stand back, Prof; real men at work." He grabbed a medium-sized shovel and gently stuck it into the wall. He pushed and then levered free a bucket-sized clod, and used the shovel end to gently mash the soil flat. "Still soft, and not even rock fragments; it's like there was a tunnel here that was filled in." He looked back to the wall. "But nothing I know of could do it that completely without leaving a trace of the excavation work." He turned to Tania. "Could you guys? The military, I mean."

Her mouth turned down and she slowly shook her head. "We've got equipment and techniques that are powerful, fast, and adaptive, but not pretty. There'd be traces of any work done by a team like ours."

"That's what I thought." Andy turned back to the wall. "Frank, give me a hand – let's see where this rabbit hole leads."

Matt watched as together the two men gently shoveled dirt from the section. Tania had her soldiers clear away the debris, piling it further along the cave. The piles grew as the hole became deeper; and after about fifteen minutes, the pair had dug about five feet into the wall. The going had been fairly easy due to the softness, but still, working in the thick suits must be hot and fatiguing.

Andy stopped. Frank was already leaning on his shovel, slightly bent over.

"Hot." He wiped at his forehead, and then growled at not being able to reach the damp skin behind the faceplate. Matt could see that Frank's face was once again very red and streaming with perspiration.

Tania obviously saw the same. "Shift change." She pointed to the two young soldiers. "Jackson, Morris, take over, and easy as you go." She turned to Andy but spoke to her men. "Mr Bennet here will supervise."

Andy handed over his shovel, and the two men set to deepening the tunnel.

After a further twenty minutes, the lights behind them had to be re-angled to illuminate the hole's depth. They had dug in close to twenty feet, the soldiers having made much better headway than the geologists.

Jackson dug in hard, and a slab of earth fell away. He called over his shoulder. "Got something." He stepped aside.

Morris did the same, and Tania ordered them out so she, Frank, Andy and Matt could crowd in.

"Like what I saw before." Andy traced the glyph with his hand.

Matt held up his flashlight, following the indentations over the whorls, dots and lines. "Well, it's definitely not a fluke of geology."

Andy blew air from his lips. "I could have told you that, genius."

Matt shook his head. "It's probably a picture language, or a talisman, but like nothing I've ever seen."

"It looks a little like Sumerian," Tania said as she crowded in close to him.

Matt hmm-hmmd as he reached out to touch the symbol. The pain was instantaneous and acute. There was a roar in his ears like that of a train approaching in the subway, and immediately he felt his gorge rise to the back of his throat, burning it with the acid from his belly.

He stepped back and coughed. As if a switch had been thrown, the pain, noise and other sensations vanished.

"Hey, you okay?" Tania grabbed at him, and stared hard into his visor.

"Whoa." He shook his head. "Weird." He blinked. "Yeah, yeah, I'm fine. Must have..." He shrugged. "I don't know." He smiled at her and squeezed her arm. "Yeah, I'm okay." He held up his hand and rubbed his thumb and forefinger together; the dirt was mushy between his fingers. "Sumerian, sure, it's certainly old enough. I mean Sumerian or Egyptian got interesting around five thousand years ago, beating out Minoan and Chinese by like a thousand years. But there were languages long before that; it's just that they didn't survive in a written form."

"Can you read it?" Andy asked.

Matt shook his head. "From one symbol? No way."

"Hey, I'm glad we brought you." Andy grinned.

Matt flipped him the bird, it not quite working in the suit's bulky gloves. He turned. "Can you get a shot?"

"On it." Tania lifted a small camera, and it flashed several times.

"There's something else in here." Andy nudged Matt aside, and lifted his flashlight. He tugged at something in the dirt, teasing it free. "Another shred of material." He looked around and scoffed. "This far in? That's freaking impossible." He handed it to the military woman.

Tania lifted it up in the light. "More shirt." She looked up. "We DNA-tested the previous sample you found – we confirmed it was definitely on Mr Anderson at some point."

Frank snorted. "Well it isn't now, and it didn't get down here via sedimentation, percolation or even via some sort of drain – way too deep. That leaves it getting in there *after* the land fell into the sinkhole."

"And that doesn't make sense either." Andy said. "But it's in there, so let's follow it." He lifted his shovel. "The trail of cookie crumbs says: *go this way.*"

"Wait." Matt held up his hand with Andy's shovel poised over the symbol. He would have loved to take an imprint, but he knew it wasn't possible in the time they had. "Ah, forget it."

Andy dug in again. Both Frank and Andy excavated for another ten minutes, stopping now and then to pull more fragments free: more scraps of clothing; a woman's shoe, split open; a wristwatch, still working; and what could have been a large clump of hair.

The soil now had the consistency of an underdone chocolate cake – soft, moist, but slimy moist. For the last few minutes the men had been scooping it away rather than digging, and the going had been easier.

"Jesus Christ." Frank staggered back as a huge clod fell away and the glare of the light revealed the object. In the harsh illumination, the back of a human head came as a shock. There was thin gray hair, the tips of ears and just the hint of a blue checked collar showing.

"Holy shit; he's *stuck* in there, goddamn it." Frank coughed wetly in his suit.

Matt grimaced as he looked at the grisly thing.

Andy placed a hand on his friend's shoulder. "Hold it together, Frank. You don't want to puke in that suit or you'll be swimming in it until we leave."

Captain Tania Kovitz stepped in close to the head. "Mr Bill Anderson, I presume. So there you are." She held up her light, moving it to different angles, illuminating the gray-haired scalp.

Matt could see that inside her mask her eyes showed no fear, but were instead puzzled and curious. She looked briefly back and around at the tunnel they were in.

"We're a good thirty feet in here," she said.

While they had been digging, the soldiers had been installing support struts of the same strong synthetic material that lined the huge pit outside, more of them in close to where they were now, as the soil looked like it was liquefying once again.

She reached up with one gloved hand and touched the hair. She shook her head. "How the hell would this guy get blasted so far in?"

Andy just shook his head, apparently not able to speak. He looked baffled, and Frank's pallor indicated he was indeed fighting against his lunch making a reappearance. Tania reached for the knife at her waist, and gently started to clear the soil away from one side of the head, bringing her face in real close. After a minute she slowed.

"What the hell...?" She dug a little on the other side of the embedded head, wiped and then sheathed her knife. She reached up again and took hold of Bill Anderson's head, and tugged. There was a wet plop, and then the skull, or what was left of it, came free in her hand. Frank got even closer to losing it, retching loudly.

"Oh god." Andy coughed and held a forearm uselessly up to the faceplate of his suit.

Matt grimaced at the thing she held. The skull wasn't a skull at all: instead it was nothing more than a cranial cup, as the front half, the half with the facial features, along with the skull's contents, was gone.

Tania stood looking down at it, her face hidden in the suit's hood. "I don't understand." She held the flashlight up, illuminating the grisly cup – inside it was coated in black slime. "Did he get blown apart?" She looked from Matt to Andy.

Frank cleared his throat and took a few steps closer. He edged around Tania and to the wall. He placed a hand on the dirt where the skull came from. "So soft; strange. Maybe before, when the sinkhole started to fall, it was almost totally liquid, and Bill sort of...sank or floated in there. When it solidified, the geo-pressure tore him apart." He shrugged. "We're a long way down."

Tania nodded slowly and looked back down at the remains of Bill Anderson in her hands. "I better bag this." She walked past Andy and Matt, carefully carrying the skull fragment. Andy looked up at Frank, who nodded, and motioned for the two young men to follow her, before turning back to the wall. The two soldiers who were with them continued to remove debris, following them out with another couple of wheelbarrows full of soft soil.

Andy caught up to Tania and Matt. "That can happen."

"Huh?" She looked bewildered.

"The soil...it can get liquid soft. If it was like liquid, he might have..."

"Really?" Matt waved an arm at the pit floor. "Look around, Andy."

The geologist didn't bother. "I know, I know, why isn't everything else coated, or destroyed? Why is it only Bill and Margaret that have been..." he exhaled and shrugged "...I don't know. Extracted?"

"He's right," Tania said. "Extracted, drawn in...and then pulled apart." She called for a sample bag, and dropped the fragment in. Her face was creased with frustration. "Still doesn't work for me, Mr Bennet. I was sent here for answers, and so far, I've got nothing."

"Back to Mr Bennet now, is it? Hey, don't get angry with me." Andy straightened his visor. "Look, I agree there's still a lot that doesn't make sense, but at least we know what happened to the Andersons now."

"No, we *don't*. We know where bits of them ended up, and that's about it," she fired back.

"Okay, okay." He held up his hands and straightened. "Tania, Captain Kovitz, I'm not sure we should go on. Getting dangerous in there. The soil is way too soft, and no matter how much we secure it, there's a growing chance it'll collapse on us."

She turned, and after a few seconds nodded. "Yeah, you're right. I'll get this sample back to the lab." She shrugged helplessly. "I'm sorry, Andy. But my boss isn't going to be happy. I'm not exactly bringing him back any real answers." She raised an eyebrow at Matt. "None of us are."

Matt shrugged. "I agree, we've done all we can today, we should..." There came a grunt from Frank, and Matt saw

Andy quickly look over his shoulder to the excavated hole, from which the older guy hadn't yet emerged.

"Frank, come on out, buddy, we're done for the day. Let's get out of here," Andy called, even though the microphone in his suit would have carried the voice directly to his friend's ear.

Andy turned back to Tania and smiled. "Friends?"

She smiled and nodded.

"Buy you a drink later? We can toss around some ideas." He flashed her a winning smile.

Matt groaned and was delighted to see Tania shake her head. "Rain check – got to get back."

More of Frank's grunts came over the radio, followed by the sound of his suit material rumpling violently.

"What the...?" Andy frowned. "Frank?" He took a step toward the hole. "He can't hear me."

Tania grabbed his arm. "You're talking directly into a two-way radio – he can't *not* hear you."

They heard more grunting and then what sounded like a sob. "Shit." Andy raced to the hole, disappearing inside fast.

"Wait!" Tania yelled after him. "Soldiers, at arms."

Matt followed Andy, as Tania waited for Jackson and Miller.

In a few seconds Matt caught up to Andy and slid to a halt. The man just stood there, as if in a daze. Matt came up beside him and saw his face was pale, and his mouth slack.

"What is it? What did you see?" Matt looked around. "Where...?"

The end of the tunnel was empty – Frank was gone. The section of wall where the remains of Bill Anderson had been found looked...disturbed, and glistened as if coated in oil or slime.

"It...took him." Andy's words were barely audible.

"Huh? What did?" Matt shook the geologist.

Andy suddenly put a hand to his head, over the microphone at his ear. He moaned. Matt knew why; they could all hear

Frank's voice, not words, but strangulated grunts, struggling and more of the god-awful sobbing.

"Oh god, he's in there...*in there.*" Andy lifted a shovel and started furiously digging. "*Get him out, get him out.*"

"*Stop!*" Matt yelled.

Almost immediately the soil above them collapsed.

*

Andy Bennet sat in a corner of a bustling meeting room with his head in his hands, still not understanding what had happened to his long-time friend and colleague. One minute the big man was right there, and the next he had been *in* the wall. He sat back. *In the freakin wall...*but still alive, and sounding like he was being dragged away. *How can that even happen?*

It can't, it's impossible, he thought. And *impossible* is what everyone kept saying. But he'd been there, he'd seen it, the *thing* that grabbed Frank, held him tight, and then pulled him struggling into the dirt. It couldn't have been real. He must have been in shock, delusional, that was it.

Andy crushed his eyes shut as Frank's struggling, frightened voice continued to torment him. He remembered the fragment of skull belonging to Bill Anderson, and his friend's screams took on a horrifying dimension. He tried to blank them out.

He sat back, feeling nauseated. In the cave-in, they'd lost Jackson, and Matt Kearns and Miller had needed to pull both him and Captain Tania Kovitz to safety. The official report was that both men, Jackson and Frank, had been lost in the collapse – much easer to understand – much easier to believe.

He groaned, not wanting to be here any more, and envied the professor. Matt Kearns had left, and he was here to try and clarify his geological findings, no matter how inexplicable they were.

Andy looked around the room: it was stuffed with military types. Tania had invited him to this meeting just twenty-four hours after losing his friend. He felt like shit, but he guessed that if there were answers to be had, he couldn't possibly say no. Besides, he liked Tania...liked her a lot.

After he was introduced around the room, he had shaken plenty of hands, sat down, and took the offered coffee. No one sat with him, no one talked to him, and he was pretty much ignored. That suited him fine.

Andy studied the crowd as he sipped his coffee. Henry Decker, the general, was top dog. He was large, square and, though the years had turned slabs of muscle to padding, he still looked formidable and sharp.

Just along from him was Major Joshua Abrams in animated conversation with Captain Tania Kovitz. The tall man turned to stare back for a moment, before nodding and then continuing his briefing or argument with his officer.

He watched Tania for a while – she was like a magnificent jewel among granite cliffs. Looking at her calmed him. Her brow furrowed as she spoke; she was obviously not happy with something the tall officer was saying.

General Decker clapped his hands once. "Major."

Abrams crossed to an open computer on the long table. Andy dragged his chair over to it and began to tap at the keyboard. The far wall lit up behind them, and the room quieted. There was a map of North America, covered in red spots – continental measles, Andy thought. He quickly recognized that many of the dots corresponded to sinkholes he was familiar with. The first thing that struck him was the number – hundreds – and a lot of hundreds at that. The second thing that struck him was that the sizes of the red dots varied.

"Too damned many," Decker said his jaw jutting. He turned to Abrams. "Do you have a time plot?"

Abrams tapped at the keys again. The screen went blank, and then a clean map of the USA was displayed. Another tap and dozens of small red dots appeared.

"One month ago," he said, and then pressed another key. The map became more crowded with dots that were twice as big.

"This is two weeks ago." Once more Abrams changed the graphic. This time they came back to the final screen; the dots were twice as big again. "And now we see where we are today."

"Exponential growth," Tania said. "As time progresses, the sinkholes increase in size and in depth." She stepped a little closer to the screen. "And as Mr Bennet has informed us, the ground, the subsurface, the entire geology of the areas varies little between most of these sites."

"You know, when we test drill a new geology, we use a small-bore drill – call it a string," Andy said. "Once we're happy with it, we use bigger drill kits. Thing is, we start small until we know what we're dealing with or we get better at it. That's what this thing looks like to me – the first ones were trials." Everyone turned to him. "And whatever is doing them is getting better at it."

The silence stretched.

"Whatever is doing them." General Decker paced toward him. "Well, that's the question, isn't it? What the hell *is* doing them?" He folded his arms, scanning the room. "Anyone?" He waited. He lifted his hands. "Well, come on, people: thoughts, ideas, theories, anything? You're supposed to be my best and brightest. That's why you're all here, goddamnit."

"Anyone know what an ant lion is?" Andy looked around the room at the blank faces. "It's a little critter, a bug, with massive jaws, that creates a pit in the soil, and lies at the bottom of it. What makes its trap unique is that the ant lion softens the soil so that any ants unfortunate enough to fall into the pit can't climb back out. They get grabbed by those massive jaws, and are pulled below the ground, where they're torn apart and eaten alive." Andy sat back feeling drained as he worked at trying to shut out his friend's screams – *pulled apart and eaten alive*. He knew he'd never really be able to shut them out.

Decker stared at him. Andy stared back. "Bugs." Decker looked from Abrams to Tania. "Well, Captain, is that what you're telling me you think it is? Bugs?"

"No sir," Tania said. "We're still analyzing the samples we found, but we're not ready to suggest any basis for the sinkholes or the other anomalies just yet." She shot Andy a warning glance.

Andy shook his head. "I didn't say it *was* bugs, I'm just saying that something weird is going on down there, and something *did* pull my friend into the hole – *right into the freaking rock and soil*, damnit." Andy was on his feet leaning on his knuckles and trying hard to rein in his frustration.

"The birds." He looked up. "Birds…Are there dead birds at all the sites? Suiciding?"

"Yes." Abrams said. "All of them…And that's another mystery. We're actually using the birds as an indicator now. The ground seismic sensors are useless at predicting these things. There's no initial disturbance, and even during an occurrence, there is little vibration. But hours before an event, the birds gather overhead, and then just minutes prior to the land dropping, they simply fall out of the sky."

"Begging your pardon, sir, but no, they don't *fall*…They dive bomb the site," Tania said quickly. "As Mr Bennet said – they suicide." Tania moved to the computer. "And that's not all." She called up another image of birds circling an area over water, and then in the next image, they were seen flying straight into it. "These are not sea birds, and they are drowning themselves. We've sent down divers and mini-subs where this happened, and we saw evidence of seafloor drop. It's happening on both land and at sea, and, once again, no vibration." She turned to Andy. "They couldn't possibly see it, but they knew."

The seconds stretched, and everyone in the room continued to stare at the image of the birds. Decker broke the silence. "How? How do they know?"

Andy cleared his throat. "Well, they have senses we don't. Birds can detect a magnetic field, that's how they migrate long distances even when there are no landmarks."

"Is this something you've come across before?" Decker asked.

"In my fieldwork, I've come across highly magnetized soil deposits...and they can certainly throw off sensitive equipment. If it was more powerful, then it might just be creating some sort of magnetic field disturbance that affects the birds."

Decker nodded. "Go on."

"Well–"

"I'm not sure," Tania cut in. "Look at the ocean shot again."

All eyes turned to the screen. Tania flicked between surface and underwater shots.

After a few moments, Decker shook his head. "I don't see anything else."

"That's right. I don't either – where are the sharks and rays? These creatures have a highly developed sense of magnetic determination as well. If some sort of magnetic anomaly is strong enough to get the birds' attention from the sky, then it should be an irresistible force for cartilaginous creatures below the surface."

Decker grunted. "Yep." He inhaled and exhaled slowly through his nose. "So, maybe not magnetic, and here we are, back at square one."

"Maybe not," Abrams said. "Captain, take us back to the time line, second to last."

"Yes sir." Tania called back up the second-to-last dot image of the country.

"Thank you, excuse me." He took over, shrinking the image slightly and then calling up a page that had been scanned in. It too was a map of the North America, and red dots had been hand-drawn on it.

"We've been fielding a lot of calls from the concerned public, and theories that ranged from alien crop circles, molemen, and death cults, to, well, you name it and we've been sent it. To date, the cover story for all the phenomena – the bird migrations, bad smells, and the sinkholes, is that they are all related to weather pattern changes due to climate change. It's holding so far, but for how long is anybody's guess."

Tania motioned to the screen. "But then this came in. Notice where they positioned *their* red dots...and then." He called up the final dot position of the country. Every dot hand-drawn on the map corresponded to an actual sinkhole location.

"As I said, this was sent before they occurred." He leaned back and folded his arms. "Last week it meant nothing – this week, it is the most compelling lead we've seen." He looked across to the general. "Someone has reached out to us...from Syria."

"Jesus Christ. Is it a friendly, or are they doing this as a warning?" Decker ran a hand up through his hair.

"They're a friendly, we think. Doctor Hussein ben Albadi – an academic – he checks out. He says the sinkholes are all part of some ancient prophecy. He also sent this..."

Abrams called up an image of a symbol. He paired it with the ones Tania had taken in the Iowa sinkhole: they were almost identical.

"Yep, we got a pattern emerging here," Decker said.

Abrams nodded. "Albadi says he's got further proof and an explanation about what's happening now...and what's *about* to happen."

The general turned slowly. "And exactly what *is* about to happen?"

Abrams smiled flatly. "The end of the world, of course." He then spoke softly. "Seems that to fully understand the prophecy, it needs to be read in its original language. Also there're some vital components that need to be obtained; he can't get to them, but he thinks we can."

"This might be the break we're looking for." Decker looked back at the screen. "You're my science officer, Joshua; get a team together, whatever you need, whatever it takes, make it happen. We are about one more sinkhole away from a damned national, no *international* panic."

*

Matt Kearns walked quickly down Cambridge Street, turned at Fifth, and then again into Thorndike. His apartment was a top floor of a weatherboard building – it had seen better days, but the street was leafy, he could walk to work, and it was well within his budget. Once he knew for sure he had a position at Harvard, he could decide then whether he would kick it up a level.

Besides, he thought, since his relationship with Megan had gone down the tubes he didn't need to feather a nest for someone else's tastes anymore. Spartan was good, in fact: just a TV, bed and refrigerator was fine as far as was he was concerned.

He opened the downstairs door, waved to Mrs Styles who always seemed to be lurking just inside, and climbed the dozen stairs up to his apartment. Inside he looked around. Spartan is good, but lonely, he thought glumly, missing Megan. Matt suddenly remembered the waitress from a few days back, and her smile. We'll have to do something about that – best cure for heartache, he thought, cheering himself.

He dropped his satchel, went to the refrigerator and pulled out a beer, twisting the top off, and then sinking into a battered brown leather armchair. He sipped, enjoying the coolness of the leather against his back after the warm afternoon walk. He had nothing on so could relax and decide later whether to go out for a few drinks or order in and then coach-potato it for the evening.

He drifted back to the job in Iowa, and how the cave had collapsed, killing the soldier. They'd nearly all been killed – they'd got lucky. But he knew sooner or later his own luck would run out. He shivered despite the warmth – the sound of the old geologist somehow trapped in the dirt wall still haunted him. He'd experienced some weird things in his time, and this ranked right up there.

Captain Tania Kovitz had invited him to a debrief with her superiors, but he had declined. The money had been good, but he was glad it had been a short job. He gulped a mouthful of beer, groaning as his phone trilled. He pulled it from his pocket, and glanced down – the caller's number was unknown. His finger hovered over the cancel button for a second or two, but then, bored, he lifted it to his ear.

"Hello?"

"Matthew Kearns?" The voice was rich, deep and cultured.

"Yes. Who's speaking?" Matt asked, sipping again and waiting for the sales pitch.

"Edward Mercer."

Matt sat forward, almost spraying beer across his room. Edward Mercer was the president of Harvard. Before he could even think about it, Matt was on his feet and smiling. He probably should even be saluting. "President Mercer, sir."

This has got to be good news, he thought, his heart starting to race. During his interviews he had meet with several of the senior faculty members and the executive team, but not the president. The man wouldn't call just to give him the kiss off

– he'd leave that to one of the plebs. He went to sip his beer again, but instead put it down and walked to the window.

"What can I do for you, sir?" Joyful expectation welled up in his chest. He wiped his hand on his trousers.

"Matthew, do you know what Harvard requires?"

"Sure." An easy one, thought Matt. "*Veritas,* or better said in the original and full Harvard motto: *veritas, christo et ecclesiae* – the Truth for Christ and the Church. Harvard requires the truth above all." He smiled. Nailed it – next question?

"Yes, that's the *motto*. But that is not the major requirement of a modern university the size of Harvard. That is not the lifeblood that nourishes it, and us."

Oh-oh, he thought. Trick question: bummer. Matt sat down and reached for his beer. He tried again. "Good teaching staff?"

"Matthew, also correct, but sitting above them all is the most important substance to a modern teaching entity." He paused. "*Money*, Matthew; it's money. With it, we flourish, without it, we shrivel and die."

"Money, of course. I was going to say that, but, you know." Matt rolled his eyes and sipped.

"I knew you were," Mercer said. "Last federal budget, the government allocated eighty billion dollars to health research and development. We need to ensure that a large portion of that funding heads toward our own department's work right here. The more we get, the better it is for our...students. Do you understand what I'm saying?"

"Yes sir, I do. It's vitally important for our students." And for a late-model AMG Mercedes pulled up in the faculty parking bay, he thought and toasted the air.

"And as Harvard educators, we should do everything in our power to keep that lifeblood flowing, right?" Mercer said smoothly.

"Couldn't agree more, sir."

"Good, very good, because you *can* help. There is one reality, I'm afraid; the fact is, there is not really an opening at Harvard right now."

Matt's stomach sank.

Mercer went on. "And I'm sorry to be commercially brutal, but it seems you need us more than we need you right now. You're a talented individual, but there are plenty of those who would kill for a professorship at Harvard." He let that thought hang.

"Hm-hmm." Matt sipped again, feeling his opportunity slipping away. He'd try really hard not to burn any bridges by telling Edward Mercer what he thought of him, and the lucre-green *lifeblood* running through his withered old veins.

"Matthew, people who succeed in life take chances, seize opportunities and make things happen *themselves*," Mercer said with building enthusiasm.

Matt waited.

The Harvard president continued. "And an opportunity has arisen. One that if seized could put you in the box seat for a full tenure, with all privileges and seniority restored. Straight back into the high-ranking fold, as it were. How does *that* sound?"

"Sounds like you've got my attention, President Mercer."

"I knew you'd be interested. Your file said you were a go-getter," Mercer said, the words clearly delivered through a smile. "There's a little fieldwork that needs to be done. Basic translation stuff, simple as that – Middle Eastern languages, ancient Greek, Latin, various other vocabularies and dialects...right up your expertise alley, I would say."

Matt shrugged. "Sounds straightforward; where's the fieldwork site?"

"Syria," Mercer said quickly.

"Syria?" Matt frowned. "Uh, bit of a war zone, right now isn't it?"

"Won't be a problem. It's away from all the major cities and the fighting – more out in the leafy suburbs. Matthew, this is urgent and important...especially for you. There's a plane leaving for Aleppo tomorrow morning. You'll be met by Captain Tania Kovitz, an archeologist, and will be introduced to the rest of the small team. You'll also have a military escort, so you'll be as safe as can be."

"Tania Kovitz? I know her." Matt sighed, feeling a knot starting in his stomach. "How long is it for?"

"In and out; probably only a few days."

Matt nodded. "And I'm guessing, seeing as this *fieldwork* will allow Harvard to improve its portion of the R&D budget allocation, that it must be a government job...military."

"Professor Kearns, *Matthew*." Matt could hear the confidence in the president's voice – the man obviously knew he was now hooked, and that it was time to reel him in. "All of that is way above my pay grade. There are people who are much better informed than me, just waiting to answer any and all questions you may have."

"On the plane," Matt said.

"Yes, on the plane." Mercer sounded like he had gotten to his feet. "Well, seems you're a man in demand; they requested you personally. Apparently you're on their books."

Matt slumped in his leather chair. He groaned. "I'm on the books," he repeated softly. "Sir, I'm not..."

"Please call me Edward."

"Edward, I'm not sure I want to get involved in any more government projects right now."

"Nonsense – a few days, a week at most, and then next thing you know, you'll be guiding young minds through the intricacies and beauty of ancient languages. Just as you were famed for doing in these halls of Harvard. You'll make a fine addition, and I personally can't wait to have you back in the fold...with us."

"If I help?" Matt said, weakly.

"If you help, yes, Matthew. It's a small thing and you can consider it part of the interview process," Mercer said, hurrying him now.

"No jungles or caves, right?" Matt held his breath.

"Not that I know of, Matthew. Straight translation work – in and out in little more than a day or so, I expect," Mercer added, sounding bored now.

Matt sighed and closed his eyes. He drained his beer. "Okay, what are the flight details?"

Chapter 6

Hanscom Air Force Base, Massachusetts

The dark blue car eased to a stop and the door pushed open. Matt swiveled his legs out of the passenger side and dropped his bag on the ground, whistling as he looked up at the massive aircraft on the runway.

Beside him the driver leaned forward on the wheel and followed his gaze.

"Yep, she's a big baby – C17 Globemaster III. That beautiful girl can lift well over half a million pounds of payload at a cruise speed of just under Mach 1."

"Wow." Matt turned. "Just how many of us will be onboard?" he asked, eyebrows raised.

The driver grinned. "Well, that there is one of our strategic airlift transports and can take one hundred and thirty fully kitted out troops." His grin widened. "Or six VIPs, you being one of them." He winked and then gave a small salute as Matt stepped out and closed the door.

The driver called, "Enjoy your holiday, sir." He spun the wheel and the dark sedan accelerated away.

"Holiday, huh?" Matt picked up his pack, and headed

toward the huge aircraft. The ramp was down at the rear, but the interior was nothing but a black hole at this distance. When he was still a hundred feet away, a figure half appeared at a tiny side door, spotted him, and came down the metal foldout steps quickly. She jogged to him, smiling, hand stuck out from twenty feet away.

"We meet again." He grabbed her hand and shook it. "Hey, it wasn't you that had anything to do with me being here, was it?"

She smiled wholesomely and disarmed him immediately. "What can I say? I'm a sucker for academics with charm and boyish good looks. Come on." She turned and headed back to the plane.

"So, Syria, huh?" he asked, looking up and up at the enormous aircraft.

She nodded. "Now you're here, we'll do introductions, and then a formal briefing when we're under way."

"I'm the last?" Matt's feet clanged on the incongruously flimsy metal steps.

"Yep, last but not least." Tania stopped just inside, and held out an arm directed past the cockpit to the rear of the plane.

Hollow, was Matt's first impression. Inside the metal skin of the aircraft, the slightly oval shape was enormous at nearly seventy feet in length, about twelve high and eighteen wide. But it was nearly empty. There were just six chairs – two by two in three rows, each fixed to the middle of the craft. There was a small bench-type structure in front of each – a small island for work and rest in a gigantic echo chamber.

A tall man stood at the front: mid forties, looking fit and only slightly army. However, either side of him there were two sharp-eyed military guys who looked tough enough to break boards with their hands *and* heads. Matt recognized the type – Special Forces. He also recognized the geologist Andy Bennet from the sinkhole at Iowa, and waved.

The tall man raised his hand. "Now, I can say: Good morning, everyone." He smiled broadly. "Firstly, I'd like to welcome Professor Matthew Kearns and welcome back Chief Geologist Andrew Bennet, and thank both of them for joining us at such short notice. Matt, Andy, my name is Major Joshua Abrams. I am the chief science officer for US STRATCOM, and I'll be the mission leader on this little trip."

Andy stuck up his hand, but Abrams shook his head. "Later. You've both met Captain Tania Kovitz, our senior archeologist. And these two big guys either side of me here are lieutenants Lester Hartogg and Rick Berry. They will be our support officers."

On face value, both of the huge men simply looked bored, but their eyes were alert. It's always the eyes, Matt thought. They were the giveaway of a killer. Berry's were dark and pitiless. Hartogg's were ice blue, set in a ruddy face with red hair and stubble – he would have made a good Viking. The men's flat-eyed stares spoke of the more brutal aspects of combat – receiving and, undoubtedly, delivering.

Matt exhaled slowly. If they needed soldiers of this caliber, then Mercer's "straight translation work – in and out in a day" talk might not have been the whole truth.

"That's all we need to do for now. The distance to Aleppo in Syria is five thousand four hundred and seventy miles, and should take us just on fourteen hours. I'm sure that'll give us plenty of time to get to know each other real good. After we take off and then have leveled out, there will be a formal briefing. Until then…" Abrams gave them a small informal salute before looking over their heads to the cockpit. Matt spun in time to see the pilots close the cabin door. Almost immediately, there was an electronic whine and the huge metal tongue of a rear ramp began to lift. At the same time, the smooth sound of the Pratt & Whitney turbofan engines came to life.

Matt turned back and saw Tania Kovitz looking at him, so he smiled and nodded. She returned the gesture. Maybe the trip might not be so bad after all, he thought. Next he leaned forward and saluted Andy. The geologist gave him a lopsided grin: he seemed to have recovered from being near buried alive. It was the first time he'd gotten a good look at the guy, what with them having spent most of their last encounter in HAZMAT suits. Andy looked only slightly older than he was, and had short sandy hair and a tan line that stopped halfway up his forehead – Matt had seen them before on guys that wore hardhats in the field.

They took their seats, Abrams and Hartogg in the front row, then Tania and Berry, followed by him and Andy in the rear two. Matt gritted his teeth as the huge machine rumbled down the runway and lifted into the air. It seemed no time at all before his ears had popped and Abrams was unbuckling and getting to his feet.

The major stood, his expression more formal, in one hand a slim electronic tablet. Now that they were sealed in and on their way to about twenty-eight thousand feet, he knew there was no backing out. He held his arms out wide.

"Our mission is one of many. In a way we are an exploratory team investigating the sinkhole occurrences happening across the world. To date, there have been a thousand significant earth-drop events across the United States, and globally the number is twenty times that...that we know of. We now know there are holes opening up below the ocean, so at greater depths, beyond our scopes, there could be many, many more."

"Thousands?" Matt frowned.

Andy nodded. "Yep, and *earth-drop* is probably a better description than *sinkhole* for what's going on. A sinkhole usually implies subsurface water – none of these have had that cause. Instead, the earth simply drops away without any discernible geological influence. It's weird."

Abrams smiled grimly. "Andy is right." He paced. "He was also the first geologist on site in Iowa for what we're calling the genesis event. Although there could have been smaller ones earlier, this was the first one where we managed to obtain samples – all of which still defy explanation. Bottom line is, we're stumped as to what's causing these events, as is almost everyone else."

"Almost?" Matt asked.

"Almost." Abrams nodded, giving him a grim smile. "And that brings us to our mission. Seems we have someone in Aleppo, Syria, who believes he knows what it is we're dealing with. He anticipated the recent earth-drop events – every single one of them – and so proved he is the real deal. We know because...well, let's just say he sent us a calling card."

"Come on, Major, no need to be coy. I'm here now, locked in with the rest of you." Matt held out his hands. "What exactly was this *calling card*?"

Abrams half smiled, and then nodded. "Okay." He lifted the tablet, and flicked his hand across the screen several times, looked at the image he'd called up, and then handed it to Matt.

It showed a map of North America, crisscrossed with something that looked like veins running over the countryside. The veins intersected at certain points, some small, some large. Red dots of different sizes were at the intersection points.

"*That* is the calling card." Abrams's face had became serious. "The sinkholes identified...*before* they occurred."

Matt snorted softly. "Ley lines."

"What?" Abrams frowned.

Andy slapped his leg. "Of course, ley lines; I thought I recognized them. We come across references to these all the time in unexplained geological phenomena. They're a joke." His grin fell away at the look on Matt's face. "Aren't they?"

"What's a ley line?" Abrams asked.

"A metaphysical reference," Matt said. "There was an English archaeologist named Alfred Watkins, who in 1921 identified a sort of connection between alignments of ancient monuments and megaliths, natural ridge-tops and water-fords. They are also supposed to have been influenced by the sun, moon and other astral bodies."

Matt looked down at the image again. "Watkins's work was influenced by an even earlier paper by William Henry Black given to the British Archaeological Association in 1870. Black speculated that there were spiritual geometrical lines which covered the entire world."

"Spiritual?" Abrams shook his head. "What we're dealing with is definitely *not* spiritual."

"I agree." Matt shrugged and handed back the tablet. "But that's what the lines represent." He looked at his colleagues, and his brow creased. "Okay, I understand why Andy is here, and Captain Kovitz, and also Berry and Hartogg, but why am I here? It can't be just because you need some Syrian translated. There are thousands of American Syrian speakers, some of them already in the military, so I'm assuming it must be something a little more complex."

Abrams paced for a moment, as if thinking through his answer. "Our contact has alluded to a document, a manuscript or a book or something written in different ancient Arabic scripts. We don't know what it is at this point in time, and he wouldn't tell us."

"Arabic?" Matt shook his head. "Are you sure? 'Arabic' includes numerous dialects and type-forms across a huge territory, stretching across the Middle East and down through much of Africa." He pushed his hair back. "In *Syria*, I think we're more likely to be looking at Syriac. That's a Middle Aramaic language, written in the Syriac alphabet. It was spoken for centuries, but it wasn't a literary language until around the fourth century."

Abrams opened his arms. "You see; you're already of value."

"No, no, no. I know when someone's blowing smoke. Any first-year languages student could have told you that. One more time: why am I here, Major?"

Abrams grunted. "Professor Kearns, I could not begin to form a satisfactory explanation for you at this point. You've seen the symbols we have been encountering in the sinkholes – Doctor Albadi has similar glyphic representations. He also said there would be critical translation work, and we needed to bring someone expert in numerous Middle Eastern dialects...and some older languages." He held up a hand. "I don't know which yet, but our new friend said some of the languages would be...challenging. He also said that our specialist needs to have an open mind. I'm loath to embark on speculation without something a little more concrete."

He looked from Matt to Andy. "So, in a nutshell: we are going to meet Hussein ben Albadi, a doctor of anthropology formerly of the University of Damascus. He now resides in a small town on the outskirts of Aleppo. He has some compelling information for us – and I believe he has something worth seeing and listening to. Something that is critical to our survival." He took a breath. "We need to hear it first hand – all of us."

Chapter 7

Aleppo International Airport, Syria

Yellow dust and broken brick, peeling paint and miles of ochre roadway: these were the impressions Matt got as they sped away from the airport. The battered minivan continued past the city center, heading west, fast.

Their plane had immediately dusted off, not even waiting for a refuel – armed men in jeeps had chased it down the runway. It would take on more fuel in Israel, and then continue home. The airport was too unstable for it to stay, and the team knew that getting back stateside would mean they'd need to travel by another route. The expedition's return plan now was for them to make it across Turkish border – A few days, my ass, Matt thought. Lucky he didn't have any houseplants.

Matt leaned forward to the driver and spoke in rapid Syrian; he grunted, nodded and then spoke out of the side of his mouth, keeping his eyes on the partly obliterated road and the groups of sullen-looking men patrolling the streets.

"*Shou-Kran.*" Matt wedged himself back in between Andy and the SEAL Rick Berry, who took up most of the seat, and, like Hartogg in front, never took his eyes off the streetscape.

"Bashnatrah," Matt said, and half turned to Abrams and Tania seated behind him.

"That's right: Bashnatrah," Abrams said, also keeping a close watch on the passing street.

"It lies on an ancient merchant caravan route between Aleppo and the Mediterranean. Mostly cultivated farming land, and one of the few towns as yet untouched by the civil war. It's where we'll find the summer place of our contact."

"Doctor Hussein ben Albadi," Matt said.

"*Ah*...he is honorable, good man," the driver said over his shoulder.

"An honorable man." Abrams nodded. "Good."

Once past the city perimeter, the driver became a little more relaxed – there was less debris, fewer bands of watchful soldiers or rebels – but still the SEALS kept their weapons ready.

"Slow down," Hartogg said.

The driver turned and frowned at him, but shrugged and then eased back a little. Andy looked out at the near empty landscape, seeing nothing. "Expecting trouble?" he asked.

"Always," Berry said from next to Matt.

"IEDs," Abrams said from behind them.

"Great," Matt whispered. Improvised Explosive Devices, or IEDs, were one of the deadliest creations of modern Middle Eastern warfare. They'd started as little more than buried mines, but as those taking defensive measures became better able to deal with the simple explosives, then so too did the bomb builders adapt. The IEDs became more sophisticated, making use of professional concealment techniques, armor-piercing shells, remote or automatic detonations and pressure or motion detection. The big ones could easily take out an armored troop carrier. Matt gripped the seat back. To a flimsy minivan, they'd spell total obliteration.

"Not Syrian." The driver slowed even more. He turned, his face furious. "No Syrian would make this type of war."

Abrams leaned forward to look past Matt and Berry through the windscreen. "That's the problem – a lot of militias now, crime gangs, and foreign fighters who hate everything and everyone."

"Al-Qaida, ISIL," the driver said. "Cut off heads."

Andy snorted. "Did I thank you for inviting me yet?"

Tania leaned forward to pat Matt and Andy's shoulders. "Don't worry boys, stay close and I'll protect you."

In another hour they began to see more green and less yellow, and soon they pulled into a large property. Stout metal gates swung open, and, after the ochers of the trip, the magnificent green oasis was a welcome sight. As the van coughed to a halt on crunching gravel, a small, round man appeared on the front porch and raised his hands.

"Welcome, welcome."

"Hold." Berry and Hartogg were first to alight, taking up positions each side of the van, their eyes moving over everything.

After a few minutes, Hartogg nodded to Abrams – the major stepped out. "Doctor ben Albadi?" he asked.

"Yes, yes, I am ben Albadi. Call me Hussein, please. Welcome." He came down the few steps, and shook hands, clasped shoulders and grabbed elbows as introductions were made.

Matt heard the van start up its engine, and he turned to see the driver mouth "Good luck" in Syrian before accelerating hard toward the gate.

"*Hey!*" Matt took a step but the van picked up even more speed, turning hard on the gravel.

"Sonofabitch." Tania started to chase it, but Albadi yelled after her.

"Forget him, miss; he was brave enough just to bring you here."

Abrams watched the cloud of dust as it disappeared, growling low under his breath. "Great."

"Someone tell me we have a Plan B to get home." Andy looked from Abrams to Tania.

Matt shook his head. "I thought *he* was Plan B."

"Work first, worry later." Abrams turned away. "Doctor, show us what you've got."

Albadi nodded and led them inside; the temperature immediately dropped ten degrees.

Matt wiped his brow, relieved to be out of the heat, and looked around at the sprawling single-level house in disbelief – it was packed from floor to ceiling with books, papers and overflowing boxes. The air smelled of mold, ancient paper and drying leather.

Albadi led them further inside to a room a little less cluttered and with a single large wooden table. He called for refreshments. Hartogg and Berry conferred with Abrams for a few seconds and then both disappeared. Albadi frowned as they left the room, and looked to the major.

Abrams shrugged. "Forgive the intrusion and rudeness, Doctor, but security is critical. You understand."

Albadi seemed to think about it for a second or two and then waved it away. "Of course, of course; these are the times we live in...and why you are here."

Matt walked to a shelf laid out with books. "This is some collection, Doctor." He turned one huge book towards him, its leather cover heavily carved and also inscribed with gold gilt and other still-vibrant colors. His eyebrows shot up. "Holy wow. This is a copy of the *Tarikh Dimashiq*. And a very good one."

Albadi grinned and came closer. "You know this book, Professor Kearns?"

"Oh yeah." Matt nodded. "The first ever history of Damascus, written by Ibn Asakir in 1170. I've read a later copy, or volume one, anyway...though nothing like this one."

Albadi glowed. "Yes, yes. The *Tarikh Dimashiq* is in seventy-two volumes and is one of most important books about the Islamic history of Syria. Asakir tried to collect everything about our city, its important people, and even their conversations. It is also one of the biggest collections of ancient Arabic poems gathered in one book."

"Beautiful." Matt ran his fingers lightly over the cover. "It's been around for nearly nine hundred years. Magnificent copy."

Albadi shrugged. "Magnificent, yes; a copy, no. *This* is the original *Tarikh Dimashiq*."

Matt's mouth fell open. "Then it's priceless." He pulled his hands back. "What is it doing here?"

Albadi opened his arms and turned slowly, taking in the stacks of books, papers and material around the room. "The *Kitab al-zuhd* and *Kitab al-fada'il*, written in 840, the *al-Jam bayn al-gharibayn* of 1010, the *Gharib al-hadith* by Ibn Qutaybah al-Dinawari of 889 – they're all here." He walked along a row of books, trailing his fingers lightly across the top of some as though they were jewels. "Remember Libya, Iraq, or Afghanistan? After their formal governments were toppled, one of the first acts of barbarism was the looting or destruction of the contents of the museums and libraries." He shook his head. "It is said some of the theft was carried out to order."

"Collectors with shopping lists." Tania Kovitz spat the words. "Bastards."

Albadi frowned at the harshness of her words, but then nodded. "And none have yet been found. Syrian treasures, which had taken centuries to find and amass, vanished within hours of the uprising."

He looked up at the group, his smile weak. "Syria is an unstable place right now. The Az-Zahiriyah Library of Damascus is our oldest, established in 1277. It has books and manuscripts dating back to the first millennium – over twenty-two thousand of them." He held up a fist. "I will not see its treasures whisked away to end up in a rich man's private collection *or* destroyed in some sort of stone-age religious purification." He waved an arm and sighed. "Here, I can keep them safe, until things...settle down."

The tea and coffee arrived and they gathered around a low table. Tania was straining to keep herself under control as a servant poured the drinks. She declined some dates and honeyed pistachio, and then couldn't hold back any more. "Doctor Albadi, you found something among your ancient books and manuscripts? Something that gives you some clue as to what is going on with the birds, the disappearances, the earth-drops and their growing size?"

"And the vermin that precede them...the roaches." Albadi held up a hand. He waited until the servant had finished his task and left the room. He shrugged apologetically. "We must be watchful. Not everyone will be happy with what we will do and say here." He sat back and interlocked fingers on his stomach.

"Roaches?" Matt asked.

"There were roaches in the Iowa drop," Andy said. "Didn't think anything of it then...should I have?"

"Have you seen anything else in the depths of these pits?" Albadi tried to seem indifferent, but his eyes were alert as he watched them.

"I thought I..." Andy grimaced. "Maybe. I don't know what I saw."

Matt saw how keenly Major Abrams watched the young geologist. There was something hidden there. Albadi also seemed to notice the major's focus.

"Major Abrams, perhaps you have seen something too?"

Abrams looked away and slowly shook his head. "We registered some anomalies, but we're still analyzing the data. Nothing conclusive enough to share at this point."

"Anomalies? Yes, *anomalies* is *a* term for them. But perhaps *abominations* is a better one." Albadi's fingers were still clasped over his stomach. "I believe what we are dealing with is something beyond ancient, beyond mankind, beyond the beasts, and perhaps even beyond the primordial ooze we all crawled from." He looked at Matt. "But perhaps we have sensed it. Maybe *the gifted* have sensed it more keenly than the rest. And other creatures with even greater senses than our own – surely they have."

"Like the birds," Tania said. "And now you're saying the roaches do too."

Albadi shrugged. "The roach is probably one of the most ancient creatures living on our world. They were here before even the great saurians, and have been on this planet for three hundred and fifty millions years longer than humankind. The world was young then, raw, and they have seen things that we could not imagine. They have seen what has come before, and perhaps they can see what is to come again. I think maybe they share an infinity with, um..." He sat back, seeming to search for the right words.

"With what?" Veins stood out on Tania's throat. "What do you know about what's going on? You predicted the earth-drops, their time, and even where they were going to occur. We're in a race, doctor, and we don't have time to talk about roach philosophy. Tell us what you know, please."

"I know but a little." Albadi stared for a second or two and then sighed heavily as he got to his feet. He searched a shelf, pulled free a roll of tattered paper, and laid it on the table, unrolling it flat. It was the crisscrossed map of North America.

"The ley lines," Matt said.

Albadi turned to Matt, toasting him with his small ornate cup. "You have an extensive knowledge, Professor." He left the map on the table, looking at each of them. "I have seen one of the sinkholes. I have read scraps of a manuscript that was beyond fantastical." He stared hard at them. "I believe we have *all* seen things that defy explanation. Little pieces of the same puzzle. We see a hint here and there – a glimpse, a scrap, or a fragment." He held up his hands. "It seems we all know a little, but none of us knows all." He put his cup down carefully. "Have any of you heard of the *Andhgajanyāyah?*"

Matt said, "The parable of the blind men and the elephant; we probably all have."

Albadi nodded. "There are many different versions, but the message is primarily the same. It is an old parable dating back to Jainism, the obscure fifth-century BC Indian religion. In essence, it is the tale of a group of six blind men in a deep forest who come upon an elephant for the very first time. They wanted to determine what it looked like, so each approached the beast, feeling different parts of the elephant's body. The blind man who feels a leg says the elephant is like a pillar; another, the tail and says it is like rope. The trunk is like a tree branch, the ear is a fan, and the belly is a wall, says three more. The final blind man feels the tusk, and announces it is a pipe of stone.

"None of them could agree on what the huge creature was actually like. It was just then that a sighted man walks by and sees the entire elephant all at once, and tells them. They are shocked, but then realize that the lesson is that while one's subjective experience is true, it may not be the totality of truth."

Matt nodded. "In another version, the men also learn for the first time that they are blind."

"And have perhaps never really seen anything as it truly is," Albadi finished. "And that, my friends, is perhaps what we are like here. Each of us has information about what we are experiencing, but none of us knows exactly what it is we are actually dealing with...and even if we did, would not see things as they truly are."

"Because none of us has seen the entire picture...including you," Major Abrams said. "So, has anyone seen the entire picture, Doctor?"

Albadi bobbed his head from side to side. "Yes, I believe there have been a few. But only one recorded what he had seen." He turned with his lips pursed to look at Matt, and he nodded, perhaps coming to a decision.

"What do you know of the *Al Azif*?"

"The Book...*the* Book?" Matt's mouth dropped open. "Seriously?"

Albadi nodded solemnly.

"The *Al Azif*, AKA *The Necronomicon*, AKA *The Book of the Dead*?" Matt shook his head. "Yeah, I know a lot. It's a fictional – what? Grimoire? – created by H.P. Lovecraft. It doesn't exist. It was first mentioned around 1924 in a short story called 'The Hound'. The author of the *Al Azif* was supposedly a man named Abdul Alhazred, known as the Mad Arab."

"Yes, the famous English writer, Howard Phillips Lovecraft. He had a copy, and found out very early that the Beast and its army would return. He was another who had seen...all of the elephant. He tried to warn us the only way he knew how – through his literary works. For all his brilliance, and his prodigious writings, he died penniless and in great pain." He looked up at Matt. "He was ruined financially, mentally and finally, physically. It seemed powerful forces tired of his expositions."

Albadi waved his arm around taking in the stacks of ancient tomes. "As for the Book; where better place for clues to be found than in one of the world's most ancient libraries?" He chortled. "The Mad Arab – some would say we're all mad, yes? I assure you, Professor, he, like the book, was, real. Alhazred was a poet from Sanaá, in Yemen, who lived during the period of the Ommiade caliphs, around 700 AD. He roamed the Middle East, visiting the ruins of Babylon and the subterranean secrets of the great southern deserts of Arabia – the Roba El Khaliyeh, the vast empty space of the ancients. He also transversed the ad-Dahna or Crimson

Desert of the Saudi Arabians, which is held to be protected by evil spirits and monsters of death."

Albadi crossed to a small, heavy wooden door set into the wall. He unlocked it, and from the space behind brought forth something wrapped in an oilcloth. He set it on the table before them. He placed one hand on it, fingers steepled.

"In his last years of his life, Alhazred lived in Damascus, and in 738, he wrote a book of pure horror and mad prophecy in Syriac, Arabic, and multiple other languages, some that could not be read. He called it the *Al Azif*."

"And you have it?" Tania's eyes burned.

"No." Albadi smiled, and turned from her, back towards Matt. "In 950, the Book was translated into Ancient Greek and called *The Necronomicon* by Theodorus Philetas, a scholar from Constantinople. This version was later outlawed, and then burned in 1050 by Patriarch Michael. However, not before it was translated from Greek into Latin by Olaus Wormius in 1228. In 1232, Pope Gregory IX banned all editions of the work, calling it 'a blasphemous script of ultimate evil'."

"Now *that's* a book review you won't see on Amazon," Andy said, grinning.

"But the book did survive." Albadi turned his back on the geologist. "A Greek edition was found in Italy in the first half of the sixteenth century, and supposedly translated into English. But this edition has never been seen, other than as fakes turning up for sale, even today on the internet."

Albadi sipped at his coffee again and then smiled. "Time is the enemy of history, my friends: sometimes it erases it. By 1050, when the Greek version of the *Al Azif* was created, the original version had already long disappeared." He shrugged. "And with all translations, the new versions lost much along the way – much of the meaning, much of the power, and also anything written in the strange languages that refused to be translated by the best scholars of antiquity." He turned back. "The original has never been found, and even a location for it remained a mystery."

"The language *refused* to be translated?" Matt asked. "What does that mean? Was it not an Arabic or Syriac dialect or form?"

Albadi shook his head. "I do not know: other than a symbol here and there, I have never really seen it, and no one else living has either. But they became known as the forbidden passages, and it is said they were not in any human language. It is perhaps nothing but the scribbling of a madman, or..." he looked levelly into Matt's eyes "...Enochian, *true* Enochian."

"Enochian?" Matt snorted softly. "I must see it."

Tania said, "Oh, please. That's bullshit."

Abrams stepped closer, glaring at Tania. "I think we need to know everything; then we can decide what's bullshit. I agree with the Doctor; these are all pieces of the puzzle, and we need to hear them all."

"Enochian." Matt rubbed his chin. "Well, no one is even sure if it's real. It's supposed to be the language of the angels as recorded in the private journals of the Englishman John Dee in the 1500s."

"Matt." Tania shook her head. "Historians and linguists have studied the Enochian symbol strings, and not one of them can decide if it's a real language or something just made up by Dee as a joke."

"They can't decide...but they never ruled it out." Matt shrugged. "Over the years, I've seen enough to know that some legends are real. It sort of fits; according to the story, Dee's journal was actually a transcript of an earlier work...much, much earlier – maybe it was drawn from the translated *Al Azif*. Enochian is also called Celestial Speech, taught to Adam by God himself."

"Language taught to the first man, by God." Albadi nodded. "But now the question is, which God, hmm, Professor Kearns?" He rubbed his hands together as if washing them of any traces of the Book. "And whether it is Enochian or the fevered scribbling of a madman is yet to be seen." He grinned. "But 'The earth shall fall' is a fairly accurate prediction for a madman to make, yes, Professor?"

"'And the earth shall fall'," Matt repeated, startled. The phrase had occurred to him as soon as he read about the sinkholes. "I know that quote. From an old Arabic saying, or so I always thought."

Albadi smiled broadened. "The words of the *Al Azif* are everywhere, we just don't realize it." He looked from Matt to Abrams. "And now to another piece of the elephant, hmm?"

Major Abrams scowled impatiently, and Tania folded her arms tightly across her chest.

"The *Al Azif* – I do not have the original, but I believe I have located fragments of the first ever copy made. A copy in native Syriac and Arabic, and far more descriptive than the one the American author, Mr Lovecraft, possessed."

"And you've read it?" Tania asked.

"Yes, and I think it is mostly safe to read. But a copy is nothing like the original. According to notes in the text, the simple act of even reading the original work is dangerous. The author, Alhazred, vanished without a trace. Some said he met with a terrible end. The man claimed in his tome to have discovered the secrets of a race far older than mankind, and far older than life as we know it on this planet. He had found the path to the Old One, Cthulhu, and their servants, the loathsome Shoggoths – and I believe it was one of these creatures that took him."

"Cthulhu, the Old One," Tania said, folding her arms, her brow now deeply furrowed.

Albadi nodded. "In the *Al Azif*, Alhazred talks of a time when our world was nothing but a boiling vision of Hell, with a black sky above, devoid of any light or hope – there was no moon, no light, no life. These great beasts brought all the hate and lust of a newborn universe with them, creating more of their kind, budding off pieces of themselves to raise as slaves and soldiers, and perhaps just to be more beasts for them to torture, maim and kill."

"There's nothing in the fossil record to confirm that at all, Doctor," Andy said.

"I know, and there wouldn't be." Albadi drew in a deep breath. "These leviathans knew dark magic, and knew how to defeat death itself. They are not dead, my friends." He stared into the distance. "The Old Ones, the First Ones, the Elder beings – bad dreams, or things of mad fantasy, we thought. But perhaps that's what they, and others, wanted us to believe."

Tania threw her hands up and turned to Abrams. "Boss, come on – dark magic now? This is turning from bullshit to *ludicrous* bullshit."

"It certainly is," Abrams said. "But so is what's happening around the world." His expression hardened. "Do you need to wait outside, Captain?"

Tania's face blazed momentarily. "No, sir." She snorted. "But…"

"Once you eliminate the impossible, whatever remains, no matter how improbable, must be the truth." Matt half smiled at Tania. "Be patient; Dr Albadi is risking a lot by even talking to us."

Albadi tilted his head. "Who said that, Professor Kearns. Was it a Persian philosopher?"

"Not quite." Matt grinned. "Sherlock Holmes…another great philosopher."

Albadi chortled. "Very good." He moved his hand to hover over the cloth cover. "And you are correct: there are mortal risks, and not just for me. I have found there are real cults of Cthulhu, whose members do not consider themselves bound

by any of the rules of the human race. We must be on guard."
He sucked in a breath and pulled the oilcloth back, displaying
a moldering pile of pages.

"Written in 800 BC, less than a hundred years after the
original – its value is in its proximity in time to that first
manuscript. The more you follow the book back in time, the
more of its core meaning is revealed." He hesitated for a moment, and then quickly lifted the leather cover. There came a
knock on the door, and one of his servants entered. Albadi
quickly flipped the cloth back over the book, and shooed the
man away. "*Shukran idrukni, idrukni.*"

The man's eyes darted around, taking in the cloth-covered
mound and each of the Americans, before he nodded and
backed out. Only then did Albadi relax. He turned to the
group and shrugged. "I am overly cautious, perhaps."

Once again his hands fussed as he flipped pages. "In Syria,
we are also experiencing the sinkhole phenomenon. But within
the fog of war, who cares if a few thousand people fall into a
pit, when tens of thousands are being slaughtered in the streets
above, hmm?" He peered up at Abrams and Tania. "But these
events are what started my search for answers among the
ancient books, and what led me to the *Al Azif.*"

He placed one stubby finger on a particular page. Matt
drew near, looking down over his shoulder.

"The sinkholes are the first doorways to the surface for the
Shoggoth. The birds are the spirits of the Earth, the enemy of
Cthulhu, and are becoming enraged in the sky; the carnivores,
the roaches, the vile lice upon the sleepers beneath us...It is all
in here. *Before they rise, the earth shall fall.*" He tapped the
book. "The sinkholes are only the start. The Shoggoth will
come through first, as well as the other vermin of the dark
deep. And they will be in the shadows, moving upon the surface now, as the few morsels that have been brought down
will not long satisfy the appetite of the leviathan below us.

Those disgusting servants of the Old One; they exist to eat and round up the food for their master."

Albadi leaned forward and started to read. "*From the darkest core, they will rise. From beneath the rock, below the soft earth and slime, they will come. The Great Old One and its army. It sleeps, powerful, all knowing, and patient beyond time itself. Cthulhu shall rule again.*" He pushed the book away, looking pale. "It is my theory, based on the prophecy in the *Al Azif*, and the signs we have seen, that the Great Old One Cthulhu is once again awakening, and we don't have much time. Its army of Shoggoth is already here."

Abrams stared hard at the Syrian but spoke almost casually. "You keep mentioning these things, Shoggoths. What exactly are they? Does it say what they are...supposed to look like?"

Matt looked at Abrams. The major's eyes held a hint of unease, and the realization struck – the man knew something.

Albadi hesitated for a moment, and then began turning more pages. "The Shoggoth – yes – their very name means *Inhabitant of the kingdom of darkness*. In the Book they are described as shapeless things – creatures made from nothing but black putrid slime, with multiple eyes that float freely over their surface. They can form limbs, mouths, and eyes whenever and wherever they will. They are much bigger and more powerful than a human." He looked up. "These will be the army, the shock troops of Cthulhu."

Abrams's face drained of color, and he turned away.

"Soon, the leviathan from the deep earth will come." Albadi sat back. "And then the time of humankind will be over."

Silence stretched as Abrams paced.

Matt noticed Tania smirked, and she shook her head when he caught her eye.

"I need to know more about this...thing, that is supposedly on its way." Abrams stopped pacing.

"Cthulhu," Matt added, now less surprised that the major didn't challenge what they had just heard.

Abrams nodded. "I want to know more about its strengths, and its…weaknesses."

"Weaknesses?" Albadi snorted his derision. "A flea could ask how to stop an elephant."

"Ever seen what the toxic bite of a Chimaeropsyllidae flea can do to an elephant?" Tania said folding her arms.

Albadi's lips compressed. "These beings are not like mortal creatures, Captain Kovitz." He carefully turned a page in the ancient manuscript.

She held up her hands. "Well, tell us about them." She looked down at the page and frowned. "That's the Caduceus – it's Greek."

Albadi stared down at the image of two intertwined winged snakes. "No Captain, it's not the Caduceus. That *was* one of its interpretations after it was adopted by the ancient Greeks. The wand of Hermes, with power over life and death." He traced the image with one finger. "But the symbol is far older. It was found on Mesopotamian cylinder seals that were over six thousand years old. It was thought to represent the earliest form of the Underworld gods."

Matt came and stood between Tania and Albadi. "It's also appeared in Babylonian script, representing the balanced struggle between life and death."

"*Balance*," Albadi said. "Yes, but the balance between two of the greatest Old Ones, brothers, locked in an eternal embrace – Cthulhu, of the dark, and Xastur, the light."

"Xastur? So there's two now…and one is good?" Tania asked, with her lip curling.

Albadi seemed unfazed. "Not good as we understand it. We are dust compared to them, and our values and lives mean nothing."

"And now they're both coming awake?" Tania asked.

"I don't know," Albadi said softly.

"But this shows two beings intertwined or fighting. How come then only one, Cthulhu, is rising?"

"Again, I don't know, Captain Kovitz. These are ancient beings of immense power. From what I can decipher in the *Al Azif*, they are currently imprisoned." He grimaced. "No, that's not right; they are currently sleeping beneath the sea, beneath the Earth, and in some versions in other dimensions altogether. When they first ruled it was for billions of years, and it was even before the primordial ooze. But something happened, some sort of great cataclysm that made the world unsuitable.

"A few, like Cthulhu, chose to await a more suitable environment – just as some animals hibernate during a time of cold, so also did the Great Old Ones lie dormant. Many perished, simply vanishing over the intervening billions of years. But the true Old Ones, the most powerful of them, slept on. But not eternally. Cthulhu was but waiting, and it had set itself an alarm clock. Not a device, but an event – it would await powerful cosmic forces aligning again, so it could be woken, and then be released to revel once more across the world and cosmos."

Tania frowned. "Cosmic forces aligning? Like what does that mean?"

Matt said, "The sun or moon being in a certain place?"

"Something like that, but a lot more powerful." Andy, who had been standing quietly at their rear, came forward. "What about *all* the planets aligning? That's about to occur soon."

"The convergence." Albadi nodded. "I think this is true. Alhazred called it *heaven's light* – all the planets in alignment would have been very bright in the sky. It is a very rare event." He rose to his feet. "The last such alignment was in 738 AD, the year that Alhazred finished writing the *Al Azif*. And the next is due…in just a few days' time."

Matt raised an eyebrow at Andy. "How did you know about that?"

Andy waved away the question. "Most modern geologists do. There are seismometers left on the moon by Apollo astronauts that record moonquakes, right? So, they occur most often during perigee, that's when the Earth and moon are closest together – once every month. It focuses a lot of gravitational energy on the geology. Ha! And I didn't even go to Harvard." Andy continued, "The Earth's gravity can trigger quakes on the moon. But being eighty-two times smaller than us, the moon's way too weak to trigger any earthquakes back here, though it is of course still enough of a force to pull at our tides. Now, what if all nine planets were brought into alignment; something that happens, once every thirteen hundred years or so? There would *have* to be a geological effect – there'd be no avoiding it."

"Yes, yes, but more than geological," Albadi said. "It *is* a very powerful gravitational force, no question. But when all the planets focus on us at the same time, what other cosmic forces would also be focused on us, pulling and tearing at us?" His face became grim. "They would draw out the old impurities, like pus from a boil."

"So, this alignment is some kind of cosmic alarm clock," Tania said.

"And it's getting ready to ring," Matt responded.

Abrams ran both his hands up through his short-cropped hair, exhaling. "Doctor, you said they'd been here before. But they're not here now, and we are...so where are they?" He dropped his hands heavily to the table. "And what happened in those times they *were* here?"

"A sensible question, Major." Albadi turned back to the pile of yellowing paper, and began flipping through more pages. "There are no times included here, but there are the ancient Syrian words for thousands and millions. I made some notes and then correlated these to what we know of the Earth's history. What I found was astounding."

He drew aside several pages of hand-written notes. "According to Alhazred, there have been five appearances of the Old Ones in Earth's past. These events occurred *after* they supposedly went into their cosmic slumber, when they were in effect *awoken*. The periods correspond exactly to the four mass extinction events punctuating Earth's history."

"I don't like the sound of this," Matt said softly.

Albadi turned one of his note pages. "The first great mass extinction event took place when our world was in its infancy, some 434 million years ago, during the Ordovician period. According to the fossil record, sixty percent of all life forms of both terrestrial *and* marine life worldwide were exterminated. Then again, some 360 million years ago in the Late Devonian period, was the scene for the second mass extinction event." He turned a page. "It goes on...The end of the Permian period, 250 million years ago, shows that up to ninety percent of life was extinguished." He looked up. "*Ninety percent.*" He sighed and went on. "Finally, and most recently, 65 million years ago, the dinosaurs disappeared – *all* of them."

"Jesus Christ." Andy leaned back against a table, upsetting some books. "But how the hell did we send them back?"

Albadi expression was miserable. "We didn't; how could we have? Even when the Old Ones were most recently here, we were barely tiny animals scurrying between the toes of the giants. No, they, *it*, went back to its slumbers of its own accord." He shrugged. "Perhaps the food ran out."

Matt snorted. "They ate everything. There was nothing left – they scoured the planet of meat."

"And we're up next," Tania said softly.

"He's damn well gonna find us a bit hard to swallow." Abrams got to his feet, but paused before turning away. "Wait a minute...why didn't they come through in 738? The planets were aligned, these things were obviously beginning to come through, given what we think happened to Alhazred. So why aren't they already here? Why didn't they *scour the planet of meat* then?"

"Yes, yes, another sensible question." Albadi pointed at the major's chest. "In fact, Major Abrams, that is the *most* important question now facing mankind. This is why you *must* find the original *Al Azif.* It alone must have the answers we seek. It is my belief that Alhazred somehow found a way to stop them." His brow creased. "No, that is not right. I do not believe that they could ever be *stopped*. But maybe he found a way to slow or delay them. Make them continue their slumber until the next alignment."

"Push the problem out to be dealt with by the poor saps of the future – us," Andy said.

"And we need to do the same to the next guys," Tania said as she came over to look down at the ancient book. "So, Doctor, here's the next million-dollar question – the Book – where the hell is it?"

Albadi smiled. "I believe it is hidden right here, in the Middle East. Where it has always been."

Chapter 8

Charles Sheldon Drummond, one of the wealthiest men on the West Coast, lay face down in the chapel. His lips moved in fervent prayer, his eyes were screwed shut and his hands spread, his mouth was cotton dry and his chest and ribs screamed in agony from the hard stone beneath him. He had been there for hours, and he would stay for hours more.

"Sir."

His prayers stopped.

"Sir."

His teeth ground and he opened his eyes. No one was allowed to disturb him here – *no one*. He looked up at the altar, seeing the large eye embedded in the center of the writhing mass of limbs – the image of the Old One, its likeness known for as long as humans could daub images onto cave walls.

"How dare you, Kroen?" Drummond started to rise.

"The Book, sir," the big bodyguard responded.

Drummond froze, waiting.

"Father says there are non-believers searching for it."

Drummond's eyes went wide, and he twisted, looking up at Kroen, knowing immediately what the huge man was referring to. Thoughts of retribution fell away like dry autumn leaves. "The Father said that?"

"Yes sir, and we have a location," Kroen said.

Drummond turned back to the eye. "Oh Great One, your return will be the mightiest event we worthless humans have ever witnessed." He got to his feet. "Where, when?" His dark robes trailed as he headed for the doors. On the way, he snatched up a bottle of Swiss mountain water, drank deeply, and then tossed it over his shoulder to the bodyguard.

Kroen caught it smoothly. "I do not know. The Father calls for you."

Drummond spun, his eyes blazing. "When...?"

"Now," the guard said.

Drummond felt the color drain from his face. "Of course..." he gulped. "Of course."

*

"And now we must ask ourselves; where in the Middle East?" Albadi held a finger in the air, waving it, as he talked. "Abdul Alhazred travelled far during his...creative phase, and said he found the ruins of Babylon, the fallen cities of Ibu, and also crossed the haunted deserts of ad-Dahna to the forbidden caves. I believe it is in one of those long-forgotten sites that he got his inspiration for the Book...where he spoke of *communing* with the Old Ones."

"Great," Tania said sharply. "If it's in a cave, we just go and damn well get it, and then get the hell out of here."

Albadi turned to her, and opened his arms. "I didn't say *the Book* was in the cave. In fact, even if you did find the cave that Alhazred used, it might be of no use to you, *now*. What I said was, the cave was where Alhazred received his inspiration. No, Captain, the Al Azif was secreted somewhere else, and I believe it is quite close – hidden – in a library."

Matt looked up. "A library...*your* library, in Damascus?"

"No, no," Albadi scoffed. "This copy refers to the Great Library of the Macedonian. Even though the Az-Zahiriyah Library of Damascus was created nearly eight hundred years ago, the library we seek was already ancient long before that. It was the greatest library our world has ever known, and at one time had collected together *all* the world's knowledge, and its secrets." Albadi smiled. "That Macedonian was Alexander."

"The *Bibliotheca Alexandrina*; the Library of Alexandria in Egypt," Matt said. "But it was destroyed nearly two thousand years ago by Julius Caesar."

"A tragedy on an unbelievable scale," Albadi said, his eyes downcast. "The most famous example of cultural vandalism in our history." He looked up. "But not by Caesar, Professor Kearns. It is true that a fire raged through the library at the time of Caesar, but the works were spared. The real cultural vandal was Pope Theophilus in 391 AD, who regarded some of the works as being heretical and decreed they be destroyed."

"Great; a dead end," Tania said, pacing away from them. "I gotta use the head; back soon."

"A dead end?" Albadi asked, brows raised at the departing woman. "The original library was an oasis of wisdom, and Alexandria became the center of the world for scientific and intellectual learning. It was also said to be the repository of many mystical wonders. Things that defied explanation for even the finest minds of their time."

"I don't know how that helps us, Doctor." Abrams looked briefly at his watch.

Albadi smiled. "It helps because the copy of the *Al Azif* I have infers that the original work is held within the great *Bibliotheca*...on the island of the Pharoes."

Abrams just stared, deadpan.

"Its impossible." Matt frowned. "The *Al Azif* was written in 738 AD, and the library was supposed to have been destroyed centuries before that."

Albadi said, "Exactly, and perhaps why it escaped destruction and remains hidden. I think that the library was moved again. To the scholars at the time, the works would have been more valuable than gold. They would have had an almost religious value. The scholars would have died before they let the entire library be destroyed again. Somewhere in Egypt, on this island of the Pharaohs, the great library still exists."

"Then the library it is." Abrams turned to Matt and then Tania, who had just pushed back into the room and was drying her hands on her pants. "Do either of you guys know the location of this island of the Pharaohs?" he asked.

Tania folded her arms. "Never heard of it."

Matt's brows were still creased. "I know a lot about the ancient Middle East, but I've also never heard of any reference to an island of the Pharaohs. Still, it sounds vaguely familiar. Dr Albadi, can I see the references to this library?"

Albadi nodded, and turned some pages, coming to one and running his finger down the archaic script. "Here."

Matt nodded as he read, and after a minute he paused. "Ha, of course." He began to smile. "Doctor, you were right and wrong at the same time. Yes, it's still in Alexandria, which makes sense. But it's not the *island of the Pharaohs*, but it's actually the Island *of* Pharos."

Albadi smacked his forehead. "Of course, the inflection on the noun." He bowed. "Your skill is truly impressive, Professor Kearns."

"Pharos?" Andy came and looked over Matt's shoulder. "Does that help us?"

"Pharos, why not?" Tania grinned. "It makes sense to move it to, and perhaps hide it in, the greatest structure of the ancient world...perhaps even as great as the pyramids themselves. It's where the Ptolemaic built the Lighthouse of Alexandria." Seeing their more or less blank faces, she went on. "Look, back then, most dwellings were single story, and very few were ever over fifty feet tall, so imagine a structure of stone standing nearly four hundred feet high, fully encased in pure white marble. At its top, a giant golden statue of Poseidon, and between his legs, a large bonfire was kept burning at night with a huge polished mirror to guide the ships into the harbor."

She sighed. "But, I'm afraid, it's something else that was destroyed. Though it did endure longer than the Library of Alexandria. It survived over a thousand years of earthquakes."

Albadi bowed again. "You too amaze me, Miss Kovitz."

"Captain," she said, and he bowed an apology she waved away. "It's gone now, of course. It was a fort for a while in the fourteenth century – those earthquakes had eroded it quite a bit."

Matt took over. "The island, Pharos, is just a barren rock now with a lot of debris below the water – there's nothing there at all." He folded his arms and paced. "I've been there, seen it. It's empty, picked clean – little more than an interesting destination for diving enthusiasts."

"And the reason it's empty is what's left is all below the water." Tania grabbed him as he went to pace by. "Think about it, Matt; what if what we seek is not *on* the island, but somewhere below it...or *inside* it?"

"But what's below the water is mostly rubble," Matt said. "And the place is crawling with tourists. It's not exactly hidden in the center of the Amazonian jungle."

"If I may, Professor." Albadi gave another small bow as he interrupted. "Maybe they just don't know where to look...or maybe, if there is an entrance, there are only certain times that it becomes apparent."

Andy clicked his fingers. "Like at certain times of the day...when the sun is just at the right angle. There's this huge rock in Australia that looks like it can change shape and colors, depending on time of day. Also some crystalline deposits can reflect light, like halogens, but only for a few minutes a day, and only during certain times of the year."

Matt spun and pointed at him. "Bingo." He grinned. "That's it. And now imagine the effect if the moon was amplified by the celestial convergence." He clapped once. "It might only be open at night, during the three days of the full moon."

"Night dive, anyone?" Andy said.

"We've got to get there, pronto," Matt said to Abrams.

"Agreed. We need to find that book." Abrams exhaled. "Doctor, we can't use the airport in Syria, and looks like our ride hightailed it. We also can't get a chopper in, with all the militants on the ground with stinger missiles. Our fallback is to cross into Turkey; can you take us?"

Albadi shook his head. "No."

Abrams's eyes became sharp. "Well sir, can you arrange for us to be taken there, as our driver took off like his ass was on fire the moment we stepped out of his van?"

Again Albadi shook his head. "No, I'm sorry."

"Oh, for fu–" Abrams ground his teeth, his face turning red. He spun away from the Syrian, and then leaned close to Matt. "Talk to him before I shoot him."

Matt turned to the Doctor, but Albadi must have already anticipated him, and waved him away.

"Major Abrams, it is nothing to do with my cowardice, or bravery, or even trying to extort your money." He waved an arm around in his library. "I have all the riches for a dozen lifetimes. But whether you know it or not, we are in a war zone. Above us, in the air, you have government planes with orders to shoot down anything that isn't personally authorized by the President. On the ground, you have too many militias and factions to count or try and negotiate with. In every second house is an informer. Major, you cannot go by road, you cannot fly, you cannot travel by any standard route and chance being seen by the population. You must cross the desert." Albadi stood beside an old map, gently running fingertips over the images of skulls and djinn...and the warnings. "And even then, it is not a good place now."

He turned, his head tilted. "I cannot take you, and I cannot give you a driver or arrange one – it would be suicide for him...and most likely for me and my family." He shrugged. "Already I risk my head just by having you here. I cannot take the chance of being seen to help Westerners." Once again he waved his arm around at the piles of ancient manuscripts. "If any one of the more aggressive anti-Western militias finds out, they'll burn everything, behead me, and then search for my relatives. Then they will come for you." His eyebrows sagged on his forehead. "Everything would be lost. Truly, I am sorry."

"It's okay, Doctor Albadi. We'll find a way across," Matt said. "I know this was a huge risk to you and we greatly appreciate it. Your assistance has been immeasurable." He turned to Abrams and raised his eyebrows, before slowly turning back to their host.

"Ah, Dr Albadi, is there anything we can do for you? As a simple gift of thanks for everything you have risked for us?"

Albadi stared for a moment, and then his head bobbed. "Well, yes; my daughter Sabeen is studying economics at Princeton University. She worries about me and wants to come home. *She must not.* If you could just...keep her there, at least until the country here stabilizes."

Abrams nodded.

"Of course. She will be safe. You have our word," Matt said.

"Good." Albadi closed his eyes and swallowed. "Professor Kearns. I do have an SUV you can take; it is rigged for desert driving, so will suit your requirements. I can give you supplies, and I can also give you directions. But the rest must be up to you."

"Thank you," Matt said.

Tania grunted, and looked from Albadi to the map once again. "Dr Albadi, is there anything else you can tell us about the Book, or Abdul Alhazred, or the library? Anything and everything is important now."

The doctor seemed to think a moment more, and then turned back to the table and the ancient tome's pages. He leaned over it, sighing. "Much of Alhazred's work was crazed, nonsensical – it is why he was called the Mad Arab. For many centuries, scholars who read the copies assumed it was *all* mad scribbling – now, current events mean we know better. Most of his essays, writings and poems have turned out to be truly prophetic. The man was given over to bouts of dark poetry, and perhaps..." He started to turn pages quickly, and then stopped and looked up at Matt.

"If you find the original *Al Azif*, it will be you who translates it, yes?"

Matt nodded. "When we find it."

"Then you must steel yourself. As I mentioned, the act of reading the original work is dangerous. It was said to drive men to suicide, make them sick, and even invite the attention of the Old One in their dreams. There is only one way to prepare – read here, and start to absorb the words." Albadi kept one finger on a page. "Alhazred gives us a clue as to what to expect in your journey. Read it, Professor."

Matt looked down at the mix of ancient languages. He started to translate. "Hmm, it's incomplete, but he talks of an underworld...and structures." He read on. "A city guarded by massive gates, and..." He felt the bloom of pain begin in the center of his brain. He shook his head. He soon felt he had been kicked by a horse, but from the inside. It slid down into his gut like a bomb.

Matt slammed a hand over his mouth and swung around frantically. Albadi anticipated him and lifted a wooden waste bin. Matt grabbed it and vomited explosively into it.

Tania rushed to him, putting an arm over his shoulders. "Jesus, Matt, you okay?"

Matt nodded, feeling embarrassed, but slightly better as soon as he moved away from the book's pages. He wiped his mouth.

"A city?" Tania said, rubbing Matt's back. "Is that what Alhazred found, and what we're looking for?" She let him go, and looked at Albadi with one eyebrow up.

"Perhaps," Albadi said. "Alhazred says that what you seek is buried deep behind mighty barriers big enough to hold back an army. It is the same as I deciphered. He says it is a city created millions of years before human beings even stood upright."

Matt breathed deeply, shutting his watery eyes for a moment. "Many of these ancient prophetic works were allegorical. It might not mean a physical city at all. Given Alhazred's mental state, perhaps he meant something like a mental construct – the walls of his mind and all that."

"Or nothing but hallucinations from a mix of hashish and a wild imagination," Tania added.

"We could hope that. But it might mean exactly what it says," Albadi said softly. "Only in the original *Al Azif* will you find the answer."

"Gates so huge they could hold back an army," Andy said softly. He looked to Matt. "Hold them back...from our armies going down, or something else coming up?"

Matt nodded. "You know, the planets have been used for both chronological and religious reasons for thousands of years. After all, archeoastronomers are still studying Stonehenge for its possible connections with planetary alignment."

"The trigger," Andy said. "The alarm clock event again."

"Yes." Matt looked from Tania to Abrams. "Given what we are experiencing, I think we should take everything seriously, and be prepared for it."

"Agreed," Abrams said.

Tania nodded, but still looked reluctant. "What about the monsters and djinn in the forbidden deserts?" she asked, sardonically.

Albadi snorted. "I wouldn't worry so much about djinn as bands of Al-Qaida fighters roaming the outskirts of the cities. You have more to fear from falling into their hands." His lips compressed momentarily and his eyes moved to Tania. "They torture and behead foreigners, and would take great delight in capturing an American – especially a female American."

"They can fucking try," Tania spat.

Abrams growled. "No one is going to be getting captured...*Soldiers!*"

Berry and Hartogg came back into the room, their eyes wolf like in their intensity.

Matt was glad they were there...and on his side.

"Berry, Hartogg, load em up, we're moving out in fifteen." Abrams dismissed them, and with a brief "*HUA!*" the men spun and then disappeared out the front.

Abrams approached the small doctor, his hand out. "I appreciate everything you have done. Thank you; I hope we see you again."

Albadi took his hand and shook it. "I hope so too. Good luck, and I pray you are not too late." The doctor held onto the major's hand. "There is one more thing. I also pray this *is* all the raving of a lunatic, but I fear it is not. And if it is not, then the servants of the Old One also exist and will be already here."

"The Shoggoth?" Matt said.

Matt noticed Albadi's eyes were fearful, and he wondered what else the man knew that he wasn't telling them.

106

"The army behind the gate," Andy said folding his arms and turning away.

"And you think they are here now?" Matt asked.

Albadi nodded. "These things were the slaves and servants of the Old Ones. They built the giant cities, gathered food for them, fed them, cared for them...and protected them."

Abrams exhaled forcefully. "Can they be killed?"

Albadi shrugged. "Are they even alive as we understand it?"

Andy spun back to them. "Well, that's just great." He went to turn away again and then stopped dead. "Hey, you said they fed the Old Ones. You mean they'll feed them us?"

Albadi's face was blank. "They feed them meat. And in this age, man is the most abundant food source. So yes, Mr Bennet, they will feed them us."

Andy groaned. "Frank, my partner, was grabbed by something under the earth...in the Iowa earth-drop." He shook his head, eyes downcast. "From what I understand, all the holes, once the land drops, anyone unfortunate enough to be inside the drop area is never seen again – they vanish." He winced and rubbed his forehead. "Oh God, I feel sick."

Matt narrowed his eyes. "Looks like food gathering has already commenced."

Tania came over and placed a hand on Andy's shoulder. "We need to make sure this stops, now."

Abrams lifted his voice. "First thing we *need* to do is stop spooking ourselves." He looked at his watch. "We've got a long way to go, and all over potentially hostile terrain." He looked Andy and Matt in the eyes. "As civilians I can't order you to come with us. But, I think we'll need you – both of you."

Matt turned to look at the mountains of old books. Staying made sense, and he could spend his time exploring ancient works that he might never get to see again. A feeling of comfort spread through him as he looked over the piles of ancient books. Staying made a lot of sense. Going with

Abrams made no sense at all. He'd seen what happened when people got involved in these insane military-type missions – they died, and damned horribly.

Abrams must have noticed Matt's wandering focus. "I think untold numbers of lives will depend on us. What I've seen, and now what I've heard, leads me to believe that a lot is at stake...perhaps everything we hold dear." He stared hard. "*We...need...you.*"

Matt sighed. "Okay." He met Abrams's eyes. "Okay, I'm in."

Andy nodded as well, anger in his eyes. "Let's fucking do this."

Chapter 9

Bristol, England

Jessica pushed the pram along Coronation Street, and inhaled deeply. The crepe myrtles were in flower and their vanilla scent filled her nose with perfume and her soul with happiness. She stopped briefly under one, letting her eyes travel from its base to its tips – she always loved the trees' magnificent streaked bark and bunches of small, tight flowers on the end of the branches.

This was her dream job – being a live-in nanny for a prominent surgeon and his wife. Trips abroad, good pay, and Jeremy, an angel to care for. She breathed in the scent of the flowers again and peered through their bouquets to the River Avon, still a little muddy from some recent rain. It was a good-sized watercourse, broad, deep, and with small ferries punting along its rippling surface.

The pram wheels squeaked, but other than that, it was still library-quiet that early in the morning. There was a single jogger and the odd cruising taxicab, but the rest of the up-market street was hers. Looking across the road, the compact two-story houses were jammed in tight together –

not a lot of land, but an expensive price tag for a view over the water. The block she lived in on Coronation was one of the biggest, at about two thousand square feet, and bordered Camden Road, Osborne and Allington. But the block more like a village, really, she thought, just as a curtain of cloud pulled back to let in golden shafts of morning light.

The first vibration tickled the soles of Jessica's feet, and she looked back over her shoulder expecting to see some large lorry approaching – there was nothing.

The next sound was different, and ugly. The wet thump was from a fat, gray pigeon as it dive-bombed into the grass of a front yard in an explosion of feathers and gore.

Ew, she thought, pursing her lips. She thanked her lucky stars that Jeremy hadn't seen the unfortunate bird's accident, but then shrieked as another bird struck the ground, then another and another. Soon starlings as well as pigeons were raining down and battering the houses, lawns, and the pavement. She grimaced at the sight, as the birds weren't just falling from the sky, but actually flying into the ground as if they couldn't see it, or were determined to strike it as hard as they could – it seemed as though they made war on the Earth.

Jessica felt frozen with indecision. There was no cover for hundreds of yards, and the tree she sheltered under was hardly thick enough to act as an umbrella against the feathered onslaught. She reached forward to pull the small canvas canopy over Jeremy, who was now sitting up, his mouth open in a single-toothed grin of delight as he watched the brown and gray birds fly into the grass and cement around them.

Jessica felt the vibrations again, the pavement shimmying under her feet, but this time there came a small jump as if everything raised and fell an inch. Car alarms started all over the city, and, looking along Coronation Street, it seemed that the vibrations, the jumping, and the birds ended at Camden, as if there were a fence of calmness just a few hundred yards further on.

Go, go, go, she thought as purpose finally jolted her into action. She sucked in a deep breath and began to run, the pram out in front, rolling over the bodies of birds and the dark cracks opening in the pavement. When she was within a hundred feet of the street corner, the ground lifted again, higher and higher, rising up as if there were a huge bubble of gas underneath them.

She started to weep. Her muscles burned and her breath became hot and tortured. She gagged as a foul gas belched up from below. She knew what was coming; she had heard the whispered rumours, seen the stories that usually vanished as quickly as they appeared. No one had believed: no one really cared. They'd all just continued with their lives – part of her mind took a moment to look at that unbelievable fact in something like wonder, or disgust, or both.

Whatever bubble had blown up below them suddenly burst. They were on a slope now, running down a hill of broken concrete and torn grass with just a few dozen feet to go to safety. Then the land started to fall.

Jessica knew she would never make it, but there was one thing she knew she *had* to do – nannies were more than just nursemaids, they were carers, playmates, best friends, and bodyguards, prepared to do anything for their charges. Jessica launched herself, pushing out her arms, flinging the pram forward, its large rubber wheels spinning as it raced down the slope, travelling at about twenty miles per hour toward the stable ground so close.

She fell flat on her stomach, but raised her head, her eyes wet as the ground beneath her dropped. Her last vision as she fell into the pit was of the pram slowing to a stop on the stable ground: safe.

Chapter 10

Mableton, Georgia, Atlanta outskirts

"Kroen, just...wait here...and leave the engine running." Charles Drummond wanted to be away quickly, as he knew he'd be uncomfortable. The street, the building, and the Father, all made him feel small and uneasy. He'd been given much, and promised so much more; still the Order was unsettling even for a high-level acolyte like himself.

He looked again at the doors, steeling himself. The Order of the Old Ones was an ancient sect that reached back to the days of Babylon and even beyond. Its sole purpose was the worship of Cthulhu and its minions, with the goal of easing the great gates of R'lyeh open so they might have rule over the Earth once again. In return, people like Drummond were made wealthy beyond the dreams of Croesus, and were promised they would be made kings over humankind for a thousand years. They would also be spared while the other creatures of flesh and blood were...consumed.

Drummond stood in the empty back street before the black double doors. There wasn't another person in sight, nor a bird perched on an eave, nor a rat, nor a single bug scurrying about. There seemed nothing living in the entire street.

Drummond pressed the bell button. There was no sound, and the huge black doors stayed closed and silent. Time stretched, but he knew to wait. After another few moments the door swung inward, and a tall shaven-headed man nodded, but said nothing. He was one of the priests of the order and was dressed in a rough cassock, made of something coarse that looked like it had been woven from long hair. Drummond grimaced, imagining what it must feel like against the man's skin.

He followed the priest in silence; no words were necessary, as he knew where he was to go. It wouldn't matter if he did feel the need to talk; he had tried to strike up a conversation once before, and it was if he and his questions didn't exist. The priests were courteous, helpful, but silent as mutes, and were both the household staff and bodyguards of the Father – nothing more, nothing less.

Drummond continued weaving along dark corridors that sloped ever downward, with the only light a single candle placed here and there in damp stone alcoves. He guessed the candles were for his benefit, as the priests didn't seem to mind the dark at all. Drummond watched the man's back for a while – he seemed to glide in his cassock, as though he didn't take steps but instead moved on some sort of conveyance that had no normal up-and-down motion of walking. Maybe he was on wheels. He would have laughed at the thought, expect he knew that his nervousness would have made it come out like some sort of insane cackle.

After another fifteen minutes of heading down ancient moss-covered steps, and along smooth stone pathways, Drummond estimated they were a good half-dozen floors below ground. It was warmer here, as though the heating had been cranked up to about eighty degrees. He pulled a silken handkerchief from his breast pocket to dab at his brow and top lip.

Eventually the priest stopped before a large archway, at another dark, sealed door. He turned and nodded to Drummond, and then stood back into a coffin-shaped alcove. Drummond knew what was expected – he was to go in alone. He swallowed, and licked dry lips. He could feel his heartbeat in his throat, and knocked once before pushing open the thick door.

The first thing that always assailed his senses was the smell – fishy, but not the scent of fresh-caught fish, but more the odor of something left to putrefy on a dead shoreline. There was also the heat, and the pervasive darkness broken only by the light of a double candle on the altar stone at the far end of the large room.

Drummond stood still, feeling perspiration run down his sides. There were other impenetrably dark alcoves at various places, and he knew they led on to further passageways. He had no idea how large the building was, or how far it descended into the Earth, but guessed whatever the size from the outside, its depths led down too many levels for him to calculate. Frankly, he thought, I'm as deep as I ever want to go.

A gust of even more fishy air: he felt the hair rise on his neck. He knew what was required of him and walked slowly to the altar, keeping his gaze averted, then got to his knees, clasping his hands in front of him. He looked up, straight ahead, feeling his heart rate increase.

"Father."

A huge figure grew out of the darkness, seeming to rise up from behind the altar stone. The Father was over seven feet tall, wearing a cowl pulled up to conceal a large head, and a dark cassock over a lumpy misshapen frame. Like the priest on the way down, the Father seemed to glide rather than walk, and was always face-on, never turning his back, as though there was only ever one side to the being.

"Charles." The voice was ocean deep and guttural. It had a bubbling quality as if the man had fluid in the back of his throat and was struggling to form words around a sluggish tongue.

"Yes, my Father. You called and your servant came."

The voice bubbled for a moment, before words formed. "The *Al-Azif*, the hidden *Necronomicon*, will be found. It is, as we suspected all along, in the land of the Egyptian kings." The Father paused as if to catch his breath or rest a strange tongue in a strange mouth. "Charles, there is a man, a Hussein ben Albadi, in Syria, who has access to the first copy made – it is quite detailed. He is talking to the Americans now, sharing what he knows. They are already there."

Drummond looked up. "Do you want me to intercept them?" He knew if he could recover the Book, his reward would be substantial.

"Not yet." There was wet wheezing for a few seconds. "Go to Syria first. But let the Americans recover it. Then take it from them."

Drummond bowed. "It shall be as you wish."

The Father glided closer, his arm reached forward. Something that felt like soft, cold fingers caressed Drummond's chin, tilting his face upward. "The last seals will be broken; the *Necronomicon* will show us how. You will speak the words, Charles." The hand caressed his face. "Bring it to us, and you shall be rewarded like no other human on this world. You will be the king of the kings. The Old One will rise, and we must all be ready."

Drummond's eyes were glassy in his pleasure, but as the Father continued to lean over him, he needed to hold his breath from the stench. The tall being shifted, and Drummond caught a glimpse of the structure within the dark folds of the cowl. He felt his testicles shrivel. Things moved in there where the face should have been, coiling over each other, writhing and twisting softly, like some many-legged sea creature moving in excited agitation.

The head leaned back, and the image disappeared in the folds of the heavy material. "Charles, they must never learn to read the book. Even those who see its fragments must be...silenced. Nothing must stop our work. Nothing must stop the final seals being broken. *Nothing.*" The hand moved to clasp his shoulder – it was viscid soft, at first. He felt the cold through his jacket, but then also felt pressure, and then pain. "*They must not learn.*"

"I...understand." Drummond knew his voice sounded a little high, as the fingers began to dig into his flesh. He crushed his eyes shut, and the pressure on his shoulder eased and then vanished. He looked up in time to see that the figure had retreated behind the altar, and then, as if by magic, it simply shrank or dropped from sight.

He fell forward and threw up, his stomach continuing to roil within him. After another few moments, he got to his feet and backed to the door. As soon as he got there, it was pulled open by the bald priest, who motioned for him to immediately follow him back along the way he had come.

Back in his car, he used both hands to wipe his handkerchief up and down over his face. He had already discarded his jacket, as the smell of the handprint made his stomach turn over again.

Kroen sat silently, waiting for his command.

"Get our Syrian people on the line. Prepare the fast jet, and a team; I'll take charge." He smiled, his eyes burning with excitement. "We can't beat them to it now, but who cares? We will let them find it, and bring it to *us*." He confidence was returning. "I want that fucking book, Kroen."

"Yes sir," the big man said, staring straight ahead.

Drummond smiled thinly. "And I want to find out what else this Dr Hussein ben Albadi *really* knows."

Chapter 11

They'd left the road hours back, and the tough four-wheel-drive vehicle was now bounding over a dry, rock-hard clay pan, throwing up clouds of yellow dust. Abrams scowled as he looked back through the rear windshield. "We're sending up a plume a mile high."

Hartogg spun the wheel. "Nothing we can do about it, sir. Place hasn't seen rain for weeks – dry as the dust in a mummy's jockstrap."

Abrams snorted and then tried to make room between the two SEALs. He turned to the other passengers. "Everyone all right back there?"

The major looked at each of them briefly before his eyes travelled once again to the rear window. Matt knew he wasn't checking their own dust plume again; he was looking for other plumes – pursuit.

Matt sat at the window to the right in the rear seat, and Tania had demanded the one on the left for security. Andy got the middle as he had scrambled to be next to her.

"Are we there yet?" the geologist asked over the sound of the engine.

Abrams smiled patiently. "About a hundred miles, but

definitely not as the crow flies – so maybe a day's driving – longer if we need to do some avoidance maneuvering."

"How will we know when we're in Turkey?" Andy continued to watch the landscape go by.

"People will be speaking Turkish…and hopefully won't be trying to cut your head off." Tania nudged him when he rolled his eyes. "Just pulling your leg, Bennet. As there's no border, and just miles of empty land, we'll have to rely on our GPS to tell us."

Andy nodded and slid down into his seat. "You seemed to know a lot about this lighthouse and island. What exactly are we looking for?"

Tania leaned back. "The Lighthouse debris is mostly underwater now, and the Island of Pharos has thousands of archeological pieces scattered over the surrounding sea floor – columns, statues and sphinxes have been lying there for ages." She turned to him. "I'm looking forward to what we can find there."

Rick Berry had his head down looking into his GPS, and then pointed flat handed to the north-west. "We need to veer five degrees to avoid a small town coming up."

Matt knew that running into possible spies was not an option for them. Though he could speak most Middle Eastern languages fluently, the group looked about as Syrian as the Bee Gees. If they ran into rebels, they wouldn't get away without a firefight.

Hartogg eased the wheel over a notch, and slowed as they hit some heavily stoned ground. Abrams looked back for a moment, grunted and then slid lower into his seat as well, and then pushed his cap down over his eyes. The dust cloud was worse, and, as they barreled along, the thick tires kicked up a huge rooster tail of debris.

Matt sipped from his canteen and looked past Tania and out her window. It was easy for the eyes to become tired, looking out over the crumbling yellowed ground, and the occasional pale spiky leaves of stunted trees.

Though they were heading into an area of higher elevation, it was still hot and dry with the outside temperature around ninety and the humidity at a moisture-sapping fifteen percent. This was not the sort of land you took to by foot. Without lots of water, you could end up dehydrated and delirious within twenty-four hours. He bet that the two SEALS, Abrams, and probably even Tania might be physically equipped for the terrain, but city slickers like him and Andy would be in a world of hurt. He was...

Their vehicle was kicked up into the air, to spin in slow motion. Matt felt his stomach lurch as light and dark swirled in and out of each other. The truck struck the ground on its roof, and his head and neck compressed. Everything went black.

*

Matt opened his eyes as he was being dragged backward, his boots furrowing the hard ground. He looked up to see the SEAL, Hartogg, smiling down at him; the big man winked.

"Nice to see you back in the land of the living, Professor."

"Wha...?" Matt's vision swam and the SEAL's white grin in a dust-and-soot-covered face stood out like a Cheshire cat's.

"Bit of a lump in the road, is all. All good now." Hartogg continued to grin and drag him.

Matt craned his neck; Tania was sitting up, hunched over and holding her head. Andy was beside her, sipping from a canteen; his face was streaked red.

Matt went to sit forward. "I'm okay."

Hartogg pulled him up next to Andy and Tania. He then let go, and kneeled to push up one of Matt's eyelids and look into his eye. After a second he nodded and slapped him on the shoulder. "Good man; you profs are tougher than I remember from when I went to school."

"You went to school?" Andy grinned at him.

Hartogg grinned back, gave him the finger, then got back to his feet and jogged to the upturned SUV. Matt sat forward, feeling his head swim momentarily.

"What just happened?" He watched as the SEAL joined Berry and Abrams in stripping the destroyed vehicle. Smoke billowed and the scorched ground indicated there had been a fire at some time. The three men worked quickly, crawling in and over the machine like ants over roadkill, and that's exactly what it was.

Tania groaned. "Oh God." She rubbed her head through her hair. She looked around quickly. "Give me a shove here, Bennet."

Andy pushed Tania forward and she got to her feet, standing with her hands on her hips but head down as she sucked in huge gulps of air. She looked across to Matt. "What happened? A fucking mine, Claymore, IED, take your pick – that happened. You okay?"

Matt nodded, and felt his neck creak.

"Good." She smiled down at him.

"I'm okay too, thanks for asking." Andy toasted her with his canteen.

"I could already see you were," she said, stretching her back.

Berry trudged back to them, unloaded some gear. "Boss says five minutes and we bug out, Captain."

"Got it." Tania sipped again and watched as the big man returned to the truck. In a few more minutes they had everything of value that was still working, and the SEALs and Abrams joined the wounded.

The major lifted field glasses to his eyes. "We need to move. Was an IED, a good one; usually means there'll be insurgents close by. They'll want to see what it was that triggered their trap. We need to be a long way from here by then."

Andy looked around. "Where to? Do we head back?"

Abrams shook his head. "Nope, we're closer to the border than home. Might as well continue. Our sat-comms are toast so as far as HQ is concerned we've gone dark. We can only send a local squirt to some friendly stations and hope we can pick up support – might be useful if we run into trouble." He continued to scan the horizon. "So, we go forward."

Andy snorted. "Did you say *run* into trouble? You mean, this is *not* trouble?"

Abrams continued to look out at the dry landscape. "You're alive, aren't you?" He turned back to the group and grinned. "But that was the good news. So, now the bad news – we do not have transport, we are in extremely hostile territory and will need to move quickly, carrying as much as is humanly possible. There will be no backup, no international communications and no more supplies until we complete our mission. That is the priority, those are our orders."

Tania dusted herself down. "The only way is forward." She turned to Matt and Andy and smiled. "Just think of it as a very long walk on the beach."

Matt scoffed and looked out over the arid, gritty land. "Yeah, and then normally the payoff is a cool dip in the surf."

"Not this time, Point Break." She held out her hand, and Matt grasped it and hauled himself to his feet. He felt a little woozy, and although his head cleared quickly, he was left with a splitting headache. He used one hand to press on his temples.

"How's the head?" She stepped in closer to him, looking deep into his face. "No concussion I can see, but you look a little pale. You need to sit down again?"

"No." Matt felt a dab of stickiness at one of his temples – blood. "Headache, but I'm okay." He winced.

"Got just the thing." She reached into her pack, jiggled something and then held up her open hand – there were two small white tablets on her dirty palm.

"Excedrin – that's it?" Matt raised an eyebrow.

She grinned. "Kearns, out here, even if you lose a freakin leg, that's it. Look around, Professor; we're not in Kansas any more."

Matt shook his head. "It's okay, I'll survive."

"Tough guy, huh?" She closed her hand over the pills and smiled. "I like it."

"My back is sore." Andy got to his feet, knocking dust from his hair.

She snorted. "You're a geologist, Bennet – an outdoor man who works with rock." She jerked a thumb at Matt. "I'm sure the toughest thing the professor has had to put up with is a fight over the last bagel in the staff room."

"Hey I..." Matt clamped his mouth shut, cutting off his protest. He'd battled krakens beneath the Antarctic ice sheets, been stalked by giant beasts up in the Black Mountains, and he'd travelled to the Amazon to trek through a hidden prehistoric jungle. He looked at Tania grinning at him, and he shrugged. At the moment he was getting special treatment because she thought him a bookworm – Why rock the boat? he thought, and grinned sheepishly. "You know me too well already, Captain."

The SEALs talked quickly and softly, with Abrams pointing in a few different directions, and then to small devices – probably GPS and ground radar, Matt assumed.

After a moment, Abrams nodded and turned. "Okay, people, let's move it out. I want to do twenty miles before we rack. Berry, take point, Hartogg, secure the rear – no stragglers, folks." He waved them on. "Take us out, Lieutenant." Berry jogged a few hundred feet out in front, and then continued at a fast walk. His neck was craned forward, and

Matt imagined his eyes would be darting over everything that could possibly conceal a sniper, explosive, or attacker. Given the hostile territory, Matt didn't envy these guys for a second.

In another few hours, the sun had started to dip, but the heat was no less intense. The only saving grace was that it was a dry heat, though even so, lips became chapped and skin chafed. Water was now at a premium, so rationing at short sips only was in force. Matt knew what could happen during dehydration – disorientation, hallucinations, headaches, and muscle fatigue, and then, in extreme cases, death.

They would walk long into the night's darkness, and rest for a few hours before sunup. Then hopefully, they'd only have another twenty-five or so miles until the border, maybe arriving by mid morning. Matt wasn't sure what this meant, when they got there – friendly faces, an outpost? He was too fatigued to ask.

A few hours later, the light had gone and Berry came back in. Matt overheard his words as he spoke softly with Abrams.

"Got a dry creek bed – only a slight depression, but gives us some shelter. Flat land outside, low opportunity for concealment on the perimeter – good as we're going to get."

Abrams nodded. "Okay; we'll rest here." He suddenly felt for his comms and looked at the small screen. He grunted in satisfaction.

"Good news, we got a return ping. There's a Mossad agent in the vicinity: Bluestar. Looks like we might have a friendly face out there about to join us." He turned to the group and pointed to the dry creek bed. "Let's get some rest. I'll take first watch for an hour, then Berry, and then Hartogg. No fires, no lights, no wandering off, limited conversation – sound will carry for miles over a flat surface." He looked hard at Matt and Andy.

"Got it," Matt said.

Later, he and Andy sat together, eating dried beef and sipping warm water. Matt felt bone tired, and Andy's eyes had dark circles showing under a layer of dust.

"Been in the desert before?" Matt whispered.

Andy nodded slowly. "Yep, Chihuahuan, Sonoran, Mojave, lots of them. But never in the Middle East – first time." He took another bite of his beef, chewing slowly. "You?"

Matt nodded. "Yeah. The Middle East is the real genesis of civilization, and the birthplace of formal language. Most of my work is done on campus, but I've been known to get my hands dirty."

Andy grinned. "Thought so. You never struck me as the sort to wrestle with other academics over that stale donut."

Matt smiled. "No, but as Captain Kovitz is extending me her personal protection…"

"Forget it; she has eyes for only me." Andy laughed. He nodded to Tania. "She's quite a looker…for a soldier, I mean."

Matt looked over his shoulder to where Tania was checking her kit. "Only you, huh? Good luck with that." She looked up and gave them a thumbs-up. Matt retuned the gesture and then turned back to Andy. "Sure, she's attractive, but I wouldn't tell her that; army chicks are usually pretty tough."

Andy's mouth turned down. "Still not sure I like them on the front line."

Matt snorted. "You haven't met some of the military women I have." He remembered the fearsome Special Forces soldier, Casey Franks, all tattoos, scars and bunched muscle. And there were others he knew even more formidable.

"Yeah, well, maybe there's one in a thousand," Andy scoffed. "But Tania's a nice girl – too nice to be doing this." He laid himself back down.

"Archeology or army? Ah, forget it." Matt also lay down, resting his head on his pack.

Andy said, "Do you really think there is a book that's going to tell us what's going on with these earth-drop occurrences?"

Matt shrugged. "A week ago I would have called bullshit. But with the holes, the birds, roaches, and seeing the pages that Albadi had, *predicting* the events we are experiencing, well, then, yeah, I think there's a good chance we'll find something."

"Good." Andy cleared his throat. "Because when I was at the bottom of the Iowa sinkhole, I saw something. Freaked me out. First time I ever felt like that in my life."

Matt stared up at the sky. There were a billion stars sprayed across the velvet darkness – pinpricks of light showing through a black blanket. Directly overhead, lighter and bigger than the rest, was a line of six dots. Matt knew there'd be two more behind the Earth – it was the solar system's convergence, and would complete within a few days.

"Yep, we'll find something," he hoped aloud, and closed his eyes and prayed for sleep.

*

Abrams, first on watch, had draped a camouflage net over his head to break up his profile. He had a long, bulky set of field glasses to his eyes and moved them over the landscape – nothing showed. He flicked them over to light enhancement and then up to thermal – a few rocks still glowed pink, as the day's heat slowly left them, but for the most part, there was nothing – not a bat, rodent, lizard, or even bug he could detect. Unnatural, he thought, as a desert night was a hive of activity for nocturnal hunters. The heat of the day forced most creatures below ground, but at night, it was showtime...Unnatural, he thought again.

He was about to move back to light enhance when a lump grew in the sand a few hundred feet out. He frowned and focused in on it – the thing was big, and moved slowly, only raising the sand by a few inches. Where it lumped the dry surface there was a red glow, as if there was intense heat being generated. He blinked to clear his vision. The small sand wave travelled for hundreds of feet. He wished the geologist was with him to ask, as he doubted it was anything artificial. As Abrams followed it with his eyes, it began to sink lower and lower, until it vanished.

"What the fuck was that?" he whispered. *Must* be related to the sinkholes, he guessed. He made a mental note to ask Andy Bennet when he woke. He exhaled, feeling unsettled. He'd feel better after they got to their destination, and at least had some cover at their backs. He put the glasses to his eyes again, and scanned the now cold and motionless desert.

*

Matt felt the toe in his ribs and looked up to see Captain Tania Kovitz standing over him. "Rise and shine, Sleeping Ugly."

He blinked; it was still dark. He felt grittiness in his eyes, and a mouth that was sticky dry. "Christ, I feel like shit. Sorry." He sat forward, his head thumping.

Tania kneeled. "How's the head?"

"Not worse." He rubbed his face. "Just dehydrated. I'll be fine when we're under way."

She punched his arm. "Good man."

Matt grinned back. "Yes I am. You should see me at my best."

"Careful, I might take you up on that." She raised an eyebrow.

Matt toasted her with his canteen and then sipped. He would have liked to swill and spit, but the water was too precious, so he swallowed it down, grit, stickiness and all. He got to his feet and saw that Andy was already up, talking to Abrams. Berry and Hartogg were nowhere to be seen.

Tania had a small pair of field glasses to her eyes and spoke out of the side of her mouth. "Get some food into you, as we're heading out soon. We're going to try and put in another ten miles before the sun comes up." She lowered the glasses. "We don't have enough water for a full daylight trek; this'll save us a few pints."

Matt nodded. "I'll be ready."

Andy joined them and Matt snorted. "Hey, you look as bad as I feel." He motioned to Abrams. "Everything okay with the major?"

"Yeah sure," Andy said. "He said he might have seen something strange out in the desert last night; like a lump or something moving under the sand. Wanted my advice."

"That sounds weird; what did you tell him?" Matt tucked his canteen away.

Andy shrugged. "Could be a lot of things. The earth can create a wave effect through seismic activity, stress vibrations, liquefaction – plenty of causes." He looked around and then grunted softly. "But I doubt any of those are in effect around here. The Middle East is geologically very old and stable. But then again, so were Iowa, Kansas, Montana, Utah, and a hundred other places where the land dropped." He grunted softly. "Nothing is making sense any more. Don't think I was much help to him."

Abrams turned to them and held up a hand.

Tania nodded in return. "Let's go, boys." She waved them on.

*

Charles Drummond walked around the man nailed to the top of the wooden table. He hummed softly as he removed objects from his pockets to lay them gently next to the prone figure. At one side of the large room, the man's servants were perched on wooden stools, hands tied behind their backs, and a noose around each of their necks – there were six of them, but three already dangled, their faces blue, eyes popping and tongues bulging like fat slugs between their lips.

Kroen stood with several men almost as huge as he was, with automatic weapons held loosely at their sides. More men were spread throughout the house – Drummond's small army had been assembled.

"So, so, so, Doctor Hussein ben Albadi, formerly of Damascus University, well-respected academic, and a man who is moderately wealthy...and now a traitor, and a thief to boot!" Drummond motioned to all the books stacked around the room. "And a very good one, by the look of this treasure trove."

Albadi mumbled through his gag.

Drummond leaned over him. "What's that, too tight?" He laughed. "That's the least of your troubles, my dear." He walked to a shelf and drew out a book. He flipped it open. "Wow, this looks old...and expensive." He looked up. "Is it rare?"

Albadi's face was red and he mumbled more frantically.

Drummond opened the book, and ripped out a page. He snorted. "Oh what the hell." He ripped out page after page, getting faster and faster. Many of the ancient leaves crumbled in his hand. At last the spine split and the book fell to pieces. "Oops, bet I get a late fee for that."

He dropped the remains and wiped his hands together. "So, dear Doctor, let's get down to business. We know that you have assisted six Americans – four of them military, and two specialist civilians. We also know you sent them out into the desert, after showing them fragments of the first existing copy of the *Al Azif*. A very valuable copy, given it has clues regarding the whereabouts of the original. But you already knew of its value and its secrets, didn't you? That's why you burned it up."

Drummond sighed. "What makes a man who has given his entire career over to books consciously destroy something of such rarity and value?" He grinned down at the doctor. "Oh, I can't tell you how irritating I found that. Irritating, but of no matter." He reached out to stroke Albadi's head. "Because we now have you, and all the wonderful secrets locked away in your brain."

Drummond patted Albadi's balding head, grinned and then reached under the plastic apron he wore to take another item from his pocket, which he placed with the others. He looked along the neat arrangement of scalpels, calipers, pincers, and bone saws and nodded approvingly. They were all gleamingly new and terrifyingly sharp. All would saw, open and slice though flesh like butter.

Drummond ran his hand along the line of reflective steel. Albadi whimpered and stared up at the ceiling, tear streaks marking his cheeks and temples. He was stripped to his underwear, with large nails pounded into the palms of his hands, his elbows and ankles, pinning him to the wood.

Drummond lifted a single instrument, a scalpel, and held it delicately like a conductor would a baton. "Beautiful." He spoke softly, catching sight of his own reflection in the polished steel. "Where did you send them?"

Albadi whimpered, and then mumbled. Drummond snickered and reached across to pull down his gag. "I'm sorry, you were saying?"

"You fool. You have no idea what you're doing. I know you don't want the Book; you want to find the gates. Do you know what will happen if the Old One rises? Do you?"

Drummond turned. "Why yes." He held his arms wide. "I'll be king...and you and your kind will be nothing more than grist to the mill, so to speak." He looked at his wristwatch and his lips compressed. "This is taking too long." He turned to look over his shoulder at Kroen, and nodded once.

The huge bodyguard kicked another of the stools away, and Albadi crushed his eyes shut, as if that would also drown out the strangulated gurgling as another life was extinguished.

Drummond smirked. "Two left. Soon we will run out of servants, then it will be your turn."

Albadi kept his eyes closed and Drummond leaned over him. "It's not very pleasant, watching a man die like that, and knowing that it's all because of you. But, Doctor, you really are missing something that is truly beautiful." He tapped the man's face with the scalpel. "I could make you watch, you know. A little incision here, and here, and then peel away the upper lids on both your eyes – no hiding then, *hmm*?"

Drummond sighed. "Doctor, or at least doctor of literature, I know the human body so well. I know how to caress it to heavenly pleasure, or take it to Hell when I expose nerve clusters and then play them like a harp." His smirk deepened. "But the music yours plays will not be to your liking: of that, I can assure you."

"Kroen." Drummond held up two fingers, and the last two stools were kicked away. He waited until the sounds died away to only the creaks of stretching rope fibers. He sighed. "I have done this dozens of times, to stronger men and women than you. They all talk, they *always* talk." He grinned. "Just to be clear: you are already dead. Your future is known and it is me who will have the pleasure of taking you forward on that journey. But the way I *take* you is up to you – swift and painless, like you are just getting tired and so cross over into a gentle sleep from which you never wake." His eyebrows went up slightly. "Or screaming for hours on end as I reduce you to a thousand slices of bloody flesh and shrieking nerve ends."

Drummond waited a moment longer, and then held up both hands, surgeon-like, with one holding the scalpel.

Albadi whimpered, and then nodded. Drummond leaned over him. "I have a secret to tell you." He snickered. "I don't really care about the Book's copy, and I know exactly where your visitors are going...I only want to make sure you tell no one else about it." He kissed the blade and smirked. "Doctor, I think we both know that I was always going to torture you." He placed the blade on Albadi's thigh, just over the femoral nerve, and then drew it down.

*

On the Lebanese-Syrian border, an Israeli agent of the elite Metsada Division stopped her roadside interrogation as she received the coded security squirt from the Americans. Her lips compressed in a tight line: she knew well the territory the Americans were in – there were Al Qaida, ISIS, the United Islamist Front, Party of a Thousand Martyrs, and a dozen other armed brigades crawling all over the area. With luck they might make it – but there was precious little of that left in Syria any more.

The man underneath the agent's boot wriggled and spat words up from split and bloody lips. The agent ignored him, and looked out to the east – the sun would soon rise, and the Americans would be exposed – not much time.

Concentration lapsed for only a moment, but it was enough – the man jerked upward, a combat knife appearing in his hand, the blade coming fast at the Metsada agent's groin. In a swift motion her foot on his neck was withdrawn, and then swung around to stamp down on the wrist holding the knife. Her slim black dagger flashed down once, deep into the man's orbital socket – he shuddered, and then lay still.

The agent wiped blood from the knife and hand, exposing a small blue star in the meat between thumb and forefinger. The blade was then expertly tucked back into a sleeve, and then she stepped away from the body and rolled it into a ditch.

The agent climbed aboard a long skeletal-looking motorbike. The LEPERD was an Israeli design for fast solo incursions – electric motor with plenty of torque delivered via a lightweight but muscular power plant. Its heavy-duty spring suspension system, adjustable rear shocks, and knobbed tire tread meant it was built for overland desert terrain.

The agent kicked up the guard, pulled goggles down over her eyes, wrapped a keffiyeh headdress around her nose and mouth, and throttled forward, accelerating quickly to seventy miles per hour over the dry flat landscape. It immediately became clear why the motorbike was Metsada's solo vehicle of choice in the Middle East – it was near silent, the electric motor giving off only a faint whine as it blistered over the predawn desert landscape.

Fifty miles – be there in an hour, thought Adira Senesh, whose name meant *mighty* in Hebrew. She concentrated on the still dark desert as she drove without lights. Her eyes were as black as pools of oil and they were narrowed in her concentration. She knew she owed the Americans nothing, but there was one man she would never forget, one who had stolen her heart, and who perhaps again one day…She shook her head and gritted her teeth. But not this day, she thought. This day she would do her job, and, as a top Metsada agent, sometimes that job was dealing death.

*

The sun was up and Abrams and the small group had long since left the creek bed. The land was flat save for dry scrub and ochre boulders in an ochre landscape, for miles upon miles upon miles. He thanked his lucky stars that the GPS unit had survived the crash – without electronics he bet even his SEALs would be hard pressed to navigate by just the huge sun.

Berry was out at point, a hundred feet ahead, hunched, and occasionally lifting field glasses to his eyes. Thermal and night-vision were of course now useless. Abrams looked briefly over his shoulder – the geologist and language professor were strolling along as if looking for a picnic spot in Central Park. Behind them was Captain Tania Kovitz with only a sidearm, but she was as vigilant as ever. Deeper back at rear point was Hartogg, adopting the same crouching movement as Berry – Abrams was glad to have both of them, but now wished for another dozen. There was something about the land here that made him feel uneasy...and he hated to admit it, but he was still a little rattled by that weird lumping in the desert he had seen the night before.

Out front, Berry raised a hand, and then lowered it slowly, palm down. Abrams felt a tingle run through his system – the SEAL had spotted something. Those guys could pick up things regular soldiers like him could never hope to. Abrams half turned; Tania and Hartogg were already lowering themselves to the ground, but Matt and Andy were just squinting back at him.

"Get on the goddamned ground," Tania hissed. Matt and Andy immediately dropped.

Berry scurried to a craggy outcrop, and was down on one knee. He had his rifle to his eye and was using the scope to scan the flat plains out to the northwest.

Abrams spoke softly into his field mic. "Talk to me, Berry."

"Movement; two o'clock – staying low now, dug in tight, but they're there." The man was cool as ice.

"*Shit*," Abrams whispered. They could win a skirmish against a few militants, but couldn't afford to get pinned down. When reinforcements came, they wouldn't be his own. And if there were more than a few dug in; they were in trouble right here, right now.

Abrams clicked on his mic again. "Kovitz, bring the civs in close. Hartogg, secure the rear."

Matt, Andy, Tania belly-crawled to Abrams, and Hartogg stayed a few dozen feet back to turn and focus on the landscape behind them.

"Clear," was all the SEAL said.

Thank God. We aren't ringed yet, Abrams thought with relief. They had grenades; once Berry confirmed how many and where, they could turn them to dust.

"Let's see what we've got. Berry, give me a count." He tried to project cool, but was anything but. He felt as if he had a lit stick of old-style dynamite in his hand, and the wick had just disappeared into the end. Nothing had happened, yet, which meant explosion imminent or nothing at all – either eventuality was possible.

Abrams swallowed; it hurt, his mouth dust-dry. He felt the rising sun begin to sting the back of his neck. Taking too damn long, he thought.

"*Incoming!*" Berry roared the word, and got down low as the RPG fizzed out of the desert, directly at him, and then over him, travelling at about six hundred feet per second.

"*Shit!*" Abrams hugged his head. It was never like in the movies, where the rocket seemed to travel slowly – in real life once they kicked from the pipe, they were moving almost as fast as a bullet.

The rocket-propelled grenade exploded in the desert, just a hundred feet past the SEAL. They all felt the heat and percussive blast wave: the plume was close enough to punish eardrums and sear skin.

Berry was immediately up, putting rounds back at the launch position. Return fire spat from dozens of concealed positions at two o'clock, just as he had said.

Another rocket sailed out and past them. They couldn't shoot these things for shit...And thank God for that, Abrams thought. But they obviously had more weapons than sense, and time was on their side. Eventually they'd hit the bull's eye.

A couple of insurgents broke from the earth and sprinted toward Abrams's position. Berry raised himself up and fired two rounds, both hit dead center and both men were blown backward. Immediately hundreds of rounds were launched toward Berry and their group.

From behind, Hartogg spoke laconically into Abrams's ear. "Got another nest, one out at four o'clock and the other making all the noise at two o'clock – reckon there's about half a dozen shooters in each, not counting those two try-hards that Berry just sent to Hell."

"Got it." Abrams held up his field glasses, and Hartogg spoke again.

"I also reckon there'll be more coming soon. Can't stay here, boss. Just say the word."

"Yup." Abrams exhaled. He knew what the man was asking – an assault – take them head-on now, before they got a lucky shot in, or their numbers grew. Berry and Hartogg would get close, and perhaps take them down. They both had M67 fragmentation grenades, but unlike the sniper's nests, theirs weren't rocket propelled – they could throw them a hundred feet, but closer was better for kill-confirm.

Abrams grimaced, momentary indecision making the gears of his mind spin uselessly. Just then Berry kneeled up and fired again, short bursts to conserve ammunition. This time, total firepower was concentrated on him, and another rocket fizzed out from behind a small outcrop of low rock.

"Incoming." Berry threw himself down.

Abrams also hugged the dirt, and watched as his worst fear was realized – Berry ceased to exist – his position was vaporized by a direct strike.

Abrams pounded the dirt with his fist. "*Fu-uuuck.*" His seconds of indecision had meant a good man's death.

Bullets came at them like swarms of bees, and another rocket exploded a few feet out from Hartogg. There would be more rockets now, and if they tried to flee, they wouldn't get a dozen feet.

Abrams ground his teeth. Trying to wait them out was not an option – nightfall would spell their death, as then they'd also have to deal with the belly-crawlers coming at them over the dark sand.

He looked back over his shoulder. Four sets of eyes looked to him, waiting for his next instruction – he had nothing.

Can't stay here, Hartogg had said. Take em head-on, now or never. He felt down for his grenades. This is gonna hurt, he thought, as he steeled himself for the suicidal assault.

He looked up briefly to check the sniper's position, and saw momentarily a rooster tail of sand and debris shooting up about half a mile out. It stopped, and he blinked, trying to determine what it had been. Maybe more reinforcements for their attackers, he thought with dismay. Abrams had surprise on his side for only a few more minutes.

He opened his mic. "Hartogg, going in, on my word – looping assault, I'll come in from the right flank, you the left on the four o'clock nest. Kovitz, prepare to give us cover from your position. Okay, people, let's blow them back to hell."

"HUA," Hartogg returned aggressively, sounding eager to avenge his SEAL buddy.

Abrams sucked in a huge breath, and looked down at the ground for a second. He said a silent prayer, and then counted down.

"Three, two, one...go."

He burst from his position, sprinting out in a loop, zigzag-ging as he came. Out of the corner of his eye he could see the huge form of Hartogg doing the same, the man moving at a speed beyond his own to take on the southern nest.

The hundred yards seemed to take forever, but as he ap-proached his target, there were no rockets or gunfire. When Abrams was within thirty feet of their enemies' position, he saw someone dressed in dark fatigues, guns strapped down on his groin in a V-shape for fast draw, and a slim black blade in each hand.

The figure – not a big guy, but wiry as heck, and faster than any human Abrams had ever seen in action – danced, spun, and kicked, slashing and stabbing at the snipers who one after the other fell around him. The desert fighters leaped at the lone figure, or raised guns, but the soldier was too quick for all of them, and soon they had all been cut down like wheat.

Abrams slowed to a stop, trying to make sense of what he was seeing. Hartogg joined him, his gun still at the ready.

"Boss, southern nest is dead – all six." He motioned to the dead snipers before them. "And now, so is this one. Who the fuck is this one-man hurricane?" He still had his gun up.

"Don't know yet, but I'm done with taking chances." Abrams held his pistol in a two-handed grip. "Soldier, lower your weapons."

The black covered figure was barely breathing hard. Dark eyes were the only feature showing in the keffiyeh headdress.

"Put...your weapons...on...the ground." Abrams spoke through his teeth.

The twin pools of dark stared for a moment, assessing Abrams and Hartogg, and then the guy leaned forward to wipe his bloody blades on the clothing of one of the dead.

"Oh for fuck's sake." Abrams felt his patience burning away.

"Boss, maybe he doesn't speak English," Hartogg added.

Abrams shouted, "This is your last warning: put your hands in the air, or I will be forced to disarm you." He felt Hartogg glance at him from the corner of his eyes. He didn't want to shoot – just wanted the asshole to comply. What's his problem? he wondered. "Drop...the..."

The lone figure spun the blades and then slipped them back into hidden sheaths. He then held his hands out, palms open.

"Don't move." Abrams advanced, followed by Hartogg from a slightly different angle. Abrams could still see little other than a pair of velvet-dark eyes. The assassin raised his arms, and stayed stock still, legs slightly apart. His eyes never left him for a second.

Abrams came in close and reached out to pull the head-covering away.

"Boss." Hartogg's voice carried a warning – too late.

The figure exploded into action, grabbing Abrams's wrist and gun, spinning him around, finger and thumb on each side of his windpipe, and using his body as a shield from Hartogg. One minute Abrams had felt in control, and then next he was disarmed, and now a hostage.

The SEAL screamed instructions, gun up, but obviously knew that he didn't have a shot.

Abrams cursed. Idiot, amateur! he thought. He'd just witnessed this person take out two snipers' nests by himself as easily as if he were ordering a burger and beer. And a minute later he was underestimating the guy.

"Be still."

The voice in Abrams's ear was muffled, but not deep. He calmed himself and they stood for a few seconds, Abrams held as a shield, and Hartogg neutralized. In another moment, the assassin loosened his grip on Abrams's throat, and let his gun slip back into his hand. Abrams was pushed away, but the point was clearly made – I could have killed you, but I let you live.

Hartogg had his gun up, rock steady. "Got a shot – say the word, Boss."

Abrams waved him down, breathing in gulps from a pinched neck.

The figure started to unwrap the covering over his head, ignoring them both now. The eyes stayed fixed on Abrams.

"What...?" Hartogg's mouth fell open.

Long dark hair fell loose around a face that could have been beautiful but for an edge of brutality that urged caution, not trust. She wasn't smiling, though there was no anger in her countenance. She was calm and totally relaxed.

For a woman she was tall, Abrams guessed about five ten at least. She looked around and then her eyes came back to him.

"Not a good time or place for a stroll," she said without a trace of mirth.

Abrams blinked. "No, no indeed, and we should be driving but ran into a little unexpected IED trouble."

"Here IED is not unexpected, but *always* expected – a child's mistake." Her eyes were hard.

Hartogg snorted, and the woman looked at him, and then to Berry's smoldering remains. "You make mistakes out here and people die, hmm?"

"Fuck you." The veins in Hartogg's neck bulged.

"At ease." Abrams cleared his throat, feeling like they, he, had been admonished enough. "Major Joshua Abrams; you mind if I ask who I might be addressing?"

"Joshua?" Her brows went up. "That is an old Hebrew name. It means the salvation of Jehovah. A good, strong name." She nodded. "Captain Adira Senesh; I got your callout."

"Israeli army?" Abrams asked.

Senesh ignored the question and instead looked around at the landscape, the sky and then back to Abrams. "Major, you are a long way from home...and not in a good place. What are you doing here?"

Abrams half smiled. The woman didn't answer his question directly, but the obvious evasion was answer enough: she was a Mossad agent – Kidon or Metsada, he bet – and, by the way she took down all of the insurgents, a damned good one.

"What we're doing here is classified," said Tania Kovitz, joining them, followed by Andy and Matt, still several dozen feet back.

Adira looked Tania up and down. "You have about an hour before a squad of terrorists arrive. Good luck." She began to walk away.

"Adira." Matt jogged closer.

She spun at his voice, squinting. Like a door swinging open to briefly show warm light, her face softened momentarily, before it swung shut once again. She shook her head. "Professor Matthew Kearns...we live in interesting times." She suddenly looked around, her eyes wide. "Is he here?"

"No, no, he isn't," Matt said, knowing immediately who she was looking for – Alex Hunter.

Her expression dropped. "Of course not. If he were here, those sniper nests would have been obliterated long ago." She sighed.

Abrams brow creased. "You two know each other?"

Matt grinned. "Yeah, kinda...we met on a mountaintop ...in the Appalachians. She gets around." He stepped closer to the Metsada woman, and turned to Abrams. "And we need her if we're going to get out of here alive."

Captain Tania Kovitz kept staring at Adira, but Hartogg lowered his rifle, and nodded to the woman – wary, but more at ease now. Abrams knew the SEAL recognized a fellow Spec Forces warrior...and he agreed with Kearns that she was one they needed.

Abrams grunted. "I agree." Tania started to object, but he just took his voice up a level. "Adira –"

"Captain Senesh," Adira said.

"Captain, we need your help. We lost our truck and need to get to the Turkish border."

"Why?" She stared evenly.

"Because –" Matt began.

"Professor Kearns." Abrams's voice carried a warning.

"She can help." Matt turned back to Adira. "We need to get to Alexandria, in Egypt, and Turkey is the closest friendly place."

"Where were you hoping to cross, exactly?"

"Reyhanlı, Hatay Province," Abrams responded.

She nodded. "I know it – on the border – stupid choice. Your information is out of date – it's now a bombsite. They distrust everyone, and you would be arrested on suspicion of being a spy. This is the Middle East, Major. Nowhere is safe for Americans."

"Or Israelis," Abrams pointed out.

She snorted. "But we are used to it, and here, we expect nothing but treachery. Keep in mind that for every single supporter you encounter, there will be a hundred more killers or informants who would sell you out in a second."

Abrams breathed evenly for a moment, and tried hard to keep his frustration in check. "Well, do you have a better suggestion?"

"Of course. For a start, you must stay away from populated areas. Get to Samandag. It's in the same province but is less populated and still mostly untouched by the war. It's also on the coast," Adira said evenly.

"Then what?" Abrams asked.

"Then, if we're still all friends, I can have someone meet us. Get you to Israel."

"We don't want to get to Israel. We need to get to Egypt, and fast."

"Oh yes, Alexandria. And you think the Turkish military is going to help you get there? The Turks and Egyptians don't even talk any more. And you think they will do more than simply detain you, as diplomatic communiqué go back and forth between your countries for weeks."

Her eyes narrowed. "I think you do not have passports, or a cover story, or even a lot of money to buy safe passage."

Abrams folded his arms.

Her head tilted. "Did I mention how popular Americans are out here?" She relented. "Major, we can provide you with cover, documentation and everything else you need." She shrugged. "One step back, two steps forward. Think smart, Major, the door is closing."

Abrams bristled, and he knew he was grinding his teeth. The damned woman had him over a barrel.

Matt Kearns came and stood in front of him, his back to the woman. "Major, that'll work. We can trust her." He shrugged. "There's no one else *to* trust."

Abrams looked past Matt to Adira. "And what's the price?"

She smiled. "No price, Major. All I need to know is what I'm getting into. What is so important in Alexandria that you would come all the way to Syria, and then cross the desert to find it?"

"You don't need to know that, and it's not relevant to you. Besides, I'm not sure at this stage that we should be teaming up with Mossad. However, guide us to Samandag, and then we can see if our plans need updating."

Adira grinned. "Ah, the warrior who won't take advice."

Matt tilted his head. "Sounds like someone else I know."

Her eyes flicked to Matt. "You are using up all of your lives too quickly, Matthew Kearns. Sooner or later there won't be someone to save you, and you'll find your head will become separated from your body."

"Probably true." He smiled sadly. "Adira, this is important. We think it might give us answers to the sinkholes and disappearances."

"Kearns!" Abrams's voice was sharp, but Matt held up a hand and continued.

"We know they're also happening in Israel. The Major might even put in a good word for you with the right people in the States."

She stared for a few moments, and then grunted softly. "Then perhaps we do have a shared goal. This is what I was sent into the desert to ascertain – whether the sinkholes had a military cause...and, if they did, to eradicate it."

Suddenly, from behind them, Hartogg roared a warning. Adira dived and rolled, and Abrams and the others followed quickly.

Abrams lifted his head. "What have you got, soldier?"

Hartogg was like a statue, gun up and pointed out at the desert. "Movement in sniper nest one."

"Impossible," Adira said and got up on one knee, a handgun pointed at the place where she had demolished the six fighters earlier. "They are dead."

Abrams waited another few seconds, licking dry lips. "Hartogg, low and easy, come in from your right flank. Captain Senesh and I will –"

Before he could finish, Adira was up and sprinting in a zigzag to the nest. She leaped in.

Andy nudged Matt. "Bit of a risk taker, huh?"

"Goddamnit." Abrams got to his feet, sprinting. Hartogg came in fast from the right.

They arrived at the same time, with Matt, Andy and Tania in fast behind them. They stood looking down into the small depression. Adira walked around the next, kicking over some scraps of clothing, weapons, ammunition, and a dusty pair of field glasses.

"Nothing." She looked hard at the SEAL.

"What did you see, Hartogg?" Abrams said, frowning.

"Corner-eye movement." He shrugged. "Bit like...a lump, or something. Thought it was..." He stopped, and then shook his head. "Where are they, then?"

Abrams looked back at where Adira stood holstering her gun. There were no bodies. He slowly turned to scan the landscape.

Hartogg jogged to the second sniper nest, and called back to the group. "Empty as well – all gone."

Abrams lifted his field glasses. "Someone's out there – must have snuck in and recovered the bodies from right under our noses."

Adira shook her head, also turning slowly to look out at the desert. "I do not think this. There were a dozen bodies. If there were enough men to carry that many away, there were enough to ambush us. They would leave the bodies and try and kill us."

"Well, they didn't just walk away," Abrams said quietly.

Adira kicked at a pile of clothing. A football-sized creature scuttled free, its claw-like legs moving quickly.

"Shitza." She pointed her gun at it.

"*What the fuck is that?*" Andy said, his face twisted in horror.

The thing was like a giant slater bug with armor-plated segments and way too many legs. It stopped its bid for freedom and instead seemed to stick to the ground. It started to sink into it, shuddering and twisting, and just before it disappeared into the soil, an eye opened on its back – not a chitinous bulb, or multi-faceted lens, but instead a brown eye, a human eye, with pupil and white around it.

In another second, there was just a lump in the soil. Adira used her boot to kick at the small mound – the thing had already sunk below the top layer.

"Was that...was that some sort of gross scarab? They're carnivorous, aren't they?" Andy said, his voice high.

"Yes and no." Matt came down into the small depression and kneeled by the hole Adira had just made. He picked up a discarded blade and started to dig into the soil: it struck nothing solid, but when he pulled the blade back it was coated in black goo. He sniffed it and then flicked it off. "They're flesh eaters, but the biggest can only grow to about five inches, I think; *that* thing was a foot long and had about ten legs. It looked like some sort of deformed aberration. I've never seen anything like that before." Matt turned, his mind leaping back to the Syrian doctor and his unsettling texts. "Perhaps *no one* has seen it before. Remember Albadi's quote? 'The other vermin of the dark deep would rise, the lice upon' or something."

"Oh great," Andy groaned. "Do you think these guys were pulled under?" He turned to Tania. "Remember how Frank was pulled into the earth?"

Tania looked from Andy to Abrams. "We should probably move out, sir."

"Yeah, we should." Abrams took one last look around. "Captain Senesh, lead on."

"You." Adira pointed to Andy, and then out to the desert. "Bring my bike."

"Huh?" Andy guffawed. "Can I ride it?"

"No. If anyone could ride it, I would. All of us cannot ride, and I do not wish to leave it for the desert. So we need to push it." She shrugged. "It's light, and you look strong."

The geologist went to complain, but Abrams cut him off. "Do it, Andy. All hands in now."

Andy groaned, but went and lifted the long machine from the sand.

*

After about an hour's steady walking, Tania sidled up to Matt, her expression set. "I don't trust her. She'll throw us over in a second."

Matt smiled. "As we've done to her in the past. Believe me, she has no reason to trust us either. But, it seems we have shared goals, so..." He shrugged.

Matt saw that Tania's gaze narrowed as she stared at the athletic form of the Israeli woman. Is there a flash of green appearing in those eyes? he wondered. Perhaps it was just a natural rivalry between members of different forces. Hartogg might have relaxed, but he had volunteered for rear point, where he could keep Captain Senesh in sight even while surveying their surroundings.

Matt nodded at Adira's back. "She knows what she's doing, and we need her."

Tania snorted. "Yeah, well, she needs us too. Everyone does." She turned to look into Matt's face. "I think I'm a little more objective than you, and my advice is, just don't get too close to her. I think you'd regret it." She dropped back, leaving Matt to trudge on alone.

The pace was hard, Adira's long legs never once slowing. She never seemed to fatigue. As well, the sun had reached its peak, so the heat began to hammer down on them. Adira had covered over her head again, leaving just a slit in the cloth for her eyes. Andy pushed the bike, and his shirt was completely wet – to his credit he hadn't complained for a second. Matt felt for the geologist, and decided he'd give the man a break soon. Before he did, he jogged up to walk beside Adira. "You look well...Are you?" he asked, glancing at her.

She turned her covered face to him. "I'm alive." Her black eyes stared for a few seconds. "And back where I belong."

"Ah, back where you belong; here." He waved an arm out at the desolate landscape. He looked back into her eyes. "I kinda missed you."

"I would have killed you, Matt...if you'd got in my way. That's what I do. You think I belong in America? I think some people might not be too happy if I turned up there." She looked away. "Did Alex Hunter survive?"

"Yeah, he survived, and he's back in the fold now," Matt said. "I worked on a job with him recently in Crete."

"So, that was him?" She laughed softly for a moment, before becoming serious again. "Does he ever...ask about me?"

Matt stared forward for a moment, not sure how to answer.

"*Ack*, forget I asked. Stupid question." Her voice had a bitter edge.

Matt trudged on beside her for another few minutes before looking around at the landscape. "Must get lonely out here with nothing to do but save us poor dumb Americans."

"It's becoming a habit." She pulled the material away from her face and reached down for a canteen on her hip. She took a sip, then replaced it. "My search for the source of the sinkholes was proving fruitless. They're happening now all over the world – but you know this."

Matt nodded. "The land is sinking globally and anyone who goes down into one of the pits never comes back up...or is found. We're also seeing people disappear who are simply in proximity to the pits."

She nodded. "Our scientists have tracked anomalies on the surface – strange things that came out of the holes. They usually return, but when we follow them in, we find nothing. It's solid rock down there. And even the deepest caves only descend a mile." She grunted. "We have both seen strange things in our lives, Professor. I fear we are about to see them again."

From behind them Andy cleared his throat, then pushed the bike up between them.

Adira grinned. "You like my bike?"

"I love it, and it only started getting really heavy about five miles back." He jiggled his eyebrows at Matt. "Still love to have a ride." He waited, but Adira didn't respond.

Matt looked over his shoulder at Tania and she flicked him a worried look. He turned back to Andy. "My turn, buddy." He grabbed the handlebars.

Andy straightened his back and stretched. "Thanks." He walked beside Adira. "I couldn't help overhearing you mention about things disappearing into the pits. I lost my friend in Iowa, and I think something was in the soil...something big."

"Did you see it?" Adira asked.

"Yes, no...sort of. The cave collapsed on us," Andy said. "Looks like we're all coming at this from different angles."

"Blind men and the elephant again," Matt added.

"Except one of the blind men is now a mysterious and beautiful Israeli agent." He turned and winked at Matt.

Matt groaned and slowed down, letting Andy weave his magic. He watched as he flashed her toothy grins and delivered a non-stop monologue. Eventually she stopped and leaned in close to him. Her expression was rock-hard as she spoke directly into his face.

Andy nodded, and Adira increased her pace, leaving him behind.

Matt caught up. "Trouble in paradise, Romeo?"

"My heart is broken." Andy snorted softly, his mouth turning down. "She said I was a little boy, and compared to the men she has loved, I am a bug."

Matt laughed out loud. "Hey, out here, I think that's a compliment. She likes you; keep at it, buddy."

"Nah." He looked over his shoulder at Tania and perked up. He looked back at Adira's tall athletic form. "Did you see the way she took apart those terrorists? She's awesome."

"Yeah, I've seen her in action before. The woman is a human weapon." He motioned to her back with his head. "Hey, I know, why don't you bring up that thing about women not being tough enough for the front line again?"

Andy groaned. "I think I'm gonna skip it."

Matt pushed the bike over a large piece of stone. "Good call; we don't want to have to carry you as well."

*

They walked and rested, walked and rested through the heat of the day and well into the cool night. The borders in the region were porous and endlessly disputed, and Syria had become Turkey many miles back. Adira only called a halt around two am, when they were ten miles from the water. In the distance the black ocean showed a line of lights right on the coast.

"Samandag; we rest here. No fires."

The group stood on the hilltop, looking out over the coastal plain and the water. A moon was setting, creating a huge silver path over the dark waves.

Matt felt tired from his scalp right down to his blistered toes. "Will there be a boat? It's still about six hundred miles to Israel, and about another two hundred onto Egypt, plus we need to pass by the rest of Turkey, Syria, and Lebanon – not going to be an easy ride."

She nodded. "Then best not go by boat, hmm?" She looked at each of the bedraggled group. "And I certainly do not think you are ready to walk into Egypt just yet."

"We're not staying in Israel," Tania said quickly.

"Okay, we avoid Israel." She smiled at Tania, but there was no warmth in the expression. "You see, I can compromise. I hope you can too." Her smiled dropped. "Captain Kovitz, Lieutenant Hartogg, scout the area and report back. Mr. Bennet, bury my bike."

Tania glared and looked to Abrams who exhaled, but then nodded to his subordinates. Hartogg took off, and Tania muttered and headed off with Andy and the bike in the opposite direction.

Adira walked off a dozen feet and spoke into a small comms device, and after a few minutes she came back over the Abrams.

"They're on their way. I've also asked that they relay your whereabouts to your superiors." She smiled flatly. "Don't want them sending another team out to blunder about in the desert, do we?"

She walked to a slight rise in the sandy soil, reached into a pocket and pulled out a fist-sized rod. She telescoped it to about a foot and then jammed it into the earth. A small green light started to blink on the top.

"Beacon?" Abrams said.

She nodded. "As I said, they're already en route. They just need to know where to rendezvous with us."

"So where are we going?" Matt asked.

She turned. "We should be in Cyprus within two hours."

"Cyprus?" Abrams recoiled. "What the hell are we going to Cyprus for...? And I thought we needed to pick up our documentation?"

"Exactly." She stood with her hands on her hips. "We have an office in Cyprus. They will take care of us. It also means we can depart via normal airlines – just a few tourists on a Middle Eastern diving holiday, travelling from Cyprus to Alexandria – sound good?"

Matt snorted and nodded, but Abrams wasn't mollified. "What do you mean, 'we'? Who exactly is this 'we'?"

She stepped in closer to Abrams. "Time for you to compromise, Major. You are not safe yet, you have not secured what you seek yet, and you are certainly not at home. You'll need support and protection. Without me you'd be picked up in about fifteen minutes."

"Goddamnit, Captain, why do I get the feeling I'm losing control of this situation?"

Adira's smile never faltered. "You're not. I'm making sure you remain *in control*, Major. Trust me."

Abrams held her gaze, and then threw his hands up.

Tania Kovitz came back in from scouting the area. She glared at Adira, but then faced Abrams. "Clear, sir."

Hartogg and Andy followed and nodded to Adira. Hartogg seemed to be enjoying the interchange between the two tough women. Abrams just sighed.

Adira nodded. "Good. Everyone bury everything we don't need."

Andy held up the few remaining items he had been carrying. "And what exactly *will* we need?"

"Truthfully, just yourself. Everything else twelve inches below ground...now," Adira said as she checked a small box.

In another five minutes, she waved an arm. "Get down – clear a space. We need to get back about fifty feet from the pulser." She walked away from the green-lit tube and crouched. The others did the same.

Matt waited; there was silence now, and the moon was sinking lower toward the water. He was conscious of the people close to him in the dark, but other than a fingernail-sized dot of green fifty feet away, there was just the hint of light from the low moon.

At first it sounded like a breeze was coming up from the sea, and then in another few seconds he heard Hartogg laugh softly.

"Nice," the SEAL said.

An odd sharp-angled shape appeared; it was impossible to make out its exact form in the darkness, as it was black against a dark night. It came in near silently, and Matt marveled at how quiet the huge machine was. Turning side on, it looked to be about sixty-five feet long.

"So quiet," Matt whispered.

Hartogg nodded. "You bet: it's one of the best hunter-killers on the military market." Matt could see his white teeth in the dark as he grinned. "You're looking at a UH-60 Stealth – it was that baby that crept into Bin Laden's backyard. The reason it's so quiet is it's got extra chopper blades, and a lower rotor speed. Added to that there's no external rivets, and an infrared suppression finish in nano paint – this bad boy is invisible and silent as the devil." He grinned again. "Like I said, it's the best of the best...and that's because it's one of ours – we sold it to em."

They squinted through the sand kicked up as the huge machine touched down like a giant dark insect. A soft red glow came on inside the cabin, and a figure waved them on.

Adira ran first, snatching up the pulser. In another thirty seconds they were moving at about a hundred and eighty miles per hour toward Cyprus.

Chapter 12

Derby, Sedgwick County, Kansas

"Sunfa bitch." Harry Wilcox's hands slipped down the slick plunger as he worked it again in the basement sink. After pushing and pulling it some more he lifted it away and in return received a *gurgle* and a *blerk*, and then a few measly bubbles popped and slid back into the metal drain.

Phew. He turned away to drag in a breath – whatever was goddamn stuck in there was now stinkin to high heaven.

"*Is it clear ye-eeet?*" The voice from upstairs carried notes of high impatience.

Harry leaned back. "Nearly, baby; I think I just about got it that time." He ground his teeth and lifted the plunger again, bringing it down over the drain once more. Their basement was the storage cellar, workshop and laundry room, and, as he and Summer had three kids all under the age of three, diapers were piling up – fast.

He sighed. When they had little Melody-Blue, their oldest, they'd promised each other they'd do their bit for planet Earth and never use those disposable ones that clog up the landfill – but then came Little Miss Mountain-Dew followed by Daisy-Sunshine, and whaddaya know, those little suckers shit right around the fucking clock.

Harry pumped again and again – if he couldn't unblock the drain, that meant no washing machine, which then meant washing by hand outside, and as Summer was still breast-feeding little Daisy-Sunshine, he'd for sure be the sap stand-ing out there with fifty pounds of brown-streaked Modern Cloth Diapers.

He stopped to wipe his brow, and then frowned. "Ah, *getouttahere.*" A huge cockroach scuttled across the concrete floor. Harry stamped on it, but immediately another took its place, racing madly towards the center drain grate. He lunged and managed to catch its rear half with his boot tread.

"Yech." Even with its abdomen flattened to a yellow and brown paste, the front half still tried to scuttle away.

He looked around for more moving targets. The basement room was a good size, about fifty feet square on a concrete slab with a drain in the center. It had a sink, dryer and washer, and storage for dry goods, plus his workbench, and a million other things that had come down there to be sealed away in boxes and forgotten.

Harry sucked in a huge breath, jammed the plunger over the sink's drain and started his dance once more – up down up down, and then rip it free, hopefully dragging loose whatever was in there – *gurgle, splurk, pop* – nothing.

Just then, he felt a small vibration through the soles of his feet, and the drain in the center of the room also popped and gurgled. A splash of inky fluid spattered the floor around its chrome rim.

"So-ooo, that's where you're hiding?" Harry lifted the plunger, spun it in his large fingers and walked toward the center of the room, keeping his eyes fixed on the drain-hole lest it disappear like some rabbit he had his sights set on. On his way he grabbed the already open bottle of Drain-Away, and then got down on his knees beside the tiny round grate.

"Bottoms up." He upended the bottle, letting the blue liquid run thickly in, smiling and holding his breath.

The bottle emptied, and he sat back on his haunches. "Let's see you chew on that." He grabbed the plunger, but would give the caustic concoction a minute or two to work its magic.

"*Now Harry? Is it clear no-ooow?*" The voice was getting shriller by the second, and he gritted his teeth.

He lifted his head. "Soon, angel pie. What do you think I'm doin down here; playin with myself?" he added under his breath.

There was a squelching sound from in the hole, and Harry peered in. Seeing nothing, he placed the rubber cap of the plunger over the drain. "It's go time." He pumped it up and down several times, his face going red and his grin widening as a thick mucousy sound started to rise and fall in time with his jerking ministrations.

Using his bodyweight, he leaned down hard for one last plunge, and then ripped it away. To his shock, a gush of glistening blackness rose in a column, splattering his shirt, face and one of his arms. He dropped the plunger and grabbed for a rag to rub at his eyes.

He barely heard the liquid sound in the room, or if he did, he wouldn't have cared. The burning gunk stung his skin and one of his eyes – mercifully it hadn't got in both, but still the shock and pain were unbearable.

Harry went to get to his feet but couldn't. He realized that something had him by the arm, and he took his hands away from his red raw face and opened his one good eye. He recoiled in horror – the silver drain cap had popped free and a thick black pipe of goo extended from it and was wrapped around his forearm.

Gaa! He yanked, but it stretched. He tried to throw himself backward, but the thing was incredibly strong. Harry whimpered. The slimy touch on his arm started to burn even more ferociously than the fluid on his face. And this had the added horror of being something that seemed alive, and was now tugging at him.

The ground vibrated again under his feet, and he became aware of Summer's yelling voice once again.

"*You better have that cleared soon, Harry, or there's gonna be tro-ooub-bbble.*"

"Summ–" was all he could yell, before something slimy that tasted like shit, oil and Drain-Away jammed itself in past his lips and worked its way down his throat.

*

Summer sat on the couch frowning at the television. Everything the young English chef baked or cooked slid easily from pans, golden and perfectly made. He turned to the screen and gave her the benefit of his usual open-mouthed grin. His tongue looked slightly too big for his mouth.

"Lovely jubbly," he yelled as he held up the plate.

"Yeah, well, you try doin that with my old pans." She wrinkled her nose; the clothes basket was full to overflowing with dirty nappies. Either they went in the washer or in the tub outside, and as she had just gotten the little ones off to sleep, and was on her downtime break, she knew who would be scrubbing shit, and real soon.

"*Ha-aarry, are you...?*"

The basement door burst open, and Harry lurched out. She sat forward – his face was beet-red, and one of his eyes looked funny – all milky-white sort of. "Harry?"

Harry opened his mouth but nothing came out. Instead he worked his jaws as if he were either trying to say something or pry loose a bone he had managed to lodge in his gums.

Her brows came together. "Are you stoned? Is that what you been doin down there?"

He lurched closer and now Summer could see that around his mouth it glistened blackly like he had been drinking engine oil. She tried to think what was stored down there that he could have been getting into.

He hadn't said a word, or even looked at her. She started to feel the hair on her head and neck rise.

"Is it...fixed?" She got to her feet and stepped up on the couch.

Harry remained standing in the center of the room, arms slightly out from his sides, and turning slowly as if trying to find something.

"Harry, you're scaring me. *Stop it*!" She put a foot up on the back of the couch.

He slowly turned toward her, and the good eye in his head suddenly went full black, as if the pupil had totally grown over all the white. He opened his mouth wide, then wider. She heard his jaws cracking. Summer was expecting the man to scream, but instead, several feet of black ribbons extended from his mouth.

Summer's throat hurt, and she realized *she* was screaming, and couldn't stop. She grabbed up a pillow and held it in front of herself, getting ready to vault over the back of the couch and sprint to the door.

Suddenly Harry just...exploded. The black ribbons came from every part of his body, growing hugely to become tendrils, pipes, and trunks of black flesh that all ended in thrashing tentacles. His eyes doubled, tripled and kept on multiplying, and then slid all over his grotesquely inflating body.

Harry, the man, her husband, just broke apart as if he were a shell casing being shed by the disgusting giant creature that now stood before her, filling the room with its bulk and its stink.

Summer's nerve broke. She forgot about her kids. She forgot everything. She glanced over her shoulder to the door, and then leaped. She had been a sprinter at high school and used to be as fast as the wind.

The thing that used to be Harry was even faster – she never made it.

Chapter 13

Cyprus, south of Larnaca

A light blinked twice on the hill.

It was still before dawn when they were dropped off on an empty stretch of coast on the southeastern side of the Cypriot island. The chopper immediately sped out over the dark water and was gone before they had left the sand.

Matt sniffed the warm air – salt, dry grass, and the beach shack smells of seaweed and old driftwood.

A tall figure appeared. "Bluestar."

"Lonewolf," was Adira's quiet reply. Confirmation received, the man turned and led them to a dark SUV waiting just back from the coastal dunes.

Their driver was introduced as Baruk. Matt noticed he spoke to Adira deferentially, and seemed a little in awe of her.

Beside the driver, Adira shared the front seat with Abrams, which meant he, the enormous Hartogg, Andy and Tania were crowded into the rear. Matt could barely breathe. Thankfully, they arrived at their destination within thirty minutes – a bungalow on the outskirts of the small town. The house looked like any normal bungalow, and surprised Matt

with its Spartan look and low external security…until he realized that was probably exactly the image Mossad or whoever
wanted projected.

They were met on the porch by a young woman, who held
the door open as they entered. She ushered them through to a
side room, where the carpet was rolled back to reveal an open
trapdoor and dark stairs leading down.

Adira went in first, followed by Abrams and then the rest.
The young woman, Marta, remained up top, shutting the
trapdoor as Hartogg came in last.

Once inside, Matt saw that it was more than a basement –
there was effectively another house underneath the one above.
In one large room, several cots were readied for them, with
clothing laid out on each. As they moved along a hallway,
Matt saw a computer room with photographic equipment, an
armory and even washing and cooking facilities.

Baruk conferred quietly with Adira, who nodded and
then motioned to the shower room. "Fast showers for all.
Once done, we can take photographs, and prepare the
travel documentation."

Hartogg started to strip off, and Andy wasn't far behind
him.

"A shower sounds perfect right about now." The young
geologist shucked off clothes that billowed yellow dust as it
hit the ground at his feet. It was only then that Matt realized
how decrepit they must all look…not to mention a few of
them still had crusts of blood on their heads and faces from
the explosion.

In half an hour they sat around eating tomato omelets
Marta had made, and sipping coffee. Matt still felt tired, but
human again. Like a production line, Marta and Baruk had
taken their photos, cropped them and expertly inserted them
into well-traveled American passports. They decided to stick
with US identities, as Adira knew that, other than maybe

Matt, none of them would be able to pull off any other nationality, and they hadn't had time to absorb an entire foreign back-story should they be interrogated.

Adira and the two agents sat at a computer screen, building up their travel history. Adira came back and joined them, and handed each a packet of documentation containing plane tickets, dive passes, and printouts of entry tokens for windsurfing, diving, water skiing, and other holiday enjoyments.

"Congratulations, you all just spent time at the Pervolia Club Resort, one of the nicest on Cyprus."

Matt checked his watch – it was still only ten in the morning, and already he was exhausted. He looked at the information and shook his head in admiration. It was perfect, and he had no doubt that many of the intelligence agencies in the world did the same thing. It made him wonder just who anyone really was any more – that man on a bus, the woman in a restaurant – a real person, or some sleeper agent gathering information or on a secret mission? Welcome to the world of espionage, he thought.

Adira sat down at the table and spread out some airline tickets.

"Twenty hundred hours tonight – ten pm – we fly out late in two groups on ALY airlines. It's a short flight of only two hundred and ninety miles, and we will be there in forty-five minutes." She pointed to the information packs. "We will need to clear customs and immigration, which should be our only real challenge. Read the information prepared for you, study it and remember it."

"Who goes with who?" Abrams asked, sorting through his data.

"Team one will be myself, you, Major, Professor Kearns and Captain Kovitz – we are two couples on holiday. Team two will be Hartogg, Andy and Baruk – you are all salespeople who have won a dive holiday, congratulations."

"Sweet." Andy turned to grin, but Hartogg ignored him, and Baruk kept his eyes on Adira.

Abrams looked at the Israeli agent opposite him. "So we've picked up another Mossad body?"

Adira nodded. "Baruk is one of our local operatives, and he knows the region extremely well. Once we are in Egypt, we will make contract with one of our local cells to obtain any equipment we need." She looked into Abrams's eyes. "Unless you believe you can secure the necessary equipment and logistics yourselves." She raised an eyebrow.

Tania Kovitz scoffed. "We can organize resources if we need to. In fact –"

"Ha." Adira waved her off. "In fact, your intelligence capacity in the Middle East is near non-existent. We know most of your offices in the region were exposed by the traitor who worked in the NSA, and are now all identified on the internet." She shrugged, and then stared hard at the American captain. "Let's not kid each other here, Captain Kovitz – there is no time, I have neither patience nor any interest in playing games. We're here to offer help – but only once."

Tania gritted her teeth, her face growing dark. Matt could tell she was going to explode, but thankfully Abrams intervened.

"We're all on the same side, and we have the same goal here. Of course your assistance is welcome." He got up from the table, still holding his coffee mug. "Now if no one else has anything else to add, or objections, I suggest we get some sack time before the flight."

"Works for me." Matt said, leaning back. His weariness dragged at his bones, and started to blur his vision. Everyone around the table looked the same.

Abrams motioned to Adira. "One more thing; I need to check in – now." His expression told her there would no argument.

*

162

"Sir," Abrams said, looking over his shoulder. He was in a closed room, but would bet every word he said was being listened to.

"About time, Major." General Decker's voice sounded relieved. "Thought we'd lost you. What happened?"

Abrams smiled, imagining the tough stocky general in his office. He bet he'd already had another team ready to go.

"We met with Dr Albadi in Syria, and got a good lead on a source of information that might be the key to the earth-drops and disappearances." It was easy to keep his briefing short seeing as he didn't want to divulge too much. "But our ride home took a hit from an IED. Had to hike it across the desert. Luckily we found a friendly...of sorts. Captain Adira Senesh, Israeli army – pretty sure she's Mossad."

Abrams heard keys being struck as the general typed the name into the database.

"Jesus Christ, Joshua. This woman is on the extremely dangerous list. She not just Mossad, she's Metsada. She even had a head-on with some HAWCs last year. If she's tough enough to mess with those guys, you better watch yourself."

Abrams exhaled. "Well, we need to get to Egypt, and she can get us there. As for trusting her, not a chance." He smiled, knowing he wasn't giving up anything the Metsada agent probably didn't already know.

There was silence, and he knew Decker was probably looking over her file. He whistled softly, but before he could add anything Abrams cut him off.

"Sir, this line is not secure." He changed the subject. "Have there been any new developments I need to be aware of?"

There was silence for a few second. "More earth-drops, more people disappearing, on larger and larger scales. We're getting information breakouts now. Had to happen. But we have a new threat. There are...things, creatures of sorts, coming up from out of the holes, and even out of the

freaking drains. Monstrous things we believe are directly re-
sponsible for the earlier animal abductions and the more
recent disappearances."

"Yes, happening here too." Abrams remembered the bodies that vanished in the desert.

"God," Decker said. "But we also think we now know
what's happening to some of them – the people. Some of them
are being...absorbed, for want of a better term...instead of
just eaten."

Abrams grimaced. He didn't like hearing the tension in the
older warrior's voice.

It sounded like Decker got to his feet. "In fact, I've got an
appointment in about an hour where we expect to determine
how we can deal with these things."

"How are you able to do that?" Abrams asked.

Decker grunted. "Because we captured one."

*

Adira talked quietly upstairs with Baruk and Marta until her
comms device pinged. She recognized the call signature and
walked quickly to a front room, looking out over a small
garden. She answered it.

"*Boker tov*, Captain." The deep wheezing voice was both
formidable and familiar.

"*Shalom*, General. We were right, they are here looking for
the *Al Azif*, and now they are taking me right to it."

"Good, good work, Addy. I knew it was right to send you.
Do they have a firm lead?" he asked.

"Yes, Uncle," she said, confidently.

He laughed, sounding more like air brakes than anything
human – he was wheezing more than usual. She could imagine
the small, grizzle-haired man almost lost in his favorite red
leather chair. But appearances would be deceptive – there was

no frailty or weakness in the old warrior. General Meir Shavit was the head of Metsada, the Special Operations Division of the Mossad, and had served his country for over fifty years in both military theatres and dedicated intelligence services.

From his headquarters in Tel Aviv, he oversaw a staff of around two thousand. Though the Mossad was classed a civilian bureaucratic security operation, it was one of the most structured and professional intelligence services in the world; and also one of the deadliest. General Shavit's Metsada was Israel's well of poison, and Adira the sharpest dagger he dipped in it.

She smiled; glad now that their relationship was as strong as ever. "We will be in Alexandria tonight. They believe the Book is secreted somewhere on or around the island of Pharos."

"Pharos? Hmm, interesting. I will have a two-man team waiting for you. But be warned, Addy, you are not the only ones seeking the Book. The man the Americans met, this Dr Hussein ben Albadi, has been killed, along with all of his staff. The remains displayed signs of extreme surgical torture. Addy, they have someone on their trail, someone ruthless."

Adira ground her teeth. "If they step in front of me, they will fall." Her face was grim as she spoke.

"I know, my dear. Show them no quarter." He wheezed for a moment and Adira waited, her concentration intense. "Addy, we must have the *Al Azif*. We must know what it contains. If there is a solution or cure for the falling earth, then Israel must be cured first. Strength, honor, and good luck, Captain Senesh."

She straightened. "I will not fail you, Uncle."

"I know you won't."

The line disconnected and Adira sat down, her tired eyes on the garden, but her mind spinning with plans. Her eyes gradually closed, and soon the plans continued in her dreams.

Chapter 14

Centre for Advanced Military Science – Deep Research facilities

General Decker stood with hands clasped behind his back and stared through the two-inch-thick military grade Perspex into the twenty-by-twenty foot reinforced cubicle. His hands were damp, and he wished some of that moisture were in his mouth.

Looking at the thing inside made him feel physically ill. He saw what it looked like now, but he had seen the footage of what it had looked like when it was captured – it made him want to vomit.

"And that...that, *thing*, is Harry Wilcox?" He couldn't help his mouth turning down in disgust. The man in the room looked wet, but stickily wet, as if he had been rolling in engine lubricant. He stood staring straight ahead. Decker knew that it was looking at them.

Eric Ford, lead scientist in their bio-weapons division narrowed his eyes. "Yes and no. Well, no, not any more." He turned to Decker and shrugged. "I mean, sure it looks like him, but now, who knows what it is? The fact is, the life form can imitate anything it comes into contact with."

Decker swung toward Ford – the man's face was grim, and contained none of the usual spark he would normally have exhibited for a discovery such as this. Ford saw it like Decker did – not a source of wonder, but a threat to life...*all life.*

He scratched his chin. "And the other family members? My files said there was a wife, Summer...and they had three children."

Ford shrugged. "All dead – consumed, we think, by good ole Harry in there."

"Consumed? He ate them? All of them?" Decker grunted, remembering the footage of the capture – at first the thing had been much bigger than it was now. "So, it's shape shifted, re-morphed back into some sort of hiding camouflage?"

"Yes, so it can move among us...its prey, I assume. But I doubt it would hold up to any sort of close scrutiny – it doesn't speak, or at least it hasn't with us. It's primitive, but we think it has a base intelligence. It's very clearly an ambush predator."

"What is it? Is there anything even remotely like it? I need something to work with." Decker's frustration started to override his nausea.

"What it is? We have no idea," Ford said. "Its physical composition is more akin to some sort of amoeba, but it's so primitive, it predates anything we've ever seen. Any trace of a close relative probably never survived in the evolutionary geological record – how could it? It doesn't seem to have bones." He sighed. "And as for where it's from, we can only assume it came from deep underground. There was a sinkhole that had opened up below the house. Traces in the basement drain indicate it came from there."

"Jesus Christ, Eric. What's it doing in there? It hasn't moved since I've been down here."

"Hasn't moved a muscle for hours. It's waiting for stimuli – let me show you." Ford pressed an intercom button. "Martin, send in a sample." He folded his arms. "This is what it's waiting for...and *all it wants* for now."

A door slid open in the rear of the cubicle, and a goat was quickly pushed in. Its ears flickered, and its nose twitched as it caught the scent of something strange. It took a few steps along the side of the room and then froze. Its nose worked some more.

"Keep your eyes on Harry," Ford said softly.

While Decker watched he saw Harry's expressionless face start to palpitate. One of his unblinking eyes started to slide – not the pupil, but the entire organ – across his face, to now be situated on his temple. It stared unblinking at the goat. Another eye formed and popped open, this one on Harry's cheek, before the head started to slowly turn.

The goat's legs started to tremble, and its head dropped. It bleated constantly as it backed into the farthest corner of the room.

In the next second, Harry opened his mouth, wide, then wider than was humanly possible. From that dark hole, an explosion of black tendrils shot at the goat. The animal screamed in a voice that was too human for Decker's liking.

"Jesus Christ," he whispered, narrowing his eyes as if to try and shield himself from the horror.

The goat was dragged toward Harry, who started to grossly inflate into a mass of writhing and squirming blackness as the Shoggoth finally revealed itself. Perhaps it couldn't maintain the pretense while it was focused on capturing its food, or needed to be in its primary shape to feed at all. Regardless, the thing now resembled a giant thrashing blob of putrid black flesh, with tentacles that were a mix of tendrils and muscular trunks. Some thrashed in the air, others pounded down on the ground, like elephantine legs. All the time, new organs formed and unformed over its bloated body – ears, eyes, mouths, not all human, and not all even from creatures the watching soldiers recognized.

A giant orifice formed on its side, and opened stickily. The goat was dragged across the cell and then stuffed inside. The hole closed over it. The animal's shape could just be made out inside the Shoggoth's form, and its screams were still loud over the speakers. Ford quickly reached out to shut off the sound just as the screaming turned into a wet crunching.

"Shit." Decker couldn't drag his eyes away from the horror. "Can it get out?"

Ford's mouth turned down and he shook his head. "The room is a level-9 containment cell – reinforced, blast-proof walls, ceiling and floor, and nonporous to even liquids and gases. Harry isn't going anywhere." He folded his arms. "We need more time to study it. This thing is the true primitive, but we know it has some level of intelligence."

"Intelligence?" Decker sucked in a deep breath, and blew it out hard, as if to expel the vision. He turned to the scientist, talking through clenched teeth. "I don't care if it's fucking Einstein; you just find me a way to kill them."

PART 2
Rise Up The Ancient Gods

Chapter 15

It was just ten-fifty pm when the two teams walked across the warm tarmac and headed for the square three-story cream building. Matt was in the lead team with Abrams, Tania Kovitz and Adira. The plane had been crowded but as it was continuing on to Cairo, only about fifty people disembarked in Alexandria – still, it was enough to give them cover, as there was a good number of Westerners in among the returning local businesspeople.

Adira looped her arm through Abrams's. "Smile: we are on holiday, remember, husband?"

Abrams gave her a grin that was more like a grimace.

Tania did the same to Matt. "Hey, you too – and don't we make a pretty pair?"

Matt grinned. "Army life, huh? One minute you're being shot at, and the next you're on a dive holiday with a professor."

"I like to think I'm ready for anything." She smiled and raised her eyebrows momentarily, before becoming serious, and looking hard into his face. "Do you trust her?"

Matt shrugged. "She's a combination of spy, agent and assassin – and she's tough as hell." He looked down at the military woman. "Don't mess with her, Tania; I've seen what she can do."

Tania snorted and looked away for a moment. "I'll take that as a no."

Matt honestly wasn't sure whether he did or not. "Look, I trust she'll do what's best for herself and for Israel. But..." he remembered the woman on the Black Mountain in the Appalachians, who went way off course for the most basic human emotion – love "...she's human and has a soft side. Well, not sure it's still there – I think she's been *re-educated*." He looked at Tania and gave her a look of mock horror.

"Well, that sounds unpleasant." Her smile widened. "Good."

When it was their turn at the desk, the sharp-looking immigration official flashed his eyes up and down at Matt, before letting them rest on Tania for several seconds. He looked back at the passports, studying them as if they were the Dead Sea Scrolls.

He stamped and read, stamped and read, and then spoke without looking up. "When were you married, Mrs Kearns?"

Tania gave him a wide smile and leaned forward against the high desk. "Twenty-twelve, in Minneapolis."

He grunted and then let his eyes flick up to Matt. "You have no diving equipment. How will you dive – hold your breath?" His mouth turned up on one side.

Matt nodded and grinned. "It's too expensive and too much trouble to cart it around. Our travel agent told us that there's a dive shop on Eastern Harbor...What was it called, honey? Alexandra Dive? We plan to hire everything we need there."

They waited – there was more stamping – and then the passports were pushed back to them, and with a brusque "Next!" the official made it clear they had ceased to exist.

In twenty minutes they were out in the front of the building, avoiding shouting taxi drivers and private car owners touting for their fares. Adira walked a hundred feet down the road to where a faded green Mercedes Benz was pulling up. She nodded to the driver, opened the door and motioned for the other three to get in.

"What about Hartogg and Andy?" Abrams asked, looking over his shoulder.

"Forget them." Adira waved him off. "Baruk will look after them. Another car will pick them up shortly. We must leave and go in different directions. Get in."

Abrams slid in the back next to Matt and Tania.

Matt grinned. "That was pretty straightforward."

Adira stopped her conversation with the driver and half turned. "Our documentation is good, but there will be GID watching – there always are."

"GID?" Matt asked.

"Egyptian secret service – the General Intelligence Directorate." She fully turned in her seat, resting her arm on its back. "But they might not be the biggest problem we have. She looked at Abrams. "Your contact, Dr Hussein ben Albadi, has been slaughtered, along with all of his house staff."

Abrams went red, before he punched down hard on his thigh. "*Goddamnittohell.* Was it the terrorists?"

Adira's face was expressionless. "No, it seems he was tortured, and the work was carried out with far too much skill for simple barbarians." Her eyes were level as gun barrels. "I assume he knew everything that you do. So now…"

"They do," Abrams finished.

"Except for this last part," Matt said. "He only knew we wanted to get to Pharos, and what we were coming to find, not how we were going to get here. They can't possibly know about you."

Adira's face betrayed nothing. "We must assume that whoever tortured Albadi is already here." She looked at each of their faces. "They are playing hard. If they take one of us, we can expect the same sort of interrogation treatment – vicious. Better to be dead."

"Do you know who it was? Did they leave any clues?" Abrams asked.

She shook her head. "None, but we do not think they were part of any militia. Like I said, these people were very skilled at what they did and the techniques they used were very precise – surgical almost. It may mean they are Westerners. With luck, perhaps we can spot them before they spot us."

*

It was late, eleven-thirty pm, when their car pulled into Matrouh Road, and eventually stopped out front of a large sprawling building. Faded letters spelled out the name *Aida* on the façade.

Adira stepped from the car, looking up and down the street. Matt, Abrams and Tania followed her out, stretching. "The Aida hotel," she said, turning to them. "Old, but just down a single road to the water and the site of Pharos Island." She shrugged. "Better than some, but not so good as to attract attention – so don't be disappointed by its rundown appearance."

"We're not here on holiday," Abrams said.

"That's not what my passport says," Matt said. "I know we're not, but best to at least look like it."

Adira nodded. "I have arranged accommodation for a week. Hopefully, we'll be gone in a few days."

Matt waved as Andy and Hartogg's car pulled in slowly beside them. "That poses the obvious question – when *do* we call it quits if we don't turn anything up? Adira's week? Longer?"

"Can't answer that, Matt," Abrams said. "Not until we've at least had a look at what it is we're dealing with." He acknowledged Hartogg and then turned to Adira. "What about the equipment?"

The driver gave Adira a small, heavy package, and she placed it in her bag. "It'll be ready for us in the morning." She checked her wristwatch. "It's late. I suggest we check in, get some rest and meet out front at oh-six hundred."

*

Matt sat in the bar; his beer as yet untouched in front him. He was tired, but knew sleep would be impossible, and hoped that some alcoholic anesthetic might help. He smiled dreamily and watched a bead of condensation run down the side of the green bottle. He followed it with his eyes, preoccupied.

The *Al Azif, The Necronomicon, The Book of the Dead*, whatever they called it, it had become the key to everything. Would it even be real? he wondered. Not long ago, he would have laughed at the suggestion, but now...

Well, we have all our eggs in one ancient Middle Eastern basket now, he thought, so it damn well better be.

He remembered reading the words of the copy of the Book, and that, as he read, images had formed in his mind – magnificent and horrible in equal measures. They had conjured up scenes of beauty, monstrous wonder, and decrepit horror. He had been a scholar of languages and words all his life, and he still didn't know how words, marks on a page really, could actually do that.

Matt knew some writing was bland and informative, and that some was powerful and persuasive. But this went far beyond that, into the realm of *words as magic*. And if what he had seen had that effect, what would the Celestial script, the actual speech of the gods, be like?

"Penny for them."

He jolted at the light touch on his shoulder.

177

"Jumpy tonight." Tania Kovitz slid onto the stool next to him.

He half smiled and shook his head. "I'm okay, just thinking about the day ahead." He nodded at his drink. "Get you something?"

"Sure, one of those'll be fine." She looked around at the remaining people sipping drinks late at night in the hotel bar. "I didn't think they'd serve alcohol here."

Matt shook his head. "There're a lot of purists who want to make Egypt totally alcohol free, but there are also a lot of businesses that rely on the tourist trade. No alcohol, covering of women, segregation of sexes might just detract from the fun in the sun holiday lifestyle. So we're okay...at least for now." Another beer arrived on a coaster, and Matt reached out and lifted his drink. "Enjoy it while you can."

"*Salut.*" Tania lifted the small green bottle and clinked it against Matt's.

He sipped, looking at her and smiled. He watched her soft lips just close over the top.

She smiled as she sipped, and held his gaze.

*

Matt woke about four, and lifted Tania's arm off his body. The room still smelled of perfume, sex, and beer. He winced as he moved, feeling the scratches on his back.

"Hellcat," he whispered.

He got up and went to the bathroom to relieve himself and then on the way back poured a glass of water and sipped it slowly while looking out over the huge central pool. It was a beautiful blue, empty of swimmers: a picture of serenity. He so wanted to dive in and wash himself clean.

Matt heard sheets move behind him.

"Hey."

He turned. "Hey."

"Come back to bed."

He padded back to the edge and slid in, immediately feeling her hand searching for and finding him. She squeezed and caressed, and once again he wanted her.

"I wish I could have read the Book." She tugged at him gently. "Tell me about it. What did you learn? What can it do?"

He sighed as her hands worked harder and faster and she started to kiss her way down his stomach.

"It's strange; it could be older than anyone thinks. It's too descriptive and powerful to have been written by Abdul Alhazred. I think he was the writer, but not the original author. Maybe he was someone who had read the original and transcribed it." He placed his hand on the back of her head and pushed her down, hurrying her.

She slid lower, plucking at his tip with her mouth, but then stopped. "Go on."

"What?" Oh, he talks of Cthulhu – the Old One – its power and its horror. But I get the feeling all the real secrets are hidden in the strange language – I haven't seen that yet. But look, if it *is* true Enochian, I doubt I'll be any help."

Her mouth engulfed him, and he arched his back for a second. He placed his hands behind his head, and began to talk softly in his bliss, telling her everything as she worked her magic.

*

At six on the dot, Matt and Tania walked from the entrance to the building. Baruk was already there with Adira, who watched them approach. Her eyes were like dark gun barrels on the pair, and Matt could have sworn she was reading his mind, and not liking at all what she saw in there.

Abrams, Andy and Hartogg immediately followed. Hartogg whispered something to Abrams and then stood a few feet out from them on the steps.

Abrams came and stood next to Adira, but kept his eyes on the water in the distance, the sun only just rising above its edge. "We have eyes on us."

Adira didn't turn. "Yes, I know: in the Mercedes. Do not worry; they're ours – a couple of field agents from our local office. After hearing about Albadi in Syria, we decided it might be prudent to have someone watching our backs. They're good operatives." She nodded to Baruk, who loaded diving gear into the back of an SUV.

"Baruk and I will be running a proximity shield defense, but if they get in that close, it will mean we will already be fighting for our lives. I want some advance notice if we have a team of butchers on our trail."

"Makes sense to me," Abrams said. "I'll let Hartogg know. Be good to have some weapons as well." He nodded to his SEAL. "He's also good."

Adira smiled. "All taken care of. Baruk has been busy."

The young, rugged-looking man closed the rear door of the SUV, stood back and waited.

Adira took one last look around, and then headed for the passenger door. "Let's go."

*

They pulled to the side of El-Geish Road, and sat looking out over the azure water. Three-foot waves crashed onto the shoreline, and there was nothing between them and the horizon.

Tania leaned forward, putting her hand on Matt's thigh as she went. "Just how far out is our dive site?"

Matt squeezed her hand once and quickly lifted it free. He had a sudden sense of panic over what Adira would do if she thought they were suddenly *a couple* – for that matter, he didn't want *anyone* in their group to get that impression. For a start, Andy would freak out, and he remembered Adira's glance on the front steps, and it still scalded his conscience.

"Closer than you think." He cleared his throat and sat forward. "Pharos was a small island about a mile off the coast. In 332 BC Alexander the Great founded the city of Alexandria on an isthmus opposite Pharos and he built a link to the island – it was so wide they used it as a walkway. But over the millennia, that silted over, and then centuries of erosion and various earthquakes destroyed the island, and what was left was buried. Now it's all under water." He pointed. "Somewhere arou-uund, *there*."

They followed his hand – to nothing but blue water.

In the front seat Adira's fingers danced over a tablet and she called up several maps – ancient and new. She adjusted size and orientation, and then lined them up one over the other. She turned in her seat, holding the screen up.

"We are *here*." She pointed to a long road running along the shoreline. "And we need to start our search, *here*." Less than a mile offshore there was the outline of the island. "This coastal section has been reclaimed from the sea, so the good news is the island is closer to us now than it would have been on the coast of a thousand years ago." She sat back. "Of course, it might not be the actual island we're looking for."

Matt grunted his assent. "She's right. Pharos itself was very small, only about as large as a few football fields together. And the entrance to the secret library could be anywhere surrounding it. A thousand years ago, it was shallows out there. Low tide might have exposed a lot more of the rock and perhaps some sort of cave entrance."

"I doubt it," Andy said. "This whole area is nothing but a layer of limestone over a bed of sandstone, the oldest ground being outcrops of metamorphic and igneous rocks. The island was created under high pressure, and therefore was a lot denser and more able to withstand the elements. Everything else would have been softer, and would wear away very quickly." He looked at each of them, eyebrows raised.

Matt grinned. "Spoken like a true geologist." He bumped knuckles with the young man.

"Benefits of a higher education." Andy wiggled his brows. "But seriously, we should start with the remains of the island – if there is any type of entrance, it'll probably be there."

"Do we dive now or wait until the sun has risen a little more?" Tania asked, her eyes on the water. "Also, this area is notorious for tiger sharks."

"We dive now," Adira replied with a smirk. "And there are always man-eaters, Captain – above *and* below the water."

Tania's jaw set. "Dr Albadi said that it might not be open or even visible until the full moon. And the first phase of that is not until later tonight."

"True, but we should at least familiarize ourselves with the territory – every second counts now." Adira turned to look at Tania; her eyes were expressionless, but there was a hint of enjoyment at the corners of her mouth. "Have you ever done a night dive before?"

A challenge welled up momentarily in Tania's eyes, but after a second or two, she simply shook her head and looked back out at the water.

Adira snorted softly. "I thought not. The underwater is a very different place at night. There is no light, other than what we bring – it can be disorienting and frightening to a novice." Her eyes slid again to Tania. "Starting the search then would be extremely difficult or impossible. We will dive this morning, and at least try and narrow our field of search. Any objections?" Her eyes moved along the faces.

"Works for me," Abrams said, his eyes also on Tania. He turned back and smiled. "It'll also add to our cover story, doing what we are here to do – enjoy the diving."

Adira nodded to a small boat hire firm on the beach. "There."

*

The faded green Mercedes Benz with the two Mossad agents in the front seat sat under a tree that grew smaller as the seven-person group chugged away from the shore in the old wooden fishing boat.

Matt inhaled the sea air, and clung on to the seat, feeling old fish scales, splinters and dried salt against his palms. The air was still cool, but already he felt the hint of the balmy day to come, as sheets of golden light bathed their wetsuit-clad bodies.

The captain, Mahmood, a little man with few teeth and the brawniest forearms Matt had ever seen, knew exactly where the sunken island was to be found and also the best dive spots, as he'd taken probably hundreds of diving tourists out from the beach. Matt placed his hand on the rough gunwale; there were a few fingernail spots of green paint still attached, but the faded glory of huge hauls of shimmering silver bodies in woven rope nets was lost permanently now to the more lucrative tourist trade.

Adira stood in the small open cabin with Mahmood, chatting amiably, and Matt watched as he occasionally pointed out different landmarks on the shore. Adira nodded, looking impressed, probably extracting as much useful information as she could from their ancient mariner.

Each of them wore wetsuits with tanks, weights, and goggles pushed up on their foreheads. Matt admired Adira's physique in the suit – long and athletic. He turned, and saw that Hartogg looked hugely bulked, like some sort of superman, and that Baruk also looked formidable. Abrams, Matt and Andy were more modestly muscled, and Tania looked tiny compared to the Israeli woman. However, her visible curves made it impossible for Matt not to think back to smooth, pale skin beneath his sheets. She smiled at him, and he smiled in return.

They travelled for another few minutes and then with the sandy beach just a yellow strip in the distance the captain turned off the engine and let the boat coast for a few dozen feet more. His eyes never left the shoreline as he lined himself up with a couple of taller landmarks, and then he called for Adira to nudge an iron pick anchor over the side. It loudly dragged about ten feet of chain and then a few more dozen feet of salt-toughened rope into the magnificent blue water. Matt watched as the rope sizzed dryly on the gunwale and rapidly sank. In another second it suddenly went limp.

"Bottom," Mahmood said in English. He turned and grinned.

Adira looked around slowly, and then spoke in Egyptian to Baruk. He nodded and took off his mask – the agent had just been volunteered for topside lookout duties.

Adira put a foot up on a seat and pointed out over the water. "Out there – Mahmood says we are just fifty feet from the island. He won't drop anchor any closer due to the underwater snags. Some places are only twenty feet deep; others can drop down to eighty. He said that the island has broken into three pieces, and the fissures are the deepest areas...but there's nothing in them to see." She waved her arm over the water. "Columns, sphinxes, and blocks are scattered in a wide area." She turned to each of them. "We start with the island, and then we can broaden our search if we need to." She stepped down and walked in among them. "Okay, we all get dive buddies – the major and myself, Matt and

Andy, Lieutenant Hartogg and Captain Kovitz." She zipped her suit to the top, and looked at her dive watch. "Stay in visual. It's now seven hundred hours. First surface in thirty minutes; clear?"

Everyone nodded. Breathing equipment was given final checks, goggles came down, and then bodies fell backwards over the side.

They swam down at an angle into the azure water, and Matt was delighted to find that it was warmer in the ocean than up on the boat's deck. He had dived many times before, but was far from an enthusiast. Matt remembered descending in inky black water – there was something about not knowing what was below you that still gave him the creeps...especially as he understood that there were things in the depths staring back at you, big things, seeing you without you even knowing they were there.

Matt shuddered; he wasn't looking forward to the night dive for exactly all those reasons. But this dive...this was more like it. The water was a magnificent blue, like tinted glass, and so warm he was sure they didn't really need their wetsuits. As he descended, he looked at his companions and smiled around his mouthpiece; the group stayed fairly close together – a school of oversized water mammals heading to the bottom to forage, clouds of bubbles streaming up behind them.

They neared the sand, and Matt spotted his first relic – a broken sphinx, probably weighing about two tons, and nearly perfectly formed. Andy swam in close to him and pointed at the stone lion creature, then gave Matt a thumbs up. Matt smiled; the geologist's eyes were round with enthusiasm behind his goggles.

They headed on towards the island, and the sea floor started to resemble a building site or a disused quarry. Huge blocks, half-sunken columns, and giant slabs of coral-coated stone were all thrown together, all encrusted with algae, barnacles, and coral of all colors and ages. Then, looming up in the distance, a small broken mountain – the sunken Island of Pharos. To Matt, it looked like the carcass of some dead prehistoric creature curled up on the sand, the leviathan body all sharp angles and weird growths.

The group hovered in the water – the remains of the island were about several hundred feet around, and Mahmood had been right, it was broken into the three. Fish of varying sizes patrolled the deep cracks that dropped beyond the sun's rays.

Adira swam on strongly and was first to the top, where she waited, floating above one deep rent. She pointed to Matt, and then to Hartogg and then into the other fissures: the meaning was clear – each take one and descend.

Thumbs up were returned, and then into the cracks each team descended.

Matt exhaled and, as the air left his lungs, his weight belt took him into the deep vent in the rock. It was wide enough for Andy to follow at his side, and the geologist nudged him, pointing out jutting edges and striations in the natural rock, and then making cracking apart motions with his hands. Matt nodded, getting it: the last earthquake must have been so huge it literally tore the island apart, and dragged the rest to the bottom as effectively as the kraken did ancient schooners.

As they dropped further, they both switched on wristband flashlights and pointed them downward. Matt was surprised and dismayed by how far their crack in the island descended, and as he kicked lower, he had to stop several times to repressurize his eardrums.

Close to the bottom now, the corals and sea grasses that relied on light had disappeared, and softer sponges dominated. Spiny crustaceans waved antennae from the rock ledges, and small fish darted in and out of Matt's light beam. He heard his breathing loud in his ear, and the occasional clang from one of their tanks as they bumped into the ever-converging walls.

Andy jammed into him, and they both slowed as they came to the wedge end. Matt righted himself and hovered, panning his light one way, then the next. He examined the walls…there was nothing that even remotely indicated humans had touched these depths, let alone some sort of entranceway or passage. Andy floated up beside him and shrugged. Matt nodded, and pointed along the length of the fissure – they'd do a slow traverse along the craggy corridor and then surface.

As Matt and Andy were coming to the end another flashlight flickered above them. They came up together to find the small form of Tania and the much larger one of Hartogg, together looking like a mother whale and its calf. Tania waved them on to the fissure she had checked and led them down into the crack. About a third of the way in they came to a stone block embedded in the fissure wall. To Matt it looked like a piece of the ruined lighthouse that had tumbled in during the cataclysm, and then become overgrown. But Tania tapped it and shook her head.

Matt guessed she meant it shouldn't be there. She should know, she's the archeologist, he thought. He moved his flashlight along its edge, and saw nothing that indicated it was anything other than what he initially suspected – a block of stone. He looked back at her and shrugged again. Andy, who was performing his own inspection, turned and made growing-over motions with his hands.

Matt nodded and hung suspended before the slab for a moment, looking at its shape and size, then reached out. As soon as his fingers touched the edge of the stone, his mind exploded with vivid images – he saw the world, Earth, but not the Earth as we knew it. The scene was so ancient there was no moon yet captured by our gravity. The sky had few stars, and our world bubbled and steamed as it still cooled.

It should have been impossible to recognize, but Matt knew it was our own. He looked out over a vast, blood-red landscape.

The seas had not yet formed, but it was not devoid of life – there were monstrous creatures, fighting and mating, killing and maiming. Things with vast evil intellects whose machinations touched the entire universe, and whose life spans could ride out a thousand apocalypses.

The sounds were terrifying: their bodies were so huge that mountains were crushed to dust when they fought, and craters were smashed into a continent's crust when they fell. Impossibly, Matt's mind registered it all, and the worst came when he inhaled and the smell of their blood and excrement filled his nostrils. He ripped away his mouthpiece and jetted a stream of vomit into the water. Immediately the murky cloud started to settle towards the bottom of the crack, and dozens of small fish shot from nowhere to pick out the larger chunks as it floated down – A free feast, pre-chewed, Matt thought.

Tania swam over, but with the images shut down, and his breakfast gone, Matt immediately felt better. He nodded and had replaced his mouthpiece. Tania pointed to the surface.

They came up together, broke the surface, pushed their masks up and trod water. Within another minute all the divers had returned, and together they swam slowly back towards the boat.

"Anything?" Adira called.

"*Nada*. Just a giant crack in the rocks that is home to plenty of sea sponges and a few nosy lobsters. The most we can get down there is a nice dinner," Andy said, and then grinned. "That's if you like fish with a touch of Kearns sauce."

"I'm okay," Matt said. "Must have been the breakfast, or something. Just got a bit sick. I'm okay." He changed the subject not wanting to dwell on the images, but knew that reading the copy of the *Al Azif* must have affected him more than he'd like to think. "The stone slab set into the wall," he said. "May be nothing, but we weren't expecting anything obvious were we?"

"Describe it," Adira said quickly.

Tania recounted the size and shape. "It was definitely Lighthouse-era stonework, and the only sign of human habitation below the island's crustal surface."

Adira looked to Matt and Andy, and the geologist bobbed his head. "Maybe. I mean it sure looked like a tumbled part of the edifice to me. But could just be where the earthquake tore open the surface skin of the island and some debris fell in."

Matt nodded. "Yeah, not sure it was anything significant. But might be worth bringing back a crowbar."

Adira looked at the sky and then her watch. "We take a break and warm up on deck. Then we have time for one more dive before we head back. We'll take a quadrant each, and expand our perimeter search."

In another few hours they were on their way back, the afternoon growing cold with a slight breeze kicking up over the water. Matt sat on one edge of the boat, Tania and Abrams in the seat next to him. "Going to be the first full moon tonight. If there's anything more to find, then this has gotta be it."

When they reached the shore, Adira froze momentarily, and then spoke in hushed tones to Baruk. He continued unpacking the boat, but his eyes slid left then right along the coastal road.

Matt eased up next to her. "Problem?"

She also continued with her tasks, but spoke softly in Hebrew, knowing only Matt, of the Americans, would understand. "Our security is gone."

Matt looked for the Mercedes that had been parked under the tree. She was right; it was nowhere to be seen. He responded in her language. "Would they have been called away?"

"If there were overriding orders, I would know. I need to call this in," she said. She looked from Abrams to Hartogg, who now seemed tuned in to her unease.

"Our time is running out."

*

"Enough."

Drummond walked from the shadows in the soundproofed basement and stood before the bound man. Kroen stepped back, breathing hard. There was a small smile of ecstasy on his blood-splattered face. The huge bodyguard wore a plastic apron and dark shirt, sleeves rolled up. Blood and specks of flesh coated the material and ran down the plastic to the floor. Sticking from the large front pocket of the apron was a pair of greasy-looking bolt cutters.

Drummond looked down – there were two seats, nailed to the ground and facing each other. They both contained naked men, one untouched but with eyes heavy with fatigue and scoured of any human emotion. The other contained a man who had been beaten to a red mess. Bits of bone showed whitely at his eyebrows and cheekbones. Both eyes were swollen closed and his lips were split, in one place so badly the remains of his broken teeth showed through. Scattered around him on the floor were ten fingers, looking like pale grubs trailing bloody tracks back to their former owner.

Drummond walked around the ruined man, *tsk-tsking*, and placed a hand on his bloody shoulder from behind. He wore rubber gloves, and gently patted his captive. He looked across at the untouched man.

"This must really hurt. The important thing is, I'm not doing this because I hate him – I don't even know Agent Herzl here. I'm not doing it for him, or Kroen, or even myself. In fact, you may have noticed that I have not asked a single question of him...although I have many."

Drummond reached up and stroked the man's sweat-soaked hair. "Many questions...but not for him. I'm not a monster...not really. Nothing like what's coming." He stifled a laugh, then spoke in perfect Hebrew to Agent Herzl. "Release you now?"

The battered head came up a fraction, and one of the eyelids twitched but couldn't possibly open through all the swelling and sticky blood. Drummond straightened. "Kroen. Show him our mercy."

Kroen, turned and lifted a huge silver bowl from a tabletop, and came and placed it between the battered man's legs.

Drummond looked to the untouched seated man. His eyes now burned like lasers beams of pure hate. The older man smiled. "Good – anger, defiance, determination – you will need it all. Agent Kahan, what you see here is nothing more than a demonstration of our resolve. Soon, you will pray to be given this merciful gift."

Drummond held out his hand, and Kroen placed a long silver surgical blade into it. In a flash he dragged it across the man's lower abdomen, causing his entire bowel and intestines to spill forward heavily and plop into the bowl. The man shuddered, and his ragged lips opened in a moan.

Drummond stroked the man's hair, almost the way someone would their favorite cat that had taken up residence on their lap. He smiled and watched as blood ran thickly, already overflowing the crowded bowl. The room filled with the smell of dark blood and the contents of Herzl's bowels.

"Phew, what *have* you been eating?" Drummond laughed with good humor. Kroen passed him a clean towel, which he used to wipe off the blade. "This might surprise you…" he went on, stepping out from behind the dying man "…but a human being can survive…well, *exist* anyway, with his bowels outside of his body, for many, many hours." He looked up with raised eyebrows. "Not a good look though, *hmm?*"

He walked slowly towards Agent Kahan. "Now, to you…and for you, I do have questions, and yes, *you* will answer them. Your only reward will be death. But by the time

I finish, it will be the most blessed reward any man on this Earth could wish for." He pretended to count for a moment. "You have ten fingers, ten toes, a nose, two ears...and a penis – plenty of things to remove, and I promise you, each will be more painful than the last."

Drummond turned and nodded to Kroen, who walked over, and grabbed the man's left hand. He levered up one finger, and held it, its joint now in the jaws of the bolt cutters. Kroen looked to Drummond, waiting.

"Question one." Charles Drummond stepped in front of Kahan. "Agent Kahan, please tell me if they believe they can read it?"

*

It was five in the afternoon and they were dry, warm and sitting together in the café inside the hotel. Matt noticed that Adira and Baruk looked on high alert, and he hated it – if the Mossad woman was nervous, then he sure should be.

Adira had called for more agents as support, and also a team to find the missing men. But they wouldn't arrive until the next morning, and the dive needed to be undertaken that night. By the morning, events would have already overtaken them, or not.

Matt closed his eyes and leaned back, luxuriating in a beam of sun that came though a tall window and bathed the rear of his neck. He tried to shut out anything remotely to do with the Book so his mind could rest. At eleven forty-five that night, they needed to be descending on the sunken island of Pharos – the moon would be at its zenith at midnight and they needed to be there, ready. If something was going to occur, they would be on top of it, waiting and watching.

"It's too dangerous; we should think about aborting, or at least waiting for backup," Andy said.

192

"No, we need the book. End of discussion." Tania snapped back.

"I agree; we can't wait," Abrams said. "It'll be another month until the next full moon." He snorted and shook his head. "Nix that, it'll be another thirteen hundred years until the next planetary convergence, and frankly, given what Dr Albadi told us, we don't have thirteen hundred hours. We need answers, now, and if, as we believe, Adira's men have been taken, then whoever did take them is only one step behind us. If we abort, we might be handing the Book over them." His face was grim. "As risky as it sounds, we have to search tonight with or without backup. We've got to believe we're still in front."

The silence stretched. All eyes were fixed on the tabletop as they retreated to their thoughts. At last Adira spoke. "Major Abrams is correct. We have no choice but to continue." She got to her feet. "Time for rest. Eat in your rooms and be down the front at nine-thirty pm. Baruk and I will be waiting."

Matt saw Tania look across at him and raise her eyebrows. He shook his head, but she just smiled wider, and nodded subtly.

Adira's voice was cutting. "I suggest we all get some rest. Focus on what we need to do tonight, rather than on our genitals."

Matt blushed, Tania looked away, and Andy's head jerked up, his brow furrowed in confusion.

Within ten minutes, Matt was flopped on his bed, feeling drained.

He punched the pillow behind his head, but knew he'd never actually sleep – the best he'd be able to do was close his eyes and try and relax his muscles, if not his mind.

There came a knock on his door. "It's me." Tania's whispered voice.

"*Go away.*" He hissed to the door.

The knock came again. "It's...*important*." The words were breathy.

He groaned...and then let her in.

*

The wind had fallen away and the sea was like a sheet of oil. Mahmood flicked a cigarette into the water as Adira came into his small open cabin. She handed him over some notes – more than double what he was normally paid. They talked quietly for a second or two and he laughed and nodded, and then turned out the single light, so they were all in darkness.

Matt sat in silence, just like the others. They were all thinking through what had brought them there, the coming dive, the missing Israeli agents, and who it was who had taken them and was probably watching them all right now.

The boat chugged directly out from the coast, and Mahmood glanced over his shoulder from time to time, lining the stern up with landmarks on the shore. It was dark, and in the cabin they could only tell he had turned when the red dot of his cigarette was pointed directly at them.

Outside on deck, there was more light – the moon was already huge as it steadily rose overhead and created a silver path on the still water that was an endless black plain. Below water, Matt knew there was more activity – movement, predator and prey, eyes already on them.

In fifteen minutes the boat slowed, and then stopped. Just as before, Mahmood let the craft coast for a moment or two, and then pushed the anchor over the side. He let out ten more feet of rope, tied off, and then lit another cigarette. He watched the shoreline for a few seconds before nodding, satisfied with his position, and then spoke a few words to Adira as he sat down to watch the divers.

Adira pointed. "The island is about fifty feet to our north. But he said there is a current running tonight, so we must take that into consideration in our dive as it can push us off course. He will leave the lantern alight on the bow – it will be our beacon, our *only* beacon: if we surface away from where we went in, just head for that."

"Do we trust him?" Abrams asked quietly.

"I trust no one. Baruk will remain with him again. But it is not our captain I would be concerned about. If another boat comes, we might not know until we surface."

Matt was looking over the side at the dark water. "Did I hear someone mention sharks before?"

"Yes, plenty," Adira said, readying her equipment. "There are great white, bull shark, tiger – all very big and aggressive. But I hear you only need to punch them on the nose, yes?" She looked at him deadpan for several seconds, before breaking into a grin. "I joke – don't worry about them, Professor. They will not bother us."

I'm not worried; I've faced worse, Matt thought

Adira looked up at the sky and then at her watch. "In about fifteen minutes, the moon will begin to be at its absolute zenith. It will pass through that apex for only about twelve minutes. If there is an opening, and we can find it, and enter it, then we will have less than that to locate the Book and get out."

"Or we spend the next thirteen hundred years waiting for the next celestial convergence," Matt finished.

"We can do this," Tania said.

Matt saw she seemed to be speaking to herself. He checked his own equipment – this time they had headlamps, wrist lights and extra handheld flashlights with a couple of large 35-watt spotlights that could be positioned on stands.

One after the other they dropped over the side, with Andy and Hartogg the first to the bottom, aided by the crowbars they carried. Anyone looking down from above would have seen the white pipes of light moving under the water, and nothing of the black-wetsuited divers behind them.

Matt felt he was holding his breath on the way down. The walls of complete blackness surrounding him made him feel tiny and vulnerable. His scalp prickled, and he couldn't help feeling he was being watched from somewhere out in the dark.

In a few minutes they were at the island that grew up out of the sand. They broke into two teams – Matt, Andy, and Hartogg, and then Abrams, Tania, and Adira – once again as directed by Adira. Matt could tell she felt the need to keep an eye on Tania. There was quite clearly a great degree of dislike growing between the women, and he doubted it had anything to do with him.

Matt's team descended into the first crevice and slowly drifted along its ravine walls, slowing now and then to inspect odd shapes or protrusions. After a few minutes they gave up and drifted to the island's surface.

They swam to the other team's position, hovering over their split in the seamount. Looking down, Matt could see the pathways of white light, but this time, he could also see the divers as the glow of the full moon was now reaching down into the bottom of the crevice. After another few minutes the divers joined up. Adira looked at her watch, and her frustration was clear.

Matt nudged Adira and pointed up at the moon – it was like a giant floating spaceship above them, and was so bright that the divers cast shadows. Everything was a twilight silver, and small plankton, invisible before, now phosphoresced like a glowing snowstorm around them. Fish seemed oddly excited and darted in and out of the cracks in the rock, and even the lobster and huge crabs were drawn onto rock ledges to peer at the divers, like theatregoers leaning out of their boxes.

Adira nodded in return – the moon was peaking, and they were about to enter the apex period – it would be like this for another ten minutes only.

Matt noticed a few of the divers had stopped using their lights, and it gave him an idea. He tapped the rock wall to get everyone's attention, pointed to his light and shut it off. After a few seconds everyone understood, and one after the other the lights went out.

As Matt expected, the lights weren't needed, and were in fact hiding more than they were revealing. Back along the rift in the island, the slab of stone they had seen in the earlier dive now gave off a faint glow. He shot towards it, and saw that there was a huge symbol showing on its surface.

He approached it, Andy at his side. The geologist went to dig his crowbar in beside it, but Matt waved him away. He ran a hand over the whorls and long strokes – there was no indentation, the symbol itself gave off luminosity like a projection.

As Matt's hand finished his tracing of the symbol, the huge stone swung as if on a hinge. They all could hear *and* feel the vibrations running through the water. Ancient coral and other debris floated away, but just inside, Matt could see huge cogs of a clockwork mechanism working. He'd seen something like it before – the Greek Antikythera mechanism. That was an ancient mechanical device, a computer, created over two thousand years earlier, and designed to predict astronomical positions and eclipses.

No technological device coming even close to it in complexity would exist for another fourteen hundred years. Who else but the Greeks could construct a hiding place such as this, and then use the world's first computer to seal it away? Matt thought.

There was a flicker of shadow, as if something above momentarily eclipsed the moon's glow, but when they looked up there was nothing.

Matt turned and gave the group a thumbs up, and went to enter, before Adira pulled him roughly back. She held a finger up in front of his face, and then turned and swam in first. In exactly one minute she returned, pointed to Matt first, then Abrams, and Tania. She held her hand up flat to Andy and Hartogg – *Stay*, it said.

Andy began to protest, but Adira pointed to both him and Hartogg and then the huge door and then made an opening motion with her hands and arms. Hartogg nodded, then Andy: *Keep the door open.*

Matt bet both men were wondering how the hell they'd accomplish that feat with a couple of crowbars, if the many-ton door started to close.

All flashlights came back on as Adira led them in and then along a stone passage to a set of stairs climbing out of the water. There was little or no growth, testifying to just how tightly the door must have been sealed – many ocean plants, sponges and algae started out as microscopic spores easily able to fit into the tiniest of cracks. That seal, coupled with the size of the machinery, meant it was no wonder other divers had been unable to detect anything other than a deeply embedded block of stone, Matt guessed.

Ancient Greek writing was carved into the corridor walls, but when Matt became spellbound by a certain phrase or image, Adira yanked him forward – they had minutes, and already time was becoming a scarce commodity.

Adira came to the steps first, and, removing the fins from her feet, climbed them, lifting herself free from the water. Matt, Abrams, and Tania followed. The Mossad agent carefully took the breathing apparatus from her mouth, and sniffed. She winced and wrinkled her nose, but then nodded.

"Stale, very, but I think not toxic," she said, waving her light around.

"I hope so," Matt said. "Because those guys sure didn't die of old age."

Piled like corded wood just past the edge of the steps were half a dozen skeletons, all in the robes and gold-fiber belts of Alexandrian scholars.

Tania kneeled beside them. "Ptolemaic clothing; must have been the curators." She turned one of the skulls. "Healthy, at least before they died. Wonder whether they decided to stay – the caretakers for eternity."

"Job for life," Matt said grimly.

Adira clicked her fingers twice. "Or they were slow and became sealed in by the door mechanism. I have no desire to be one of the next skeletons." She spun. "Professor, we need to find that book, now. Everyone spread out."

The flashlight beams lifted higher. Tania gasped, her mouth hanging open as she slowly panned her large light. "This is truly the Bibliotheca Alexandrina." She laughed softly, tears, not salt water making her eyes wet and shining in the darkness.

They found themselves on a walkway built into the side of the hollowed-out island. A huge central room was sunk into the floor, and now it became clear why the ocean had to be kept so thoroughly at bay – inside was bone dry, and contained a treasure trove from the ages.

Matt didn't know where to start – he could see magnificent statues, some of Greek gods intermixed with Egyptian and Roman. There were rulers, other great figures of the time, in marble, polished granite and coated in gold. There were onyx sphinxes, milky alabaster Anubis sculptures, many startlingly different when compared to each other, and not possibly done by the same artist or even in the same era.

Tania held her arms wide. "The riches of all the known world."

"Not just the riches; also the knowledge," Matt said, walking slowly down the steps and then in among artifacts.

There were shelves and shelves piled high with scrolls. He groaned. "Just for a day down here, just one day. I wish Dr Albadi could have seen this."

He moved his light around the room. Golden caskets with depictions of rays of light causing armies to fall; ornate oil lamps with warnings of djinn; a huge age-tarnished bronze urn, a dozen feet across, inscribed with the image of a hideous face screaming in fury, and covered in coiling rope or serpents; there were statues of monstrous Cyclops; and so much more.

Matt turned, feeling exhilarated and near overwhelmed. "The caretakers, I don't think they were locked in. I think they stayed on purpose – they valued knowledge over life."

"*Move it!*" Adira's screamed words reverberated around the large room, echoing the chastisement back at them, over and over.

Their hunt sped up – caskets of golden objects were ignored, silver weapons, some studded with brilliant stones, or intricate machines were all now knocked aside. Matt found a long table stacked with scrolls that fell to pieces in his hands, but from the dry scraps of Egyptian and Greek he read, he knew they were not what he sought.

Tania smoothed out a large sheet of some sort of hide that was beautifully decorated with a map. "You're not going to believe what this is – it's a map of *Aztlan* – That's the ancient name for Atlantis. You're not going to believe where it is…"

"Forget it." Matt snorted. "Seen it."

"Here!" Abrams called from the far end of the chamber.

Matt sprinted, leaping over chests and skirting marble statues. The major shone his light on a small coffin-shaped box that was so dark and polished it looked like black glass. He had pushed the lid aside, and now stood back.

Matt came over and peered in – inside there was another box, this one gold, and on its lid the same sort of strange glyphs he had seen in the sink holes. He reached in and gently lifted the lid. Immediately he felt a wave of nauseating dizziness, as if some sort of radiation had been released from the confines of the receptacle.

There was a single item – a book – it was about a foot in length, and just less than that in width. The cover was of some sort of soft-looking leather, heavily tooled, the image of an inhuman face set into a boiling mass of coiling tentacles in the center. The craftsman had used large polished rubies for the eyes; this managed to imbue it with a lifelike quality that was both beautiful and unsettling.

"I think this is it," Matt said weakly.

"Grab it, bag it, and let's go." Adira's voice was urgent.

Matt shut her out, and reached in slowly, his hands shaking. Beside him, he heard Abrams shake out a plastic bag and hold it open. Matt's fingers flexed, but it felt as he were holding a strong magnet, and approaching another of an opposing pole. His fingers tingled as they hung over the odd leather.

Just then, from the sunken steps, there came a dull *clunk*. Everyone froze and Adira sucked in a breath, before roaring over their heads, "*The door!*"

She pushed past Matt, grabbed the book and jammed it into Abrams's bag. The major rolled it tight, and then stuck it into yet another plastic bag. He unzipped his suit and pushed it inside. He was already starting to sprint for the steps.

"Let's go, let's go, let's go."

They all ran now, flinging priceless relics out of the way, Abrams shouldering aside an ancient wooden crucifix, dark stains on each of its arms, and then all throwing themselves into the water. Vibrations filled the chamber, and they could feel the dull thunk of heavy metal and stonework gears grinding against each other right through their skin.

Matt remembered the corridor was about twenty feet long – short, but narrow, so they could not all travel side by side –

someone would be last. He tried hard to remember how long it had taken the thing to open – five seconds, ten, twenty? Please be twenty, he prayed.

Up ahead, Matt could see a light waving back and froth – Hartogg or Andy, signaling – so close. They came to the end and the huge door began its slow swing. Matt turned and saw the massive stone cogs working over each other as the clockwork machine worked to draw the gigantic slab up tight against the crevice wall.

Adira went through, and she dragged Abrams with her, keeping him close – Of course, thought Matt, he now has the prize. Matt shoved Tania forward, and she swum torpedo-like through the rapidly narrowing gap. Hartogg reached in and held the crowbar between the wall and door, waiting for it to impact with the inch-thick hardened steel. Matt kicked furiously, and, as he swam through the gap, the slab reached the crowbar and crumpled it as though it were a soda can.

Matt breathed hard, feeling dizzy from the exertion. Andy swam over and grabbed his arm, his eyes troubled behind his mask. Matt nodded in return, but the geologist pointed up, and he realized the concern wasn't for him.

The moon was still a distorted glow high above the crevice, though it had passed its peak, and the first thing Matt noticed was all the sea life had disappeared – then he found out why. Overhead, a huge shape glided past. Then another.

Hartogg grabbed Adira, and used his hands and eyes to try and convey the trouble. She simply nodded, and from her calf drew a long diver's blade. She held the knife up to them, pointing at each. Together the divers drew forth their knives, and followed Adira as she swam up and out from the island shelter.

At the very edge of their rocky fortress, she stopped and turned, holding up three fingers – she counted down, three, two, one, and then brought her fist down. She spun and started to propel herself fast toward the position of Mahmood's boat.

Matt felt his stomach flip inside – though the moon still gave them a faint twilight, the ocean at night meant that the depths of their vision ended in shadows that moved behind curtains of darkness.

Each of them swam like seals as they rocketed out of the fissure in the sunken island, along the bottom, and headed for the safety of their boat. They moved fast, huge diving fins paddling strongly, but where they were like seals, the things coming out of the darkness were living torpedoes.

Matt was thankful for the glow of the moon, as he could at least see the sharks' circling, some small and under six feet, moving erratically and agitated, working themselves into the mindless mass that would become a feeding frenzy. But further out, at the very extent of his vision, he could make out larger shapes, huge, as thick around as a draft horse, and longer than their boat – the ocean's apex predators, the great white.

A shark peeled off and lunged in toward them, seeming to pick out Abrams as its target. Hartogg slashed at it, his blade pummeling the tough hide, but not opening or even denting its rough skin. It turned away, but another immediately took its place.

Again and again, they came at Abrams, and Matt knew why – it was the Book. These primordial creatures, 450 million years in the making, were either seeking to attack the Book itself, or were perhaps trying to defend it from the mammalian apes that sought to steal it.

There came a thud, a grunt and an explosion of bubbles. Matt saw Andy tumbling in the water as a seven-foot bull shark flicked away.

Adira was first to the anchor rope, and looked up. The ascent was where they would be most vulnerable: especially in the moment they would need to look away and lift themselves from the water. The image of kicking, dangling legs among all the man-eaters made Matt feel sick from fear.

Adira pointed up, and then held up five fingers. She swam away a dozen feet, and then used her knife to open a slit in one of her palms. Black blood immediately clouded the water around her.

Matt knew what she was doing – drawing the beasts to her. With blood in the water they could expect the furious eating machines to be driven into a frenzy of attack.

Adira turned and furiously pointed to the surface. Abrams pulled on Tania's arm, and the two of them started guiding the groggy Andy up the anchor rope to Mahmood's boat. Hartogg ignored Adira, and swam towards her.

The Mossad agent looked to Matt as she hovered in the water. She seemed to offer him a slight bow. Hartogg saluted, and Matt bet that behind his breathing equipment the big man was grinning. These people have no fear in them, he thought. He began his own swim upward, but couldn't leave the soldiers to their fates. He paused, hanging by the rope, looking down.

As he watched, a monstrous shape loomed out of the darkness, the silver moon just lighting its grey-blue upper hide and the deathly white underneath. Its muscular barrel shape was easily twenty feet long. Matt marveled at the way the great white could sail through the water with only the smallest of flicks of its huge tail. Its mouth hung open, a dark pitiless cave made more horrifying by the row after row of finger-length teeth. Triangle daggers, designed for ripping, shredding and sawing through meat and bone.

It circled once more, and Hartogg and Adira got back-to-back. A small knot of human flesh with just two blades, silver teeth, for defense. The shark turned and came at them, accelerating with a single flick of its six-foot scythe-like tail.

Hartogg slowly lifted his arms out and leaned toward the huge creature. The diving knife seemed a futile weapon against the approaching monster.

Matt felt a tingle run up his spine as animal-fear made every inch of his body seem like it had electricity running through it. He could feel his heart beating in his throat, and he wondered whether Hartogg felt the same, or if instead, there was nothing but ice in his veins as he faced the giant man-eater.

The massive creature barreled in, and at just at a few feet from them, turned a degree and rolled, to look at the pair with one black, soulless eye. Hartogg struck out with his knife, using all his great strength to bury the blade into the hide.

The shark veered away, wrenching the SEAL's arm, and pulling the knife from his hand. There was no blood from the great beast, and Matt knew that even though the tough hide was breached, the skin and muscles on its back were inches-thick leathery armor.

Hartogg hung there, fists balled, but now without a weapon.

The shark turned, and both the Special Forces agents swiveled in the water, Adira nudging the SEAL around behind her – it was her turn.

Adira never twitched, but simply floated, arms extended, silver blade clamped in one hand. The other sharks stayed back, seeming to give this ruler of the deep its killing space. Hartogg, Adira and the giant shark were in the center of a twirling tornado of grey hide, black soulless eyes and serrated teeth.

The team had ascended to the boat, and Matt could hear above him the sound of bodies, tanks and belts being pulled over the gunwale, as he hung mid-water to watch. He wanted to do something, anything, to help. He knew there was nothing he could offer, but was condemned to at least watch the pair's stupidity or bravery. Whichever it was, they knew they had done their job – distracted the sharks to give the team time to escape.

The great white flicked its tail once more, turning and accelerating. It came at her like a miniature submarine, and when it was within a dozen feet, she pushed away from Hartogg and pulled herself into a ball. The giant mouth opened, easily wide enough to consume her entire frame, but suddenly, she unfurled and pivoted, and then one hand shot out, and caught the top of the snout, and she pushed down so it changed course and started to pass her. Her other arm flashed around and the thin blade dug into its softer belly; she held onto the knife handle with both hands, as the forward momentum of the beast allowed the eight inches of toughened steel to traverse the belly, unzipping the softer part of its hide, and spilling guts and blood into the water.

Adira and Hartogg immediately burst into action and frantically made for the surface, as the huge injured beast turned again. But her attack had worked, the blood and trailing organs were enough to attract all its primitive cousins – they shot towards the hemorrhaging beast, and a true frenzy began.

Matt had started for the boat as soon as Adira's knife made contact with the shark's belly, and, when he had just one hand on the rope net ladder over the side, he flung himself up and onto the gunwale, surprising himself at just how fast one could move when they needed to. Fear gives wings, he remembered.

Abrams grabbed him and pulled him onto the deck as if he were a stranded dolphin. He lay there momentarily, stunned and gasping, and feeling his fatigued muscles still buzzing with adrenaline. Hartogg came next, but immediately turned and reached back to grab at Adira and lift her over the side. She went down on her knees, breathing hard.

She pulled off her goggles. "I lost my knife." She grinned up at the SEAL.

Hartogg threw his head back and roared his laughter. He looked down at her, still out of breath himself. "I'd kiss you, but you might do the same to me as you did to that shark."

Matt reached out to her. "We'll buy you a new one." He squeezed her arm. "Thank you."

She nodded, and he sat up beside her. "Hey, I thought you said they wouldn't bother us."

Her grin widened. "And they didn't really, did they?" She looked at Andy, whose arm bled, and she shrugged. "A scratch."

She turned to the captain. "Mahmood." She pointed a thumb to the shore. The old man saluted, and flicked his cigarette into the water.

Hartogg helped Adira to her feet. "Not bad at all, Captain Senesh."

Adira nodded. "It's what we do, right? You can repay the favor by pulling in the anchor. I think it's time to go home."

"I heard that," the big man said, turning to the thick rope.

Abrams came towards her smiling and holding the still-wrapped book. Adia snatched it from him and unwrapped it, momentarily examing the cover. She snorted and then handed it to Matt. "It better be worth it."

*

Drummond and Kroen sat in the Mossad agent's car and watched as the boat powered back to shore. Kroen held a pair of powerful field glasses to his eyes. "They have it."

"Good." Drummond unfolded his arms to look at his watch. "Make preparations to leave; I want to be home by tomorrow…with the Book." He refolded his arms, smiling dreamily and almost hugging himself. "The Father will be so pleased."

*

Adira squinted, frowning as they approached the shore. She turned to Baruk and nodded toward the distant shape of the faded Mercedes as it pulled away from the sidewalk, and then disappeared around a corner.

"They're back?" He said to her in Hebrew, keeping his eyes on the disappearing taillights.

"Very unlikely." Her eyes narrowed. "We need to be most on guard."

"Always," the big man responded.

"What was it?" Matt asked in Hebrew, joining her.

Adira pulled in a cheek in annoyance. "Remind me not to bring any more language specialists on my missions. Probably nothing; just looked a little like our missing agents' car."

"Your face tells me you didn't think it was *nothing*," Matt said.

She smiled sadly. "In my business you learn quickly to discount coincidences."

"Great," Matt said in English, and then sighed. "We should leave immediately."

"Yes. But our problem is, we cannot afford to break cover and put ourselves at risk of being exposed to the Egyptian authorities. They only need to slow us down, and they've won." She turned to look him in the eyes. "We stick to the plan. I suggest you start work on understanding that book immediately – every second may count." She leaned in close to him. "You must keep me involved…this is vitally important to me."

Matt stared back for a few seconds, wondering if the woman was under any sort of pressure – Probably, he thought. She had risked a lot for them, no, *everything* for them. "Don't worry: I promise to share the results with you."

She nodded. "It needs to be guarded. For now, where the Book goes, Baruk goes." Her implacable eyes moved from Matt to her compatriot. They gave no hint of compromise.

Matt shrugged. "Sure, sure, no problem."

The boat scrunched up onto the sand and Adira stepped over the side, holding her swim fins. She checked her watch.

"It's two am." She paused. "The first flight to the United States is not until the afternoon. We must all stay safe until then." She turned and headed for the car.

Baruk leaped over the side, landing softly. He held the boat steady as the others came over the side, and then he smiled at Matt. "Just pretend I'm not here." He followed them to the car.

*

Matt sat at the desk in his room, bent over the ancient book. The copy that Albadi had shown him was impressive, but contained only a fraction of the words and verse that the original did. He had no doubt that the hide covering the book was human, as there were open pores, hair follicles, and what looked like a mole still evident on its surface. It didn't bother him, as he knew that it was not unusual for ancient tomes to be bound in human skin –anthropodermic bibliopegy dated way back to ancient snake-worshipping Scythians.

Inside the Book, the work was a mix of Syriac, Arabic, Greek, and a mélange of other ancient languages. But there was also another, the one that Dr Albadi had referred to as the Celestial Speech – it was supposed to be the language of the angels, or gods – *Enochian*. But in the Book, Abdul Alhazred called it *the tongue of the underworld*.

"Nice," Matt had said softly to himself, causing Baruk to momentarily look up from a magazine he was reading.

Matt dived back into the pages of weird script – whorls, strokes and curved lettering so elegant and beautiful it ranked with that of the finest Japanese calligraphers. It resisted all his efforts to be understood.

He knew its secrets were there, but just at the edge of his consciousness, dropping hints but then dancing away, like a shadow glimpsed from the corner of the eye, gone when you turned to look. It was unlike any language ever constructed by a human hand or mind. Of that he was sure. For some reason, Matt had the impression it was strings of blasphemic spells, and incantations, secrets whispered by some race or species that might have touched humankind long before. But it remained impenetrable to him.

In the end, maddeningly, Matt had to skip over the strange passages, and instead work at translating the chapters that had been omitted from Albadi's copy of the *Al Azif*. Even then the ancient prose was revealed to him as impressions, and it spoke to him, directly into his mind, and more. When he closed his eyes to rest them from the rush of fantastic information, he saw everything, every page, every word, he had read. It was if the thing were imprinting itself on his mind, once his eyes had captured their images.

Several times it became too much, and he had to rub his eyes hard in a vain attempt to banish images that tore at his sanity. Periodically he felt light-headed, as if he were on a rollercoaster rising and falling, and becoming dizzy from vertigo. Baruk had come over once and laid a hand on his shoulder, checking on him. He had brought water, and Matt had thanked him, having sometimes forgotten he was even there. Though the rooms were small, the proximity of his personal bodyguard hadn't bothered him at all. Baruk, true to his word, had remained silent, and near invisible. But then, Matt thought, the passages had been absorbing; unless he was grasped he would have missed a fire alarm.

The hours sped by as he sat hunched over. His back and neck screamed but he was transfixed. He had never seen anything like this material before, and the current events of the earth-drops, disappearances, and monstrous emergences had made the fantastic things described all the more horrifying.

Matt learned of the things that came before – the Elder beings, the Great Old Ones, a race of creatures or entities that once ruled the Earth and who now slumbered deep below the crust of the planet, or deep in the dark, fathomless seas. There were Xastur, Azathoth, Ghatanothoa, Shub-Niggurath, Yog-Sothoth, Nyarlathotep, and the vilest of all, the great Cthulhu, hidden behind colossal red gates of a lost city.

He read how they were worshiped by humans and non-humans alike, mentioning the crawlers in the filth and the great eaters of flesh, which Matt took to mean the roaches and sharks. He then read of the Shoggoths, the hapless monstrosities that were like the fleas on the hide of the Great Old One: they were its servants, its workers and slaves. And finally, he learned more of the giant form of Cthulhu itself, the slumberer beneath them all – *beneath us all.*

Alhazred had tried to describe the being, calling it some sort of immense, near immortal thing that was like an octopus, a dragon, and a deformed parody of the human form. There was a pulpy, tentacled head whose face was a mass of feelers atop a grotesque, scaly body. In other passages, he talked of a giant many-limbed worm of vast intelligence, not dead, not alive, but aware of us tiny things on the planet's surface. It waited, to wake, every few millennia, testing and checking to see if the bounty of Earth had replenished enough for it to pour forth from the pit like some sort of rupturing infection and consume us all.

How could it hide, or remain undetected? Matt wondered. Perhaps it was too deep for us to see with our primitive instruments, or so large, we thought it nothing but some sort of massive underground ocean.

A touch on his shoulder.

"*Jesus.*" Matt jumped.

Baruk smiled. "Sorry, Professor. But it's time to get ready."

Matt smiled weakly at the Israeli. "I was lost – a million miles underground. Alhazred has been there; he described it in a poem." He slumped for a moment, before looking up again, feeling slightly befuddled. His eyes wouldn't refocus on the man, as if they longed to be back on the page. "What did you say?"

Baruk handed him another glass of water. "I said, we need to get ready. Final briefing before we depart." He snorted softly. "You haven't moved for hours."

"Hours?" Matt checked his watch, a little alarmed at the time. He nodded. "I'm nearly done." He turned back to the last few pages. It was there, and it wasn't. The information sat in his mind unprocessed. The languages, the warnings, and the poems – all would have meanings that needed to be dissected and analyzed.

"I need more time. There's some I still can't understand." He read on, hurrying now, searching for, and then finding, what he was looking for – where the Great Old One would come next, and how.

A jagged pain ripped through his skull, and Matt sat back pressing his temples. The pain passed, but there was a residue of screams and howls in his head that was like a tornado loosed from hell. There were voices, not just human, but of things that existed so long ago they were now little more than bones pinned together in museums. They were all trapped, in both the pages of the Book, and within the monstrous con-sumer of all things, Cthulhu.

And with its image, came its plans. "There's a poem here." Matt now knew where. "The Gated Deep; *his gate...*" Matt pointed to the page. "It's why the original caves were useless to us. It moves – his portal of return will be where the convergence is closest to the Earth, *right now*." Matt turned to Baruk. "What part of the earth will be facing the celestial convergence when it is at its absolute peak?" He closed his eyes. "Because that is where Cthulhu will rise again."

*

Adira gathered everyone for a final briefing in Abrams's room. In a small kitchen off to the side, an electric stovetop glowed red underneath a coffee pot – the major was probably running on little more than adrenaline and caffeine by now.

Matt accepted a cup and spent ten minutes telling the group what he had found, but finally stopped, and held the Book open at a block of magnificent script. He tapped the page. "Here...Alhazred called it 'The Path to the Gated Deep'. It's a poem of sorts." He looked down at the text and licked dry lips. He cleared his throat and read.

"*They slumber, a race far older than man's first word,*
In a city more ancient than Lemuria's first brick.
The sleepers in the dirt, the burrowers below us all."

Matt felt the increasingly familiar pain behind his eyes. He ignored it, and continued reading.

"*We who climb down into the depths find not just caverns of wet and slime,*
But carved faces beautiful in their hideousness, carrying not one visage of mortal man."

Matt swallowed, feeling a ball of nausea roll in his gut. He blinked away tears and continued.

"*Pathways spiral ever downwards to hopelessness and eternal blackness.*
There, find mighty columns, towering edifices, and streets too wide for a sapiens's feet.

A primal city long past anything the tiny human mind could comprehend."

He groaned and screwed his eyes shut, and then placed a thumb and finger into them rubbing hard. "Headache."

Tania grabbed his arm. "Go slowly; you're doing great."

Matt shook his head and blinked rapidly. "It's strange; feels like a bad vodka hangover." He winced again and continued.

"Gates of red granite so huge they could hold back an army. Now swung wide.

Past them the Old Ones eternally slumber – dreaming, and still reaching out to us.

And the Earth shall fall before they rise."

"So, this thing has a base." Adira's voice had a satisfied edge.

"A city...underground?" Abrams pulled at his chin.

"As I said before, it could be just allegorical. I'm not sure I really undestand it. It could mean something else entirely," Matt added still feeling lightheaded.

"I think you've read enough now." Tania said, squeezing his arm.

"For today." He agreed; the descriptive passages of the Book threw back monstrous images and a sense of hopelessness, not to mention the physical pain, which still lingered.

Tania surprised him by not pushing him on the strange language. He guessed her concern for him overrode her archeological background and her desire to understand more of the historical oddities of the *Al Azif*. Matt stumbled, and briefly held on to a chair back. Tania grabbed at him. "You're freezing...and pale as a sheet."

Matt nodded. "Just a little dizzy." He leaned forward. "The celestial convergence of our solar system – how can we find out what part of the Earth will be closest at its absolute peak?"

Tania went back to her small computer tablet and typed furiously for a few seconds. She snorted softly and sat back. "Back home…it's back home." She looked up. "Sort of. It'll be over the USA – Kentucky, to be exact."

Andy nodded and sat forward. "That's interesting, and maybe only a coincidence, but you know what else is in Kentucky? Mammoth Cave – the largest cave system in the world. It's about four hundred miles of caves, caverns, and slide holes – some of it still unexplored."

"How deep?" Abrams asked.

"Deep, but not too deep," Andy said. "From what I remember, its deepest point is about four hundred feet." He clicked his fingers. "But there's a pretty good-sized sinkhole in it…" He looked up, brows raised. "The sinkhole itself has been dated to about thirteen hundred years ago."

"Look's like it's about to drop again. We need to be there, with the entire army if that's what it takes." Abrams got to his feet. "Are we done here?"

"No." Adira, who had been leaning back against the wall, watching everyone, strode to the center of the room. She stood before Matt. "How did Abdul Alhazred put this thing back to sleep?"

Matt shook his head wearily. "I don't know."

"*Think!*" Adira's voice was like a slap.

"Lighten up." Tania got to her feet, and the look that passed between the two women bordered on the volcanic.

Matt held up his hand, waving them down. "It's just that there are some language elements that defy description. I think some of it is Enochian, but it's not based on any linguistic construct I, or anyone, has ever known. They're symbols, but I know they have meaning." He shrugged. "I mean I might know, and just not realize it. Or maybe I just need to look at it from a different perspective…one I don't fully understand yet." He had the *Al Azif* on his lap, his hand on its soft surface. "I need more time."

Abrams stared for a few seconds, his jaws working. "We have the flight home – fourteen hours, and then, 'different perspective' or not, the celestial convergence will be at its peak, and over the USA. Whatever is going to happen will begin there. We will have something we can use to stop this thing rising, or..." he shook his head, face grim "...or we prepare for war."

Adira paced for a moment, and then turned. "We meet downstairs in twenty minutes."

"One more thing." Abrams nodded to Hartogg and stood straighter. "Captain Senesh, we want to thank you personally, and on behalf of the United States, for all your assistance. But if you can get us safely to the airport, then your job is well and truly done."

Tania smiled, and folded her arms. Hartogg looked pained, clearly bothered with the new orders.

Adira's face was untroubled, and she just tilted her head. Matt didn't think for a moment, that Adira thought her job was "done'.

*

Matt felt sickly and weak, the effects of the Book still pulling at him. Baruk was hurriedly packing for him, or rather tossing his stuff into a bag, and pushing it down hard. It didn't matter, he didn't have much: most had been lost when the SUV was blown up in the Syrian desert, and what remained was part of his cover story.

Matt sat forward. "What now for you?"

Baruk turned, and looked as if he was going to ignore the question for a moment, but then stopped what he was doing. "All agents are being recalled for defense of the State."

Matt raised his eyebrows. "What, the earth-drops?"

Baruk shook his head. "No; what is coming out of them." He smiled sadly. "It seems we are also at war, Professor Kearns."

"I'm sorry," Matt said.

Baruk shrugged. "Home defense; we are used to it."

Matt sighed and sat back. "Home defense...against the end of the world."

Baruk zipped up his bag. "Done." He grinned, and held out his hand. "Where's my tip?"

The Mossad agent's smile froze on his face and he stood extremely still, as if listening.

The door burst open.

*

Adira spoke softly and urgently to her uncle, General Meir Shavit. As always she imagined the old man in his favorite chair, chain-smoking his cigarettes, one eye half closed from the curling smoke.

"I cannot just take it from them," she said, beginning to pace.

The old soldier's wheezing formed into his usual slow words. "You could, Addy, if you wanted to. But I agree this might become messy, that is, if the soldiers foolishly decide to put up a fight." A cough, and what sounded like a long pull on a cigarette.

Adira stopped at the window, and opened the curtains a crack. "I believe Professor Kearns is the only one who can decipher it. Even if I secure it, it might end up being useless to us...and then too late for anyone else."

There was a low chuckle. "You give the Americans too much credit, and us too little." There was more wheezing. "So then, Addy, I think if this *Al Azif* book won't come with you, then you must go with the Book, hmm? I already have a seat for you on their flight." He laughed slushily, and then coughed. "Just tell them you are there for their own protection, as we have heard there will be an attempt on the Book...and their lives." He shifted in his seat. "After all, we don't yet know who tortured Dr Albadi, or removed our agents. So this is probably true."

"I agree, Uncle." She shivered slightly at the thought of being allowed by the Agency back into America.

"Addy, the new agents I have sent will conduct an investigation into the disappearances, but by now, it is likely to be more a body recovery than a rescue." She listened as the general breathed laboriously in and out for a second or two. "This is the business we are in." He sighed and his voice grew distant. "Contact me when you know more. Good luck, Addy."

The line went dead.

Adira held the phone for a second or two in her hand, her mind working. From down the hall there came a crash of splintering wood.

*

Matt felt his breath catch in his throat as the largest man he had ever seen came through the door. For such a physical giant, he moved quickly, his dark eyes missing nothing as he took in Matt, the Book, and then, Baruk.

The Israeli agent also moved fast – the Glock pistol was in his hand in a second and two shots were discharged. The giant ducked the first, but took the next in the chest – it didn't stop him; in fact, he didn't seem to feel it, even though there was a smoking hole in his shirt.

He crossed to Baruk in two steps, chopped at the gun hand and struck him under the chin with such force that the agent flew backwards into the wall. Baruk was highly trained and sprang back, shrugging off the hammer-like blow and diving for the big man's midsection.

The giant clasped his hands together and brought them down like a pile driver between the Israeli agent's shoulderblades. Matt could feel the impact of the blow right through the soles of his feet and it jolted him into action. He leaped up, dragged his chair with him and broke it over Baruk's opponent's head and shoulders. That was his plan, at any rate: it didn't break like in the movies, it just bounced off as if he'd simply struck the wall.

The giant ignored Matt, reached down to Baruk still hanging on at his waist, and grabbed his head. In one swift movement, he span the skull so quickly and violently that the Mossad agent's head was now facing the roof.

Matt nearly gagged: Baruk had a startled look on his face as if he suddenly realized he was dead.

The giant held onto the body and turned to the door. "Sir."

Another man stepped in, flanked by two brutal-looking Egyptians carrying long blades. This one was wearing a tailored suit, his silver hair brushed back in an expensive haircut, and movie-star teeth on display in a wide, satisfied smile.

"You *must* be Professor Matthew Kearns. It's truly a pleasure. And I am Charles Sheldon Drummond, a fan of sorts." He gave Matt a small bow, and then turned to look up at the giant next to him. "Kroen, let's get ready to receive our visitors."

Drummond turned back to Matt. "Oh, Professor, did you hear what happened to poor Dr Albadi?"

Matt nodded, wondering what the man was playing at.

"Yes, your Syrian informant wasn't as cooperative with me, and needed to be punished – in fact, punished to pieces. So, you sit quietly over there and don't make a sound."

Drummond's face hardened, and Matt saw something behind the eyes that told him that this suave little man would like nothing more than the chance to *punish* him.

Matt sat still. I can wait, he thought. Opportunities always present themselves.

Kroen picked up Baruk's gun and then came and stood in front of Drummond, his huge body effectively shielding the doorway. He pointed to the two Egyptians and ordered them on either side of the door. Their trap was set.

Drummond then looked out at Matt and smiled broadly. "Professor, move to the other side of the room, and don't say a word. Remember, I don't want to hurt you, so please don't make me."

Kroen then took the limp body of Baruk and twisted the head so it was back in the right position. The sickening crunch and crackle of vertebrae made Matt wince. When the huge man had finished, he held the Israeli's body up in front of himself, one hand on the collar and the other holding the head straight.

Matt went and stood against the wall. Hartogg came through first, and looked briefly at Baruk, and then at Matt. He sensed the danger a second too late, and before he could spin, Kroen had hammered the side of his head with the gun butt. The SEAL dropped to the ground. Abrams came next, followed by Andy and Tania together. Kroen and the Egyptians grabbed one each and flung them to the center of the room.

Kroen threw Baruk's body aside like a sack of rubbish, and rolled his shoulders. Slabs of muscle, on top of a deep chest and huge arms ending in sledge hammer fists. The man was a born killer of men.

Drummond stepped out slightly, a small pistol now in his hand. "Weapons on the floor, and up against the wall." He leaned forward, looking out into the hallway. "Oh please, come in, Captain Senesh, no need to be bashful." He waited two seconds. "I'll shoot one of them." He smiled his megawatt smile and pointed his gun at Andy's face.

Adira came in, arms straight down and slightly out at her sides. Her eyes flicked to Baruk's body. Matt had never seen a look of such pure hatred on her face before; this had just gotten personal.

She stood in the doorway, her eyes flicking from Matt and the team, to Kroen, sizing him up, and then to Drummond before looking down again at her fallen comrade. She looked back to Drummond, her face impassive, but her eyes burning with a molten fury.

"Now, now." He grinned at her. "I know what you're thinking – can you take out Kroen, and my two men, and *then* get to me before I can fire?" He shook his head. "The answer is no. I'm a crack shot, and I *will* hit you at this range. Kroen will also snap the American woman's neck as punishment. All your exertions will achieve is two more bodies, one of them being your own."

Drummond turned to Matt. "Time to finish up. Professor, the *Necronomicon* if you please."

"Don't give it to him," Adira said.

Matt froze.

Drummond turned and fired at Adira. The bullet whizzed past her face, grazing her cheek, and leaving a line of red. She didn't flinch.

"That will be all, Captain. Or the next will be between your very angry eyes." He turned back to Matt. "The Book, now."

Matt looked to Adira, and then to Abrams, trying to elicit some sort of word, plan or even the indication of a plan – there was nothing from them. He felt helpless. Hartogg was still unconscious, and Abrams, Tania and Andy were bailed up against the wall, with Adira just inside, but up on her toes, her arms still straight down at her sides, fingers beginning to flex.

Drummond's lips compressed in annoyance, and the muzzle of his gun started to travel toward Matt's thigh. "Now."

Matt held it tight in both hands. "You won't be able to understand it. It will be useless to you," he said quickly.

"Really? Then you won't mind giving it up." He pointed the gun muzzle at Matt's groin. "This is going to hurt *me* a lot more than you." He flashed his smile. "I'm kidding of course, this is *only* going to hurt you." He leveled the gun.

The throwing blade entered the back of Drummond's hand, but didn't pass right through the meat as it hit the metal of the gun. He howled in shock and dropped the weapon. Kroen spun, but before he could fire, Adira's leg lashed out, kicking the gun up to discharge harmlessly into the roof.

She dived for the Book, her hand flashing out to it, and her palm slapping down on its cover, just as Kroen brought one of his pile-driver hands down on her back between her shoulder blades.

The two Egyptians went to launch themselves at Adira, but were immediately set upon by Abrams and Andy. Matt joined in, leaping onto the back of one man and pummeling his head. Tania pressed herself against the wall, apparently unsure which of their attackers to target.

The major quickly knocked his opponent down, and then kicked him unconscious. He turned to help Matt and Andy, who struggled. Andy took a kick to the chest and flew back to hit the wall hard and sit slumped and unmoving. Matt then took a backhanded blow to the chin and was knocked against the table, where he sat dazed for a moment. Abrams then traded blows with the last Egyptian, standing toe to toe.

Drummond grimaced, and wrapped a rapidly reddening handkerchief around his palm. He spat his words. "Quickly Kroen, kill her."

As if it were a dream, Matt watched the mad dance that Adira and Kroen performed in the light of the doorway. The big man outweighed the Metsada agent by one-fifty pounds at least, and in his hands he had produced two ancient-looking curved blades, that looked like a combination of Macedonian Kopis blade and boning knife.

Matt was once again amazed at how the big man moved – fast, fluid, and professionally, the knives apparently part of his body. He knew his art.

But so did Adira. Her black spike knives had materialized in her hands, and she parried, blocked and ducked as Kroen's trunk-like arms swung and thrust.

The giant jabbed with one arm, while spinning and thrusting with the other – he was blindingly fast and caught Adira on the bicep, opening a line of red. But even before the big man could recover from his extended arm thrust, Adira had slid down, and jammed one of her eight-inch spikes deep into his inner thigh.

She ripped it free, and her target, the large femoral artery, spurted like a tap.

Kroen fought on, but already the carpet beneath him was becoming sodden. He lunged again, becoming more furious, possibly knowing that his biggest advantage, his great strength, was leaking away. He was an imposing figure, huge and maddened, but though he would have had no trouble disposing of any other adversary, the person he fought that day had been trained in a dozen different fighting techniques, many of them designed to combat and kill bigger foes.

Kroen's hand, gripping one curved blade came down fast. Adira blocked it, and then swung high, and around to jam her remaining spike into the back of his neck. His eyes widened, and his mouth hung open in shock – revealing to Matt the tip of Adira's blade in the back of his throat, like some sort of sharp metal tongue.

The spike had severed his spinal cord, and Adira leaned in as if to caress him, with her lips just brushing his ear.

"For Baruk." She pushed the huge lump of dead flesh from her, and watched it fall heavily to the red carpet.

Sirens sounded from out in the street, and then jarringly loud in the small room was the sound of gunfire. Adira went down hard. Abrams leaped to his feet just ahead of Andy. The two Egyptians were unconscious, and Matt pushed one off and crawled over to the fallen Adira, turning her over, he saw the blood on her body – it still pumped. He pressed his hands on the wound and looked up at the shooter. Tania.

Drummond was edging to the door, and Abrams, who hadn't seen what Matt had, roared to Tania. "Captain Kovitz, take that man down."

Tania turned and fired – at Abrams. The bullet went past him and he froze, his face screwed in confusion.

Drummond walked to her, and took the gun. "Thank you, darling. Pretend time is over now."

Tania walked calmly to the table and took the Book. She turned to Matt and smiled. "You talk better than you fuck."

Matt knew he looked like a stunned fish, but he just couldn't get his mouth to close.

The sirens stopped just outside, and they could hear the sound of car doors opening.

"I bid you all a good evening." Drummond panned the gun around the room. "You haven't got the Book, but you do have your lives." He gave them his Hollywood smile. "At least until the Great Old One rises."

Tania motioned toward Matt. "He's read it."

Drummond shrugged. "The Father said the ape wouldn't understand it even if he did read it. It's of no matter now. Without it, they can do nothing but wait and become more...cattle." He looked out the window and then at his watch.

"The police are here, and I'm betting you all have a lot of explaining to do – especially with those bodies and fake passports." He looked down at Kroen's body. "Kroen, you're fired." He looked up and grinned. "One needs to retain one's sense of humor, right?" He gave them a small bow, and went out through the door.

Tania turned and blew Matt a kiss, and then followed him.

*

Matt cradled Adira's head. Her eyes opened, and she sprang immediately to her feet. He tried to reach for her.

"You're hurt."

She looked down, pulled her shirt open.

"Ach, it's nothing." She looked around quickly, and then went to leave the room.

Abrams caught her. "Forget it; they're gone. We need to tend to your wound." He looked to the door. "And the police will be here in about thirty seconds."

She punched her thigh. "Shitza!" She pressed the wound in her shoulder. "Stick to the cover story, it's solid." She pulled out her phone and walked away a few paces, speaking rapidly in Hebrew. She listened, grunting now and then, and keeping her eyes on the street outside. She disconnected and turned.

"We were attacked, robbed." She pointed to the two unconscious Egyptians, and Kroen's body. "There were five of them. We overpowered three, but the rest shot at us and escaped." She growled and lashed out with her boot, kicking Kroen's body and cursing again. "I wish you were alive so I can kill you all over again." She rounded on Abrams. "Your security is worthless. How did this Kovitz woman infiltrate your ranks?"

Abrams's mouth worked for a moment, surprised by the attack. He shook his head. "Captain Kovitz was assigned to me just months ago. She was competent, friendly, just… normal."

Hartogg shrugged. "I didn't notice anything unusual about her." There was blood covering half his face. "She must have been deep cover – no amateur."

Adira bared her teeth. "*Ach*, a sleeper. This has been years in the planning."

"Remember what Albadi told us?" Matt asked. "There're cults that still worshipped Cthulhu. I bet they had infiltrators in every country, every government body, just waiting to see who got the first lead."

"What do we do now?" Andy asked. "We've lost the Book."

Silence stretched and Matt rubbed his eyes, the images flashing like a reel of photographs. "We don't need it." He leaned his head back, feeling the dull throb behind his eyes. "I can still see it – every page, every word, every curl, dot and stroke."

"Can you recreate it?" Adira asked, walking closer to stand over him.

Matt opened his eyes, focusing on her. "I think so…yes."

She smiled down at Matt. "Good. Then we must get you home – *you* are now the prize." Adira looked at Abrams, her eyes level. "Until the Professor is safe, he is still under my guardianship."

Abrams seemed to think for a moment, and looked briefly at Hartogg, who nodded. He turned back to her. "Okay, until then."

"Now what?" Andy asked, rubbing his own head and wincing. "Home?"

Adira crouched down to Matt, looking into his eyes. "Yes, and we find this *Father*…he seems to be their leader. We also need to find out exactly what is going to happen in Kentucky, yes?" She placed a hand on his shoulder, leaving a print of her own blood. She looked at her hand and then felt the wound on her shoulder again.

"*Ach*." She stood and went to the electric stovetop. She removed the coffee pot, took a large spoon from a drawer, and rested it on the red coils. She turned back to Matt.

"What do you need?"

Matt thought for a moment. "Paper, lots of it. It needs to be written in Syriac, Arabic and Greek. Ink, pens, and then...peace and quiet."

Heavy footsteps sounded just outside. She turned. "Remember the cover story – it will work. As we're foreigners, they'll want to sweep this under the rug – we can be out of here in a few hours, and still make our flight." She turned back to the now red-glowing spoon. She snatched it up and then held the flat end against her wound. Smoke curled, and it sizzled as the flesh sealed over. She never flinched.

Chapter 16

Mammoth Cave National Park, Kentucky

Big Ben Jorghansen inhaled deeply through his nose. Instead of the sharp smell of cold, dry stone, there was an odd, burning odor. Not the hint of a clean fire: instead it reminded him of the time they were at Hank's cookout and, for a laugh, Hank threw a handful of deer gut on the flames – it stunk to high heaven.

He wiped his wet brow. And what was with the heat? It was always cool down in the caves, but today he could feel the perspiration running down his back and sides – it had to be damned eighty degrees.

He sighed and checked his watch again, wishing he were out in the fresh air. The heat didn't worry so much as confuse him. Mammoth Cave was formed by hydrological means, not volcanic. Water seeping through holes in the sandstone layer above the limestone had eroded away the caves over millions of years. There was no geothermic activity – or at least there shouldn't be.

Ben took his position up on a rocky ledge looking down on the shiny sweat-soaked faces of his guests on today's tour

– the group was only half what it should be. People were just staying home. He wasn't suprised with the sinkholes closing roads, and he'd heard a few sad sacks had even fallen into them. The government had been telling people it'd be best to stay indoors at night. Guess a giant hole is harder to see in the dark, he thought. He sucked in a deep breath, trying to ramp up his enthusiasm.

He had done this many times, and it was as informative as it was theatrical. He'd turn on and off lights, showing different formations in the huge bowl-shaped cavern, and then take them over to the bottomless pit – it was only about a hundred and thirty-five feet deeper than where they were, but the lighting made it look like it fell away forever.

To finish up it'd be off to the cave pool and point out a few of the blind crawlers in the glasslike water. Then he'd round em up, herd em out, and get ready for the next bunch, if there were any. He checked his watch; Not long now, he thought with relief. He usually loved being down in the caves – the peace and quiet, the coolness and sense of strength and permanence. But today, strangely, he wanted to be out in the air, or fishing, or home with his wife. Today, he just wanted to be anywhere but down in the Mammoth Caves.

"Ladies and gentlemen." He waited.

Heads swung towards him and murmurs fell away. There was silence, except for the wheezing of a kid with a red face who looked like he enjoyed his dessert just a bit too much.

"Ladies and gentlemen, this is one of the lowest points in the Mammoth Caves. Just to your right, you can see the railing that guards the bottomless pit, the *Gateway to Hell*, as it has been called, and a very sacred place for the previous locals dating back many thousands of years."

No questions, please no questions, he secretly prayed.

"It's not really bottomless is it?" one big, surly and hot-looking guy asked.

"No, but it is a deep sinkhole dropping away further into the depths." Ben looked over the heads, keeping his smile in place.

"Well, how deep?" From red and beefy, again.

"About one-thirty feet, or *all the way to Hell*, whichever comes first." He winked, and started moving.

"Please walk carefully to the railing, but secure all loose objects."

"Wouldn't want then to end up in Hell, right?" said beefy.

Oh fuck off, Ben thought, keeping his smile tight.

The group moved quickly, almost rushing, even though there was enough room for twice as many at the railing.

"And please..."

There came the sound of a plastic bottle banging against rock, once, twice, three times, each strike getting fainter and fainter as it fell. Ben sighed. There was always some asshole who just *had* to drop something. He didn't want to think how much shit was down in that hole by now.

He placed his hands on the light panel, and flicked the first switch – lights came on about fifty feet down. He cleared his throat, lowering the timbre of his voice to give it the right gravitas. "And down we travel into the very bowels of the Earth."

Ben flicked another switch, and a light came on about a hundred feet down. "Abandon all hope, ye who enter here." A few *oohs* and *aahs* let him know that at least some of the group were still impressed by nature's wonders.

He hit the third switch for the final ring of lights, about one-thirty feet down, and so just up from the bottom. He compressed his throat, ready to speak in a baritone he knew would resonate in the stone chamber. He was set to deliver his lines about Hades and the Underworld when the red-faced guy had something else to add.

"Hey, Ranger Jorghansen, there's sumthin down there."

Ben groaned. Probably the bottle you just dropped, jackass, he thought, wishing he could say it out loud.

"And I think it's coming *u-uuup*." The big guy leaned out over the railing, straining to see down into the depths. "It looks like oil."

"Huh?" Ben came down from his perch, and walked quickly over, trying to maintain his cool and his command, in case he was being pranked. Camera phones were being pulled out, ready, even though photography was banned in the caves.

"Hey, please don't..." Ben knew the high intensity light could damage the mineral composition of some of the delicate formations. "That's gonna –"

There was a yelp from one side of the hole, and then a short, sharp scream, before the crowd started to push back – hard. The people at the rear couldn't see what was happening, so reacted slowly. The people at the front were still jammed in against the railing.

Ben started to increase his speed to get to the hole before there was an accident, but thought his eyes were beginning to play tricks on him – people looked to be leaping over the railing.

"Stop that!" he yelled pointlessly. The red-face guy was at the back now, shoving and elbowing hard, when what looked like a lasso made of licorice flung up out of the pit and wrapped around his neck. He screamed, the voice much higher than a man that size should have been able to manage, and then he was pulled onto his back, and dragged backward.

Ben stopped dead with his mouth open. The guy must have weighed an easy two hundred pounds, but he was yanked up and over the four-foot-high railing as if he were a child's balloon.

People were running now. Screams of panic subsumed all of his warnings, and groups broke away into myriad dark chambers, not caring where they went as long as it was away from whatever was coming up out of the pit. Ben was frozen in indecision, his mind trying to make sense of what he was seeing.

He started to back up, all the way to his perch, and then turned to look back down on the hellish scene.

Something dark that at first looked like a huge black cake covered the entire width of the bottomless pit. Once it reached the rim, it exploded into separate fragments – ten-foot-tall amoebic blobs of shiny blackness, covered in eyes and all thrashing limbs. The things took off after the fleeing people.

Ben's eyes were so wide, they threatened to pop out of his skull, and he was transfixed as one charged toward him, rolling, scuttling, gliding on centipede legs one moment and a slimy slug foot the next.

He held up a hand, his mind now fully short-circuited. "Call the police," he said softly as the thing loomed over him.

*

"I want it sealed off – the entire area." General Decker paced as he spoke into the phone to Perry Logan, the base commander at Fort Campbell in Kentucky. Logan's base was a big one – an army installation known for the 101st Airborne and 160th Special Operations.

Decker stopped to look back at the live feed from the satellite of the Mammoth Cave's main entrance. There were the flashing lights of the local police blocking all the roads.

"And Perry, pull those local cops back; they have no idea what they're up against." He snorted softly. "For that matter, I don't think any of us do."

He listened some more to the local commander, and his eyes closed. Sealing the area off was a pipe dream – there were hundreds of miles of caves, and literally hundreds of entrances. They were still finding new ones all the time.

Decker exhaled. "Okay, Perry, let's assign flamethrower units at all the major entrances – I'd like to try and at least contain them."

He disconnected and then checked his watch. Major Abrams was due to touch down soon, and he had a chopper waiting for him and his team to bring them straight to the compound.

Decker now ran the entire US operations, called Project Underground. He had sent the President, safe for now in the sky on Air Force One, a recording of the interrogation of the thing that Ford had locked up in his deep containment cell and had been immediately given the green light on everything and everyone he wanted – unlimited resources.

Decker stood back from his screen – the Mammoth Caves event was not the first. Across the country, *across the entire globe*, there were more attacks, bigger attacks – and huge seizures of all populations.

General Henry Decker knew he was fighting on two battlefronts – one was the public's right to know versus his obligation to keep them safe. His duty won out. National security protocols had now been brought to bear on all information traffic to shut down the collecting, reporting and dissemination of news associated with the sinkholes and mass disappearances. He had to believe he was doing good by blindfolding the masses. If not, the public would panic and then surge – but to where? The phenomena were occurring from coast to coast, and country to country. There was no safe haven any more, and he just couldn't afford millions of people on the move.

He sat down heavily and tapped one hard fist on the desk. And then there was the second battlefront. The public didn't know it yet, but they were at war...at war with ground troops the likes of which they had never seen. He sat back and closed his eyes, letting his mind work.

And these were just the forward troops – What comes next? he wondered dismally. He hoped Major Abrams was bringing him something they could use.

*

Matt felt he was in a dream – he saw the pair of hands working furiously, daubing the long lines of ink onto the pages and turning them into script of multiple ancient languages. The hands didn't stop, or rest for even a few seconds, and the stack of pages began to rise. Blisters rubbed where he held the pen, but it didn't matter – they weren't his hands, and it was all a dream.

The story flowed smoothly, along with the poems of beauty and horror, and the insightful advice about beings long dead, or never dead at all. But the strange symbols were not there: the fast-moving hands were not managing to recreate every curve, cross and dot – the Celestial Speech of the angels or of Hell itself, or whatever it was, remained immune to his translation or memory.

He knew this Book, *The Necronomicon*, or *Al Azif*, or *The Book of the Dead*, was more than just a collection of thoughts from a Mad Arab. It was a book of war and warning about cruel elder beings, and spells and creatures that had once inhabited our world, and sought to do so again. The Book was both the poison and the cure. It was also a guide to Hell itself.

Matt dimly became aware of the shaking of his arm, firm, then firmer, and then the voice. He blinked and licked lips that were parchment dry. Adira sat next to him. Abrams and Hartogg in front and Andy Bennet behind.

"Huh?" He felt groggy.

"We land soon." Adira leaned around in front of him, trying to look at his eyes. "You've been at this non-stop for twelve hours. How are you doing?" She handed him some water.

Matt took the cup and drained it. He knew exactly what she was asking – the question wasn't so much one of concern for him, but for his progress.

"More time. I need more time." He waved her away and picked up the pen again. Once more he felt himself slide back into the dream. Time passed and he would not remember it. Instead, what Matt experienced was a world to come. He saw the images of what had been before, and what was *to* be for the human race – vile creatures herding humans like long lines of cattle into caves and holes and basements. The things like many-limbed amoebic blobs, eyes and mouths forming and unforming on their disgusting hides, towering over their human stock, uncaring, unfeeling, little more than army ants for a monstrous leader yet to come.

From time to time, one human soul would break away, but would be quickly chased down, grabbed, lifted and stuffed into a puckered hole that opened in one side of the dark horrors.

Matt wept as his hand flew across the page. The lines of people were endless – thousands, hundreds of thousands, and many more kept corralled in yards, waiting, waiting. The other billions of humans fled in panic, but nowhere would be safe, as they too were part of a grand new plan.

And then that too became clear. A huge living thing lifted itself from the Earth, its size beyond anything in human memory. It grew and grew, squeezing forth from the underground like a huge mass of pus from a wound torn open. Alhazred had tried to describe what he saw, but his words fell short of fully describing the horror. It was wormlike – a pulpy, rubbery-looking body, pulsing with enormous strength, that barely supported a grotesque octopus-like head. But the worst of all was the thing's face – masses of eyes dotted the head, spider-like in their tight clusters, and each one glistened with a frightening but pitiless intelligence. Matt could already feel its malevolence, and its...*hunger*...as it rushed upward to sate its lust for flesh.

Matt placed hands over his ears as the scream of countless people rang out when the huge head dropped down upon them, its maw open wide.

"*No!*"

He was caught then, trapped, the tentacles wrapping around his body; he fought, but the bonds were unbreakable. There was a sharp slap across his face, and he opened his eyes. There were arms around him, and he found Adira gripping him and holding him in his seat. Hartogg and Abrams leaned over their seat backs and stared down at him.

Adira grabbed a towel and dabbed at his forehead. "You were crying out. I've been trying to break your trance." She wiped his hair back with the damp towel. "We've been worried."

"I'm okay." Matt didn't feel okay, and he could feel his heart careening in his chest. His stomach still felt like it was swollen with a poisonous liquid.

"It's the Book, I..." He looked down. There were hundreds of pages written in Syriac, Greek and Arabic calligraphy. "Did I do that?"

She smiled. "You've done nothing else." Her forehead creased in confusion. "You don't remember?"

Matt shook his head. "All the people, the entire world is doomed if we don't stop it."

She gripped his arm. "Did you find something?"

Matt closed his eyes for a second or two and willed himself to calm down. "I saw it, and it will consume us all like grains of rice."

Adira's fingers dug in, and her gaze intensified. "Professor Kearns, *did...you...find...something we can use?*"

Matt searched his memory, rifling through the images. At last he slumped. "No."

"Ach." Adira let him go and leaned back into her chair. She breathed calmly in and out for a few seconds. Abrams and Hartogg sat back down in their own seats.

She smiled sadly. "Buckle up; we're landing." She seemed to think for a while, and turned her head. "Matthew, I think you do know, but perhaps you just don't know it yet. The answer is there. Alhazred found a way – you will too."

Matt sat back. "I need to rest for a while."

Abrams's voice floated back immediately. "Sorry, Matt, not yet; we need to report straight back to base. And you'll be coming, Professor." He stood up to look at Adira. "And we'll be on home soil and safe. Captain, you have been of enormous help, but there are too many people who do not want you roaming around the countryside. I'm afraid you don't get to leave the airport, and will be on a turnaround plane within twelve hours." He sat back down.

Adira closed her eyes.

Chapter 17

Moore Observatory, Oldham County, Kentucky

"Amazing, simply amazing. You can almost feel it." Walter Brayshore held out a hand, flat, and flexed stubby, white fingers, wiggling them in the air. "They...tingle."

"Huh?" Geoff Swartz didn't look up from the screen. "Pringles? None left." He continued tapping keys and rotating the powerful 24-inch Ritchey–Chrétien telescope to follow the celestial body convergence occurring almost directly overhead.

"No, *tingles*." Walter swung in his chair to stare at his fellow astrophysicist. The bearded scientist leveled his thick-lensed gaze at his colleague. "Tingles, I said." He held out a stubby arm and shook the hand in the air. "See?"

Swartz turned, and then let his gaze run from Walter's face to his hand. He held out his own for a second or two, shrugged, and then swiveled back to his screen. "It's not related. *Focus*."

Walter blew air through his lips and went back to his own screen. *Focus*, he repeated softly. Geoff was right; this was important. The Moore facility was tiny and its primary responsibility was to measure transiting exoplanets – a fancy name for mapping celestial bodies as they move over the face of another. And what was happening right now, in their own astronomical backyard, was big news.

Walter swung back again. "This won't happen again for another thirteen hundred years...and we, my friend, are in the box seat." He whooped, fist pumped, and then grinned, his tiny teeth just showing through his straggly beard.

Geoff wiped a hand up over his brow, continuing up and over his thinning hair. "Jesus, man, I'm hot; are you hot?"

"Huh?" Walter shook his head. "Not really." He lifted one meaty arm; there was a huge wet ring under it. "Maybe a little." He went back to his screen.

A line of dots was strung up overhead – some the size of grapes, and others little more than pinpricks of light. Geoff sipped from a bottle of water. "And in twenty-four hours, when the big cheese rolls around, we'll have them all in a line."

Walter clapped once, and his feet stomped under his seat. "I can't wait, I can't wait, I can't wait."

Geoff stood up, frowned, and then kicked off his brown slippers. He clawed his toes on the floor – three feet of solid concrete foundation for telescopic stability. "Hey, I knew it." He clawed his toes some more. "This is where the warmth is coming from – the floor. It feels like it's heated."

Walter turned and blinked at him. He stared for another moment, and then got his feet. He stepped out of his prized Australian sheepskin boots – *Uggs*, he called them. He also clawed his toes. "Holy shit, man; you're right." He looked up. "You don't think...?"

Geoff shrugged and looked at his feet. "Why not? With that amount of focused gravity it absolutely *could* cause crustal friction. The displacement alone would throw up a few extra degrees." He looked up. "Is it a problem?"

Walter pursed his lips. "One or two degrees...now. But what about in twenty-four hours when the moon lines up as well?"

Geoff winced. "We better tell someone."

"I'm not going outside; way too much weird shit going down." Walter sat down and went back to his screen. "So, I agree, *you* better tell someone."

*

Fort Benning, Columbus, Georgia

Matt felt overwhelmed by the assembled military crowd packed into the room. Abrams had brought them directly to Fort Benning, the new command centre, and one of the largest army posts in the US, with over twenty thousand active-duty military. According to Abrams, it could deploy combat-ready forces by any delivery medium at a moment's notice. Matt guessed if there was one place you wanted to be when preparing for a home-turf war, it was right there.

A long table had been set up on a platform at the front of the hall-like room. Abrams sat next to Matt and Andy, and along from him was the general, Decker. Hartogg had showered, shaved and was down the back. When Matt caught his eye, he nodded and gave him a you'll-be-fine gesture.

Dozens of seats were lined up and filled by various military personnel. Most sat talking in groups or with arms folded, eyes like hawks trained on the team at the front.

"Ladies and gentlemen." Decker's voice boomed, shutting down the chatter. "We are enacting War Plan Red." The general's eyes moved across the senior people in the room. None flinched at the term for a strategy to deal with a mainland invasion.

"We envisaged a non-indigenous force would one day seek to either occupy the mainland territory, or try and decimate the population through a weapon of mass destruction. We always envisaged that invasionary plan would be human foreign-power enacted. The ground has shifted under our feet – literally. Ladies and gentlemen, here are the facts."

Decker clasped his large hands together. "An enemy force is already among us, capturing, subverting and killing our people." Decker nodded to the rear of the room and the lights dimmed. The wall behind him lit up, and then the horrors appeared. The screen showed the Shoggoth in the containment cell. People sat forward, faces twisted in disgust, and there was angry murmuring.

"Jesus Christ, what the fuck is that thing?" came from one large man in the front row.

The thing was shown feeding – its body bloating as it consumed the flesh. Pulsating eyes popped open on its glistening dark hide, and ever more mouths opened as it consumed its prey, ripping it first to shreds, and stuffing the pieces of dripping meat into the holes.

The crowd shifted uncomfortably. Decker's face was impassive. "Like I said; things have changed." He jerked his thumb over his shoulder at the images. "What is it? Hell if I know. It's called a Shoggoth. But as for what it really is, our best and brightest have no idea. We can analyze its characteristics and make some educated guesses." He lifted some notes. "High percentage of water, amorphous striated muscle that's enormously strong and pliable. Has a toxic mucous layer in cells that are like chromatophores, except they don't just allow the thing to change color, they also allow it to change shape." Decker looked over his shoulder, his face like stone. "When this...*thing* was brought in, it looked like a man. The closest we can come up with is that it's more closely akin to some sort of giant, semi-intelligent slug than anything else."

241

Decker exhaled between his teeth and moved to the next image. This one was a film that started rolling as soon as it appeared. It showed an aerial shot of a large and deep sinkhole, with dozens of people milling around, some taking pictures. The people stopped moving, and all stared in the same direction – toward the rim of the pit.

Something came up out of the dark hole. Matt expected it to be some of the horrifying Shoggoth, but the thing's body kept coming. At first it looked like dark scaffolding: long shiny legs gripped the edge of the pit, claws digging in to the concrete, and then it dragged the rest of itself free.

Long insectoid legs, shining in the sunlight, and all spiked and barbed like a monstrous locust. It rose higher and higher, gaining a height of about three stories. Its long body was that of a primitive reptile with short stubbed tail, and it had a mottled hide more like bubbled flesh than scales or skin.

It seemed to lack eyes, but the enormous head swiveled toward the people, who were all apparently rooted to the spot. They finally started to flee, but the creature moved, fast – too fast for something that size. It quickly ran down its prey. A long sticky tongue shot out, lapping at the fleeing bodies, and, like ants on an anteater's, people were glued to the long tongue and reeled back up and into the open mouth.

"That's enough," Decker said softly. The image froze behind him, and the room sat in silence for several seconds."

"The National Guard took this monstrosity out… eventually. Had to blow it to pieces and burn what was left. Like the Shoggoths, it is – was – we believe, a primitive form of life, but not mindless. These bastards are moving to a plan…under orders. They're feeding, yes, but they're also stopping us from entering the sinkholes."

"Where the fuck are these things coming from? Are you saying they've been under our feet the whole time?" asked another granite-faced military man, chin jutting. Matt saw he had enough bars to cover most of his left breast, and sat with folded arms across a button-popping frame. Matt had been introduced previously – he was Fort Benning's Commanding General, James McAllister. To date, he had seemed most pissed off because Decker, of equal rank, had been given mission seniority.

Decker shook his head. "I don't know where they were, or where they're from. Our seismology teams are getting readings from across the globe of activity about a mile down that are not related to anything geological. We're also getting data in now, on the planet's crust starting to warm. Probably related." He shrugged. "The issue for today is, these things are here, now, today."

"*Whose orders?* You said they were under orders?" McAllister asked.

Decker nodded to the man. "We believe there are two distinct forces at work against us." He nodded again and once more images appeared behind him. The smiling tanned face of Charles Drummond filled the screen.

Decker's mouth turned down as if he had just smelled something bad. "Charles Sheldon Drummond – movie production, publishing, media consulting – in the field of entertainment or communications, you name it, the guy had his thumb in it. Seems he's been financing some sort of global cult that intends to aid and abet whatever is occurring right now. Drummond has also shown aggressive intent to slow down our efforts to even understand what is going on. My team was attacked in Egypt – people were tortured and killed. More worrying is that it showed us we have been infiltrated. One of our own people was a sleeper agent for Mr Drummond. This group has now gone to ground. Whatever is occurring is at point of culmination."

McAllister shifted in his seat. "The sinkholes, the quakes, the weird creatures, the people attacked, and also disappearing

– I can see the effects; they're as plain as the nose on my face. But that doesn't tell us what this culmination point is, or what's about to occur."

Decker sat back for a moment. "We had an interesting conversation with some of our observatories yesterday. Seems the celestial convergence that is occurring now is producing some physical manifestations – abnormal gravity effects causing crustal friction resulting in a rise in ground temperature. Also, the sinkholes have begun to outgas nitrogen – by itself nothing serious. But in combination with other phenomena, it starts to build a picture." He turned to Abrams. "Joshua, do you want to take it from here?"

"Thank you, sir." Abrams sat forward. "Our Earth was formed a little over four and a half billion years ago, and the Moon formed about thirty million years after that. At that time, the Earth was nothing but an ocean of magma. When the Moon did coalesce and first form, it was very close to the Earth, possibly as close as twenty thousand miles away – still sounds a lot until you realize that the moon is currently more than ten times that away now. That lunar proximity would have had a tidal effect even on the seas of molten rock."

Abrams interlocked his fingers on the table. "Once the world cooled, it was another billion years before even single-cell life appeared...and then it took four billion more before the first rudimentary animals evolved. Those missing billions of years have always perplexed scientists – there should have been something...*more*." His face was grim. "Now we think there might have been. In this primordial stage of the Earth's life, we believe there may have been a rise of other life-forms in the nitrogen-rich, high-gravity, high-heat planetary climate. Something that rose to dominate the world, and then, for whatever reason, fell away either into death or long-term hibernation."

"Below the crust," said Don Mancino, McAllister's senior officer.

"Below the crust, below the ocean." Abrams shrugged. "Whatever this race was, it attained a civilization of sorts and also had a high level of intelligence. Now, the Earth is unique among the terrestrial planets in having a large satellite, and we know the emergence and development of life has been strongly influenced by the presence of the Moon. It affects our oceans and tides. It affects our planetary rotation, and it can even affect our moods. Well, this effect is about to be increased ten-fold by a planetary line-up, a celestial convergence. The planet will be warmer, gravity will be altered, and perhaps the atmosphere itself will change – the higher nitrogen is indicative of the planetary atmosphere of about four billion years ago. In effect, the environment *will* be altered..."

"Terraforming," Mancino said, matter of factly. "The environment will be temporarily more primordial."

Abrams nodded but then turned to Matt. "Now, another piece of the puzzle. Professor Kearns..."

Matt nodded, feeling light headed, the lack of sleep dragging on his frame. From a satchel he pulled free the manuscript he had completed, now bound with simple boards. He opened it, knowing exactly where he needed to go.

"We met a brave man in Syria – a Dr Hussein ben Albadi, the former Doctor of Anthropology at the University of Damascus. He gave his life to impart certain information about the location of an ancient book that foretells the events we are now experiencing." Matt looked down and saw the words, but then lifted his head, not needing to read, as each of the letters, words and syllables, was imprinted on his mind forever.

"*From the darkest core, they will rise. From beneath the rock, beneath the soft earth and slime, they will come. The*

Great Old One and its armies. Where man rules, sure of himself and comfortable in his vanity, they know we are but caretakers for the true master. It sleeps, powerful, all knowing, and patient beyond time itself. Cthulhu shall rule again."

Matt felt the same heady rush when reading or speaking the words, and he licked his dry lips before continuing. "This book, written nearly one thousand, three hundred years ago, originally known as the *Al Azif*, and also as *The Necronomicon*, or *The Book of the Dead*, or even *The Book of Old Ones*, contains a prophecy, and all the signs we are seeing bear out the fulfillment of this prophecy...and that is, the Great Old One, Cthulhu, is once again awakening." He rubbed his eyes then looked along the faces in front of him – they displayed a mix of alert concentration and disbelief.

"This thing is an ancient being of immense power. From what I can decipher, this Cthulhu and its...minions...are currently sleeping beneath the earth, and beneath the sea. When they first ruled, it was for billions of years, and it was even before the primordial ooze. But something happened, some sort of great cataclysm that made the world unsuitable for them. Some died, some left, and some, like Cthulhu the Great Old One, hibernated."

"Cu-what? Is this a joke?" McAllister's features seemed to have screwed themselves into a knot on his face.

Decker held up a hand, and nodded to Matt to continue. He did.

"According to the Book, and to Dr Albadi's research, there have been five appearances of the Old Ones in Earth's past. These appearances correspond exactly to the five mass extinction events throughout Earth's history." Matt looked along the line of faces again. "When this thing rises, nearly all life on Earth vanishes."

"Bullshit." McAllister turned to Decker, his jaw thrust out. "That's what we're working with now; fucking voodoo?"

"Voodoo?" Matt's brows went up. "Are you shitting–?"

Decker leaned forward. There were cords standing out on his neck as he glared at McAllister. "You think we're making this up?" He jerked a thumb at the image of the long-legged creature frozen on the screen behind him. "Maybe that's just a lot of Russians in a big fucking suit?" His head seemed to extend on his neck even further. "You got better intel, thoughts or theories, then why don't you impress us with your own insights? Come on up, and take the floor, General."

The silence hung thickly. McAllister sat stunned, his face reddening. "It's just..."

Decker continued to glare, and Abrams leaned forward.

"Thank you, Matt." He looked McAllister in the eyes. "That's what I thought at first, General; that it can't be real. I didn't want it to be real." Abrams raised a hand to the rear of the room. "But it is." Once more the screen behind them came to life. "This may help us understand what we are dealing with. We have determined that the nearest Earth point of the celestial convergence is approximately over the state of Kentucky. We rerouted one of our VELA satellites and used ground-penetrating radar at maximum over the area – this is what we came up with..."

Images flashed on the screen one after the other – the first showed a high-altitude shot of Mammoth Cave National Park, then each successive shot peeled another surface layer – soil, limestone, sandstone, and then, deeper, there appeared a dark stain. Even more layers were stripped away, and the dark stain seemed to shift, and pulse with life.

"What in goddamn hell is that? Is it a lake, oil or something?" General McAllister asked, his forehead folded into deep clefts over his brows.

Abrams looked from the screen. "We're not sure what it is. But it's about ten miles down, for now, and seems to be coming to the surface."

"That thing is enormous – what the hell size is that mass?" Don Mancino asked.

Abrams exhaled and looked at the screen. "It covers a distance of approximately five miles."

"Five fucking miles?" McAllister said, his face turning beet red all over again. "What happens when it gets to the surface?"

Matt felt like he was going to black out, and felt Abrams hand still grip his forearm. He closed his eyes. "Have you not been listening? When they rise, it will be the end of us all."

"How much time?" Mancino asked.

Matt opened tired eyes. "The peak planetary convergence is tonight – in about twelve hours." He smiled sadly. "It will be a new dawn for Cthulhu...and the last for humanity." He slipped out of consciousness.

Chapter 18

Adira Senesh sat in the hard wood and plastic chair, staring straight ahead, and with one wrist handcuffed to the armrest. The two police guards, Deck and Bill, she had learned, stood a dozen feet back against the opposite wall, facing her. Both had grown tired of trying to eyeball the tall woman, and now spent their time chatting, while occasionally glancing in her direction. Time passed at a glacial speed.

She focused, thinking through what needed to be done. Drummond had eluded them and was in the possession of the original Book. The traitor Captain Tania Kovitz had been worried that Matt Kearns had read it – whatever it still contained, and whatever it was that Kearns could not yet understand, must have extreme value to them. They had traversed oceans and countries to maim and kill to ensure they took it from them…just so they couldn't read it – bottom line, if they wanted it, then she wanted it more.

Major Abrams had dealt her out of the game – she'd expected that. Now it was time to change things up. She looked up, her eyes half lidded. "Water."

"What?" The guard closest to her, the one called Deck, turned to frown at her.

"Water. Thirsty."

Deck looked at his partner after a moment and shrugged.

"Please, I'm thirsty." She stared straight ahead again.

Bill shook his head. "Forget it. She's not leaving the room, and neither are you. You want to give her something, then she can have the rest of yours." He turned to stare hard at Adira.

Okay, she thought. So you are the tough one then. She looked up, her expression one of defeat and fatigue. She slumped, making herself small in the chair.

"So thirsty," she pleaded.

Deck reached into his pocket and pulled out a half-full plastic bottle of Mountain Lake Water, and unscrewed the cap. He held it out.

Adira looked at the bottle hanging just two feet from her face. A Spec Ops soldier would not have even engaged with her. An experienced soldier would have put the bottle down and just kicked it over. Her eyes flicked from the bottle to the hand – only an inexperienced soldier would allow any part of his body to come within reach of an enemy opponent – especially one who was extremely well trained.

Adira exploded forward, dragging the chair with her. She grabbed Deck's wrist with her unchained hand, and forced it back. The big man bent backward, and she shoved him hard into his more alert companion. Both collided with the wall, and by the time they had regained their feet, she was ready.

She swung the chair into Bill, and rounded on Deck, punching him twice rapidly in a two-knuckle blow to his temple. Bill went for his gun, but by then she was close enough to launch a vicious kick up under his chin, which caused him to bounce into the wall, and then pinball back toward her. She hit him again – a flat strike to the bridge of his nose. She could have killed them both, but it was enough that they would be unconscious for hours.

Adira stood silently, not even breathing hard, just listening – no sounds from outside the room. She kneeled quickly, finding the handcuff keys and freeing herself. She then stripped the men of their guns, money, both their two-way radios, heavy torches, concealed weapons and anything else she could fit in her pockets. She then tied their hands and legs behind their backs.

She picked up Deck's water and sipped as she got to her feet, cracking the door a fraction and looking out and down the empty corridor. She eased out and moved quickly to an exit – escape from airport security would be simple. She was already on the inside of the secured area. US security provisions were extremely tough and effective against people trying to get into airports, not break out.

In another ten minutes she found the carpark, and jacked a small sedan. The parking card was in the glovebox.

"I love this country." She shot out into the street, and turned hard onto the main boulevard. In a few minutes she was moving toward the city center. She knew the town, and knew there was a Mossad safe house nearby.

She needed to find Drummond, and for that she needed a connection to him – she needed Matt Kearns.

*

General Decker called for a break in the meeting so the group could grab coffee or food, or just generally stretch their legs.

Matt and Andy decided to walk for a bit in the huge grounds of Fort Benning. The secure grounds they were in was part of a massive complex the size of Rhode Island – offices, accommodation, restaurants, training fields, firing ranges, with huge tracts of land for field exercises and jogging tracks. In some areas, you felt you could have been in a secluded forest, and it would have been too easy to get lost.

251

The pair headed off for a quick head-clearing walk, and maybe a coffee and donut if they could find one. Once out in the fresh air, Matt felt better immediately.

His phone buzzed in his pocket, and he pulled it free, frowning down at the small screen.

"Trouble?" Andy asked.

"Nah, but more a bolt from the blue – it's from my ex, Megan– haven't heard from her in a year or so." He read the message.

"What's it say?" Andy tried to see over his shoulder.

Matt blocked him. "Urgent news. She wants me to come to the front gate; they won't let her in." He raised his eyebrows. "What's that about? And how did she find me? Jesus."

Andy snorted. "I miss you, honey...and it's time for you to say hello to Matt Kearns Junior."

"Oh piss off. It's been ages...Still." Matt grimaced at the thought Andy had planted in his head. "Nah, impossible. Something's not right." He looked around, seeing where he was in relation to the front gates – only about ten minutes. They only had thirty minutes, but his curiosity was over-whelming his good sense.

"Want me to come?" Andy asked with a lopsided grin.

"No way, it's –"

"Forget it, buddy, I'm coming. Any chick who'd put up with you for more than five minutes is worth seeing." He slapped Matt on the shoulder and pointed. "This way."

It took them twenty minutes to pass the front gate, explain they were going for a walk, and then another ten to find the small car parked by the roadside. When they approached a hand came out and waved. Matt slowed, Andy at his side.

"You've got to be shitting me," Andy said and snorted. "Do all your women friends look the same?"

"So, Megan?" Matt folded his arms at the car window.

Adira lowered her sunglasses. "Matt, Andy; sorry for the subterfuge, but I needed to talk...and yes, it is urgent."

"I thought you were confined to the airport?" Matt asked, scoffing.

"I convinced them I can be of more assistance in the field. So..." She shrugged, and then looked at the military facility. "So, how's it going in there? Have they ordered a nuclear strike yet?" She smiled. "They will, you know."

"On home soil?" Matt shook his head. "No way."

"Professor, Matthew, when a man has a hammer, everything needs hammering. This is the military you're dealing with – to them, everything has a military solution."

Matt exhaled and looked around. He knew she was probably right. He could tell the way the mood in the room was shifting toward a conclusive response.

"There is another option," Adira said, pushing her sunglasses back up on her nose. "Get in." She motioned to the seat next to her. She looked up at Andy. "You don't need to come, Mr Bennet."

"Nice one, and I missed you too," Andy said with one brow up. "But if my buddy is going, then I go too."

Matt got in and Andy jumped in the back, and rested his elbows on the seat between them.

Adira turned to Matt. "The Book, the *Al Azif*, is in your head. But the answers have not been made apparent to you...yet. Charles Drummond wanted that Book for a reason – even if it was just to make sure we didn't have it. I want to know why."

"I don't have the copy I made." Matt held out his hands.

"The copy is in your head. But what you wrote down was incomplete – you are missing many of the symbols, I remember you telling us. We need the original." Her eyes became flint hard. "And for that, I want to talk to Charles Drummond – one on one."

*

General Decker, Fort Benning's Commanding General James McAllister, Major Abrams, and Sergeant Major Don Mancino shared a coffee as various teams ran some tactical response scenarios.

McAllister nodded his thanks as Decker topped up his coffee. He sipped and then looked at his officer. "No one saw this coming."

Decker shrugged. "Yes they did. Unfortunately, we didn't know they did, as they've been dead for over a thousand years." He exhaled. "They way I see it; we've got an immediate threat to the population in these goddamn creatures rising up and attacking our people. They're hard to kill, and there are more of them by the hour. But the worst of it is, we have the greater threat in this giant...*being* rising to the surface of our planet. We need to break our problems down." Decker looked to Abrams. "Major, your job is the Shoggoths – get down to the containment cell and pull that freak apart and find out what makes it tick. I want to know how we can kill or at least hurt it. Also, keep on that Kearns guy's back – he's the only one who's looked at the Book, and I think there's more we can learn from him yet."

McAllister nodded at Don Mancino. "Don will send a team after Drummond, and this traitor, Captain Tania Kovitz – if they're in, on, or under our country, we'll find em." He looked up the screen; it showed the faint image of Cthulhu underneath Mammoth Park. "That thing reminds me of some sort of giant infection under the skin. You know what we do in the field if we get a growing infection in a wound." His eyebrows went up.

Decker nodded slowly. "We cauterize."

"It's a big infection, so we'll need a big instrument." McAllister's face became grim. "You thinking Castle Bravo?"

Decker smiled. "Way ahead of you, Jim: we're upgrading a B83 as we speak. It's our best nuclear earth penetrator – big-end-of-town bunker buster. Normally, we can punch out about one point two megatons – not enough. We're scaling it up for a twenty-megaton strike. It'll be about a thousand times more powerful than the atomic bombs we dropped on Japan. When this thing detonates, it will form a fireball almost five miles across, and scour a crater five hundred feet deep."

Mancino whistled. "Let's hope that does it. What about fallout?"

Decker exhaled and his lips compressed momentarily. "We can expect a mushroom cloud rising to forty-seven thousand feet with a contamination plume expanding to a diameter of sixty-two miles within ten minutes." He looked at each of the men, his jaw set. "Conservative estimates are that it will onward expand at more than two-twenty miles per hour, and that around a hundred miles of the state will be significantly contaminated, and a thousand square miles of land mildly contaminated."

"Jesus Christ." Mancino grimaced. "That's most of Kentucky – four and a half million people. We need to get them out."

Decker nodded slowly. "We're gonna do our best." His face was grave. "But if this thing starts to break through, then either the B83 drops, or we say goodbye to everyone and everything on the planet anyway."

McAlister blinked a few times. "Then I pray we don't have to use it."

Chapter 19

Charles Drummond and Tania stood in an antechamber, outside a huge door, awaiting their audience. The Father would not be rushed, would not be at anyone's beck and call. Two of the shaven-headed priests stood up against the wall, their eyes on the floor – they didn't move or even seem to breathe. Since the two had led them into the room, it was if they ceased to be alive.

Tania held the *Al Azif* under one arm and shivered despite the heat.

Drummond looked across at her and smiled. "Don't be nervous. You are given a great honor to meet the Father; not many of our flock even know he exists. In fact, not many would even get to meet me, let alone know about me."

She grinned nervously. "I just don't know what to expect. Maybe I'm just overexcited to meet someone who has actually communed with the Great Old One," she said, trying hard to stop her teeth chattering.

Drummond watched her face for a moment – he could almost smell her fear. The freckles across her nose and cheeks were more prominent against the cold pallor of her skin.

"Like I said, he asked to see you…perhaps a reward is in order. Your service as a sleeper agent, working within the military for nearly ten years, has been exemplary. We couldn't have monitored the Americans or obtained the Book without you." He nodded and smiled again. "Whatever you receive, it will be a gift; just remember that."

She sucked in a deep, juddering breath.

Another thirty minutes passed before one of the priests stepped forward and opened the door, and pointed. Drummond steadied himself, and once again, was nearly overwhelmed by the rank fishy odor. He almost chortled at the thought of what the woman was experiencing, it being her first time. He half turned.

"Follow my lead, bow your head, and do not look at the Father unless he asks you to."

Tania nodded jerkily and stepped forward on stiff legs. The huge familiar figure was already waiting for them. The cowl pulled over the large head was a portal into utter darkness. The Father beckoned them to the ground before him, and Charles immediately went to his knees. Tania followed.

"Charles, you have done well." The Father looked down at Tania. "And Captain Tania Kovitz, you have something for me."

Tania kept her head down, nodded, and held out the Book. A priest came and took it from her, and disappeared back into the shadows. Drummond didn't even know the man was there, and it made him wonder who or what else was lurking in those darker alcoves, watching them.

The Father held forth his hand to Tania, and she stayed still unmoving, not knowing what was expected of her.

Drummond felt his irritation rise at her inexperience, and he hoped the Father wasn't as insulted as he was. "Kiss it, you stupid bitch. Show your obedience."

Tania's head came up, and she saw the hand for the first time. Drummond heard her rapid intake of breath, and he smiled. The hand was a mottled greenish-black with lumps and protrusions all over the boneless-looking fingers. Tania reached out slowly, and Drummond could see her own hand shook – the Father's beauty was not for everyone.

Her head started to tilt upward, slowly, jerkily, her eyes rounder than he thought possible. Hold yourself with dignity, he prayed.

The woman's mouth opened wide in a silent scream, and he saw her tongue retreat to the back of her throat. The Father leaned forward and she now looked directly into his face. The dark folds of the cowl rippled as things inside the hood coiled, writhed and twisted, like some many-legged sea creature moving in agitation.

Drummond watched from the corner of his eye, becoming tense, as it looked for a moment she might snatch her own hand away. But instead, the Father's hand continued to reach out, those long boneless fingers extending, impossibly long, and coiling around her wrist and forearm. She looked down in horror at first, and then pain, as the sting began. Drummond saw the skin on her wrist redden.

"I...am...your servant," Tania hissed between tight lips and gritted teeth.

"Yes, you are. And you will be forever." The voice was watery, bubbling, made by a tongue and vocal chords not meant for surface speech. The grip tightened and the skin on her wrist began to blacken.

Tania's resolve snapped and she began to scream, a long siren sound that rose in pitch and intensity. Before the noise became unbearable, there came explosive movement from under the cowl. Black whipping tendrils shot out to wrap around her head and neck, holding her tight, and dragging her closer.

Charles got to his feet and backed up a step. He'd never seen this before, and felt his own fear tingle his spine. The masses of rubbery strands, pipes and limbs forced themselves into her mouth, nose, ears, and ripped away her clothing to find other egress into her pale body. She seemed to swell, and angry red fissures opened all over her as if her insides were growing too large for the delicate outer sheath of her skin.

Then, to Charles's horror, she just burst apart – she didn't explode, exactly. It was as if her outer shell were violently cast off. The discarded bits of her face, head and body flew to the corners of the room, and then she, *it*, stood there, bloated, glistening black, and her once-beautiful blue eyes were still there, but now many more formed and popped open. They slid along her bulging body and its ever-sprouting multiple limbs – some human arms, some whipping tentacles or crab-like claws. Just as quickly as she had become the grotesque thing, she began to reform back into a Tania shape. A few shards of her former self still hung wetly to the new, false pink skin.

The Father released what had been Tania, and said words to her that were in a language Drummond had no hope of understanding or ever being able to form with his own primitive tongue. Tania stood next to the Father, naked, and glistening as if coated in oil.

Drummond felt his mouth go dry. Years ago, he had been asked to serve the Father, and in return for saying yes he had been rewarded with immense wealth and power. Further, he had been promised he would be a king among the remaining peoples of Earth, after the Great Old One arose. Now he wondered whether his final reward might in fact be something far different.

"Charles." The voice bubbled up again. "The great Old One will soon breach the weak skin of this world. But first a human must say the words to break the final seal." The Father lifted his boneless hands once more, palms up; his head tilted back as he seemed to look up through the ceiling above them. "I can feel it now, the pull of all the planets; the gates will open."

The hands dropped, and the Father glided backward toward the rear of the room. "Stay with us Charles. We need you, and need to protect you...our future king."

Charles could have sworn he heard a sound like a wet laugh, but was more concerned about not being able to leave. Tania remained where she, *it*, was, and two of the priests appeared and murmured something to her; she nodded and then looked at him.

Charles knew now what the priests were, what everyone in this place was: vile Shoggoths, the mindless protoplasmic beings that lived to feed the Great One, and themselves. They need me to utter the last incantation, but then, how long will I remain human? he wondered. A sudden wave of fear rippled through his gut, making him feel lightheaded. He pushed it down, straightening his spine. They want me to rule over what is left of the human race...and I *will* rule. He swallowed, his mouth dust dry.

The priests came over and motioned for Charles to follow him – *down*. Tania followed.

*

Outskirts of Franklin, Kentucky.

Hours passed, and Adira still drove hard. She had left the Interstate 85 Highway long back, skirted Atlanta and Birmingham, and now was roaring up the 65. She drove as if their lives meant nothing, and Matt wondered what would happen if a local cop decided to try and pull her over.

Andy was in the back, his head now resting on the seat, and he watched the blurred scenery speed by as if in a trance.

Matt looked down at the woman's waist – she had two guns strapped to her front.

"I assume negotiated diplomacy is going to be done Mossad style?" he asked.

"There will be no negotiation." She smiled humorlessly as she drove. "As soon as Charles Drummond ordered my colleague killed, he signed his own death warrant. While he talks, he can live." Her face became hard again. "And then he dies."

"Franklin," Andy said. "Coming up."

Adira nodded, and slowed for a moment to look down at a small box in her lap. She grunted, and looked back to the road. "Not far now."

"What? You're tracking him...how?" Matt tried to see the device she was using.

"Not him," Adira responded, looking at the device one last time and then stuffing it back into her top pocket.

"The Book, you're tracking the Book. Of course; when you made a grab at it in the hotel room." He shook his head. "You could have been killed."

She looked at him, her smile flat. "But I wasn't, and it was a worthwhile risk."

Andy cleared his throat. "I don't mean to rain on any parades, but we should tell Major Abrams where we are. We're not exactly the Seventh Fleet, are we? We need backup." He sat forward. "Matt, we need backup."

"Yeah." Matt turned to Adira. "He's right, you know. If you've got a lead, you must share it. We can't afford for Drummond to get away. And I'm sure the major would love the opportunity to bring Tania, ah, Captain Kovitz, in."

She kept her eyes on the road. "If I see Captain Kovitz, I will kill her."

"Whoa, whoa there. This is America you're in now." Andy leaned further over the seat back, his face twisted. "For all we know, she might have been brainwashed or blackmailed into helping Drummond. So none of this shoot first crap, okay?"

"Then you keep her out of my way, Mr Bennet. For believe me, if she even looks like she might be a threat, I will put her down." She half turned. "As for Drummond, I will just need a few minutes alone with him...and I don't need backup."

"Great." Matt exhaled between compressed lips. "And then we can call in the major? I mean, when you've had your minute."

"He can have what's left." Her smile was devoid of any humor. "When *you* call him."

Matt felt a dawning realization. "Oh Christ; you're not even supposed to still be here, are you?"

She turned briefly and smiled. "I don't think any of us are supposed to be here, do you, Professor?"

Chapter 20

Westerville, Ohio

Billy Jenkins turned into State Street from Lincoln, and breathed a sigh of relief. Creepy as all shit, is how he was planning to describe it later to his friends at the Mall. He pedaled harder; still a few papers left to toss, and then back to the shop for his pay. His mom had told him they were all grounded, but today was payday, and hell if he wasn't gonna get his money.

He took a corner, sharp, and frowned as he remembered the blocks of tomb-quiet streets he had just left behind – the usually friendly residents weren't out and about like they shoulda been. This was a midday delivery, and he should have seen people walking dogs, jogging, hosing lawns or washing cars – it was summer: people were outside in summer.

Not today. Today, the few people he *did* see, stood still as sticks just inside their houses, standing behind windows, or at doors half cracked open, just...staring at him. And they were all wet, as if they'd just stepped out of dirty showers. And what was with the clothes? Most just wore rags, like they'd been in a freakin bomb blast or sumthin, their shredded clothing just hanging on their oily bodies.

Just up ahead was Krozer's Groceries, and he quickly lifted his arm to check his watch – he had time to grab a quick choc-mint shake before finishing up his run. He turned into the store parking lot, and had rolled toward the front door, coming to a stop next to a power pole he was going to prop his bike against, when he froze.

Billy stared, his brow creasing as he tried to understand what he was seeing – inside the store there was a maelstrom of chaos and confusion. Shelves were tipped over and the dozen or so people inside – checkout guys and girls and customers alike, were all stuck in something. The thick, soundproof glass out front stopped any noise escaping, and the electronic doors were shut, but he could see there was some sort of black ropey stuff all over them, and they were immobilized, like they were trapped in a web thingy...but a living web thingy. The coils were wrapped tight around arms, necks, legs and waists, and it was slowly dragging everyone toward the rear of the store, where Billy knew was the entrance to the cellar's coolroom.

Fishing – they're all in a fishnet – caught, was what came to mind as he stared with his mouth gaping.

The black stuff tugged again, and they were all dragged another few feet. The faces of the trapped were terrible – all screwed up in pure horror. He wheeled his bike a few feet closer to the glass and saw Mrs Hornsby, Jake Hornsby's mother, extend a hand to him, as though trying to reach for him. Her mouth was almost a perfect circle: she was probably screaming her lungs up. Just then, another black length of wet rope lashed around her free arm, and then the net was jerked some more.

Billy started to back up. One by one all the people disappeared between the fallen shelves toward the entrance to the cellar.

Krozer's Groceries was finally still. Billy looked around – the carpark was empty, and he wondered what he should do. Just then the electronic doors pinged, and one of the slimy bits of black rope started to creep out into the carpark.

Billy dragged his bike around and jumped down hard on the pedal. He rode and rode hard – fuck the shake, fuck the paper-run, fuck his pay, he was going home.

*

Abrams watched Decker as he took the call he was waiting on from the Secretary of Defense. The general gathered a few notes and then snatched up the phone, his face grim. The greeting was short and pleasantries near nonexistent.

"Yes, ma'am, whole towns are now off the grid – everyone gone." Decker's eyes flicked down to read the reports, and then came up to stare into the distance.

Abrams could see the frustration in the older man by the way his jaws clenched, and answers became shorter and sharper.

"No, ma'am – no, ma'am – unlikely, ma'am – no, ma'am." Decker exhaled and turned to shake his head at Abrams. "Begging your pardon, ma'am, though we believe these things have a base intelligence, they couldn't give a hoot in hell for negotiation with us. I can't tell you what else they want right now, other than what they're taking – us. It seems we –"

Decker's fingers tightened on the phone. "For meat; they want us as meat, or they want us to become like them. We've shot some of them so full of holes you'd think they were Swiss cheese, but they don't go down. We've burned them, crushed them and blown them to bits – then the damned bits just disappear into the ground – we're not sure they were dead even then."

Decker closed his eyes. "We're still working on that, ma'am. We've got just about every military laboratory involved in weapon research, but so far we have a single one in containment, and the others are evading capture for testing."

He moved around his desk, and tilted his screen back. He then called up a live feed from the deep containment cells. Abrams saw the general's jaws clench and knew the man was feeling the same revulsion and anger that he did when seeing the creature.

The cell now looked like the inside of an abattoir; its surface streaked with blood, mucus and other body fluids torn and spattered from the animals that had been pushed inside.

The Shoggoth had drawn itself back into the Harry Wilcox shape and stood passively in the center of the room, its wet nakedness incongruous in the red mess of once-living creatures that surrounded it. The thing was a marvel, a perfect copy of the man it had been, except for one thing; two of its eyes were fixed on the glass panel in front of it, and there was also another eye, perfectly formed, on the side of its head, that kept an unblinking watch on the sliding door.

Ever hungry, Abrams thought, with a twist of nausea in his belly.

"Fucking monster," Decker whispered with enough hate written deep into his features that Abrams bet he wanted to walk in and try and tear the thing to pieces with his bare hands.

He pushed the screen away as the Secretary of Defense's voice lifted from the handset once again.

"That is the only option we think has a chance of success," Decker said, his voice low. "We've initiated convoys and airlifts of the Kentucky population. We'll move mountains to get as many men, women and children out." Decker exhaled slowly. "We don't have much time, and that's why I need the Presidential authorization. If we're having trouble with things that are only a few times our size, what happens when a monstrosity breaks through that's the size of a mountain? He looked at his watch. "We lose Kentucky or we lose the planet; in about ten hours. Ma'am, I need the President to approve the B83 burn, *now*."

Abrams leaned in a little closer, but heard nothing – the Secretary of Defense had gone quiet. Finally there was a few final words spoken, and Decker nodded.

"Yes, ma'am, I hope it won't come to that either." He hung up and turned to Abrams.

"She'll seek immediate authorization. However, COOP is being enacted, and I've been requested to join them."

Abrams knew what the initiative was – in times of significant threat from any sphere, be that biological, geological, or military, the government must be able to continue to function. COOP was this perpetuation plan, and stood for Continuity Of OPerations – all senior White House officials and military heads would be gathered in the massive underground city deep within Mount Weather in Virginia. It was basically a hollowed-out mountain, hermetically sealed, and designed to withstand anything nature or humankind could throw at it.

Abrams knew, however, that what they were facing was neither natural nor the result of any human endeavor.

Decker looked up at the tall major. "I will refuse the request to join them. Joshua, we need to find something, anything we can use against these goddamn things."

The phone buzzed again and Decker lifted it and barked into the receiver. "What?" He gritted his teeth and listened for a second, shaking his head. "This just keeps getting better." He handed it to Abrams and then walked to the window with his hands clasped behind his back.

"Major Abrams here." He listened, and couldn't help groaning when he heard that the police guards stationed to watch over Adira Senesh had been found bound and gagged. "Thank you." He hung up, and Decker turned to him, his expression flat.

"She's gone," Abrams said.

The general grunted. "I don't care. We've got enough on our plates without having to worry about a single Mossad agent on the loose." Decker turned back to the windows.

Abrams stood, thinking through what it meant: the woman had been free for hours. What would she do, where would she go? he wondered.

A thought struck him like a thunderbolt, and he snatched up the phone, dialing the front gate.

"Major Abrams here; has Professor Kearns left the camp?" He closed his eyes, knowing the answer before it was even spoken.

"*God-damnit-alltohell.*" He turned to General Decker, who was already watching him from under lowered brows.

"So, looks like we should care after all," the general said with a humorless smile.

Abrams nodded. "She's on the road, and I believe she now has Matt Kearns with her."

"What?" Decker's face drained of color.

"And I think she's going for Drummond," Abrams responded.

"Not until we've finished with him." Decker's face went a shade redder. "Find them...we find her, we find them all."

*

Adira turned from North Street into Willow Lane, one hand on the wheel, the other holding the tracker. She slowed as the device's screen glowed red. Looking up she saw they were abreast of an old building, incongruously well kept in the run-down area, fronted by almost church-like black double doors. Adira sat staring for a few seconds, and then drove on to the end of the street.

She sat holding the wheel, her eyes focused on the horizon as a huge yellow disk was becoming visible.

"Moon rise," Matt whispered.

"Then we have little time," she said and looked back at the black doors.

"It's dead." Andy was looking out of the back window. "There's no one around."

Adira turned the car at the end of the lane and pulled in. "That two-story brownstone with the double doors. What we seek is in there."

"Now what?" Matt had sunk low in his seat.

"Now we find a way in." Adira sat forward, looking up at the blacked-out windows, the walls and roofline. "No problem."

Matt turned from the building to Adira. "Really?"

She sat back and stuffed the tracker into her pocket. "Hand me that bag." She pointed at his feet, and then checked each of her guns.

Matt handed it to her, and she quickly unzipped it, removing two police walkie-talkies. She threw one to Andy in the back and shouldered open her door.

"I climb up to the roof, and find a way in there – no one ever locks rooftop doors or skylights. And then you, Professor, will come in through the front door."

Matt jumped when his phone buzzed with an incoming call.

"Ignore that," Adira said harshly.

Matt checked the incoming number. "Oh shit; it's Major Abrams." The phone seemed to ring ever more insistently, but Adira glared so hard he almost felt physical heat on his face. He let it go, until it gave up. In another second a text came through, and he read it.

"He knows you're here." He looked up at Adira.

"Then we better get moving. Wait at the front door – I'll let you in."

"Hey, what about me? What do I do?" Andy asked through the open window.

Adira started to cross the street, but turned to lift her walkie-talkie. "You, my geologist friend, are the backup."

Chapter 21

Abrams had been pissed off that Kearns had not taken his call, but any feelings of hostility or frustration was wiped away by what he looked at in the containment cell...any feelings other than revulsion, that was.

He stood at the thick glass viewing panel, and stared in at the thing inside. Beside him, Eric Ford's face, like those of all the other scientists in the room, was drawn with exhaustion.

"It's quite impervious to projectiles – it's not made up of the same cell structures as we are. Our cells, human cells, as well as most animals, have a membrane as their outer boundary – the cell wall. This wall is surprisingly strong for something so tiny. Basically they contain something called a cytoskeleton – like scaffolding to maintain the cell's shape."

Ford folded his arms. "But not this guy; its cells do not have a cell wall, just a membrane. In fact, it's more like water and mucous than flesh and blood. One minute it can disassemble and then tighten its cells and create a shape like poor old Harry in there, and then the next it can expand to fill the room." He exhaled. "Damned tough sonsofbitches too."

Abrams stepped in closer. Immediately Harry's mouth opened and what looked like a length of dark, wet rope flew

271

out to strike the window in front of the major's face. It stuck, the suckers working – puckering and unpuckering.

Abrams jerked back. "Jesus Christ."

Ford nodded. "Gotta watch that. It can't break through, but it certainly knows we're here."

As Abrams watched in horrified fascination, he saw that the suckers continued working on the glass, tiny tongues in the center of each that licked at the smooth surface. Surrounding the tiny orifices were hooks that closed like teeth, also scraping at the glass. Abrams grimaced as he imagined what it would be like if one of those things got hold of his skin.

"Eric, give me something I can work with. If we can't even put a dent in *one* of them, what can we do against thousands?"

Ford exhaled, compressing his lips. "Bullets just go right through." He paced away from the glass. "It shies away from flame, but doesn't really seem to burn, probably because it's coated in some sort of slime – ancient, primordial, and more like something you see coming out of a garden slug."

"Yeah, well, if it was a freaking garden slug, I'd put my size twelve boot on it...or cover it in salt." Abrams ran a hand up through his sweat soaked hair. "And why is it so goddamned hot in here?"

"It's hot everywhere now." Ford stopped pacing. "Hey..." his head tilted "...what you said."

"What, the heat?" Abrams half turned.

"No, no." Ford spun back. "You know, most gastropod bodies are made up mostly of water – just like this thing. And slugs produce two types of mucus: one is thin and watery, and the other thick and sticky. The thin kind is what it expels for sliding on, but the thick mucus coats the whole body of the slug – again, just like this thing." He began to pace in front of the glass. Harry's eyes followed him – all of them.

Ford stopped, and looked back at the Shoggoth. "The other thing we've found is that this creature has a weird mineral balance, with the concentration of salts inside its skin almost non-existent. Once again, similar to a garden slug. The body of a slug has cell membranes designed to keep the nutrients and minerals inside but which allow water through." He turned to Abrams, his face splitting in a grin. "You know why slugs go crazy when you salt them? Because the imbalance forces the water inside the gastropod out to try and dilute the salt concentration on its outside – the rapid movement of fluid rapidly dehydrates the slug to a point where it simply turns to mush."

"Salt?" Abrams stared in at Harry. "Well, we've tried everything else."

"Indeed we have," said Ford. "How about a little Trojan Horse test first?" He turned to one of the scientists furiously taking notes on a tablet. "Neil, prepare a rabbit carcass; introduce a hundred grams of sodium chloride solution under its skin."

The man nodded and hurried away. Ford folded his arms, staring at Harry. "Could it be that simple?"

Abrams joined him. "Could we be that lucky?" He checked his watch. He remembered Dr Albadi's warning in Syria about the previous mass extinctions – all major species wiped out, probably eaten alive. The thought that human beings might end up as just another footnote in the fossil record scared the shit out of him.

Abrams's attention was drawn back to the glass as a small slot was pulled back at the rear of the room and a rabbit carcass was slid in on a tray. The door slid closed. Nothing appeared to be happening; Harry and the dead rabbit were unmoving at separate ends of the room.

Ford nudged Abrams and then pointed to one of the screens that showed an image from the rear of the Harry thing. "Look."

A single eye formed and then popped open in the back of Harry's head. It moved along the scalp, parting the hair like a small shiny animal moving through a field of long grass, and then stopped to fix on the rabbit. Immediately, Harry's back burst open. A ragged maw swung wide like a bear trap, and from within it, dark cords fired toward the small dead body, enveloping it and snatching it up, and then reeling it back into the huge mouth. The glistening tentacles and the rabbit whipped inside the black hole, which then snapped shut. The savage maw seemed to dissolve back into the body, and in seconds had disappeared without trace.

"Now, let's see." Ford leaned forward and Abrams felt his heart rate kick up a notch. Please, please, he silently prayed.

In another moment the skin on Harry's face and body blackened, and then his human shape first swelled, and then burst open. He continued to balloon in front of their eyes, growing quickly into a massive bulb of glistening black flesh, multiple limbs, eyes, mouths that issued all manner of screaming, hooting, cawing and hissing. In another moment, the mangled body of the rabbit was spat onto the floor, and then great gobbets if slimy flesh began to be hived off as the creature tried to expel all traces of the salt that had contaminated the flesh from inside its body.

While they watched, Harry's flesh shriveled, blobs dropping from him to hiss and steam on the floor. In a moment they were just puddles of stinking black mess. The Harry thing backed away from them, and in its eyes Abrams was sure he recognized the most basic of human emotions – fear.

"So, you *can* be hurt," he whispered. He turned to the scientist. "Cover that damn thing; I want to see if it can be killed."

Ford shook his head. "I'm not sure that's a good idea. This is the only creature we've been able to capture. If it's dead, then all our opportunities for study will die with it."

Abrams gritted his teeth and slowly turned. "I like you, Eric, but tomorrow this time, we estimate there could be millions of these things running wild on the planet. And if that's not bad enough, soon their boss will make an appearance: a creature about five miles wide, and we have no idea how deep." He stood in front of the scientist. "Who knows; when they take over, maybe it'll be you in the containment cell with these things on the outside, experimenting on your body." Abrams stood closer to the man. "So kill the fucking thing, that's an order!"

Ford's head bobbed. "Okay, okay, I just..." He shook his head. "Okay, got it." He spun, yelling to his colleagues. "I want the gas vents packed with sodium chloride dust. Let's give old Harry here a salt shower."

In another few minutes, a powder so fine it could have been mist started to float down onto the top of the creature. If there was a perfect image of Hell and madness, then Abrams reckoned the inside of the containment cell over the next five minutes was it – the creature expanded to twice its size, bulges formed, and hundreds of eyes popped open, mouths screamed and other pustules and protuberances bulged, formed and unformed, as dark fluid sprayed. The Shoggoth pounded on the walls and glass, the blows so strong Abrams felt them through the soles of his boots.

A huge crack appeared down the center of the many-inches-thick screen in front of the men, and Ford and Abrams began to step back. In one final act of madness, or perhaps defiance, a huge mouth on the end of a column-thick limb struck the glass, and suckered on. Dagger-like teeth dragged down the screen, gouging deep pits into the specially toughened glass.

The Shoggoth began to shrivel and melt away; steam rising until all that was left was a soup of black primordial ooze.

Abrams fists were bunched and his teeth bared. He turned to Ford, his eyes blazing. "Weaponize it."

Abrams rushed back to his office, and was joined by Hartogg in the hallway. "Lester." He reached out to shake the big Special Forces soldier's hand. "Sorry to pull you back in, but you know what we're up against better than most, and I need experience real close to me right about now."

"Any time, sir." Hartogg fell into step with the major as he moved quickly along the hall.

Abrams turned to him. "We've got a weapon against the Shoggoth. It works: I've seen it."

"Let me at it." Hartogg's face was grim. "What is it?"

"Salt." He shrugged. "Plain old table salt – melts em right away."

Hartogg half smiled. "Sounds too easy. What about the big bastard coming up under our feet? Will it work on that too?"

Abrams frowned. "Don't know, but anyway the general's gonna be taking that one head on. However, we need a Plan B...and that's what we're about to go looking for." He pushed into his office, pushing the door wide for his lieutenant to follow. "By the way, Senesh is off the leash. She broke out of captivity and either took Matt Kearns hostage or encouraged him to travel with her."

"Like who couldn't see that coming – that woman's a tornado. She was always going to break out," Hartogg said.

Abrams looked away. He'd underestimated her, again. "Well, we got a visual lead via various CCTV cameras and satellite images. It's being sent to me now. We picked her up as soon as she exited the airport carpark."

Abrams went behind his desk and sat down. He pushed his screen to the center for Hartogg to see, and then called up some data packets from their surveillance group. The film started with a view of the airport carpark, and the woman walking quickly to a small sedan and opening the door. The image jumped from city block to block – the car approaching and driving down various streets until it left the city entirely. The images then switched to the occasional building security feed, traffic camera, and ATM, each one picking up the same car as it sped along the highways.

Hartogg leaned in. "That's Tarver Road."

Abrams folded his arms. "Yep, just outside of Fort Benning, and where she probably contacted Professor Kearns and the geologist, Bennet – both of them went with her."

Hartogg nodded. "She could have made them go with her if she wanted to. She could have also killed them without blinking. But my bet is she told them something. Gave them some news that made them *want* to go with her."

Abrams nodded. "That's my assumption."

"But what could she tell them?" Hartogg frowned at the screen images. "She's out of the loop."

"Unlikely." Abrams pulled in a cheek. "Mossad has a powerful network in every country, and she'll have tapped into that. As for what would she tell them, well, we know Matt Kearns is the only one to have read the Book, and maybe he still has an attachment to it. Maybe she told him where he can find it."

Hartogg straightened. "She's going after it…and Drummond."

Abrams got to his feet. "She'll kill him before we have a chance to interrogate him. Damnit, if someone is going to kick that guy's ass, it should be us – especially on our soil." He turned back to the screen. "And here's where we pick her up again." Once again the images of the car jumped from street to street, from corner to corner, sometimes swapping to high altitude as the satellite took over. The car finally entered a small street in Franklin, Kentucky, and then pulled over.

Hartogg chuckled softly. "She's tracking him somehow."

Abrams smiled tightly. "Yep, must have bugged him – kept that little bit of information from us the whole time."

Hartogg smiled, his brows raised. "She's good; can't help admiring her." His eyes slid across to Abrams. "Wish she was on our side."

Abrams spoke through gritted teeth. "That's just it; she is. We're all in this shit sandwich together. If that thing breaks through to the surface, then it's the whole goddamn world that'll go to hell – Israel, America, Australia – the whole freaking box and dice."

"Do we have a team on her?" Hartogg asked.

"McAllister is trying to run her down, but he wouldn't know what to look for. And besides, unless they've got shoot-to-kill orders, Adira will ignore them, or send them home in body bags." Abrams turned. "But I'm sending a team – leading it myself – a small one...one with experience."

Hartogg smiled and held his arms wide. "Ready when you are...and don't forget the salt."

*

Abrams paced while talking into a phone. The Sikorsky S-97 Raider helicopter's rotors were already turning on the tarmac; Hartogg was leaning out, watching.

The major disconnected, and stood, hands on hips, neck jutting, as he stared at the weapons research division building. In a few more minutes, a jeep sped toward them, cutting across roads and bouncing over green grass slopes as it careened their way. It skidded to a halt, and Ford nearly catapulted out carrying a steel ammunition box and a duffel bag. Abrams turned to Hartogg and waved him over.

Ford placed the box and bag on the ground and opened both – inside were dozens of preloaded clips, knives and, in the large metal box, larger clips for Hartogg's HK-MP5N assault rifle.

The scientist motioned with his hand. "Compressed salt rounds. We used calcining lime and clay, mixed with water to form a salt-based mortar. It's hard enough to survive as a projectile as it exits the gun barrel, but will break open in the target, delivering the salt packet into whatever you hit – man, beast or...Shoggoth." He pointed to the larger clips. "Same as the larger rounds, so you got enough for a small war, boys." Ford stood, and then shrugged. "These are our test batch, and you're our test subjects...our *only* test subjects. So unless we hear different, we'll be mass producing them for the troops."

Hartogg unsheathed a knife and tested its edge against his thumb – it cut, and the SEAL sucked at the wound. "Stings." He smacked his lips. "Salty – nice."

Ford smiled. "A little something extra if you're in real close. We upped the binding compound, giving the mortar extra strength. Still mostly salt, but it'll cut through flesh and retain its edge."

Hartogg nodded, resheathed the knife, and then strapped one to his leg. He then took the bag and box to the chopper, and Ford stood back and saluted. "Good luck, Joshua." He snorted sadly. "But frankly, I hope luck is the last thing you need."

Abrams shook his hand. "Thanks, Eric." He smiled. "Hey, it's not every day you get to make war on a god, right?"

Abrams jumped into the chopper and it immediately lifted off. He placed the phones over his head and heard Hartogg's voice in his ear.

"What's the plan, boss?"

Abrams thought through his next steps, and then half turned. "This S-97 Raider will get us there in a little over an hour. If Senesh is still out front, we stop them, and find out what they know. But if they've gone in, then we go in. I want Drummond, I want the Book, and I want Matt Kearns. Everyone and everything else is expendable."

Hartogg nodded. "Copy that." He started to slide the spare magazines into pouches on his pant legs and vest, and then handed Abrams a bundle of handgun clips.

Abrams looked at them – six, with ten rounds in each. He removed his own weapon – a large HK45C, and ejected the existing clip, sliding in one of the salt-based ones. He slid the rest into the pockets of his Kevlar vest. Sixty shots to save the world, he thought grimly.

He pulled his phone out and started to key in rapid words. If Kearns was still in communication, then he needed to listen, and right now.

Chapter 22

Matt watched Adira as she calmly disappeared around the block to scale a few fences and then try and make it to the brownstone's roof. From there, she said she'd find a way in, and then come down through the building and open the door for him – simple.

He waited for what seemed like ages, and then turned and shrugged at Andy, who was sitting so low in the front seat of the car he was now just a hairdo and a pair of eyes floating over the dashboard.

Andy held up his hands, in a I-dunno-what's-going-on mime, and then pointed at himself. Matt shook his head and waved him down. In turn, Andy shook *his* head even more forcefully. Matt ground his teeth and waved an arm. *Do as you're told*, he scowled in return.

Matt turned back to the building. She'll skin you alive if you fuck this up, he thought. He liked Andy, but the guy's hormones needed to be recalibrated. So far he'd made a play for Adira – rebuffed, and then Tania Kovitz – ignored. He was batting two for none. At least he wasn't a quitter, that's something, Matt guessed.

Thinking about Tania made Matt wonder about how long the military woman had been playing the double game, watching them and informing on them every step of the way. Oh god, he had slept with her – not that he'd got much sleep. Hellcat, he remembered. He had kinda liked it at the time, but now that he knew she was just doing it as a job, it made him feel he'd been deluded about his own prowess. So much for his abilities to win her over with his fantastic love-making. His face felt hot.

He turned his focus back to the doors. He had to wipe his brow – it wasn't just his face feeling hot, the heat seemed to be radiating up from the ground itself. He didn't want to think about what could be causing it. He remembered an old literary quote from his high-school days – *Hell is empty and all the devils are here* – not quite yet, he hoped.

It was taking too long, he thought, and shifted from foot to foot, trying to act casual, standing out the front of a pair of huge double doors in a strange street that was still as death. He started to contemplate edging back to the car, or calling Adira on his phone, or at least texting her to keep the noise down.

Just then one of the huge doors eased open an inch or two and the stripe of blackness was broken by Adira quickly motioning him inside.

"Did you –?"

She hushed him. "Speak quietly or not at all." She shut the door, plunging them both into darkness.

"This way." She grabbed his hand and placed it on her shoulder and then together they eased forward along a dark hallway. He wondered how she could navigate so easily and then remembered this was a top female agent in Mossad's Metsada unit who had had to ferret terrorists out of their tunnels as they tried to burrow into Israel. She had vision like a nighthawk and was totally devoid of fear.

Adira suddenly turned into a room that had a little more light peeking in through slits in heavy drapes. Matt looked around. It was a normal sitting room, with thick comfortable-looking chairs and sofas, a piano, wooden mantelpiece and wall tables set with vases and candelabras.

"Is anybody home...I mean here now?" he whispered.

She snorted softly. "There's dust on the chairs. No one has sat on them or been in this room for many years. This way." She led him into another room that looked like a kitchen pantry. It was fully stocked with tinned and packet food – everything to prepare a meal, but nothing half opened or used at all.

"It's like a studio set, a prop, to give the impression of habitation, nothing more." She looked around slowly. "No one has lived here for years...if they ever did."

Adira crossed to a bench top where a knife block stood and drew out the largest of the carving knives – new, unused, and the blade more than a foot and a half long. It was as much a machete as a carving implement. She held it up, turning it in the air as she examined it, and then looked back at Matt, a humorless smile touching her lips for a second before she tucked the knife somewhere behind her back.

Adira then reached into her pocket and drew out two black flashlights and handed one to Matt. "Only use in utmost darkness, and point it to the ground...never at me, or at my face." She leaned in close to him.

"Okay, okay, got it." Matt looked around. "So where's Drummond?"

"He's not upstairs. There's nothing but dust-covered beds, wardrobes full of clothing, all unworn, bathrooms with untouched soaps in dishes – all as fake as it is down here. He must be somewhere else, and I'm guessing it's the basement."

"Great." Matt always knew it was going to mean heading deeper.

*

Andy kept his head down, alternately playing a game on his phone and occasionally flicking his eyes up at the black double doors. The windows in the car were down, and he could feel the radiant heat coming in off the road.

Twenty minutes back he had cracked the door and reached out to lay his hand on the asphalt – it was hot, and not just from the day's fallen sun. He would have hated to have to run down the street barefoot. As a geologist he was intrigued, especially as he knew the area was old, stable, with no volcanic or geothermal activity for millions of years.

He tried to get more comfortable, failed, and sat brooding for a while – he wished Frank was here, and immediately felt a knot of regret turn inside him at the realization his old friend was gone for good. He shuddered at the thought of what happened to him and he prayed that it had been quick.

He checked his watch and shifted in his seat again. Over an hour – time was dragging and he couldn't shake the feeling he was being watched. He wished he had some field glasses so he could zoom in on the windows at least. Though they were all as black as bottomless pits, he couldn't help the crawling sensation that someone was peering through a crack in the shades or whatever they had drawn over the panes.

Andy's phone pinged with an incoming message. At last, he thought. He flicked off his game and read – it was from Major Joshua Abrams and contained two words: *Turn around.*

Huh? Well, that makes no sense, he thought. Too late, we're already here, big guy. He was wondering whether he should respond or maintain Adira's radio silence when his phone pinged again. He read. *Look behind you, numb nuts.*

Andy frowned and swiveled in his seat. Up close to his car, a dark SUV had glided up to within ten feet of him. In the front seat he saw Abrams and the huge frame of the SEAL, Hartogg. Abrams looked pissed, but Hartogg was grinning.

Andy waved. Abrams pointed at him, and then beckoned.

Fuck, what do I do? Andy groaned and gave up. He got slowly from the car, and walked casually to Abrams's window. "Small world, huh?" He grinned, but immediately regretted it.

"Shut the fuck up." Abrams voice was like a knife. "Where are they?

Andy cleared his throat. "Ah, you mean Matt?"

Abrams growled. "Get in."

Andy slid into the back. What did he have to gain from shielding Adira, and for that matter, why, and how else, would they have gotten here? He saw the tightness in Abrams's jaw, and immediately decided that playing dumb would be plain stupid.

Abrams swung in his seat, and glared, his eyes drilling right into Andy's soul. Andy cleared his dry throat; Abrams's glare intensified.

Andy knew his rights, and he certainly wasn't in the armed forces, so couldn't be ordered around like some wet-behind-the-ears private. But out here, alone in the street, confronted by a furious army major and an enormous Special Forces soldier, he suddenly felt very vulnerable – And these are the good guys, he reminded himself.

Abrams glare was like an icepick. Andy gave up, and exploded. "She came and got us, said that she needed to get the Book back; she'd bugged it in Egypt, but never told us. She also said –"

"Enough." Abrams voice was like a punch.

"Hey, Major, listen, there's no –"

"Son, I have full take-down authorization under the homeland war protocols, and right about now, I'm getting the urge to execute those orders. You understand what I'm saying?" Abrams red face seemed to extend on his corded neck right into Andy's.

Andy nodded.

Abrams sat back. "Where are they?"

Andy pointed to the black double doors. "They went in there...about an hour-twenty ago."

Abrams turned and said something to Hartogg, who immediately grabbed up a bag with something heavy in it.

"We're goin in...and you're comin."

Andy nodded – he had wanted to go in anyway. At least now, he figured, he had two professional bodyguards.

*

Abrams led Andy and Hartogg up the few short steps to the door. He lifted an electronic lock pick to the door, inserted the pins and pressed the trigger. The pins vibrated a second or two, and then Abrams turned the gun – the door opened. He looked back at Hartogg, who had the ammunition bag over his shoulder and his rifle hanging loose at his side. The big man nodded, his eyes shining and intense – he was ready. Abrams then looked to Andy, who also nodded, but looked scared shitless.

"Stay behind us, okay?"

The geologist nodded again. Abrams eased open the door, and went through the gap quickly, followed by Hartogg and Andy. He shut the door silently, bringing down a veil of darkness.

Abrams switched on a small flashlight and Hartogg flicked on his barrel-mounted beam, and they snaked their way down the corridor. Abrams held up a hand flat and then stayed still and silent. Hartogg and Andy froze, listening to the sounds of the tomb-quiet house.

The major sniffed – dust, mold, the ocean maybe – Weird, he thought...and so silent, like it was soundproofed – he couldn't hear the ticking of a clock, the soft whirring of a re-frigerator or even the sound of wood settling in the old beams or dry wall. It was as if they had stepped into a vacuum. If Adira and Matt were close by, they must be concealed.

Abrams waved them on, and together they went quickly from room to room, finally coming to a door set into a wall – thick, strong, and ajar. He pushed it half open; there were steps leading down. He turned and raised his eyebrows. "Basement?" he whispered, and turned back to the door and pushed it wider. A blast of warm air, carrying an odor of mold and something disgusting like bloated bodies covered in fungus rushed up at him.

"Jesus Christ – stinks – dead fish...or whale?" Andy grimaced and put hand over his face.

Abrams shrugged, and then pulled his sidearm. "Ready?"

Hartogg nodded.

"No," Andy said.

Abrams went in first.

Chapter 23

Matt followed so close behind Adira he had to keep a hand out so he wouldn't keep bumping into her every time she stopped or slowed. He wished she'd let him use his flashlight more; just because she had the vision of a cat, he did not.

After passing down into and through the empty basement, they had then entered something far more complex than whatever underground storage facility one might expect beneath an old brownstone apartment block. Already, they had descended for what Matt felt must have been many stories below the earth, and the temperature rose with every step.

Sometimes they had passed through heavy stone corridors, the stone blocks huge, green and smoothed by untold ages, and at other times they crept between rough-hewn rock walls that looked chiseled by hand. Occasionally, there were alcoves holding torches embedded into the wall – none were lit.

Once, Adira had stepped in to one of them and pressed on the stones with her hand, looking for secret passages. She had dabbed a finger into the extinguished torch and rubbed thumb and forefinger together. "This was alight not that long ago."

"Maybe when Tania and Drummond came through," Matt responded in a whisper.

"Yes, I think so. They went down and never came back up," Adira responded.

She motioned forward and once again they continued moving down along the slanting corridor. They next stepped through a large archway with wide-open thick wooden doors, and found themselves in a cathedral-sized chamber. The walls were covered in the symbols Matt had seen in the original copy of the *Al Azif*, and even now, they remained a mystery to him. As he stared at the glyphs, which were all in a reddish-brown paint, he felt the nub of a headache begin to bloom in his skull. It was if the images alone were like flickering strobe lights acting on some pain center deep within his brain.

Adira slowed and Matt nearly bumped into her. She turned. "It's getting hotter, and the smell is stronger."

Matt felt the perspiration running down his body, and he'd noticed the same thing – a corrupt fishy odor permeated the atmosphere, as if they were heading down to some dark beach where the tide was out, and strange slimy grasses and the bloated bodies of sea creatures had been left to rot under a hot, sunless sky.

"Look." Adira clicked on her flashlight and pointed it.

Matt, relieved to be able to use his light, did the same. There was an altar at the far end of the room, and behind it and around the room's edges, hidden until caught in the glow of the flashlights, were dark alcoves, these ones entrances to more rooms or passages.

The entire room had a sense of menace about it, and Matt felt his legs trembling. "This place gives me the creeps."

Adira's light caught something on the floor. "Hmm, not good."

Matt frowned and crossed to the glistening fragment. He used his boot to flip it over, and immediately recoiled.

"Gack." He backed away. It was a part of a face, or skull – an eye socket, eyebrow and nose. He felt his stomach flip.

"Is that...Tania?" He put a forearm over his mouth.

"Maybe." Adira seemed unfazed by the grotesque body part. She looked up at Matt. "If it is, then this is nothing more than leftovers from something's lunch." She stepped over it. "Forget it; let's go."

"But..." Matt grimaced, both admiring and fearing the woman. "Wait." He stood his ground. "Adira, there comes a point where courage starts to cross over into downright stupidity. This is more than we can handle."

She stared for a moment, and then nodded, her face softening. "I'm sorry; I had no right to bring you down here, Professor. This is not a job for a civilian." She smiled sadly. "But it is what I do. This is what defines my life." She pointed to the archway. "Go back to the car and wait with Andy. I will scout a little more down here, and then I'll come back up and meet you."

She stepped closer to him, and Matt could see how her eyes burned with an intensity that he only ever saw in the eyes of elite soldiers on the eve of a mission. She put her hand on his shoulder.

"Thank you." She went to turn away, but Matt reached out and grabbed her.

"Wait, wait." He felt almost a physical pain as his conscience wrestled with his innate sense of self-preservation. "Forget it, I'll come with you."

She held a hand up. "No, you are right. You should not be here, and this is bigger than we expected. You need to go up and outside, and then call in Major Joshua Abrams and his team. Tell them what we have found. Tell them to come, and...to be ready."

She turned and vanished behind the altar without once looking back. Matt shifted his weight from foot to foot. In the end he looked down once more at the piece of face.

The empty staring eye socket decided for him. "I'm outta here."

Chapter 24

General Decker looked again at the updated satellite images of the Mammoth Park topology, now from only about three thousand feet. From this height, that part of Kentucky was usually emerald green. He exhaled, shaking his head.

"Goddamnit."

The entire area over the national park was a bilious smudge of black. Not just the dry ashen cast of forest-fire remnants, but a case of some sort of slimy malignant fungus that had caused everything to rot.

Much as he hoped it would all just go away, or get better by itself, the evidence was now impossible to ignore. He reached forward and toggled some keys. The satellite images shifted to another spectrum: stratigraphic sonar representations.

"Cthulhu; it's real." He blew air through his lips. There it was, the deeper smudge now taking on a definite shape – there was a huge central body, like some sort of coiled parasitic worm, except this horror had enormous branching arms reaching out beneath the skin of the planet.

"And when you break through..." He turned away from the screen and looked out at the parade ground, knowing what he needed to do. "...God help us all."

*

Matt retraced his steps, keeping his flashlight usage to a minimum, and cursing softly as he occasionally bumped into a wall or protrusion he hadn't remembered. He felt like a cowardly creep for letting Adira go on by herself. Of course he knew very well he wasn't equipped to offer her anything other than company, and frankly calling in backup was the most logical and sensible thing to do. "I'm doing the right thing," he whispered. "No, I'm a cowardly creep."

Matt froze. There was a sound – no, a *hint* of a sound, from up ahead. He flicked off his light and stayed motionless, holding his breath, remaining that way for many seconds, until his head started to pound. He eased out the air in his lungs, feeling the blackness fold around him. He suddenly remembered there were things that preferred the dark, and saw far better than he in its stygian deeps. He switched his light back on and looked up just as something large collided with him, ramming him up against the wall.

"Clear." The pressure on his neck eased as Hartogg stepped back. "It's our missing professor."

An electric shock of fear had nearly caused Matt to black out, and he had to gulp to pull in air over a galloping heart. "Shit." He coughed, and looking up saw Abrams and Andy standing back in the shadows. Their lights came back on as well. Abrams stepped up and grabbed him, one handed, lifting him slightly.

"Where the fuck have you been, Kearns, and where's Senesh?" The man's eyes were furious.

Matt felt his heartbeat ease – regardless of the fright they had given him, and Abrams's fury, he was glad they were there. "I was coming up."

Abrams let him go. "Where're Senesh and Drummond? What have you found?"

Matt rubbed his neck. "I came back to get you – reinforcements. Adira went on to look for Drummond." He remembered the facial fragment. "I think we found Tan–" he looked quickly at Andy, and changed course "– *someone*, or what was left of them."

"What?" Andy's face contorted. "Was it Tania? Did you see her?"

"No, no; I don't think so." It was only then that he realized that the geologist still held out hope that Tania was a hostage and not a willing participant in Drummond's plan. Perhaps the fool even had feelings for her that had existed somewhere other than his groin. Matt shook his head, and looked to Abrams. The major understood exactly what Matt had meant.

He gripped Matt's arm. "Well, Professor, we're your reinforcements." He gave Matt a push. "Show us where Captain Senesh went."

Matt walked them back along the passageway that changed to a tunnel, and then to rough-hewn cave, and back again, until he found the large cathedral-like room with the altar. He waved them on, making sure to avoid the shard of human being on the floor. Matt saw that Hartogg spotted it, but didn't mention it: instead the SEAL nodded his acknowledgement to Matt, and held his gun a little tighter.

"The smell; getting stronger," Andy said. "The sinkhole in Iowa smelled a bit this way. But this is different too. Moldier. Stronger."

"She went through there." Matt pointed past the altar to the dark curved passageway behind it.

Hartogg moved quickly around the stone altar and leaned in. He slowly moved the barrel of his gun and light beam in and around the dark hole. He turned and held up his hand, Abrams nodded, and then the SEAL slipped in.

They waited.

Andy sidled up to Matt. "You think she's dead? I mean, was that her you found?" he asked in a stage whisper.

Matt shrugged. "No, not a hundred percent, but it kinda looked like a woman...sort of."

"*Sort of?* What does that even mean – sort of?" Andy's voice had gone up a notch, and Abrams briefly looked across to them before going back to work on his comms device.

Matt winced. "Andy, look..." Ah, fuck it, he thought. He's a big boy, and this might get a lot worse yet. "Look, you remember Bill Anderson in the wall of the sinkhole? How we only found bits of him?"

Andy's lips started to curl in distaste. Matt decided to pull back a bit on the details. "Well, we found something that might, and I mean *might*, have belonged to her."

"She's dead? Fucking hell. Drummond tore her apart?" Andy's voice echoed.

Matt held up his hands. "Andy, we don't know tha–"

"*Hey!*" Abrams shushed them as Hartogg stepped back into the room.

"Just more passage, but the decline is increasing to about twenty percent." He looked at a large dial on his opposite wrist. "We're already half a mile down."

"Well, we've lost contact now – too deep." Abrams looked at each of them. "Looks like we're as good as it gets as far as the cavalry goes. So..." He nodded at the dark tunnel. "Only way is down."

Hartogg grinned, and headed back into the tunnel.

They travelled on, ever deeper, once again through tunnels of brick, rock, ancient green stones, some wide, some train-tunnel sized.

Abrams stopped to shine his light around at the walls and ceiling. "Professor Kearns, the house above us..." He frowned as he stared at the tunnel walls. "Those old brownstones are usually about a hundred years old, but these tunnels..."

"The house is younger than the tunnels. Andy, what do you think?"

"Huh? What?" Andy still looked a little dazed.

"The rock." He panned his light. "The house seems younger than the tunnels."

Andy nodded. "You got that right. The geology in Kentucky is some of the oldest in the country and dates back to the Ordovician age – about 450 million years. The state was once a warm shallow sea full of trilobites and cephalopods."

"Cephalopods, huh?" Matt felt ill.

"Yeah, they're ancient types of octopus things," Andy said, turning back to the walls.

"I got that," Matt responded weakly.

"Anyway," Andy continued. "To me, it's pretty obvious that the tunnels were here first, and the house was built over the top of them. This underground structure is old...very old. And it's not easy to work this rock – it's like iron."

Matt added his light. "And if you're going to work the rock, why create passageways in these shapes? They're not like anything I've ever seen before." Matt pointed to some arches stretching along the tunnel and away into the dark. "We make doors and passages based on our physical form – we're upright bipeds. These doorways are wide, bulged in the middle, and enormous."

Andy shrugged. "There are mansions with big doors and passages." He shone his flashlight down the gloomy passageway. "We're down a long way."

"We need to keep going," Abrams said quietly. "This is leading us somewhere, and if Drummond is involved, it might be his home base, so I doubt he'll be by himself."

"Adira said we needed to be ready," Matt added, looking up at the formidable arches overhead. "These structures were built by an advanced race that was here a long time ago."

Matt's vision turned inwards as he sought the words – but they were already there – they always would be. The verses tumbled from his mouth, whether he wanted them to or not.

"They slumber, a race far older than man's first word,

In a city more ancient than Lemuria's first brick.

The sleepers in the dirt, the burrowers below us all.

We who climb down into the depths find not just caverns of wet and slime,

But carved faces beautiful in their hideousness, carrying not one visage of mortal man.

Pathways spiral ever downward to hopelessness and eternal blackness.

There, find mighty columns, towering edifices, and streets too wide for a sapiens's feet.

A primal city long past anything the tiny human mind could comprehend."

Abrams exhaled slowly. "Streets too wide for a sapiens's feet, huh?" he grunted. "Well then, looks like we must be on the right path." He nodded to Hartogg, who had been silently watching the forward and rear passages. The big SEAL shouldered his weapon and headed off into the dark again.

Abrams put his hand on Matt's shoulder. "You next, Professor. Andy, you're my rear guard; okay?"

"No problem," the young geologist said, looking nervously over his shoulder.

Ever deeper they went, minutes turning into dozens of minutes, into hours, and the passageways turning to tunnels and once again to huge caves. The ancient symbols were always with them, pressed into the stone now and not daubed upon it, but carved so cleanly it looked as if they grew from the very rock surrounding them. Their meaning still tugged at Matt's mind, needling his brain, mocking him.

At last they came to a split in the tunnel, and Hartogg held up a fist. He turned to Abrams. "Want me to scout em, Boss?"

Abrams shook his head. "Send a pulse."

Hartogg pulled what looked like a flashlight from a pouch on his thigh and aimed it down the first tunnel. It pinged a few times, and then he read from a small screen on its top. He shook his head. "This one; nothing, no movement, and no blockages. Just goes on until the downward curve makes it drop out of sight of the sonar." He moved to the next, and did the same. Once again the pings sounded for a moment until he turned to them and shrugged. "Same. We got miles of tunnel and a choice – toss a coin?"

Abrams looked down at the floor of the tunnel mouths, and clicked his tongue. "Ground is too solid for any footprints." He checked his watch. "No idea which way they went. We don't have time for dead ends."

"Then we split up," Andy said. He pointed to the left cave. "I'll go down that one." He gave them a crooked smile. "I want to get his over with as quickly as possible. We give it twenty, and then come back, okay?"

Abrams cursed and stared off into the blackness of the right-side tunnel. Matt knew he was weighing his options – there were very few, and the time running out was making wrong decisions costly, and potentially deadly – not just for them, but perhaps the entire world.

They didn't have a choice – Matt knew Andy was right. "I agree; we don't have the time to check them both out."

"Okay. Andy and Hartogg, you take the cave to the left. Professor Kearns and I will do the one on the right. Back here in twenty whether you find something or not; agreed?"

Hartogg nodded, and he and Abrams synchronized their watches. The SEAL then waved Andy on, and they vanished into the blackness.

Matt looked down into the impenetrable darkness of their chosen tunnel. His cavalry had now shrunk to one man. He took a shuddering breath.

Abrams, watching him, said, "I know, Professor...*Matt*. I'd prefer to be anywhere else right now as well."

He turned and entered the tunnel. Matt followed.

*

Hartogg and Andy moved quickly, the SEAL travelling fast, almost at a jog, chasing the spot of light emanating from his gun-mounted flash. Andy stayed as close he could manage, looking back over his shoulder every few seconds – the hair on his neck was on end the whole time.

They entered another chamber, and Hartogg eased in, walking cautiously for a few paces before he froze and held up his fist. "We got company."

The words jolted Andy. "What? Where?" he whispered back, feeling a tingle of fear run up his spine to his scalp.

"Ten o'clock." Hartogg brought the barrel of his gun and light slowly around toward the figure.

Andy did the same, and as the illumination crept around the corner of the chamber, he could just make out someone standing about twenty feet to the forward-left, up against the wall, back turned to them. "Hey." Andy lifted his light a little more. The skin of the figure was milky white and smooth. He raised his light fully onto the figure as Hartogg started to crab to the side, gun up. Andy sensed what Hartogg was doing and moved to stay in front of him.

The body almost shone in the glare of his flashlight. Andy's mouth dropped open. She was naked, and...beautiful.

"Tania," he whispered. He edged forward. "Tania, it's us."

"I wouldn't recommend that, Mr Bennet. Please stand aside." Hartogg had his light beam on the former captain, and was unblinking in his concentration. "Captain Kovitz, you will place your hands on your head immediately." He lifted his rifle to sight along the barrel.

"Help me."

The voice was barely recognizable. It had come from Tania, but didn't sound like her. It was if she was speaking while holding a mouthful of water in her mouth.

"That's why we're here – to help. Everything's going to be okay." Andy took another few steps, and got to within ten feet of her. He held his hand out – it was shaking – he couldn't stop it. It was Tania, but something deep inside his brain screamed at him to stop, and back away.

He ignored the little voice in his head, and took another step. "Tania, you're safe now. It's me, Andy, Andy Bennet, remember?"

She turned.

Andy sucked in a breath, and then smiled, struck by her shameless beauty. Even though he had seen her naked form in his fantasies ever since he first met her, he could never have imagined such perfection. Her breasts were small, high and firm, her stomach flat and below that her pubic hair glistened like curls of silk in the beam of his flashlight.

He swallowed, feeling slightly aroused even as his heart raced with fear. He turned to Hartogg. "Lower your weapon – get that light out of her eyes." Andy moved again to stay in front of Hartogg.

The SEAL ignored him, keeping both his light and gun pointed at the woman.

Andy saw that her blue eyes seemed darker than normal, and that she stared unblinkingly at him. Then it clicked why – her pupils were fully dilated, even though Hartogg's light was aimed directly on them. And she still hadn't blinked.

"I think she's drugged." Andy took off his shirt, and shook it. "Let me put this on you." The material was dripping with his perspiration, but he was determined to give her some modesty. She'll thank me for it later, I bet, he thought.

"Don't." Hartogg's voice was loud in the silent room. "Mr Bennet, please move aside, sir. *Now*."

"Here." He held out the shirt, anticipating laying it around her shoulders. His fingers trembled as one part of his brain couldn't wait to touch her, and the other screamed at him to flee.

"Mr Bennet, something is *wrong*. I advise you not to move any more." Hartogg's voice raised a notch, and he edged in a little closer, the gun up and now pressed hard into his cheek.

Andy moved sideways again staying between the edgy Hartogg and Tania to avoid a reflex trigger pull making a fatal mistake. Tania's lips parted.

"*Help me.*" Her lips hadn't moved to form the words, and once again the sound had a strange bubbling quality. Her mouth didn't close, but now hung open, even wider.

"*Get the fuck out of my way!*" Hartogg's voice was a roar. "That's not –"

Andy leaned forward. "Yes, Tania?"

A black tendril shot from her open mouth. In the blink of an eye it flew past him, travelling the fifteen feet across the chamber floor to Hartogg and striking him in the chest. Andy's head whipped from Hartogg to Tania and back again. The SEAL was thrown backward, but not to the ground. Instead, he was suspended in the air, the black pipe having speared him in the chest. His rifle was out of his hands, and Hartogg gripped the thing impaling his body, his face contorted in pain.

"What are you doing?" Andy's brow creased in utter confusion, and his mind refused to make sense of what he was seeing. "What's happening?" He spun back to the woman. Her face was devoid of any emotion or sensation. It was as if she were an unresponsive machine that had somehow speared the SEAL like a fish, and was now...reeling him in.

Hartogg made agonized gurgling sounds. As Andy watched, the SEAL dropped one hand to reach for his sidearm and lift it free. Immediately, the glistening tendril in his chest widened. Hartogg dropped the gun, throwing his head back in agony. The sickening sound of ribs popping and splintering filled the dark room, even drowning out the SEAL's grunts of pain. Andy rushed to him, but the man was already gurgling blood.

Andy went to take hold of the arm-thick pipe, but saw that Hartogg already had his hands wrapped around it, and where he had gripped it, the black mass was now spreading over his fingers.

Andy's hands hovered, indecision almost causing a short-circuit in his mind.

"*Matt!*" he screamed. "*Major Abrams!*" His voice bounced away down the dark passageways without response.

He picked up the handgun, ran back and grabbed at Tania. She was at least four inches shorter than he was and he guessed he outweighed her by sixty pounds, but he might as well have been trying to tug on a block of stone. Then he felt the pain – where his hands grabbed at the woman, there was a burning sensation that felt both hot and toxic, like a marine jellyfish sting. Andy looked at Tania's face, and saw she was still facing Hartogg, but, grotesquely, one of her beautiful blue eyes had slid around to be positioned where her temple should be – and it was watching him.

Andy's heart thumped so hard in his chest, it made him feel physically sick. He let her go, and backed away, his head shaking. "*What's – happening – to you?*"

Another dark tendril of oily-looking flesh shot from a newly opened hole in her belly, this one wrapping around Andy's neck. It tightened immediately.

Andy's eyes watered from the pain and the despair. Just then, beautiful Tania burst apart, revealing the bloated creature inside.

Andy's fingers involuntarily tightened, and the gun went off in his hand. The shots and his last screams echoed along the ancient walls.

*

"Did you hear something?" Matt stopped and half turned.

Abrams came back and joined him, tilting his head.

"It's gone now," Matt said. "But it sounded like gunfire."

Abrams grimaced. "Maybe." He checked his watch. "If we head back now, it'll still take us fifteen minutes to reach them – whatever is happening will be long over by then. Don't worry about it. I trust Hartogg; that guy can deal with anything. We've got another few minutes, and then we can turn back. One way or the other, we'll find out what the noise was then." He waved Matt on. "Come on, let's finish our search...and pick up the pace."

They marched on, descending another few hundred feet as they went. Around them, they could now hear the shifting and cracking of rock as though they were moving along some deep fault line, and the heat and humidity became more unbearable with every step they took.

Matt laid his hand on the rock wall. "This is impossible. The earliest traces of modern man arrived here about thirty thousand years ago. But this system looks as old as anything in Egypt or Troy – this shouldn't be here."

"So who built it?" Abrams was shining his light deeper along the tunnel.

"I think we're about to find out." With his hand, Matt traced some more symbols in the stone. An image flashed into his mind of a dark sea, so still that it could have been black ice, except for the vapors hanging over its warm surface. Without knowing, he had the feeling it was fathomless, but that still, down in that inky liquid, something watched and waited.

Something far older than humankind, or anything else that ever lived on the planet.

"We're going the right way," he said.

"How do you know?" Abrams asked, turning and shining his light back at Matt's feet so as not to ruin his night vision.

Matt stared off into the dark, wondering that himself. "I don't know how I know, I just know."

"Well, might have been nice to make the announcement before we split up." Abrams looked at his watch. "Two more minutes." He turned and moved quickly along the edge of the wall, with Matt following. A hint of breeze sprang up, and in another minute, it seemed to increase.

"Something up ahead, I think." Abrams started to pick up the pace, and then in the next moment, he stopped dead, his arms pinwheeling in the air.

Matt lunged forward and grabbed him by the collar, holding on – the man's toes were already over the edge of a cliff. He dragged him back, the major falling onto his ass.

"*Jesus Christ.*" Abrams got to his feet, and leaned up against the wall.

The path had simply ended, and their tunnel had opened out into a larger cavern. The size was unknown, as their lights couldn't find either the other side, the roof or, coming to the edge again, the bottom.

"Wow." Matt put a hand over his face. Wafting up from somewhere deep down in the blackness was a foul breeze that once again reminded him of dead fish and bloated drying bodies on a beach.

"A fucking cliff." Abrams was still shaken, but he came forward and peered over the edge. "Hey, thanks, Matt. I knew you'd come in handy." He straightened. "I guess this is as far as we go."

Matt shook his head. "Look over there."

Starting beside them, and then set in along the wall, was a wide pathway carved directly into the stone. It circled along and downward, spiraling along the outside of the enormous vacant space, until it disappeared in the dark. The path crossed over in front of other darkened tunnels just like their own, each with the same strange alien shape that Matt had earlier noticed.

Abrams reached into a pouch and pulled free a glow stick, cracked it and then shook it. It phosphoresced a bright lemon yellow, illuminating the entire platform they stood upon. He held it out. "Get ready to start counting." He dropped it over the edge.

It fell, and fell, and eventually struck bottom as a tiny dot. "How long?" Abrams asked.

"Eleven seconds – what does that make it?" Matt asked.

"Not too bad," Abrams said. "Given things fall about thirty-two feet per second, and ignoring wind resistance, I put it at about three-fifty feet down."

He leaned out even further over the edge and looked down. "What the hell?" The dot of yellow light was moving.

"Well, someone is home," Matt said, feeling his stomach flip nervously at the thought of who, or what could be down there. "Could be Drummond...or maybe it's Adira," he said hopefully. "We should get Hartogg and Andy."

Abrams nodded. "Agreed; at least to see if they found anything." He went to turn away, but stopped. "Hang on; looks like we don't have to." He pointed.

About two hundred feet down and further along the wall, standing still as a post in one of the cave doorways, stood Andy and Tania, side-by-side, entwined, and naked. They stared back at them.

"What the hell is this?" Abrams growled in his throat.

"I thought she was dead." Matt felt confused, and recalled the piece of face in the upper tunnel. "Maybe it wasn't her."

He looked up and snorted. "Andy sure didn't waste any time." He waved, but neither Andy nor Tania returned the gesture. "Can they see us?" He lowered his arm. "If they've found Tania, maybe she can lead us to Drummond, and the Book."

"Where the hell is Hartogg?" Abrams lifted a small pair of field glasses and focused in on the pair. "You know, I've seen something like this before."

"Andy." Matt only raised his voice above a whisper, but it still bounced around in the huge cavern, and should have carried to the geologist. The young man didn't seem to hear, or if he did, still didn't acknowledge them. He just stood there, hugging Tania, and staring back as though he was a wax dummy.

"*Help me.*"

The words floated up to Matt and Abrams. Matt swung to the Major. "Did you hear that? That sounded like Tania."

Abrams was frowning as he pulled the glasses away from his face. "Oh no, god no…"

Matt started to jog down along the path.

"Hey." Abrams took off after him, keeping close to the wall.

Andy and Tania stood in the cave doorway, waiting. Both had turned to Matt as he approached them along the steps. Matt held his flashlight out, lifting it from the path to the naked pair. He noticed they hugged each other tightly, and seemed to glisten in his light beam.

Matt stopped a dozen feet back, breathing hard. They just stood watching him, or at least facing in his direction. Neither moved a muscle and he started to feel a slight rise of the hair on the back of his neck. "Hey buddy, how are you?"

"*Help me.*"

Matt turned to Tania. Was that her? he wondered. Though he had been looking at Andy, he hadn't noticed her speak. Her lips were slightly parted, but she could have been catatonic for all the expression she was giving him.

"Andy, where's Lieutenant Hartogg?" He took a few more steps.

Matt felt a hand ease down on his shoulder, and he nearly leaped off the walkway. "Shit." He spun. "Are you trying to give me a heart attack?" He turned back, shrugging Abrams's hand off.

Matt went to step closer, when Abrams grabbed him. "Don't...fucking...move." The major's hand was like a vice. "Professor, we need to back up, now."

"Huh?" Matt couldn't understand why Abrams wouldn't want to ask them where his SEAL was. He half turned. "But..." He saw the look on the major's face – determination, dread, and worst of all, fear. Abrams's eyes were wide and fixed on Andy.

Matt's head spun back, and he moved the beam of his light over the pair.

"Oh shit." He saw now what Abrams already knew. The pair weren't just intertwined in some sort of lover's embrace, but instead seemed to have melted together. Where their ribs, thighs and arms touched or overlapped, the flesh had merged, as if the skin, muscle and bone had melted together like some sort of protoplasmic wax.

"Oh." Matt took a single step back just as an explosion of thrashing black tendrils shot from the figure of the geologist – not just from him, but burst from his face down to his belly-button. He opened like a clamshell to disgorge a countless number of the whipping appendages.

Matt was covered instantly, and Abrams fell back, holding up an arm that was quickly enveloped in the greasy ropes that had also now shot from Tania.

Matt cried out as his skin burned. The touch of the revolting mass was like a combination of venomous sting and scalding hot-oil burn. He could see through the mess that Andy just stood there, arms by his side, face and gut split wide as more and more of the waving arms unloaded. He was a bottomless pit of the stuff.

"*Shoggoth!*" Abrams screamed.

The tendrils thickened, and then Matt started to feel them begin to work their way into his skin. Beside him, Abrams was almost totally enfolded, and his grunts and strains told him that the major wasn't going to go down without a fight.

More coils wrapped around Matt's neck, and he held tight to one and noticed a bulge form on the limb. The lump then popped open and Matt was horrified to see it was an eye. The bulb swiveled toward him, regarding him with the pitiless stare of a predator.

Jus then, there came a staccato burst of gunfire and the Tania half simply exploded in a geyser of black jelly. There came more gunfire, and Andy, who had been as immobile as a storefront mannequin, started to shiver and dance as holes appeared all over his naked body.

The greasy mesh that covered both Matt and Abrams fell away as another figure stepped out of the tunnel mouth, and let loose another burst from her machine gun directly into the rapidly expanding Andy. His human skin split away and he started to rapidly inflate. Dozens of mouths broke open all over the putrid bloated body, each one screaming in agony.

Adira strode toward it, lifted her leg and kicked what had so recently been Andy Bennet off the ledge. She watched it plummet into the darkness. Her teeth were bared, as her eyes followed it all the way to the bottom, where it exploded like a balloon full of toxic fluid.

She turned, her face ferocious, and approached Matt and Abrams. She held the gun dead level, its muzzle moving from Matt to the major. "Speak."

Abrams held up his hands. "Don't shoot, Captain Senesh. It really is us."

She turned the muzzle on Matt. "You too...*Now, quickly!*"

Matt opened his mouth, but no words would come. Instead, there were the whispers, chants and screams of an ancient race. There were images of burning lands, monstrous beings, and things whose size defied nature and sanity itself. The burning touch of the Shoggoth and its intrusion into his system, even only briefly, had united with the traces of the *Al Azif* he had absorbed, and they mushroomed into meaning.

"Last chance." Adira had moved the gun muzzle to Matt's face.

"I..." Matt got to his knees. "I'm okay." His vision cleared. "Adira...I'm okay. It's me."

She fired.

"*Fuck!*" Matt grabbed at his head. Blood ran from between his fingers.

"Okay, it *is* you." She lowered her gun and held out a hand.

"You shot me? You fucking *shot* me?" Matt looked at his bloody hand, his mouth hanging open in disbelief.

"Don't be a baby; it's just a graze." She shrugged. "I had to be sure."

Beside him, Abrams breathed a sigh of relief and wiped at his face.

Matt grabbed the outstretched hand and she pulled him up. Adira then turned to Abrams who was already on his feet and now vigorously rubbing his hands over his face.

"*Yech*." The major spat something onto the ground, and then wiped his hands on his pants. There were still glistening snail trails all over his body and in his hair.

Matt guessed he looked the same, but it was what was *inside* him that worried him the most. He winced as he dabbed at the red graze on his cheek.

"Salt, huh?" Adira cradled the gun in her arms. "I could smell it in among the nitro discharge – worked a treat – especially on a few *men of the cloth* I ran into."

"Salt...yeah." Abrams ran a hand up through his slick hair. "These things are closer to slugs than animals, so salt turns them to mush." He looked back at her. "Hartogg?"

"Dead," she said evenly. "I came across what was left of him in the cavern." She motioned to the cliff edge. "Captain Kovitz there, or what she had become, was waiting for you, Professor. Seems you're more a threat than they thought. Poor Andy was just another way to get close to you. They obviously didn't need Hartogg, so consumed...most of him."

She handed Matt a sidearm, and only then did he notice she had strapped on the man's knives, which were now hanging on her belt with her own guns. Her pockets bulged, and reaching in she pulled an extra magazine and handed it to him.

"You got twenty shots – choose your targets carefully. We've got a long way to go."

Abrams looked over the edge. "You've been down there?"

She walked to the edge of the walkway. She seemed to have no fear of the height. "Only part way. There are...things down there. More like Andy and Tania, but I saw other creatures even worse." She turned to Abrams and lifted her gun. "Let's hope they're also like slugs." She looked down. "In my years, many people have told me to go to Hell." She stepped back from the edge. "And now, I do."

*

General Decker put the phone down and sucked in a deep breath, his chest swelling in his uniform. He held it for a second or two and then eased it out, before turning to the room. Most of his Forward Command was assembled, waiting on his instructions.

Decker was now in charge, and his reporting line was to the Commander in Chief – the President, and *only* the President. The fate of the country was now in his hands.

"That was the President of the United States. By executive order, we have been given the green light. God bless America." There was a round of applause.

Decker lifted the phone again – it went straight through to bomber command. "Executive Order Fox-Delta-Orion-Victor-nine-nine-three-seven-two-one-nine – we have green light." He placed the phone back on its cradle and then switched on a large monitor on his wall. It showed a view from an air-force control tower, and a colossal plane beginning to move slowly down a runway.

Decker felt his heart swell with pride at the sight of the massive bombing arsenal – the B52 Stratofortress. The winged monster weighed nearly half a million pounds and could deliver its payload from fifty thousand feet. Which was just as well, as conservative estimates were that the twenty-megaton bomb would produce a cloud to forty-eight thousand feet with a significant EM-pulse.

Two F22 raptors would accompany the bomber to the drop zone to ensure air superiority over a clear flight path. Nothing would be allowed to get in the way of the flying fortress's mission. The raptors would peel away before the drop and rely on their 1.82-mach speed to get them well away from the magnetic disturbance or radioactive corruption. At least that was the plan – both pilots were volunteers, and knew the risks.

Decker was already counting down the seconds. It would take them thirty minutes to reach the drop site – *lock and load*, as they say. He sat down, his hands unconsciously crushing into fists. The men and women behind him, the noise, the heat, all of it, meant nothing compared to that plane and its destination.

*

Abrams stopped and peered over the edge of the path. They had been winding around the outside of the pit, moving quickly, and descending ever lower. Many smaller tunnels finished at their path and, though they were empty, Abrams had the impression that someone or something lurked back in the darkness. He could have thrown another of his glow sticks into any of them, but the truth was, if they were being left alone, then he'd leave them alone. Still, the skin on his neck crawled with warnings as they went past every one of them.

He looked down at his watch once again, and grunted. "It's time. If General Decker has received approval, then he'll be on his bombing run."

Matt stopped and stared for a moment, but then just nodded.

"Good." Adira scanned the pit's bottom and then half turned. "If everything is obliterated, then we won't care any more. Until then; we go on."

Chapter 25

The raptors flew over the drop site, taking several images and then peeling away, stepping on the gas and leaving nothing but vapor trails. Decker looked at the aerial shots as they appeared on his screen. The slimy mess that had been the verdant Mammoth National Park was now like an anthill, crawling with the amoebic Shoggoth monstrosities.

The General ground his teeth, feeling an almost physical pain as he saw the lines of people being led into the holes in the ground. He couldn't save them – they didn't yet have enough ammunition to mount a successful ground operation against the Shoggoth. These people were already lost; all he could do was stop them from suffering.

"I'm sorry," he whispered as he got slowly to his feet. Then his jaws clenched. "But I promise every one of you that you will have your vengeance."

"*Counting down to drop.*" The laconic voice of the pilot of the Stratofortress came in as he began his final run. "Five, four, three, two, one…payload away. Returning to base."

The aerial shot was taken from maximum height, where the national park was just a field of green, with a black smudge as a target in the distance – with a drop from fifty thousand feet, the amount of forward movement of the bomb would ensure it travelled many miles before reaching its mark. Military technology allowed a calculated precision that would mean a strike within a dozen feet of what they wanted to hit.

The big plane turned like a super tanker in the air and started to wing away. It would take several minutes for the bomb to detonate, as it was designed to be the biggest bunker buster in the history of mankind. Its goal was to penetrate deep into the bowels of the massive monstrosity making its way to the surface.

Decker held his breath.

"Detonation."

The rear cameras of the plane whited out and they lost their images. It was just as well, as no human eye could withstand the white-hot heart of nuclear detonation. He turned to look at the feed from the banks of seismometers dotted throughout the state to detect earth movement. The lines measuring the seismic waves barely registered anything above a normal background range.

"What the hell?" Decker frowned. He had expected the machines to scribble widely as they either registered the massive hammer-blow to the earth, or the sensors were destroyed – the digital feeds registered neither result.

"What's going on here? What just happened?" He turned to the room and was met with confused stares.

"*Goddamnit*, give me the VELA feed, *now*."

Decker's screen flipped to high-altitude images from the satellite, and he drilled down to the black stain over the Kentucky landscape. He had expected to see a towering mushroom cloud of heat, and the debris of the earth, the burrower beneath, and vaporized human souls rising into the atmosphere. There should have also been a massive shock wave obliterating everything in a giant ring growing out from the detonation point. Decker knew that a nuclear detonation of that size would have achieved temperatures of around 180 million degrees, about ten times that of the surface of the Sun. Everything should have been slag. Ground zero, the melt zone, should be nothing but a crater like something only seen on another world.

But instead, it was as before. Decker leaned forward, squinting – not quite. The ground moved and heaved, like a monstrous blanket stirring with a waking sleeper beneath.

"Did we not get burn? He spun left and right. "Well? Talk to me."

A military technician at another bank of screens shook his head. "No, it detonated. It just..." he stood back "...I don't know...but the device definitely triggered."

"Jesus Christ." Decker felt like his head was going to explode. "Give me the VELA feed from the time of the drop – back it up."

In a few seconds, the data froze and then swapped back to a silent view from space. A timer at the bottom of the screen counted down from the bomb release until it reached zero – impact. The digital counter continued, but this time it measured progress as the massive B83 bunker buster drilled its way down through the rock and soil. But just when it was milliseconds away from its target depth, the ground below it appeared to open. There was a surge as something huge grotesquely blossomed like a gargantuan tentacled flower, and then the counter stopped. There was an orange glow, and the oily smudge of the underground monster visibly swelled, but then, nothing.

Decker fell back heavily into his chair. "It...swallowed it." He leaned forward and clawed his fingers up through his hair. He looked up into the screen, now back to real-time, and his mouth dropped open. "Oh god no." As he watched the earth became a window into Hell. The massive stain was still there, closer and now with substance. A miles-wide head could be made out, and surrounding it, titanic arms moved beneath a surface that was still as yet unbroken. But what horrified Decker the most was the giant single eye the size of a city block.

General Decker opened his mouth, ready to issue his next orders. Instead, he stayed silent, his mouth hanging open for several seconds. He slowly closed it. He had no more options.

Chapter 26

Adira was first down at the base of the enormous pit. With the small lights they each had, there was no way to really judge its size; they could only estimate based on the winding stone steps they had come down. About a hundred feet away, there was the faint shine of the dying glow stick. Its lemon yellow was incongruous on the black stones of the cavern floor.

Matt took a single step before a muffled boom, like the beating of a titan's drum, thundered down through the huge cave. He, Adira and Abrams were thrown flat to the ground, as car-sized boulders hit the stone floor around them, followed by showers of dust and debris.

The tumultuous echoes pounded away into the deeper tunnels, and the trio stayed down, hugging the stone floor.

Abrams was up first, then Matt on one knee first, before getting warily to his feet. He dusted himself down.

"We're still here." He looked confused. "The detonation was a long way away, but still, we shouldn't be."

"And if *we're* still here..." Adira stayed down "...then so is our problem."

Abrams coughed as the rock dust created a fog of fine silica particles that floated in the beam of their lights. He looked

316

down at Adira, still prone on the stones, one side of her face pressed to the floor.

"Must have only been a partial detonation. You okay?"

She shushed him, and held up a palm to them. Both men froze, waiting.

She sprung to her feet and wiped her face. "The floor; it's hot, *very hot*." She wiped her cheek again. "And there's movement below us – grinding and sliding, like something heavy being dragged across rocks."

"Must be the deeper effects of the nuke." Abrams shook his head. "Can't be Cthulhu, we're miles away from Mammoth Park."

"We don't know that," Matt said. "We have no idea what the true physical form of this thing really is. Sure, we're a long way from where we think it will emerge, but for all we know the thing stretches below the earth like some sort of giant worm and spreads for miles – hundreds of miles."

Matt shut his eyes. "*And the leviathan that is Cthulhu, the oldest of the Old Ones, will rise. The Earth will crush, and the seas drain as the flesh of mortal beasts will be but paste for its bowels.*"

"What the hell was that?" Abrams asked reaching out to steady Matt, who was about to topple over. "Was that in the book?"

"Yes and no. I mean it was in the book all the time, I just didn't know it because I couldn't read it," Matt said, steadying himself.

"The symbols...now you can read the symbols," Adira said.

Matt nodded. "I think so."

"*Now* you get it?" Abrams asked incredulously.

"Must have been the Shoggoth's touch." He looked across at them. "I can feel it now – the celestial convergence – it's like waves of energy, pulling at everything on the planet, drawing these things from below the earth. It's all focused on this place, right here, right now." Matt pointed. "We need to go lower and find the gates...and then find the Book. The answers must be hidden in its pages – I must see them again."

"I thought you didn't need it?" Adira asked.

"The symbols: I didn't read them all. I skipped most of them. I couldn't understand them so they were useless to me – that was then. It's like some sort of Rosetta Stone, converting the language of the Old Ones into a physical form. These things respond to sound, and the words when spoken create that sound."

"The Celestial Speech; the language of the gods?" Abrams asked.

"Not of our god. This is what Abdul Alhazred found out. He also managed to decipher the words. There are the words of worship that smooth its path and let it know that now is the right time for it to rise, and...feed again. There are also mystical locks, and words are the keys." Matt wiped at his brow, feeling like he had a fever coming on. "There must also be words that do the opposite. Tell it that it's *not* time – they *must* be there."

"And these words can send it back?" Adira asked.

"I don't know for sure, but if it can be called, then it can somehow be denied. Alhazred must have said something to stop Cthulhu rising." Matt grimaced. "But by now, we might be too late to send it back. It has almost broken through, and once it does, then it's all over for us."

Abrams raised his gun, ejecting the clip, checking it, and then smacking it back in before re-holstering. "If the Book can help, then let's go get it."

"Wait." Matt felt more images slide greasily into his mind. "Drummond is waiting for us...and he's not alone."

"As far as I'm concerned, Drummond is just another slug." Adira looked along the barrel of the HK-MP5N, as though lining the businessman up in her sights. She pointed. "That way." The light from Hartogg's barrel-mounted flashlight illuminated huge glyphs carved into the curved stone lintel of a train-tunnel sized archway. Adira lowered her gun and looked to Matt.

"What does it say?"

"*I am forever.*" Matt snorted. "*Worship me.*"

"Not fucking likely," Abrams said.

Adira smiled humorlessly. "Hmm, vanity? A mortal weakness we perhaps can use." She headed for the tunnel, gun held loosely in her arms, her finger on the trigger. "Let us meet these vain gods, and introduce ourselves." She turned to Abrams, her face severe. "But remember, Charles Drummond is mine."

Chapter 27

Captain Gerry Hensen looked up at the sky, feeling tears dry on his cheeks. The moon, huge and yellow, had risen, and was only a few hours from reaching its zenith. The darkness and the pull of the celestial convergence were reshaping the world – tides were lower than they'd ever been, the ground was hot to walk upon, the air smelled weird, and there was a gentle tug he could feel at his metal fillings and even on the bones in his body – it all felt wrong.

He looked along the dark street – it was all so quiet now. The intial wave of panic had overwhelmed police stations, councils, hospitals, and anywhere else that could possibly provide protection or refuge. But there was no such thing any more.

People had initially fought back, but their bravery was rewarded by them simply vanishing. They'd left then, by road, sea, on foot, but only ended up being trapped in long lines of stalled traffic, or in their march to safe havens, encountering people coming the other way. Those who were stuck outside at night just proved easy pickings for the things that now owned the darkness.

There were few people on the streets, and those who remained huddled inside their houses were locked in rooms, basements, or even garages. But these refuges were not secure, because the things that boiled up from every subway, drain or cellar were able to reach in under locked doors, and even thread themselves through keyholes.

The army had deployed, and those that had only been issued standard ammunition managed to keep the Shoggoth at bay for a few minutes at best, before they too were overwhelmed and either eaten or converted to become the next lump of amoebic flesh to terrorize the neighborhood.

As a final insult to the human race, men, women and children were now being herded together, guarded by rings of the massive blobs of protoplasmic flesh. And *herded* was the appropriate term – Captain Hensen had dated a cattle farmer's daughter when he was in high school, and one weekend he had visited her family's ranch in the holidays. This is what the people gathered there reminded him of – cattle, in pens, awaiting shipment to the abattoir.

Hensen's squad were some of the lucky ones – they had taken delivery of the compacted salt ordnance – the hardened salt rounds worked a treat, clearing the disgusting creatures from their path. Those that were too slow and took a hit either exploded or melted away, leaving nothing but foul-smelling black puddles of goo.

They'd freed hundreds of people, and many were now being led back to secure camps. But in their eyes was shock and horror. As in all of the guarded fields Hensen and his squad came across, the people inside this ring of monsters were listless and resigned to their fate. They had obviously seen what happened to those who tried to rebel or escape. He knew what would happen as well – he'd seen it with his own eyes – the horror of the things feeding.

Hensen wiped his eyes and held up a fist to signal the next move to his soldiers. For every ten souls they freed, there were thousands more being consumed, or led down into the bowels of the Earth to suffer whatever fate these monstrosities from Hell had in store for them.

*

Adira held up her hand, causing the small group to halt. "You hear that? Smell it?"

"For the last few minutes – water lapping…" Abrams sniffed deeply "…salt water. But we're miles from the ocean."

"Miles from any ocean we know of," Matt said. Up ahead he saw that the tunnel looked different.

"Wait here." He approached slowly.

"What is it?" Adira lifted her gun.

The air shimmered in front of him, like a curtain hanging across the passageway. He held out his hand. His fingertips touched the wall of distortion and passed through it. The air swirled around his fingertips as if it was a sheet of floating oil.

He pulled his hand back, looking at his fingers, rubbing them together – there was nothing on them. Matt leaned forward, pushing his face into the swirling wall – beyond he saw a watery landscape with a twilight atmosphere. He pulled back, shaking his head.

"In there is not, ah, *here* any more." He stepped back. "In there is not really our world at all. It is some other place. Perhaps another dimension entirely." He stared at the shimmering barrier, but his vision was turned inward as his mind worked. "I think this is why these things can exist below the earth, but not be found. That world, *their world*, is beyond the physical, and maybe partway between here and some sort of metaphysical existence – what some would call *the beyond*." He turned. "And what others would call Hell."

"You mean it's always been here, below this building?" Abrams asked

"No, no. I think this place that Cthulhu comes from has always been in the same place, but the *entrance* is different. This time it's America; last time it was the Middle East. It might even open below the ocean."

"It's the planetary lineup, the convergence, isn't it?" Abrams asked.

"Yes; this place only exists in our imagination, or race memory, until it *wants* to be seen." Matt nodded. "The convergence is the catalyst, like a chronological lock and key that lines up a maze so we can enter."

"So the gateway only exists while the convergence is taking place. What happens when this convergence, the planetary lineup, starts to break away?"

Matt smiled without humor. "Then I think whatever happens, we need to be in and out before the convergence concludes or we could be trapped in there forever."

"Then what are we waiting for?" Adira stepped through.

Matt grinned and shook his head at the woman. "Sure, after you, Shrinking Violet."

Abrams was next through the shimmering curtain. Matt briefly looked over his shoulder and then followed.

*

Matt almost fell to his knees from the heat. While it had been extremely warm and humid as they descended the pit, beyond the shimmering border it was like an oven.

"Oh god." Matt pushed his hair back of his face. "It's got to be one-twenty degrees in here."

Together they stood on the shore of a dark beach under a sky of blackness. It was impossible to tell whether there was a cavern roof overhead or if they had instead crossed over into another dimension that had a starless sky stretching away into infinity.

There was a body of water before them; its far edges were hidden in darkness so any other landfall could not be made out.

Abrams stood with his hands on his hips. "Lake or ocean?"

Matt walked a few paces towards the water. "Whatever it is, it's extremely salty; I can smell it."

The surface of the oily water was only at times still. At other times the surface bubbled and rose as small waves lumped up from hidden things that moved beneath its surface. Far out from the shore, perhaps at its center, the water, or whatever it was, rose in a huge column many miles wide, and disappeared into the air. It twisted and pulsed with a strange life.

Matt turned to look along the cliff walls surrounding them. In the far distance he could see multi-colored waterfalls emptying from many caves on the cliff walls for as far as he could make out – there could have been hundreds of them emptying into the dark water.

Matt frowned. "Can anyone else hear that? Weird sounds, like howling wind, or...voices?" He turned slowly. "The voices of the damned in Hell."

Abrams nodded. "I hear it – yeah, like wind blowing, but there's not a breath of it down here." He panned slowly. "I have no idea what it could be."

"Shit." Adira jumped aside and pointed her rifle at the ground.

What looked like a long-legged trilobite had lifted itself from the coal-dark sand and proceeded to scuttle toward the water.

"Just like in the terrorists' camp," Matt said.

The thing only managed to wade in about a foot before something rose up from out of the depths and, using a long talon, speared it, and then silently pulled it back out into deeper water.

"Jesus." Matt backed away from the water.

"You're right, this is *not* our world any more," Adira said softly.

Abrams switched off his flashlight. "Save your lights: there's enough illumination for us to see." He swiveled. "Nothing, no plants, no mosses, nothing growing at all."

Adira snorted. "You must have missed that thing in the water."

"No, I mean, there's nothing as the basis of the food chain – no sun, so no life should be able to exist," Abrams responded.

"I wish that were true," Matt said. "There are other forms of energy that can cause life to spring up. Deep-sea thermal vents are one. We have no idea exactly what's below that water."

"And I, for one, have no interest in finding out," Adira added.

"Me either." Matt pointed into the distance. "We need to go there – close to the first waterfall – I think that could be a structure." He frowned, trying to understand the weird fluid in the falls. There was a constant stream falling from the caves to splash into the dark water beside the massive barriers. The sea boiled and frothed as it was struck.

Abrams lifted his compact field glasses. "Well I'll be damned. Looks like doors."

They walked quickly, their feet sinking into the dark granules. As they neared, they could see now that set into the cliff wall stood a massive pair of red granite gates. Each of the doors would have towered half a mile in height and twice that across.

Matt stopped. "*Gates of red granite so huge they could hold back an army.* Remember Alhazred's poem." There were raised glyphs carved into their mighty edifices. "It was all true."

They could just make out a pinprick of light at the base of the portal.

"That light – it's got to be Drummond," Matt said.

"He's waiting for us." Abrams lifted field glasses to his eyes again.

"If he's expecting us, he'll be ready for us," Adira added.

"Can you see anything?" Matt asked.

"No, no movement." Abrams responded evenly and turned just as beside them the sea thrashed: something heavy rose and fell back below the surface. Matt had the impression of a whale breaching and then dropping back, but doubted it would have been anything as benign as one of the giant sea mammals.

Cautious now, they edged along the rock face bordering the sea – sometimes there were expanses of sand, and others the beach nearly disappeared entirely, forcing them to walk within inches of the inky water. Together they moved in a crouch, shoulders hunched, as if expecting something to land upon them at any moment.

As they hurried forward, Matt was sure he felt things shifting beneath his feet. He ignored it, hoping it was nothing more than movement in the silky grains.

"We've got company," Adira said, matter of factly.

"Where?" Abrams had his gun in a two-handed grip, and had it pointed at the water, and then spun to aim it behind them. "I've got nothing back here."

"It's not up here, it's below us – keeping pace with us under the sand." Adira was keeping the barrel of her gun pointed at the ground.

"Under us?" Matt asked the question, but he already believed her. He also had his gun ready, and now pointed down at the sand. He had felt something under his feet before, and now, when he concentrated, he was certain he could still feel some sort of muscular contractions going on. It was if something was sliding, lengthening and contracting, worm-like, below him – and he didn't think there was just one of them.

As from a signal given, more of the long-legged trilobites lifted from the sand and started scuttling toward the dark water. Whatever Adira, Matt and Abrams could feel, the bugs also sensed, and it seemed they were smart enough to get the hell out of there.

Matt spun at a soft, sticky sound behind him. He was in time to see something rise from the dark sand like a weird plant. It bloomed, opening a bulb-like end. There were no eyes, or any sensory organs he could see, just a puckered hole that was tightly closed.

Adira fired a quick burst at the thing, and as if on a spring it was quickly pulled back beneath the ground. The same sound came again, repeated from a different position, and more of the worm-like stalks rose slowly around them, like dark blooms opening to an invisible sun, the petals shivering as if tasting the air.

In front of one of the worm-flowers, a slow trilobite moved quickly around the small forest of stalks. The bloom end slammed down on its back like a hand, and stuck there. Then the hapless creature was dragged, mewling, below the ground.

"Shit." Abrams fired on a few of them, but whether he hit them or not wasn't clear, as they disappeared so quickly it was hard to tell if there was any damage. More of the creatures rose to take their place.

"Save your ammunition," Adira said, while keeping her gun up.

Like rippling waves, Matt saw that the sand was lumping and rolling toward them – they were attracting more and more of the creatures. He turned to Adira. "There're too many of them and more are coming. We need to be away from here." When he turned back, it was to stare directly into the face, if that's what it was, of one of the muscular segmented worms. Once again it bloomed open, the edges of its petals shivering slightly. The puckered hole opened inches from Matt's nose, and he saw rows of tiny, needle-sharp teeth, all pointed inward and disappearing down into its throat. This was a mouth designed for gripping and holding on, something Matt had no intention of experiencing. He fired point blank.

He hit it; he had to have at that range. But the thing still shot forward and momentarily gripped his shoulder. The pain was excruciating. He punched at it, and tugged, but the neck was like a cross between leather and rubber, giving a little, but not breaking away. It suddenly let go, and withdrew below the soil, taking with it a small chunk of his flesh.

"*Ah, fuck it!*" Matt gripped his upper arm, dripping blood onto the sand. The effect was instantaneous. The ground began to boil beneath him.

"Run." Adira charged, putting her shoulder into him, to barge Matt forward. She aimed her gun down at the sand and loosed a dozen rounds into the agitated surface at their feet. She then turned and aimed at a few of the trilobites still making their way back to the water, and fired again, killing some and injuring several who bucked and flipped on the dark grains. The movement was enough to attract the worm-like predators. Adira ran hard, dragging Matt along with her.

Abrams followed, turning to fire back at the feeding frenzy, and yelling over his shoulder as he pulled the trigger. "This place is a nightmare."

"And it will be like this on the Earth's surface for the next few thousand years unless we send this thing back."

As they neared the speck of light, the water beside them at first smoothed and then lumped again – not just in one or two places, but the entire surface became uneven, as if there was something under the water that couldn't break through. Matt felt his heart race. "I don't like the look of this."

"Forget it," Abrams yelled. "Unless whatever that is comes out, it's not our problem." The major caught up with Matt, shielding him on the water side, with Adira on the other.

They slowed when the small fire was in sight. "I don't understand; the red gates should be open if Cthulhu is free. It doesn't make sense." Matt turned one way and then the other. There was still no one at the fire.

He stopped. For the first time he could hear clearly the noise of the waterfall. Underlying the constant splash of liquid was another sound. Matt frowned as he concentrated. He stared for a moment and then backed up a step.

"Don't stop; what is it? What do you see?" Abrams stopped with him, looking around.

"Give me your field glasses." Matt held out his hand, dread in his gut.

Abrams handed them over, and then he and Adira, kept watch for any danger while Matt lifted them to his eyes.

It was as he imagined. *No, it was worse than he imagined.* The sound they could hear: it wasn't just some strange noise caused by rushing water or air movement against deep cavern walls. Instead, it was wailing, crying, screams of horror, terror, anguish and hopelessness. The waterfall wasn't water at all. It was thousands of tumbling bodies, people, falling through space.

"Cries of the damned." Matt lowered the glasses. "When the Shoggoth have been herding the people below ground, this is where they have been bringing them."

He felt sick to the stomach. A living cascade of people voicing their last screams as they jumped or were pushed from the rim of the giant cave mouth about half a mile up on the cliff wall face.

Matt could see that there were hundreds of these falls, and he followed the stream of people from one of them down to where they fell to the dark water, and where the thrashing was occurring. Whatever was in that dark ocean was either consuming them or converting them, as no heads bobbed back to the surface. Instead they were totally swallowed up and disappeared. But maybe only vanishing as what they once were ... the lumps Matt had seen before. They couldn't have been just some freak phenomenon. The dark ocean was coated in protrusions like dark boils trying to burst free– there were thousands of them, hundreds of thousands. Perhaps they would soon be newly birthed as Shoggoths.

"It's people," Matt said softly.

Adira and Abrams stared.

"Not an ocean." Matt staggered back. "And not water at all. That dark mass is part of Cthulhu itself." Matt felt tears of futility on his cheeks. Perhaps the Shoggoths, monstrous things to us, were just like some sort of tiny symbiote that existed upon the Great Old One. As it woke, so did they, dropping from its huge body like some sort of horrifying lice.

He felt a building rage in his gut. "A nightmare?" He looked up at Abrams and wiped his face. "No, this truly is Hell."

Adira made a noise deep in her throat that sounded like a growl. "I have heard men and women die before. This is what it sounds like." She turned away from the stream of humans falling to their death. "Don't look at it. We cannot save them, but perhaps we can stop many more suffering the same fate. Let us finish what we started."

But Matt couldn't tear his eyes away. The people, human beings, the rulers of the world, reduced to little more than a stream of meat for some near immortal beast that lived in this underworld. As he watched he could make out strange creatures like a cross between lizards and spiders, dotted with bulging eyes, enormous in size, crawling along the sheer rock face, and letting long tongues unfurl, dipping them into the falling mass of humanity to lick up some of the bodies and then scuttle back to cling to the rock and digest their easy prize.

Matt felt the victims' hopelessness and would have cried out in despair himself but he felt a strong tug at his arm, and so shook his head to clear away the dark thoughts. Adira was right; it was too late now for these people.

"The doors." Adira motioned to the massive red granite gates.

At their base, four figures now stood. One was unmistakably Charles Drummond; a second was easily a foot taller with a cowl pulled over its head; and before them was what looked to be a pair of children.

"Come; here is where we settle this." Adira ran toward the odd group, Matt and Abrams following. The dark sand made a dry squeaking beneath their feet, and Matt breathed hard, working overtime to try and shut out the cacophony of tormented wails that surrounded them.

Abrams had his gun up, and Adira had the muzzle of her assault rifle pointed dead center at Drummond as they came to within fifty feet of the foursome. Matt still couldn't make out who or what it was with the cowl up over its head, but the smaller figures were unmistakably girls, no more than ten or eleven, perhaps even twins. They wore matching dirty pyjamas and clung to each other, their faces streaked with tears, and their garments with blood.

Drummond held up a hand. "Welcome." He flashed his luminescent smile. "Professor Matthew Kearns, Major Joshua Abrams, and of course, the warrior woman, Captain Adira Senesh. I'm so glad you could all make it...this far."

Adira and Abrams spread to either side of the figures. Matt saw the girls' eyes light up, perhaps with something like hope. One mouthed a word to him – *Help*.

Matt stayed stony-faced – he'd heard that plea before, and it hadn't been from a human.

Drummond waved an arm around. "Don't be so gloomy. Yes, it *is* hot, and yes it *is* dark, and sure, it's very noisy." He grinned. "But these are all small prices to pay to be witness to a new dawn...or perhaps a very ancient one. Cthulhu rises, the Great Old One. His physical form is taking shape as we speak. At the peak of the planetary alignment, his physical form will combine with his spiritual essence, and then a page will be turned on this world." Drummond smiled apologetically. "Humankind's turn is over." He shrugged. "And as well as the human sheep, so will go the real sheep, and the cattle, elephants, whales, and just about anything that proves a good meal." His smile widened.

"Aren't you forgetting something?" Matt asked. "You're one of the sheep. What do you think you'll get out of this? You'll be president, king, is that right? That's your plan, to be king of a graveyard?"

Drummond's smile never faltered. "Better to rule in Hell than serve in Heaven. Isn't that how the saying goes?"

"Who the fuck is that?" Abrams pointed his gun at he huge figure in the cowl.

Drummond looked at the tall being beside him, and then to Abrams. "Please, show some respect. This is the Father; he is the gatekeeper, and a personal attendant to the Great Old One. Some courtesy and deference is in order."

"How about we show our respect by putting some holes in him." Adira raised her gun.

Drummond reached across and dragged one of the girls in front of himself. "Careful you don't hit these little beauties." He stroked the hair of one of them. "I chose them myself. They were going to be a delicacy for the Father here, but I thought they might come in handy during our...discussions."

"You want to negotiate?" Matt said. His head throbbed and he couldn't take his eyes off the tall being beside Drummond. He knew it watched him back just as intently.

"Negotiate? Does the plankton negotiate with the whale?" He shook his head. "You're already dead, and just don't know it." He grabbed the collar of one of the girls and shook her roughly, causing her to scream and dance like a puppet in his hands. She cried and covered her face. Her sister reached out to her, clinging on, and was also shaken.

"But if you really want to play a game for the last few minutes of your lives, then so be it. Let's see, hmm, you can have one of the girls if you give up your guns." He waited a few seconds, and then shook the child even harder. "Come on, throw them down. It's a good deal – flesh for steel."

"Both girls," Matt said evenly.

"Ah, well, for both, I'll want something else…I want one of you." He looked directly at Matt. "You."

Matt felt his legs go weak.

Abrams shook his head. "Nope, it's me or nothing."

Drummond grinned. "Ah, the sacrifice of the soldier patriot." He looked across to the tall figure. No words passed between them, but Matt knew they spoke just the same.

Drummond shrugged. "Okay, we'll play…for now. After all, we'll be having all of you soon anyway."

Abrams looked at Adira, who shook her head. Her gun muzzle drifted across to the tall figure, and then travelled down to the girls.

"Why would we want a pair of your disgusting Shoggoths? We've already had the pleasure of their company." Adira's eyes carried a challenge. "I killed them both."

Drummond's head rocked back and he roared with laughter. "Oh, you mean Tania?" He laughed even harder, and then he wiped his eyes. "Put on a bit of weight, didn't she?" He grinned again. "She was a good soldier. Enlisted Mr Andy Bennet…but you know that now."

Drummond's mouth curled in a delighted smile. "I assure you these two are still human." From behind him the tall figure lifted a hand and ran a talon down the cheek of one of the girls, who screamed in pain and fright. Blood dripped to her chin.

"Shoggoth don't bleed, don't feel pain, don't feel fear, and only lust for food and to serve the Great Cthulhu. These two are human all right." He waited, then shook the girl again, treating her like a rag doll, to draw forth another shriek of terror. He looked to Adira. "She's very frightened."

Adira didn't flinch, her gun pointed directly at the cowled figure. "I don't care, killing them might be the most humane thing."

Drummond's smile faltered.

Adira's gun muzzle edged up toward the dark cowl. "Let's see what's under there."

Drummond picked the girl up and stepped in front of the tall figure. He used one hand to reach around and grip her throat. He squeezed, hard. She started to choke.

"First one is for you then." Adira's face was like stone.

"Stop." Matt held up his hand, and then pushed Adira's gun up. "We're better than them."

Adira glared, and simply brought the gun around again. "I don't want the girls; I want the Book."

"The *Al Azif*? You want that…now?" Drummond threw his head back and roared with laughter. "To do what?"

A sound started up, deep, bubbling, and it took Matt a while to work out what it was. The cowled figure was also laughing. It leaned forward and spoke again to Drummond.

Drummond cocked his head to listen, but this time Matt heard, and understood, every word.

The words have already been spoken, and the final seals removed. It is of no use to them now. This amuses me; taunt them.

Drummond snorted and nodded. "We will *consider* your offer. Your weapons and the soldier, for the girls *and* the Book."

The cowled figure drew the tome from his robes and held it out. Matt noticed the hand was little more than a slimy flipper that ended in sharp talons. He felt his gorge rise.

Drummond grinned and took the Book from the flipper, and held it up. "A deal is done." He shook the girl one-handed; her face was now blue. "The weapons, please...on the ground." He looked at the child. "Oops, she's going...going...going..."

Abrams looked at Adira and nodded. He threw his handgun onto the dark sand. Matt did the same with his. Adira's fingers looked unwilling to release their grip.

Matt turned to her. "It's what we came for. We have to risk it."

She growled and then tossed the machine gun onto the sand.

"And the others, please," Drummond said softly.

Adira threw four more guns down.

Drummond's eyebrows shot up. "Well, well, you really are a one-woman war, aren't you?"

The cowled figure leaned forward again to speak in his strange bubbling tongue. Drummond listened and then threw the girl to the side. Her sister scuttled over to comfort her, and then quickly dragged her away toward the cliff wall.

Drummond held out the book. "You stupid bugs. What would you do with this anyway? It's too late: the seals are broken. Where can you go? What can you do? Even if you made it back to the surface, the world you know will have ceased to exist. You are not even specks of dust compared to the Old Ones. They have slumbered below the earth and between the slim sheets of reality for nearly as long as this tiny world has existed. They have dined on the massive saurians, the megafauna, and billions of other forms of life who rose to believe they were the rulers of the surface domain." Drummond's face was contemptuous. "You are but caretakers, squatters, until the time is right for the Great Cthulhu – and that time is *now*."

He stepped to the side. "Show them, Father. Show them the true face of beauty."

Beside him, there came the bubbling viscose sound again, and finally the cowled figure reached up and pulled back the cloth.

Matt heard Adira draw in a breath at the revelation of the creature's form. It was the first time he had ever heard the woman issue even the tiniest sound of trepidation.

Drummond looked over his shoulder, and then back to Matt, Adira and Abrams. His eyes shone with a manic love. "I'm so rude; of course you haven't been formally introduced. I'd like you all to meet the first Father of us all." He clasped his hands together like a teenager meeting a pop star, and he beamed up at the thing.

An octopus, Matt thought. The creature defied reality. It gave the impression of being bipedal with a vaguely humanoid shape, but now that Matt looked closely, he couldn't actually see where the feet touched the ground, or if there were feet at all. As he stared, the thing actually looked *embedded into* the dark sand as if it grew up out of it. Upon its shoulders, there sat a bulbous, pulsating sack with two lidless, yellow eyes that stared dispassionately at the three of them. There was no nose: just a couple of slits for air holes. Below that, the real madness began, with a nest of tendrils and suckered tentacles that writhed and squirmed. In among the coiling mess, there was a dark hole that opened wide.

"Behold the beauty of our kingdom. You will serve us as Shoggoth or your meat will be our food." It lifted an arm, and at first Matt thought it was going to point back along the way they had come, but instead, the dripping paddle-shaped hand extended long slimy fingers. To his horror, the fingers kept coming, shooting forward, splitting in two, and two again, then thickening to become branches. The first dark branch scooped up their guns and flung them away toward the rock face. Then the other appendages came for Matt.

Matt held up his hands across his face, but Adira never flinched. She just turned side on into a wide-legged combat stance and let one of her own hands flash out. The compressed salt dagger shot at the tall being nearly faster than the eye could follow, burying itself into the center of its disgusting face.

"Eat that." Her face was calm as the whip snapped back from them. There was a horrifying eldritch scream that made Matt's hair prickle on his scalp.

Drummond looked panicked, and the hand holding the book snapped back. "What have you done?" He looked from the creature, whose face was now a knot of massed tentacles as they pulled at the dagger's hilt, and then back to Adira Senesh. "He will be angry."

For the first time Adira's lips curled up into a smile. "So, he *can* be hurt." The Mossad agent spun, picking up momentum, as she crossed toward Drummond almost faster than the eye could follow. When she within three feet of him, she finished her turn, and in her hand was the long carving knife.

"*Ha!*" she yelled as it flashed down with blinding speed and great force across Drummond's wrist. The limb parted and fell to the ground, the fingers still clamped around the Book.

Abrams had sprinted to retrieve the guns, and Matt leaped for the Book at the creature's feet, a seed of confidence taking root in his chest.

But then the unthinkable happened. One of the tentacles drew forth the dagger and dropped it to the ground. Black blood oozed, but the writhing settled and the yellow eyes glared balefully at Adira. The Father seemed to inflate slightly.

Drummond grimaced in either shock or fear, clutching a wrist that spurted dark blood onto the even darker sand. "Heal me, Father, heal me." He spun to scream at the trio. "You insects; how dare you?! When I am king, I will have you tortured for the rest of your lives. I will torture you, then heal your wounds, and then torture you again and again and again and again."

The Father seemed to grow another foot taller. The hand started to rise again.

Abrams distributed their guns, and Adira immediately shouldered the rifle, a grim smile on her face.

"We need to get the hell out of here," Matt yelled, backing up, but flipping through the Book hurriedly, attempting to catch up to where he had stopped trying to understand the symbols. He read quickly while keeping one eye on the creature growing before them.

The Father pointed again, this time the long boneless fingers dripped with black blood. "You will be stripped of your flesh, and boiled in the acid bath of my belly for eternity. But first, I will make you watch as I consume your world. By the time we have finished with the planet, there will be nothing left save the worms in the earth."

Drummond half turned, his bloody stump still extended. "Except for my kingdom. There will be subjects and some servants in my kingdom: you promised."

The yellow eyes shifted to the man, and the writhing alien face carried a look of such derision that Matt very clearly saw the moment Charles Drummond finally seemed to realize where he stood in Old One's plans. His arms dropped to his sides and the color drained from his face.

"You...promised." The words were pitiful.

Matt knew the man's role had ended; his purpose had been served. He had spoken the words and broken the final seal, so that nothing could come between the new celestial convergence and the rise of the beast. His work was done.

"*You – fucking – promised.*" Drummond ground his teeth. "I risked my life a thousand times. I gave you everything." He stamped his foot like a child.

"Not quite *everything*, Charles." The Father reached out, fingers growing once again into long tendrils to wrap around Drummond's neck and torso. It was then that the Father started to grow, taking the struggling man with it.

The little girls by the cliff screamed and turned away, sprinting madly back along the dark beach.

It lifted higher and higher, increasing in size, so that the shawl it wore shredded and burst from its expanding frame. With the Father's form revealed, they could see that it hadn't been *standing* on the sand at all, but was instead actually growing *out* of it.

"I could have told them, I could have told them." Drummond's words were faint now as the thing lifted higher, pulling free more of itself that was buried beneath the sand. The huge pipe of flesh trailed into the water.

Matt's mouth hung open as he saw Drummond beating at the cords encircling him for only a few seconds more before he was simply pulled inside the pulsating mass, his yells of protest turning to a pitiful scream at the last.

The Father tilted forward, its huge face looking back down at them.

"You think I am simply the servant of the great Old One? You think I can be hurt?" The voice bubbled and frothed in its anger.

"Good Christ," Abrams said backing away. "The Father is not a servant of the Cthulhu: it's a goddamn part of it."

Adira grabbed Matt's arm, backing him up.

"The vanity of the gods." Matt was already out of breath. "They never thought we could read it. Never believed we were ever significant enough to be a threat. But there is something in here –there must be." He looked up. "Abdul Alhazred, the Mad Arab, before he lost his life, took great pains to inscribe a warning, and perhaps his weapon or fortification against this growing horror. He hid it away, for us, for the next time that the beast attempted to rise. He *must* have."

Matt flipped page after page as the column of flesh that had been the Father moved out over the dark water. Whether the being was like an appendage of the great beast rising toward the surface, or some sort of intelligent symbiote that Cthulhu had picked up in its eternal slumber, they couldn't tell.

"This thing is not immortal. We have already proved it can be hurt." Adira fired a full magazine into the dark flesh, but it absorbed the compacted salt bullets with little effect.

"*Ach,* we need a cannon," she said, ejecting and then jamming in another magazine. "Time to go home, I think."

"What home?" Matt said. "We die here or we die there. Unless we find an answer right here, right now, our home, our entire species, will be gone before we even make it back to the surface."

"Ah, shit." Abrams backed into them. "Whatever you're gonna do, now would be a good time, or we're about to end up like Drummond." From the cave mouths along the shoreline, the Shoggoth, the bloated bags of amoebic flesh, now poured forth. They came quickly, moving on slug-like pads, insect limbs, and in some cases the arms and legs of human beings. Adira and Abrams got back to back, ready to fight, and die.

"Pick your targets," Abrams said, and then half turned. "You've been a pain in the ass, Captain Senesh...and a pleasure to work with."

Adira snorted. "You too, Joshua...and I will save one last bullet for myself. I have no plans to end up like your Captain Tania Kovitz."

Abrams nodded. "I *heard* that." He then half turned to Matt. "Come on, buddy."

Matt pointed to the red gates, and the huge symbols upon them. "The language of the Underworld, the Celestial Speech." He looked at each of the towering glyphs. His altered mind now rearranged the huge symbols, making sense of them. He spoke the strange words:

"*Ph'nglui mglw'nafh Cthulhu R'lyeh wgah'nagl fhtagn!*"

"Huh?" Abrams frowned.

The words would have sounded like gibberish to anyone else, but to Matt, and in this unholy place, their meaning had the weight of mountains – *In his house at R'lyeh, dead Cthulhu lies dreaming.*

He read the next. "*Hunwgli odururn wnghui Xastur.*" Matt's mouth dropped open at the implication: *And with him dreams his brother...Xastur, the Unspeakable One.*

"Xastur – the Caduceus – the intertwined gods. We've seen this name before; I know it." He looked up briefly. "There is another one." Matt flipped pages and then stopped. The Enochian glyphs flared like neon lights before his eyes. He absorbed their meaning, symbol after symbol.

"Great, so there are *two* of them." Abrams shot several of the Shoggoth creatures, and Adira sprayed one of the approaching flanks.

"Cthulhu is engaged in an eternal rivalry with another ancient creature, called Xastur, the Unspeakable One." He looked up again, feeling a little crazed. "It's his half brother."

"This thing has a brother?" Adira asked, firing another few rounds.

Matt shook his head. "Yes, maybe, I don't know if it's a brother like we understand it, or if a single being separated in some sort of monstrous splitting and budding process. Only Cthulhu has sought to rule the universe by himself, without Xastur...that's why he keeps trying to rise."

Adira fired another few rounds into the approaching mass of Shoggoth. "One is more than enough."

"No." Matt shook his head. "Don't you see? They held each other in an eternal embrace, an *intertwining*, waiting for the end of time. But somehow, the celestial convergence allows Cthulhu to slip way and...feed." Matt looked up. "We need to release the brother."

"Are you mad, Kearns?" Abrams turned briefly to yell over his shoulder. "You want another of these things loose, because you think, maybe, just maybe, it will somehow help?"

Matt frowned, and pointed to the growing thing that was the Father, now joined with the massive trunk of flesh growing from the lake and disappearing up toward the invisible roof of the cavern.

"What the hell have we got to lose?"

Abrams looked to Adira; she just shrugged in return.

"I've already made my peace." She turned and fired again.

Abrams gritted his teeth. "What do you need?"

Matt turned another page. "I think I need to...call to him...*just*...call him."

"Where is he?" Adira asked.

Matt pointed to the massive red gates. "Behind there, in the ancient city of R'lyeh. That's where Cthulhu came from. That's where he must be sent back to."

"You better hurry." Adira backed toward Matt and Abrams. They now had a wall of the Shoggoth on three sides and the black ocean on the other.

"Getting low." Abrams emptied his gun, and smoothly ejected and jammed in another magazine.

Matt looked around, beginning to panic. Fear was making his mind a fog of confusion. Everywhere he looked, the cliff walls, sand, and the dark water moved with hellish life forms. Things scuttled, lumbered, and slithered toward them. Monstrosities with too many eyes, thrashing limbs, and sucking or needle-fanged mouths like creatures from the bottom of the deepest ocean trenches, all now descending upon them.

Matt looked down at the page of symbols, crushing his eyes shut and saying a silent prayer for his thoughts to clear. He exhaled and opened his eyes. The strange circles, dashes and dots formed sounds deep in his mind. He looked up at the huge gates and sucked in a huge breath, yelling the words.

"*En Dooain Bolape Page Od Aziazor Ph'anglu Dooaip Ananael...Ol Vinu Od Zacamc...Auriel Ol Bolape A Noco Eglo Olapireta Ark-Pi Unkwa Padda Enoch Xastur.*"

Matt waited for several seconds. Nothing – no sounds or emanations from the colossal gates.

Abrams fired off three more shots. "I'm out." He tossed his gun to the ground and pulled out his compressed salt dagger, the tiny weapon a joke against the approaching monstrous hordes.

Matt looked down and read again. "*Xastur Ug'lu Cthulhu.*" Please, please, he wished. "*Cthulhu Enk Unhug'li.*"

Matt looked up at the doors. There was still nothing. He felt his gut knot, but read again, louder.

"*En Dooain Bolape Page Od Aziazor Ph'anglu Dooaip Ananael...Ol Vinu Od Zacamc... Auriel Ol Bolape A Noco Eglo Olapireta Ark-Pi Unknown Apila Paid Enoch, Xastur.*"

He screamed the final two sentences.

"*XASTUR UG'LU, CTHULHU!!*
CTHULHU ENK UNHUG'LI, XASTU-UUUR!!"

Matt fell to his knees, his head nearly bursting from pain. Blood ran down over his lips and chin, and he felt a warm dampness at his ears. He looked up through bloodshot eyes. The gates remained in place. He shook his head.

"What did I do wrong? I said the words. What did I miss?" He punched the sand, feeling the harsh grains scour his knuckles.

"Listen!" Adira had now backed all the way up to him.

Matt lifted his head and held his breath. There was nothing – *absolutely nothing* – strangely, no noise, and no movement. Everything in the underworld had stopped, and had now turned...toward the mighty gates of red granite.

Then there came a faint noise, but not from the column of glistening dark flesh that rose from the abyssal ocean. The noise came again, soft at first. There was a shifting, popping sound from behind the gates as if layers of pack ice were cracking and then breaking away.

Matt got slowly to his feet.

There was an ear-shattering boom, followed by another, and another. Footfalls of the gods, Matt thought. Another sound, louder than the first, and then unbelievably, the giant red gates began to bend outwards.

"It's..." Matt spun to his friends "...it's working." He grinned at Abrams, his fists clenched.

The major made a fist and turned and grinned. "I think we –"

The huge outgrowth of flesh, the appendage of Cthulhu that the Father had become, crashed down upon Abrams, flattening him to the sand. It then retreated back to the water with the squashed body stuck to it like some sort of tongue. A trail of glistening red was left behind in the deep furrow in the sand.

"No, no, no." Matt grabbed at his head. "Not now, please not now."

The towering Father seemed to shiver in delight, ominously leaning over them.

"Move." Adira turned to fire as a cacophony of screams burst through the huge cavern.

As if from a signal, every manner of beast rushed toward them – worms burst from the sand, huge scuttling beasts descended from the rock walls, and the loathsome Shoggoths were pouring down from the caves like so many bloated army ants intent on doing their master's bidding.

Matt bumped into Adira, who had stopped running. He spun and saw why – they were trapped.

"And so, we have run out of places to go, and luck, my friend." Adira wore a grim smile. He admired her courage and perhaps even loved her a little at that moment. There was no braver warrior than this woman who had literally fought her way into Hell for him.

She had the HK-MP5N rifle held in one arm, and in the other a revolver. She lifted the handgun, and looked at Matt, her eyes level.

"I lied; I have saved two bullets – it will be painless and far quicker than what is in store for us."

She waited. Matt knew that one word, or even the hint of a nod, and she would put a bullet in his brain. He smiled at her, feeling a calm come over him. I've had a good life, he thought. He drew in a deep breath.

A sound like planets colliding physically knocked them off their feet. The giant red gates of R'lyeh cracked open. Matt turned and threw a hand up over his face, but nonetheless saw the magnificent hideousness of the city beyond those titanic barriers.

Bioluminescence shone from within, revealing greenish stone blocks of an incomprehensible age. Matt's face went slack with dread, and he beheld visions that were never meant for human eyes. There were great carven statues of weird shape and form; the geometry of R'lyeh was abnormal, non-Euclidean, and loathsomely redolent of spheres and dimensions apart. Everything Matt could see was gigantic, towering and colossal, insanely so. And then, the pale light of the hidden city was shadowed as something vast made its way to the stone gates.

Matt remembered more of the secret language of *The Book of the Dead*, or whatever people had called it over the millennia, and he whispered the words:

"*That is not dead which can eternal lie – and with strange eons, even death may die.*"

Massive things like monstrous hands gripped the gates, and pushed them wide. Matt got slowly to his feet, pointing.

"Behold, Xastur."

Chapter 28

The world was at war, and Decker led them all.

Rows of big howitzers, tanks, and mobile rocket launchers ringed the far edges of the park in a circle of steel and fire. Eric Ford had worked overtime on the munitions and the front lines were fully armed with hardened salt shells that they loosed in a constant barrage into the seething masses of Shoggoths.

Like a wound bursting open to spill its infection onto the skin, the site of Cthulhu's rise was a many-miles-wide lump that had broken open to spill bloated monstrosities across the Earth's surface in wave after wave. The soldiers, Decker hoped, didn't realize that at one time the creatures they fought so hard were once their fellow human beings.

Countless Shoggoth ran, crawled and slid on slimy pads toward the soldiers. For each hundred that were turned to lifeless jelly, more simply boiled to the surface to take their place. And in among the Shoggoth, other huge monstrosities came to fight, feed, and throw themselves at the lines of humanity.

Soldiers scrambled about, firing at anything that moved, but still, many of the creatures made it through.

Huge towering spiders, centipedes as long as trains ending in vicious scorpion stings or suckering mouths, and ambling towers of pustulant flesh bulging with sightless eyes also fell among the troops, simply toppling forward onto the men like mighty redwood tree trunks, squashing them flat and then *absorbing* their bodies.

General Decker stood in his command center, watching the mayhem. High overhead surveillance planes circled delivering him multiple spectrums of his battle – none of them was promising. The plane passed over the ground-zero crater once more and he felt his stomach lurch. The thing, "Cthulhu" they were all calling it now, had finally riven the earth. Mile-long fissures were unzipping as it broke free. Decker didn't feel fear. Instead his stomach knotted with frustration that he couldn't simply stamp it out with all the traditional firepower he had.

"We've got fucking lasers, EMP devices, microwave weapons, rail guns and a hundred other ways to mete out death to our fellow man, and we're fighting these things with *salt*. Taking them out one by one. *Fuck it*." He brought his fist down on the desk so hard everything jumped an inch. "Well, we aren't finished yet." He turned. "Ready those heavy thermobarics. Let's see it choke down a few hundred two-thousand-pound exothermic blasts."

Before him the screen was becoming cloudy. "What the fuck now?" It filled with dark specks like the battlefield was in a snowstorm. He turned to the room. "Get someone in to clean up this fucking image."

"It's not the feed, sir."

Decker frowned. The image wasn't getting any clearer, and in fact was becoming more covered over. Looking down from the aerial shot, he saw that the specks began to swirl like a tornado over the site.

"Give me resolution on that new mass." Immediately, the focus pulled back to about a thousand feet above the blast zone. Decker leaned forward and snorted softly. "Well, I'll be damned."

The tornado of specks could now be seen for what they were – *birds*. The swirling storm of wings and feathers was getting thicker by the second as more and more joined in. At the center of the eye of the feathered tornado, moving almost faster than the eye could follow, were the smallest – sparrows, honeyeaters, and warblers. Then came the starlings, gulls and pipers, and furthest out, moving slower, were the cranes and eagles. There were so many, Decker had to blink to make sure his eyes weren't playing tricks. The sky was now becoming so filled, it began to cast shade over the ground.

He nodded to the screen. "Yes, this thing is a threat, not just to mankind, but to all of us and every living thing."

Beneath the swirling birds the ground finally broke open, and a red gas vented into the air – it was the bow wave of the colossal creature finally emerging from the depths of hell itself.

As if on command the birds started to descend – not fall or mindlessly strike the ground, but instead each turned itself into a missile – arrows of bone, blood and feather that spiked down into the massive center of the emerging eye.

Decker straightened, the scene reminding him of bible class from half a century before. "And on the last day, the smallest of us will rise up and join the fight against the beast."

Decker shouted over his shoulder. "Cease fire."

He turned to watch the hurricane of furious animals dive into the creature from below.

Chapter 29

Matt and Adira stood back to back, trying to avoid the rush of the monstrosities that swirled around them. As soon as the shadow of the Unspeakable One had moved to the red gates, the beasts of Cthulhu's realm started to retreat back to their master – first, one by one, and then in their thousands, they went like dark rivers of shuffling horror. They poured back into the central mass, joining with it, merging and becoming yet more of the dark jellied muscle that was vainly straining to reach our world.

"It seems stuck – not moving any higher. Something is stopping Cthulhu from breaking through." Matt grinned. "Maybe General Decker was able to halt it."

"Then, we can do no more." Adira spun to drag him along the sand until he managed to right himself.

Matt turned to look back at the gates. Something blood red was emerging like a mountain of pulsating muscle. Once past the barrier, it shot forward, colliding with column of black greasy flesh in the center of the dark ocean. The shockwave of the impact knocked Matt and Adira forward off their feet, and they both rolled to look back.

Xastur had wrapped itself around its brother, and, like a giant fist, it squeezed.

"Xastur will not let Cthulhu rise. It knows it is not their time," Matt said.

The thing that had emerged from behind the red gates extended out and around the mass of Cthulhu, but its end was still lost somewhere deep inside the city of R'lyeh. Matt brought his hands up to his head to cover his ears, as there came a wailing from the million mouths, jaws, beaks and toothless maws that had formed across the dark mass of Cthulhu.

Matt looked at his watch. "Oh God, the convergence is concluding. We need to be out of here, or we're staying."

"Then see you at the top, Professor." Adira started to sprint along the shoreline. Matt followed, both of them heading back to the cave mouth they had used to enter Cthulhu's realm.

They still needed to weave around all manner of hideous creatures that poured forth from the caves – there came the Father's priests, the shaven-headed humanoids, also stick-like insectoid things with grinning human faces. There were slithering worms with spiked fangs and sides dotted with black eyes, skinless centipedes with running sores, and lumps of muscled flesh that hopped on massive elephantine stumps. All continued to pour back into the core of their master.

The screams of rage rose, and chancing a look back again, Matt saw that the huge column had begun to be dragged from the ceiling, and was being slowly tugged toward the massive gates of R'lyeh.

Finally, from out of the darkness above them appeared the head of the beast. Matt felt an animal fear shoot through his body at the vision of the monstrous ancient being. The *Al Azif*'s description was accurate, but still could never fully describe the horror that Matt witnessed. He had impressions of an octopus, a dragon, and even a human caricature with a pulpy, tentacled head surmounting a grotesque and scaly body.

The face, or the front of the being, carried a huge central lidless eye surrounded by dozens of smaller black orbs, and then around these were masses of feelers. The thought of their world ever having something like this on its surface threatened Matt's sanity.

Cthulhu emanated pure evil, and perhaps its slumbering dreams had touched humankind ever since he had crawled from the swamps and stood on hind legs. It had always been there, the evil presence influencing and haunting us – Satan, Diablo, Lucifer, Baal, Cthulhu – they were all the one being...and it was real.

Cthulhu arched down. Its flailing tentacles, thicker than city blocks, bloomed apart to reveal a huge beak that it tried to bury in the flesh of its brother. Whipping tentacles smashed rock from the walls, and specks fell from its body – the servants clinging to its skin were being shaken free like fleas from a dog.

The two mighty creatures had wrapped tentacles around each other in what was far from a loving family embrace. Each exerted impossible pressure on the other's form, but slowly, Xastur was dragging Cthulhu back toward the red gates.

A huge chunk of stone the size of a battleship fell from somewhere overhead to strike a far stretch of beach, crushing flat hundreds of the swarming creatures and creating a tremor beneath their feet.

That settled it for Matt and Adira: they were sprinting now for their lives. Gradually, the planets were moving out of alignment, and whatever labyrinthine maze had been opened to reveal this dismal place of abominations would soon be shut.

Adira had her gun up, but the beasts they passed ignored them in their haste to return to their master. Amongst the dark, reeking mass, there was a flash of red, and Matt zigzagged towards it, increasing his speed.

"Hey!" Adira angled after him.

The lump of red looked up. The twins in their dirty pyjamas clung to each other, their faces streaked. Matt jinked past something that looked like a dog-headed spider, and then bent and reached out, while trying to not to slow his pace. He grabbed up one of the girls, who immediately clung to him. The other, he snatched and just held under his arm, and accelerated once again.

"Go, go, go." Adira pushed him in the back, and then sped to get in front of him and force open a path. The Mossad woman's long legs pumped hard on the dark sand and Matt gritted his teeth, his head already swimming with exhaustion as he tried to keep pace.

They ran hard now, bouncing off walls as time moved rapidly against them. Adira was first to the shimmering curtain between their worlds, but when she went to run through, she bounced backward. It was now less like a bodyless separation than a wall of glass. She collided with Matt and knocked him to the ground. The girls screamed, and rolled from his arms.

"Shit no." Matt got to his feet first, the twins already clinging to him again. He helped Adira up.

Her nose was bloody and she shook her head. "Shitza. That was like hitting a wall." She rubbed her face, smearing blood.

Matt reached out and touched the wall. He pushed at it, but his hand refused to go through. "It's closed; we're too late."

"Over my dead body." Adira planted her legs and lifted her gun, firing a dozen rounds into the wall. The last few passed right through, striking the rock tunnel beyond. She turned and grabbed Matt, and one-handed, fired again, upsetting the wall's stabilization just enough for them all to dive through.

The distortion wall immediately reformed, and then like some sort of gigantic digestive system, the rocks walls began to soften, pulsate and ripple like the peristaltic motions of a giant animal's gut. Then, they too began to collapse. Just like the soil in the sinkhole in Iowa, Matt thought, getting to his feet.

He sprinted now; first beside Adira and then behind as the weight of the girls slowed him and the ever-narrowing tunnel forced them into single file. In another moment, he saw a tiny dot of yellow – the dying glow stick lying at the bottom of the pit. The walls now were barely further apart than his shoulders, and he yelled until his voice was rasping.

"Dive, dive."

Adira did just that, and Matt followed. They both landed hard. Matt spun in time to see the walls coming together like lips, swallowing everything that had been behind, and probably below them. The huge stone lintel with the carvings remained in place above them, but beneath it now there was nothing but a blank wall.

Matt remained sprawled on the ground, the girls still with their faces buried in his chest. Adira was lying on her back, breathing hard. He closed his eyes, and concentrated, reaching out with his mind, trying to *feel* the monstrous presence – there was nothing. The sensations he had felt after the touch of the Shoggoth, the second sight and connection with the Beast, seemed gone. He looked down at his hand – the Book was still there.

"Is it over?" Adira rolled her head to look at him.

He smiled, seeing just how battered she was. "Over? I don't know if it will ever be over. Maybe for this millennium it is. We need to see what happened above us – see what's left."

"Call me a cab." She shut her eyes.

Matt grinned, and looked across to the tiny dot of yellow that was fast fading. "I'll call you mad, if you want to be down here when the lights go out."

She groaned and sat up. "Suddenly, I want to see the sun again."

Matt got to his feet and pulled her up. She pointed at the Book. "That thing is trouble, it should stay here...or better yet, be destroyed."

Matt looked down at the cover. The glyphs, the Enochian – the language of the angels or the Underworld – none of it made sense to him any more. The power to read them was gone.

"No. It's not for us to decide that. It is both a sword and a shield – it needs to be protected – for the next time." He craned his neck to look upward, but felt a tug on his arm. He looked down. One of the small girls looked up solemly.

"We want to go home now."

Matt nodded. "Good idea; let's all go home."

*

"What the hell?" Decker watched in disbelief as the Shoggoths retreated like army ants pulling back into their nest. They ignored the soldiers firing at them, even though they exploded into black goo when struck. The very last seemed to become confused, ambling about, and then didn't even bother trying to make it below ground. Instead, they simply started to fall apart, becoming an oily sludge that steamed and ran into the cracks of the earth.

Beside him, Don Mancino was amazed. "Did we...win?"

Decker stared for a full minute, and then shook his head. "Win? No. We didn't beat them, or the thing rising. We never laid a freakin glove on it. Something or *someone* else stopped it...and for how long?" He snorted. "Ask me again in another thirteen hundred years."

"What happens now?" Mancino asked.

Decker exhaled. "Damned if I know. Put the world back together, might be a good place to start." He snorted softly and then turned to the room. "Pull everyone back...and find me Major Joshua Abrams. I'm betting that he and that mad professor of his had something to do with this."

"What about Captain Adira Senesh?" Mancino still stared at the screen.

Decker thought for a moment, and then shook his head. "Sergeant Major, right about now, I wouldn't care if we made her the next President of the United States. Leave her be." He saluted and headed for the door.

Epilogue

Arkham, Essex County, Massachusetts

Matt walked slowly across the quadrangle of Miskatonic University's grounds. Tucked under his arm was a prize that was beyond value – the Book. It was both a curse and a salvation for the human race.

Abdul Alhazred, the Mad Arab poet of Damascus, had been shown insights into the world that could have been, and, even though it had cost him his life, he had written down the strange symbols and words, and then ensured those words remained safe for when they would next be needed.

Where those thoughts and words originally came from was a mystery. Perhaps there were other great beings, Elder Gods, less inclined to destroy and consume life than the more odious things that slumbered somewhere deep beneath our feet.

And now, it was Matt's responsibility to keep it safe. The original Book could never be taken back to the library of Alexandria, but it still needed to be hidden away in a repository – somewhere secure, and off the beaten path. He knew just the place. He had learned that the "ole Misk", the Miskatonic University, had a deep vault below its old science lab.

It was strange: the university, though a prestigious one, would not have been his first choice for storage of something so valuable and, without doubt, critical to the survival of the human race. But it was if the Book had decided for itself, guiding and then compelling him to bring it here. Perhaps to be hidden away and forgotten for another thirteen hundred years.

Just touching the strange leather of its cover caused images of the abominations to swirl like mad dervishes in his mind, along with the passages in Syriac, Ancient Greek, and Arabic. There were also the symbols of the first angels, though they were now impenetrable to him. He knew he would never be fully free of them until he performed one last duty.

Matt entered the university's stationery shop, selecting the most expensive vellum paper he could find and a fountain pen. He needed to write, to add in their battle, and how they managed to push back the Old One. He had to quickly get it down, tell the story of Cthulhu, the Shoggoths, and the other abominations. And he needed to include his own warning, before his mind was blank to it all.

He smiled as he pushed out of the store, making the small bell tinkle overhead. He headed to the Miskatonic vaults, but first he needed to find a place to write.

"Maybe one day they'll refer to me as the Mad American – *Mad Matt*." He grinned and turned his face to the sky, catching a ray of sun on his face. Overhead a bird circled, and as he watched, another joined it, and then another.

As he passed across the campus a small cloud of birds formed above him…following.

Author's Notes

Many readers ask me about the background of my novels – is it real or fiction? Where do I get the situations, equipment, characters or their expertise from, and just how much of any legend has a basis in fact? In the case of *Book of the Dead*, there is one absolute reality – its real creator: the American author Howard Phillips "H.P." Lovecraft.

My book, most of the creatures described, and even my hero being a professor in search of science and knowledge, are drawn from Lovecraft's mythos universe.

This book is where I pay homage to the man. I hope he would have approved.

Howard Phillips "H.P." Lovecraft

Lovecraft was born in Providence, Rhode Island, on August 20 1890. Today, he is considered one of the most influential fathers of monstrous and macabre horror, though it was only years after his death that he received the recognition he and his work deserved.

A young Lovecraft spent his early life being cosseted by an overprotective mother, as his father was confined to a mental institution. His grandfather turned out to be a significant influence, as much of the time he was with Howard was spent telling him fantastic make-believe stories, and this soon became their favorite pastime.

It wasn't long before an eight-year-old Lovecraft began composing his own rudimentary horror tales. Then later, when in high school, he began to involve local children in elaborate fantasy play-acting, only stopping the projects just prior to his eighteenth birthday. At school, Lovecraft abhorred many of the traditional subjects, but developed a keen interest in history, linguistics, chemistry, and astronomy, and obtained a deep understanding and knowledge of each of these. Though his intellect was being honed, his lack of interest in traditional topics led to him failing to graduate.

Lovecraft began to withdraw from the world, and soon was living a near nocturnal lifestyle. However, his writing, if mostly just personal, continued. At twenty-three, his literary flair was seen in the letter pages of a story magazine and he was soon invited to join an amateur journalism association. This was the trigger he needed and he soon began to send out more of his works. At the age of thirty-one he had his first formal publication in a professional magazine.

Lovecraft's life seemed to be thrown open then – he lived in New York, married an older woman he had met at one of his journalism conferences, and, by thirty-four, was a regular contributor to a new fiction magazine called *Weird Tales*.

Lovecraft returned to his home in Providence in 1926, and over the next year he produced some of his most fantastic works, including "The Call of Cthulhu" (first published in *Weird Tales* in 1928), which was the authoritative basis for the Cthulhu Mythos, so named by a contemporary author by the name of August Derleth.

A recurring theme in Lovecraft's work is the utter unimportance of us, humankind, when faced with the true horrors that live in the Old Ones' universe. Lovecraft made many references to these Elder Gods and Great Old Ones, who were described as a race of ancient, powerful deities from the cosmos who once ruled the Earth long before humanity's oldest ancestors had even crawled from the ooze. These titanic monstrosities are now in a deathlike sleep, hibernating, but still reaching out to us. This reaching out was first spoken of in "The Call of Cthulhu", in which the humans were sent mad when they even had a glimpse of what exists in this shared universe.

Sadly for H.P. Lovecraft, fame and fortune eluded him and he was never properly able to support himself as an author. Once again he began to withdraw from the world, and as he never promoted his own work, many of his pieces were left unappreciated, unsold, and unread for decades. With his inheritance completely spent, in continuing ill health, and deeply troubled, he died at the age of forty-six. Today, he is regarded as one of the most significant twentieth-century authors in his genre, and a genius well beyond his years.

H.P. Lovecraft's literary gifts to us remain vibrant to this day, and his influence has been remarked upon by authors such as Stephen King, Clive Barker, Joe R. Lansdale, Neil Gaiman, F. Paul Wilson, Ramsey Campbell, and Brian Lumley. All have cited Lovecraft as one of their primary influences.

As do I, in this book, *Book of the Dead*.

Cthulhu (Khlûl'-hloo, or Kə-thoo-loo)

H.P. Lovecraft's Great Old One and monstrous god from the Below. Lovecraft gave several pronunciations for the name, but his favored version was "Khlûl'-hloo" – the first syllable "Khlûl" is pronounced gutturally and harshly. So try: "Klul-loo'. However, the pronunciation has changed, and today it is more common to hear it pronounced as "Kə-thoo-loo".

After "The Call of Cthulhu", Lovecraft's evil deity went on to be featured in numerous popular culture references, from books and movies to online games.

In "The Call of Cthulhu", H.P. Lovecraft describes the Cthulhu as follows:

- A monster of vaguely anthropoid outline, but with an octopus-like head whose face was a mass of feelers; a scaly, rubbery-looking body; prodigious claws on hind and fore feet, and long, narrow wings behind.
- A mix between a giant human, an octopus, and a dragon, depicted as being hundreds of feet tall, with human-looking arms and legs and a pair of rudimentary wings on its back.
- Similar to the entirety of a giant octopus, with an unknown number of tentacles surrounding its supposed mouth, able to change the shape of its body at will, extending and retracting limbs and tentacles as it sees fit.

A Shoggoth – vile servants of the Great Ones

The Shoggoth were first described in Lovecraft's 1931 Antarctic adventure novella, *At the Mountains of Madness*. (Note: that was one of my own influences for *Beneath the Dark Ice*.)

In the story, Lovecraft describes them as huge amoeba-like creatures made out of glistening black ooze, with multiple eyes that formed and popped open all over their surface. These eyes could float freely over the lumpen body mass. In another description, they are said to lack any formal or base body shape and instead could produce limbs, eyes and mouths at will (if you have ever seen John Carpenter's movie *The Thing* you'll get an idea of the influence Lovecraft had on this film director's work).

The character of the Mad Arab, Abdul Alhazred, found the mere idea of their existence on Earth to be horrifying enough to drive a person to insanity.

The Gates of the Hidden City

R'lyeh is a fictional lost city that first appeared in "The Call of Cthulhu". R'lyeh is sunken deep under the Pacific Ocean. Lovecraft put the coordinates at approximately Latitude 47° 9' S, Longitude 126° 43' W. The water there is impenetrably deep, and warm.

In 1997 Navy sensors detected a very large noise, picked up on two different marine sensors thousands of miles apart, being produced at Latitude 50° S, Longitude 120° W, close to Lovecraft's R'lyeh. This sound (known as a Bloop) is not thought to correspond to any known living or non-living source.

To this day, the phenomenon is still unexplained, and no agreed or adequate explanation has ever been provided.

Forbidden knowledge

Secrets and knowledge that are buried, sunken, long forgotten or forbidden, is a recurring theme in Lovecraft's works. Many of his characters (usually scientists or professors) are driven by curiosity or scientific endeavor, and in many of his stories what they uncover in their searches usually proves to be a Pandora's Box, with the secrets they reveal (release?) usually destroying their discoverers both physically and mentally.

The Old Gods' influences on us

The creatures of Lovecraft's universe will often have humans who act as servants. Cthulhu, for instance, is worshiped as a god by many secret cults in both the Western world and among the Greenland Eskimo (Inuit) and the voodoo covens of Louisiana.

Lovecraft was like many of his turn of the twentieth century contemporaries, in that he saw modern man as being closer to science and rigid thinking, and the indigenous natives as being closer to the spiritual-supernatural knowledge unknown to civilized man. This closeness to the natural world was what he saw as making the "savages" the keepers of the ancient (and long forgotten in the modern world) lore.

Miskatonic University

The university where Matt Kearns finally deposits the Book first appeared in Lovecraft's 1922 story "Herbert West–Reanimator". It is a fictional university located in Arkham, a made-up town in Essex County, Massachusetts. It is named after the Miskatonic River (also made up).

Miskatonic University was supposedly known for its fantastic library collection of ancient occult books. The Miskatonic library also holds one of the very few surviving copies of *The Necronomicon*. But this wasn't the only fantastic tome it held locked away in its vaults. It was also said to include the mysterious *Book of Eibon* – that strangest and rarest of occult volumes that was said to have come down through a series of translations from a prehistoric original written in the lost language of Hyperborea.

And now it contains the original *Al Azif* as well. It is locked away in its deep vault; hopefully it'll be there when next we need it!

Printed in July 2021
by Rotomail Italia S.p.A., Vignate (MI) - Italy